REVOLUTION WORLD

THE ILLUMINATOR SERIES

BOOK 2

PHILIP GINN

Cover Design: Vivid Covers
Font for Titles: Ancient Geek by Matthew Welch
Interior Book Design: Joan Frantschuk, Woven Red Author Services
Content Editor: Alyssa Hall, Red Adept Editing
Line Editor: Kate Birdsall, Red Adept Editing
Proofreader: Virge B., Red Adept Editing

Thanks to William Ivry for poker tips and terminology.
The phrase: "Battleground for tattoos and muscles" was coined by Andrea Landaker.

Revolution World/ Philip Ginn—1st Edition
ISBN Paperback: 979-8-9857702-2-3
ISBN Ebook: 979-8-9857702-3-0

Visit my website and sign up for my newsletter: https://philipginnwriter.home.blog/

To my editors, Alyssa, Kate, and Virge.
I could not make this journey without you.

Chapter 1

Pop Rocks Candy

"I need the Razzleberry-flavored Pop Rocks. This is the only place that has them!"

Silas let out a groan. "Okay, Gavin. Let's just get the candy and go. We're already late for our dinner reservations at Gusto's." Even though Silas put on an air of impatience, Abigail could tell he was eagerly awaiting some of the candy that Gavin couldn't shut up about.

She walked with Silas and Gavin to the candy aisle of the convenience store. Gavin walked with his usual bounce. As they stood in front of the assorted flavors of Pop Rocks, Abigail noticed a peculiar spark in Silas's aura that she'd never seen before. The colors radiating around him showed fear mixed with what she thought was a swirl of courage, almost as if the two emotions were battling each other.

He stood still and seemed dazed as he faced the candy, so Abigail gently reached out to touch his arm. Upon making contact, she saw a flash of what he was thinking. She was surprised by the vivid image of what she guessed was a memory from his childhood. The setting had a nostalgic feeling to it, as if it were from an old photograph—the colors were off. The convenience store faded away, and she looked down to see two skinny white legs covered by knee-high socks and short brown shorts.

The experience reminded her of when she had joined the alien Taurian collective and relived all of their people's experiences, but she was in the body of a small boy—Silas.

Gavin piped up again with something about "Razzleberry," pulling Abigail from her trance. She raised a finger to her mouth and gestured to Silas, who was still studying the assortment of colorful packets. She wanted to know more about what he was experiencing and wondered if perhaps her ability to see into his memories was an ability she'd adopted from the Taurians, who shared their experiences on a kind of collective memory platform. She hadn't experienced anything like it since her genetic transformation.

With a slight twinge of guilt that she shouldn't be probing into someone else's mind without their consent—a feeling she brushed away because she wanted to know more about Silas and maybe help him—she focused again on his thoughts and tried to send a message though their connection, prompting him to continue thinking about his memory.

A particular summer day from his childhood came into view, and it felt like she was right there, living the experience. His big mission was to walk to the convenience store with his allowance to buy some candy. Once he had made it to the Circle K and purchased the candy, the second phase of his mission was to walk home and avoid the neighborhood bully. Unfortunately, the second phase had ended badly. He had planned for it, though, by hiding some Pop Rocks packets in the tops of his tube socks. The other candy he would lose as a casualty of war. The knowledge comforted him, even though he was terrified and in pain when Billy Rogers pressed his face against the fence. He wanted more than anything to fight back against the larger kid.

Silas snapped out of his daze, but Abigail maintained her grip. She was no longer reading his thoughts, but a wave of assurance replaced his pain and fear, as if he was reminding himself that no one was ever going to bully him like that again. That was interrupted by a flash of another more recent memory of being tied up and coming very close to dying at the hands of an angry mob. Abigail still had nightmares about it, and apparently, he was still traumatized by it.

She squeezed his arm. "Are you okay?"

He blinked. "Oh, yeah. Let's be sure to get some of the watermelon Pop Rocks. Those were my favorite as a kid."

Abigail was amazed that she had just accessed some of Silas's memories. She released her grip and gave him a reassuring smile. She wanted to remind him that everything was okay, but he seemed to be realizing that on his own. She wished she could go back in time and protect him from his childhood bullies.

Gavin nodded. "Watermelon *is* almost as good as Razzleberry! Grape is pretty good too." He was holding more packets of the candy than were possible to keep a grip on, occasionally dropping one then struggling to reach down to collect it off the floor without dropping more.

Abigail wondered whether all the excitement over a sugary treat was justified. Gavin kept saying the crackling pop of the candy would change her life forever.

She wanted to remind Silas of his accomplishments and that she would be there for him. They had traveled to Mars and beyond and saved the remnants of an alien civilization. He had worked tirelessly to construct the ship for that mission and to make a difference in the world with his electric vehicle venture. She was delighted to see how resourceful he had been as a child, appreciated the man he'd grown up to be, and imagined how the kid who hid his favorite candy in his socks would have loved to see what a capable adult he had grown up to become.

That was more than she could communicate with him while shopping for nostalgic candy, so she settled for keeping her hand clasped around his shoulder. She tried to convey a message of support through the contact, vowing to herself that she would do everything she could to protect him.

As they passed the chip aisle and walked toward the checkout with their spoils, Abigail saw a dark-red aura surrounding a figure heading toward the register. "That guy is up to something," she said through gritted teeth as the man, who wore a black hoodie, walked up to the cashier. She could see his harmful intent from a mile away.

"I think he's going to hurt someone," she whispered. She had only seen auras with that swirl of dark red a few times before.

Both of her friends moved in on the tall man to intervene. She was surprised that they walked toward someone who she was sure had harmful intentions. She felt glued to the floor, watching as they took initiative to get involved with the stranger.

Gavin rushed up to the guy. "Excuse me. Have you ever tried these candies? I swear, they will change your life!"

At that moment, the man pulled a gun. Silas instantly grabbed for it, but the guy pulled it away and whipped it at Silas's head with a sickening thud. As he fell to the ground, the man turned and said, "Nobody move, stay where you are, and be quiet!" He pointed his gun at the cashier. "I'll take all the money in the register and a pack of Marlboro Lights. Put it in a bag."

Abigail was just a couple of feet away when the man turned to face her, pointing his gun in her direction. She was too far away to shock him without hitting Gavin and the cashier. She needed to get closer. She raised her eyebrows at Gavin, who nodded.

Gavin tossed his armful of candy packets at the man. "You really gotta try these Pop Rocks. I'm telling you—"

In an instant, Abigail leapt at the man and heard the gun shot. As soon as she made contact, she sent an Illuminating jolt of electricity into his body. She didn't have the time to compose her Illumination in the way she had done before. Instead, she tried to send a message in a single jolt, similarly to how she had shocked the large crowd in Texas. He fell to the ground in a daze. Once she'd laid him on the linoleum floor, she rushed to Gavin to see blood soaking through his shirt on his shoulder.

She put a hand on his wound to slow the bleeding. "Call 911!" she yelled to the cashier. She looked at Silas, who was also on the floor, then back at Gavin, who had gone pale. She couldn't believe that in an instant, everything had turned from carefree candy shopping to both of her friends being badly injured. She was frustrated that she couldn't reach Silas, who was unconscious, since she didn't want to let go of Gavin. Her hands were covered in blood.

It had been a long night with an ambulance ride, talking to doctors and the police, waiting, and worrying. Gavin had been rushed into surgery, Silas had been stitched and bandaged, and both lay in hospital beds in a shared room. Gavin was allowed to doze off, but Abigail's job was to keep Silas from sleeping for long periods because of his concussion. She could only entertain him so much, so she decided to turn on the television. She felt awkward about having entered his memories, and a terrible guilt weighed on her because she had let him get hurt moments after she had vowed that she would protect him.

She used the remote to surf through the stations. Every cartoon that flashed onto the screen elicited a "Hey, let's watch that!" from Gavin, who was wide awake. He pointed his good hand at the TV then went back to clutching his shoulder. Abigail wondered if his pain meds were wearing off.

She stopped scrolling when she found a news channel.

Onscreen, a sharply dressed woman sat behind a news desk. "Good evening. I'm Primrose Abernaki, and this is *News Flash at Ten*. Tonight's top story: video footage from a security camera captured Abigail Montrose, hero from the Gemini Infinity space mission, preventing a robbery at a Los Angeles Quick-Mart. With the help of her friends, Silas Rutherford and Gavin Azberry, who were also members of the famed space mission, she disarmed a man who was holding the cashier at gunpoint. Azberry sustained a bullet wound to the shoulder but is reported as stable at the LA General Hospital. Rutherford was admitted for a concussion due to a blow to the head from the perpetrator's handgun.

"As is visible from the surveillance video, Azberry and Rutherford appear to have confronted the gunman before Montrose grabbed the distracted man and used some sort of martial arts move to stun him. After the interaction, the perpetrator became cooperative and gave up his weapon."

Grainy surveillance footage flashed onto the screen, showing Abigail rushing up to the man and stunning him at the same moment Gavin fell to the ground. She was glad she didn't shock him from farther away for all of America to see, as she had once done to people on the beach, but she wasn't sure if this was much better. She had Illuminated the man on camera, so anyone watching was reminded of what she could do. It was a skill that she thought should be kept secret, though Gavin thought she should come out as The Illuminator and be some sort of superhero.

The anchorwoman came back onscreen. "In a related story, a few months ago, Montrose made headlines by surviving an attempted execution by a group of extremists then rescuing five others, four Taurians and Silas Rutherford, from a potentially gruesome death by electrocution. The police who responded to that incident reported complete cooperation by the perpetrators."

A photo showing over a dozen police cars on a grassy field appeared. The newswoman continued, "One of the officers stated that if the group had resisted and held their captives hostage, the day could have ended in a bloody shoot-out."

An image of the president, with his pearly white teeth and rosy skin, flashed onto the screen. His hair had a natural salt-and-pepper look that suited him much better than the artificial shell of black hair he'd donned when they first met. Abigail jolted upright in her chair. "Oh, great... I was hoping this story would fade away and the country would move on."

The reporter continued, "In the last year, claims have surfaced, accusing Abigail Montrose of brainwashing the president to bolster government support for Silas Rutherford's space and electric vehicle programs. The president also turned a new green leaf regarding his policies for stronger renewable energy bills. Many are now considering a possible connection between her influence over the president and her ability to keep criminals from escalating hostility, like she did in the Texas incident and with the perpetrator in tonight's attempted robbery. My opinion is that if she has some sort of superpower, the world needs a hero like Abigail Montrose now more than ever."

Gavin hooted at the TV—maybe his pain meds hadn't worn off yet. Silas let a smile shine from his partially bandaged face. Abigail rested back into her chair. The anchorwoman's statement was surprising. Maybe there was hope she could be accepted, even celebrated, as a person with special abilities and good intentions instead of being viewed as a freak of nature to be feared.

The anchorwoman smiled then continued on to the next story. "In national news, two more states have voted to join the president's new federation. New Hampshire is the last Northeastern state to join, making a solid group of member-states that extends down to New York, New Jersey, and Pennsylvania.

"In the Southwest, Arizona is another of the latest states to pledge to meet the requirements for Federation membership and is the first red state to join. Although as of the last election, it is considered more of a purple state. People in Arizona have yet to vote for their three representatives. This brings the total number of member-states to fifteen. We'll keep reporting as more states vote to join."

Abigail thought that sounded promising and hoped the concept of a global federation would catch on so the world could someday be unified. She had a feeling, though, that bad news was sure to follow.

"In other parts of the country, groups are protesting the New Federation. Some are calling it a crime against the Constitution. Many groups are also protesting the inclusion of the Taurians in the government, citing that they are nothing more than illegal immigrants."

The screen flashed to footage of a group holding signs with messages like "America should be run by Americans" and the common saying "Send them back!"

Gavin reacted from his bed. "Booo! They were here first."

He was referring to the fact that the Taurians' ancestors were related to the dinosaurs and had been relocated to a new planet before a meteor struck the Earth some sixty-six million years before.

The newswoman continued, "Ex-senators and congressmen in Texas, Arkansas, South Carolina, and Georgia, among other states, are rallying to resist the Federation."

A video feed of an older white-haired senator came on. "They can't just kick us out of the Senate and tell us we've been laid off! Those were our jobs!"

The anchorwoman came back onto the screen. "Hmmm... American workers getting fired from their jobs... now, that's a story that's all too familiar." She smiled. "Thanks for tuning in, and have a good night."

Abigail clicked off the TV. "I guess that could have been worse. And you both could have ended up in worse shape too." She glanced at them in their hospital beds, feeling guilty at the sight of them being laid up. Gavin used his good hand to eat from three different bowls of Jell-O—each a different flavor.

Silas scratched the bandage on his forehead. He looked pale, but he was smiling. "I'm glad those senators lost their jobs!"

She sighed with relief that they were going to recover. "You know, you both could have distracted him without getting beat up and shot by him."

"Who knew he had issues with strangers entering his personal space?" Gavin asked around a mouthful of green Jell-O. "Although he did specifically say, 'Nobody move. Stay where you are!'"

Silas scrunched his face. "Well, I don't remember him saying that. Actually, I don't remember a lot from tonight. How did we even get here? The last thing I remember was asking for watermelon Pop Rocks."

Abigail was relieved to hear the two young men bantering like normal.

At that moment, Ives, their friend, bodyguard, and personal trainer, walked into the hospital room with two hot beverages. He handed one to Abigail then set his cup on a tray table. Ives, whose arms were a battleground for tattoos and muscles—Abigail was unsure which were winning—walked up to Gavin and mock punched his bandaged shoulder. "Wow, kid, you've got some real street cred, getting shot in LA!"

Silas said, "Yeah, maybe we should start a rap group."

Ives gave Silas a pretend punch too. "You gotta admit that getting shot is pretty legit—what with that scar he's gonna have and living to tell the tale." He drew a pretend line on the side of his own forehead. "You're gonna have a legit scar too." Abigail could tell from the look on his face and the colors in his aura that he was proud of them.

Silas shook his bandaged head. "Why am I always getting hit or punched? It really isn't a pleasant experience."

Abigail had witnessed a few of those punches and was well aware that Silas had a history of ending up on the wrong end of a flying fist. She'd also just seen a memory of him being bullied as a kid. That mind connection was something she would have to try again.

Maybe Gavin would volunteer as a test subject, although that could be a bad idea because she wouldn't want to uncover something private. She believed that everyone's minds should be personal and private spaces, free of intrusion. She supposed she would probe another's mind only if it was totally necessary.

Gavin turned to Silas. "Maybe you just have a very punchable personality." He then opted for a bite of orange Jell-O, but it slid off his spoon and onto his tray. He had been rotating through the three flavors and was attempting to slurp the orange clump from the tray.

Silas rolled his eyes. "Thanks, Gavin! I'm sorry you got shot. Next time, I'll take the bullet, and you can have the concussion. Does anyone else feel the room spinning? And can someone bring me another bedpan to barf into?"

Abigail was relieved that her friends were going to be okay, but her smile faded as guilt set in. "I don't know how I would feel if this had turned out worse. If one of you had been killed, it would have been my fault. It was a mistake to let you both get involved. I should have jumped in before you did. I'm not any sort of superhero if I let my loved ones get hurt. I'm so sorry." She had confirmed to herself that she was not, in fact, a superhero. "Or maybe it was wrong to interfere in that robbery at all. If we had just stayed down, no one would have gotten hurt."

Gavin slurped a glob of red Jell-O off his spoon. "I think the problem is we all want to be heroes. We also want to do what's right at the moment. Thinking about future consequences is important, but I think the best we can do is what feels right at the time. What if we had done nothing and someone *else* got hurt, like the cashier?"

"That's a good point, but it doesn't change the fact that I'd be responsible if something worse happened to you."

Ives cleared his throat. "Isn't there a saying, 'With great power comes great responsibility?'"

Gavin glowed. "Wow, and you're not even a fan of comic books! That *is* a very relevant quote."

Abigail cut in. "This isn't a comic book. This is real life, and once you're dead, you're really dead."

Silas spoke up. "Abigail, if I'd died today, I would have lived a more meaningful life because of you. I want to keep doing good in the world, and I accept the risks involved in doing so. Please don't hold all the weight of the world on your shoulders. We're in this together. And at some point, I swear, I'll be throwing the punches instead of receiving them!"

Abigail thought that was a sweet sentiment. She also remembered how brave he'd been during his encounter with his childhood bully. She hoped she was there to see the day when Silas would stand up for himself and not get hurt.

Ives cracked a grin. "Okay, we have our work cut out for us when you're both recovered and can return to the gym. Throwing punches will be in our training program in addition to getting better at dodging 'em."

Gavin looked at Abigail. "After all that trouble, please tell me you saved the Pop Rocks!"

Abigail rolled her eyes. "Yes, I saved the candy."

"And? What did you think? Amazing, right?"

"Yes. My life will never be the same."

Chapter 2

Dr. Cynthia Roberts

A young man walked into Dr. Cynthia Roberts's office in Los Angeles, California, and shook her hand. "Thank you for seeing me, Dr. Roberts. I am so grateful for what you did for my sister, Abigail."

"Yes... Eliot! You've grown since I've last seen you." She felt embarrassed for not recognizing him sooner, but she quickly saw the family resemblance—like his twin sisters, he had dusty brown hair, brown eyes, and freckles. Studying genes between siblings was, after all, her main focus. "How can I help you?"

Eliot took a seat at her desk. "I haven't really talked about this with anyone, but I'm having issues similar to the ones I think Abi suffered from. I'm just having a really hard time."

"I see. Your sisters didn't mention you were having problems with anxiety or depression." Cynthia remembered them saying that he had been extremely selfish as a child. "Have you seen anyone else, like a therapist or doctor?" She was already pretty sure it was a ploy and he was lying about his state of depression.

"No. All they would do is prescribe medication. I would actually like to be considered a candidate for the procedure you performed on Abigail."

Yep. This makes perfect sense. She nodded. "When I altered your sister's DNA, it was as a last resort. She was at the end of her rope and had exhausted the resources available to her. I have delayed treating anyone else in the same manner until I am one hundred percent certain there are no adverse side effects. The president and my sponsor are in agreement about holding off as well."

"My sister seems to be fine. In fact, she's better than okay. I would like to assure you that I am 'at the end of my rope' as well."

The doctor peered over the top of her glasses to study Eliot. He was looking down at his feet as if afraid to make eye contact. She was sure he was lying. "There are concerns of how recipients of the alteration can fit into society. It's a sensitive issue. Abigail has used her advancements responsibly, but there's no guarantee that others won't abuse their powers. I'm compiling a list of people who may someday be in line for the treatment, but for now, I'm holding off on altering anyone."

"I understand. That's an issue I hadn't considered. I guess assurances that I don't have any harmful intentions wouldn't mean much, but please, could you just put my name on the list?"

"I will. But in the meantime, I'd like to refer you to a specialist who may be able to help. Their evaluation would also be needed to ascertain the extent of your condition. I would also like to talk to concerned family members. A doctor's and your family's input could help to get your name to the top of the list."

Eliot tensed. "I'm really not interested in bringing my family in to discuss this. Nor do I wish to be evaluated by any of your therapists."

She checked his form to see his birth date and determined that he had recently turned eighteen. He was a couple of years younger than Abigail. She looked back at him. "Okay… There's another option. There's a plan to offer treatment to clinically depressed individuals who wish to start a new life on the Polaris colony. We may not be ready for super-advanced humans here on Earth, but the Taurians think they would make a fine contribution to their colony society. It sounds like we are a ways off from sending people to another planet, but it might be a great opportunity for those who want to start over in a new place."

Eliot twiddled his thumbs. "I'll have to consider that. I've heard the colony is going to be a socialist society, and there will be no form of money. I'm not sure I could live that way."

She pursed her lips. "I think it makes sense. The idea is that everyone will contribute in whatever ways their skills allow, and in return, all of their needs will be met."

"Yeah, but what would encourage a farmer to innovate and increase production if he doesn't see any monetary gain from it?"

Roberts wished she had Abigail's ability to see people's auras so she could get a better clue about what was going through this kid's head. "Don't you think providing food and supporting the colony so it thrives would be a reward in itself? What if the farmer's child became ill? Should the farmer be burdened with medical bills? The doctors and medical staff will offer their services to those who need it, and they, in turn, will rely on the farmers to produce food. If you were to join the colony, you would need to consider what assistance you could provide instead of focusing on how to make money."

"I'm not sure what skills I might have to offer. It doesn't sound like they'll need accountants. Keeping track of money is my favorite thing, and I'm good at math."

"Maybe you could offer your assistance as a colony debt collector, to force the farmer to pay his medical bills?"

Eliot leaned back in his chair and smiled insincerely. "Ha ha, very funny. I think I'll stay on this planet, where hopefully, capitalism doesn't go extinct. But with the way things are headed, I'm worried."

Roberts rested her pen against her notepad. "Aren't you excited for the future? Your sister has done so much to lead the world in a new positive direction. She and Silas Rutherford have worked toward transitioning the country to clean energy, they brought the Taurians to Earth, and they have worked to protect the environment. These are all amazing accomplishments."

"I'm not so sure those things are heading us in a positive direction. Restrictions placed by the government only hurt businesses, and the Taurians aren't exactly stimulating our economy. They didn't show up with pockets full of money—not that they have pockets."

Roberts took off her glasses and pinched the bridge of her nose. This kid was giving her a headache. "But they did bring advanced technology and a new form of democracy. They're helping our world evolve in a new direction. Also, let's say you wanted to join the colony. A Taurian pilot would fly you up to the orbiting colony ship, and they wouldn't charge you a penny. That alone is a worth-while contribution."

Eliot smirked. "Yes, but if they were smart, they *would* charge for their services and become rich. I think I'm going to stay on this planet, but I would like to be considered for your treatment. I know we don't agree on some issues, but that's the beauty of America. We're allowed to disagree. Please don't hold it against me just because my beliefs differ from yours."

"I will keep that in mind, Eliot. Thank you for coming in. I've got your name on the list."

Eliot winced as if he knew what she actually meant—*not a chance, kid*. His frown faded, though, and he looked her straight in the eye then left the office. She wondered what was going through his head and wished once again that she could study his aura. Despite his physical similarities, Cynthia had a hard time believing the boy was related to Abigail. She was sure he wanted the genetic enhancement only to help himself and wasn't really concerned about anyone else.

Chapter 3

Federation President

The President of the United States—or rather the New Federation—greeted Abigail with a handshake as she entered the Oval Office. She came alone because Gavin and Silas were still recovering from their injuries, and she had a feeling he had summoned her to confront her about the Illumination she had performed on him.

He kept his emotions pretty well hidden and put on a tight-lipped smile. "It's good to see you, Abigail. It's been too long."

She took a seat. "It's good to see you, too, Mr. President. We've all been busy, and it sounds like you've had your hands full lately with the New Federation."

"Remember, it's Russell or Russ to my friends." He smiled. "Yes, there's quite a lot happening. I feel like every time I'm watching the news, I'm watching history unfold. I saw your latest display of heroics. I hope Silas and Gavin are recovering from that altercation."

A pang of guilt hit her. "Yes, they're doing fine."

He cleared his throat. "There are a few recent stories of particular interest that have me thinking about what really happened when we first met. I have come to realize that when I first met you, I was affected by more than just the dream I thought I had in the night."

Abigail knew the day would come when she would have to confess what she had done to the president. She still couldn't tell if he was angry or happily accepting what she had done to him. His aura revealed only that he had many things on his mind.

She tensed. "You have to believe that you really left me with no other choice. I mean, you tried to have Silas and me killed by a hit man."

He let out a deep breath. "I know. I was a terrible monster, and I don't blame you for doing what you had to. I know it may have been a hard choice for you to make."

Abigail's nerves only slightly eased. Although she could see he wasn't angry, there was more on his mind. "I realize it was a violation to Illuminate you without your consent, even though you really left me no other choice. I did have the welfare of the planet to consider, and you had us locked in your basement."

The president let his smile grow, and his aura brightened but still swirled with a few concerning shades of darker colors. "The world is a better place because of the action you took, and I have lived a much better life because of the change you made to me." He did look to be healthier than when they'd first met. She liked his natural salt-and-pepper hair, too, changed from the artificial solid black it had been. "What do you call it—Illumination? I could not imagine going back to the way I was before you interfered with my brain. Although I wonder just how much you changed."

Abigail gave him a reassuring smile. "I simply opened new pathways in your brain, but you've maintained those pathways by using them. All I did was open your mind to a higher state of awareness. It's not like I hypnotized you or brainwashed you. You are the same person, just with more insight."

"Well, I've felt like a new person, and I'm very grateful. I've never been healthier or happier. You've probably added twenty years to my life because I've turned it around."

"I'm glad to hear about those side effects, but the well-being of the world was my main concern."

The president shuffled the papers on his desk. "Speaking of which, I believe the world is in need of your services again. I've called you here because I have a list of people who require new perspective, like what you gave me. I know firsthand that there's an issue of consent, but in all of these cases, there really is no better option. Each target has a list of helpfuls who, like my wife did with me, will assist you."

Abigail already felt conflicted about the few times she had performed Illuminations without the recipients' consent. She was also worried about unforeseen consequences of Illuminating a world leader. Like what if he got impeached, removed from office, and replaced with someone worse?

He laid out a sheet of paper with a long list of names. "For starters, there are judges on the Supreme Court who refuse to get on board. I've been dealing with backlash for dismantling Congress, even though the Federation Legislature is functioning smoothly. There are some ex-senators who didn't get elected to be Federation Representatives—big surprise—who are raising a stink. The Federation has grown in size over the last few months, which is good, but that creates concern for others. We have some hardheads who need new outlooks. Funny, it sounds like I'm hiring a hit man to break their kneecaps!"

Abigail wasn't sure if she liked where he was going with this. Illumination wasn't some magic wand she could wave to get everyone in line. She felt that it should only be done to people who were actively causing harm.

He leaned back in his chair. "I've put the more local targets at the top of your list. Then you will need to travel to Texas for a few oil executives. Oh, and there're a few other CEOs on the list. I've also got a list of more international targets. We would like to send you to Russia, China, Israel, Syria, Iran, and Zimbabwe, among other countries. Are you up for the task?"

"To be honest, I'm not comfortable with this. Even after my transformation and with some of the extraordinary things I've gotten to do, I never foresaw adding 'secret-brainwashing agent' to my résumé. I feel that my ability should only be used to prevent people from causing harm."

The president placed both palms on his desk. "Every single person on this list is causing harm. Anyone who is greedy and making billions of dollars off the backs of hardworking Americans is taking advantage of a system that benefits them. Just imagine what a difference some newfound perspective would make if powerful and rich people started looking out for everyone else. Isn't there a saying—I think I've heard your friend Ives say it—'With great power comes great responsibility'? There's a handful of people with too much power, and they're taking advantage of it without helping anyone."

Abigail bit her lip. "Listen, I admire your goal to get everyone to coexist and care about each other. Believe me, if I could shock the entire world into caring for one another, it would be very tempting. Illuminating the world isn't the right way to accomplish that, though. I want the world to become unified under its own free will. Now, if an angry mob is out to kill me and my friends, and I'm left with no other option, I'll do it, but I'm afraid I can't just Illuminate everyone who doesn't agree with you."

The president's smile faded as the deeper colors in his aura darkened. "How can you sit there with the power to bring peace to the country and to the world and do nothing?"

She raised her voice. "I *have* been working to accomplish peace, but in this case, it's only hard work that will get us and the world to where we need to go."

He cocked his head and glanced down at the list. "There are some people on this list who *are* causing physical harm. Leaders of countries who are mistreating others, even their own citizens. Would you at least consider looking through it and using your best judgment as to who needs your treatment? And will you take a trip to remedy some of these situations?"

Abigail thought that sounded like a reasonable compromise. "Sure. I'll look at your list and research each contender. Silas has been wanting to get back to Iceland. I'd consider taking a trip if we could start there and shut down the whaling operation."

The president beamed as he pushed the list across the polished mahogany desktop. "I will authorize whatever resources you need for the trip, especially if you would continue on to some of these other countries."

"Thank you, Mr. Pres—Russell." Abigail couldn't wait to tell Silas they would move forward with a mission to stamp out the whaling operation. "I'll look at your list and consider which leaders need enlightenment."

"I'll let you make that decision on your own. Sending you out with a naval force sounds like a good start to address some of the world's problems, like the whaling in Iceland. You know, Silas's business ventures could serve as a cover for getting your foot in the door to some of those countries where your help is needed." He gestured to the list in her hands. "He's a bright young man. You both have gotten in and out of some tough situations."

"Yes. Remember when you locked us in your basement?"

Russell nodded. "I do. I was a different person then. If only I had worn my tinfoil hat while I was sleeping, you would have never succeeded!" He gave her a wink.

Abigail was relieved he'd lightened the mood with some humor. She picked up her list and stood to shake his hand, smiling. "I'm glad I wasn't defeated by that tinfoil hat."

Chapter 4

The Observer and the Overseer

Ringlow wasn't accustomed to sitting across from someone who held such a high position, but he could get used to the morphing chair that sensed his thoughts and adjusted its fit accordingly. He had only to think, *I'd like to recline a bit more*, and the glob of glowing purplish-blue material would comply. Or if he wanted to face more directly toward the enormous screen in the cave-like chamber, it would rotate almost before he was aware of his desire to turn that way.

The Overseer stared at Ringlow with a cold glare. His eyes remained dark with large pupils on an oversized face that resembled their species' natural form with no horns, hair, or any prominent features but his leathery blue-gray skin. Ringlow expected the Overseer to morph at any moment, which he had heard was a common sight.

Sure enough, horns began to surface on his brow. "Don't get too comfortable. Very few Observers ever see any sort of promotion. Any promising civilization you observe will likely collapse or destroy itself before it can make any significant developments."

Ringlow willed his seat to elevate him into a more upright position. "I believe I have been observing a world upon which there is a race who I believe will overcome the Species Advancement Barrier Filter." He had fallen in love with a newly discovered planet that in his opinion had the perfect balance of conditions—size, composition, distance from its star, among other qualities. The blue planet had plenty of water and one large moon that stirred its soupy oceans with life.

The barrier filter to which he was referring was a well-known law stating that advanced civilizations were extremely rare because such developments typically led to overconsumption of resources, destruction of the livable environment, or straight-up self-annihilation. The law, which they also called the Great Filter, additionally took into account outside forces that could disrupt a civilization, such as natural disasters or cosmic events such as collisions or nearby supernovae. All of those factors diminished the chances of a species' survival, making it extremely rare for any to advance to a level at which they achieved space travel.

The Overseer's horns grew larger. "Whatever planet in whatever system you have found will be no different than countless others. They will inevitably fail to advance—or if they do advance, they will not survive long enough to make any progress toward interstellar travel. You may continue your report, but know that the only reason you're in my presence is because your parents were exceptionally gifted, and you come with high recommendations. Other than the privilege of reporting directly to me, don't expect any special treatment. I believe your parents might have put some false hope into you by naming you after the ring that circles our star. It must be disheartening to think that you will not likely live up to the significance of your name."

Ringlow took the criticism in good spirits. He knew that the Overseer's gruffness was a tactic for keeping observers from becoming overconfident and making mistakes. Ringlow also liked his name and hoped to accomplish much to prove he was worthy to hold it. The glow of their system's ring was a sight unmatched by any other in the galaxy.

He nodded and began his report. "The intelligent beings in the system X-47892 inhabit that system's outermost terrestrial planet, a red planet which has experienced a loss of sustainable habitat due to a thinning atmosphere and a growing scarcity of water, as was predicted. The planet's magnetic field has weakened over time as well.

"They have adapted by settling under the surface, and our Central Processing Unimatrix calculates a high percentage of success for the long-term survival of the small population who remains, although they may cease to be a space-faring species because of their lack of resources. The inhabitants of the red world sent ninety-eight percent of their population on two colony ships. One ship with the majority of their population is leaving the system, and the other has journeyed to their neighboring planet, X-3, which is liquid-water-abundant, thus making it a blue planet."

The Overseer conceded. "This species has persisted beyond an obstacle that would normally wipe out a slightly less advanced race, but all they have managed to do is postpone the inevitable, which is that their civilization will end in one catastrophe or another."

Ringlow nodded again. He knew he was taking a chance by bringing the system to the Overseer's attention. If the civilization ended because of their own ineptness, it would mean ridicule and little chance of his promotion. "Yes, but there was an unanticipated event that occurred before any colony activity began. Before any members of their species attempted to transfer to their neighboring planet, they sent a large asteroid to eradicate the animal life on their inner blue neighbor. After waiting for the planet to become habitable, they sent a small colony, who were met with a number of challenges and failed. That colony ship returned only to deliver corpses."

The Overseer clasped his long pointy fingers together. "What a barbaric development! It only foreshadows their demise. You may want to abandon hope of this species' survival and save yourself a millennium of tedium. I am not surprised they annihilated life on their neighboring planet instead of trying to coexist. They sound very barbaric indeed."

Ringlow was determined to observe the developments that the species was bound to make. "C-PU has calculated the probability of success for the initial colonization attempts to be rather low, but the transfer from the red planet to the blue planet was inevitable after many attempts were made."

An impatient frown appeared on the Overseer's massive head, which had morphed into that of an animal's face with larger nostrils, fur, and more elaborate horns. "Well... have they succeeded in the colonization of their neighboring planet?"

Ringlow cleared his throat. "Their final colony attempt did succeed in establishing a cluster of dwellings. From their landing site, their seed village would surely have spread to cover much of the planet's surface in giant cities, but an inexplicable event has interrupted their development. The individuals in the colony arrived, but they have scattered and have somehow lost some of their evolutionary advancement, but I am certain they will evolve into perhaps something more extraordinary than they once were."

The Overseer's frown deepened. "Why are you wasting my time with this? It sounds as if their colonization attempt has failed." He continued to tap his elongated fingers on his armrest. "I will admit, though, that I am slightly curious to know what happened to the species upon their arrival and to see if there is any possibility for their rise to a new level of advancement, since they have already overcome so many obstacles."

Perfect. I've managed to hook the Overseer's curiosity. He smirked to himself but put effort into not showing it outwardly. "I am not certain of the cause of their devolution, but I do wish to remain at my post and observe the blue planet further." Ringlow had only recently been assigned to the system. Other systems he had studied in the past had long periods of minimal activity, so he felt fortunate to have witnessed these developments so far. "There is still time for their future progression. Their yellow star is young, and we see no projected supernovae in their region for the next fifty to sixty eons."

The Overseer's appearance morphed back to his genetically given form with no horns or fur. The only alteration Ringlow saw was a ridge across his brow that would surely erupt into horns if he was agitated again. Their kind had collected and assimilated the genetic makeup of countless species and incorporated it into their own DNA. One had only to think of changing one's appearance to morph with little effort. Ringlow put effort into preventing any morphing of his own.

The Overseer let out a deep breath. "The Galaxy is a large expansive place, and we need to be aware of any species who defies the odds and advances with space-faring capabilities to the point at which they might someday appear in our system. We both know the chances of that are close to zero, but your department exists solely to predict any such surprise."

Ringlow worked to keep his appearance unchanged, deliberately wearing his most neutral face, revealing the least amount of emotion, but deep down, he was thrilled that despite the Overseer's irritability, the meeting had gone well.

Ringlow stood. "There was one more interesting incident. Before the meteor strike against the blue planet, a ship traveled from the red planet to collect multiple forms of animal life then left the system. I would like permission to follow that ship's progress and track its location so we can oversee the developments that arise from that rescue and relocation."

The Overseer reclined into his morphing chair. "Perhaps the life that has been relocated will show more promise than the group of barbarians you have decided to invest your time into. You may follow the progress of both, but I warn you that if I authorize the allocation of resources to do so and they both fail, you will be sorting data files for the rest of your career."

Chapter 5

Enterprise

Abigail sat behind the yoke of Silas's private jet, her friends strapped into their seats as they headed to land on what would become their new home for the next few weeks, an aircraft carrier named *Enterprise*.

Silas hadn't slept much the night before, and Abigail had been sure he would nap on the flight, but he stayed alert the whole time. She was pretty sure he was counting down until the day they would shut down Victor Dagurson's whaling operation with a substantial military force.

They'd enlisted Gavin, who'd jumped at the chance to travel with them. It had been all too common to leave him behind during past trips. She hoped it wouldn't be too awkward to have Gavin along— early on, he had expressed having a crush on her, and they had gone on a date, but nothing had really developed since then. She supposed she was waiting for him to grow up just a bit more.

Abigail wished one other person was aboard the small plane— her best friend, Evvie, who was in orbit, preparing her mega ship, the *Harkin*, for their trip to scout a new colony world in the Polaris system. Abigail supposed the trip across the ocean would keep her busy until the ship was ready, at which point she looked forward to traveling to a new star system. The Taurians had offered to upgrade the *Harkin* with new technology, and a large crew of Taurians and humans were up there now, working on the ship and training for the mission. Their departure sounded like it would still be at least a couple months away.

The aircraft carrier they were flying out to meet happened to be one of the longest naval vessels ever built. The team didn't necessarily need the largest ship, but Abigail did need the longer runway to land the plane, which they would also be using for some of her Illuminating missions. Landing on an aircraft carrier with this type of aircraft would be challenging, since it was not equipped for catapult takeoffs or the use of arresting wires when landing, so she would have to take off and land unassisted. The plane had, however, been modified with additional boosters so it could accelerate more quickly. She had become quite the pilot but still spent much of the flight worrying about her first aircraft-carrier landing.

They had just cleared the East Coast and were flying over the Atlantic Ocean. Abigail began lowering the plane's altitude. The carrier had gotten a head start and began traveling out from the coast a few days earlier, so they had some ocean to fly over before rendezvousing with the ship.

She followed the coordinates she was receiving over the radio and continued to drop altitude. At last, she spotted the ship as just a speck on the horizon. She called in, "*Enterprise*, come in. *Little Dipper* requesting permission to land." She shook her head with an eye roll at having to announce the plane's name. Gavin had named it, and while she thought it was a cute name, she was a little embarrassed by it. She wondered if flight controllers in other countries would think it was cute and not take them seriously. Or maybe it could be a good thing to sound innocent and unthreatening. She thought *Enterprise* was definitely a great name for the aircraft carrier.

She received her clearance. As she approached, the ship proved to be huge, but she didn't think there was enough space to land. She wished she had practiced more short-distance landings.

The ship was turned so that her approach was headed into the wind, which would be helpful. She dropped in for her landing.

"You got this, right?" Silas squeaked from behind her.

"Piece of cake." Her voice stayed firm, hiding her doubt. The aircraft carrier was getting closer every second.

Abigail thought she was pretty well lined up to land, but she overshot the beginning of the runway and touched down in the middle of the strip. There was no way she had enough space or time to come to a stop.

Both Gavin and Silas let out concerned gasps from their seats, but she tuned them out. Realizing she couldn't make the landing, she hit the boosters, and her body was forced back into her seat. The plane flew off the end of the carrier and plummeted toward the sea. She saw the surface of the water coming very close to the bottom of the plane as she hit the extra boosters, and the additional force jolted her.

She exhaled only once the plane boosted away from the water and regained a little altitude. "Okay, let's try that again."

Without taking her eyes off of her piloting, she could see Silas's aura flashing with concern in her periphery. "Um, do you think you'll have better luck on your next attempt?"

"Don't worry. I've got this." If only she felt that sure.

She circled the plane and gave herself plenty of distance to line up with the ship. The real trick was going to be to touch down as close to the leading edge as possible to give her the most time to decelerate without dropping the plane off the other end of the runway and into the water.

The guys didn't make a peep. A little silence was all she needed. She reminded herself that she had flown spacecraft to other planets. "You can do this," she murmured to herself. She just had to come in at the right angle and speed to touch down at the *beginning* of the landing strip.

She wondered if she was coming in a little too fast, but she set the plane down and hit the reverse thrusters along with the air brakes, and the plane jolted. Her straps dug into her chest. The sensation of fast braking lasted a half second longer until the plane came to an abrupt stop. Out the cockpit window, they had a view of nothing but the choppy ocean. The plane was successfully parked on the ship's deck and not in the water, so she gave herself a mental pat on the back.

She began to shut down the engines while Silas fumbled with the hatch to exit the plane.

When she stepped foot on the deck, he pointed at the front wheel of the plane, perched on the edge. "Just one more inch, and my plane would have become a submarine."

Gavin shook his head with a grin. "That was close, but I never doubted you."

A group of men in uniforms came to greet them. "That was quite a show you put on," said an accented voice. "Welcome aboard. *Mi barco es tu barco.*"

"Thanks for having us aboard, Captain…"

"It's Admiral… Admiral Fernando Rendón at your service. I think you may have made history by landing a civilian craft on this ship without the use of arresting wires to catch your plane and prevent it from falling into the sea. We are all very impressed."

His crewmates flashed amused smirks that were quickly replaced by stern neutral expressions.

Abigail studied Rendón and thought he appeared too young to be an admiral—maybe thirty. "Admiral" conjured an image of some stuffy old man with a cigar.

Gavin piped up. "Well, you should have seen her land that Mig-21 straight onto a moving Jeep right as I jumped out."

"Yes, I have heard about that stunt as well. Your reputation precedes you. We'll get your plane towed to a better parking spot and strapped down." With eyebrows raised, he peered at the plane's front landing gear. "It will be interesting to see you take off as well. Our fighter jets use a catapult system that I do not think your plane is equipped for."

Silas spoke up. "I've customized it with extra boosters that will do the job."

Rendón smiled. "We'll have a crew ready to fish this bird out of the water, just in case."

Silas's face turned a little red. Abigail thought he might continue to explain more about the modifications his team had made to the small plane, but he kept quiet.

Rendón dismissed the officers who had accompanied him. "You must be tired after such a long flight. If you'll follow me, I'll give you a quick tour and show you to your bunks." He led the way, glancing back at Abigail. "So you're going to work some of your magical powers around the world while we stamp out whaling operations and other infractions?"

"It's called Illumination." Abigail felt her face heat. "The president gave me a long list, which I've narrowed down to the ten most harmful dictators."

Silas rushed forward to follow right behind the admiral. "I think our first stop should be to Iceland to stamp out the whaling operation there. I've got some unfinished business with Victor Dagurson"

Rendón nodded. "*Sí, Señor.* That will be our first stop. My men will apprehend the man. You do know that I can't have civilians getting in the way of a military operation or getting hurt."

Abigail watched Silas's aura shift and his face turn redder. He began to open his mouth when Rendón continued, "You will, however, act as advisors and help oversee the operation. I hope that will be preferable to getting your hands dirty with a bunch of whalers?"

Silas huffed. Abigail knew that he wanted to apprehend Victor Dagurson personally.

They followed Rendón up a set of narrow stairs to the command station. "This is where we will discuss plans for every stage of the mission and where I'll give the orders to make it happen."

Gavin walked to the center of the control room and peered out the windows. "This view is awesome!" The room was lined with work stations and a crew focused on their tasks. Abigail knew Silas wanted a little more authority over the mission, and she could tell he was a little resentful, but she hoped he was realizing that with the help of this ship and crew, they were going to make a real difference in the world.

"Sir, we have something unusual coming up on our scopes," came a call from a crew member. "It appears to be some whales."

Rendón scoffed. "What is so unusual about whales? We see whales on many occasions."

"Sir, there's a large number of them, and they're swimming in formation. And they're headed straight at us."

Abigail looked over the crew member's shoulder to see the dots that were indeed in a V formation like geese flying as they migrated.

Rendón asked, "Can we see anything on visual?"

"Nothing yet, sir."

Rendón grabbed some binoculars and gestured for the three to follow him. He went onto the balcony overlooking the ship's main deck and the ocean.

While they peered over the sea, Gavin proclaimed, "It would be awesome if a pod of whales came to offer their assistance! We could use them for reconnaissance missions, and your Navy SEALs could ride them when they need a stealthy way to sneak into enemy territory. Or maybe dolphins. Dolphins might be better than whales for slipping through blockades and stuff."

Rendón chuckled. "That would be a fine addition to our forces. I still can't see them."

They waited, and Abigail wondered what the approaching group of whales was up to. At last, they broke the surface and were somewhat close.

Rendón gasped. "Now, there's something I've not seen before." He handed the binoculars to Abigail.

It took a moment for her to zero in on the lead whale. Once she did, she saw a figure on its back, grasping its dorsal fin. "We should go down to the main deck to greet them. Do we have some sort of rope or ladder?"

"Of course. Do you think they're friendly?"

She didn't answer as she rushed down the narrow stairs to get to the lower deck.

It was a sight to behold—nine or ten whales off the port bow. Standing on the back of the closest one was none other than their friend Tkla the Taurian.

"Permission to come aboard, Captain?" he called.

"Um, it's Admiral, and yes, permission granted." The well-composed and suave admiral lost a little of his poise. It was refreshing to see how he processed Tkla's unconventional arrival.

Tkla ascended the rope ladder gracefully, water streaming down his scales and off the tip of his tail. He climbed onto the deck and shook his body. Abigail grinned as she saw Rendón receive a splash of water on his uniform. She ran up and hugged the monstrously tall figure. "I knew you would be joining us, but how did you connect with a bunch of whales?"

"It is a pleasure to see you, Abigail. The boat on which I was a passenger came into the path of my new friends, who volunteered to transport me the remainder of the distance so the boat could continue on its way."

Admiral Rendón nodded. "Welcome aboard. And I thought Abigail made a fantastic entrance!"

"Thank you, Captain." Tkla approached the admiral, who this time, did not correct him on his rank, and gave him a firm handshake. "It is a pleasure to be aboard." He turned. "And to see you both, Silas and Gavin, is a pleasure I've been anticipating." He kept his hand out to shake each of theirs, but they brushed it away and bombarded him with hugs.

Gavin asked, "Did you bring the whales to help out with our mission?"

"They are aware of what we aim to accomplish, and they would indeed like to offer assistance in any way possible."

Rendón raised his eyebrows. "You know, a group of whales to escort us for a ways would not be a bad thing, and I will have to give the crew an opportunity to visit with them, but when the time comes to deploy on our first mission, I would prefer to keep any civilians out of danger."

Abigail peered into the water to see the pod of whales. She was thrilled that they were about to make the waters safer for their kind.

Chapter 6

Whaling Operation

After journeying for a few days, the aircraft carrier had traveled to within visual range of the coast of Iceland. It was early in the morning, and the crew was preparing to land. Rendón asked Abigail and her friends to meet in the command tower.

Silas glowed with excitement. "I think we should bring *Enterprise* all the way into port."

Abigail gazed out the window as the ship approached land. Gavin sat on a stool that spun so he could rotate to get a 360-degree view. The coast of Iceland was not too far off in the distance.

Rendón shook his head. "We have enough space aboard our two smaller boats to deliver enough man power." He turned to his lieutenant. "Drop the *Orca* and *Nimoy* into the water and prepare to transfer troops to those vessels."

Silas cut in. "Those boats don't have any clout. The *Orca* is our science vessel, and while *Nimoy* is a little more formidable, I don't think it will convey the message 'Give up. You're way outnumbered and outgunned.' We need the big ship to let them know we mean business."

Abigail was impressed with the way Silas stood up to the admiral. She had to admit that after the run-in they'd had with Victor Dagurson the last time they were here, she thought watching him pee his pants at the sight of the aircraft carrier would be very fulfilling. She decided to let Silas's point stand without adding to it.

Rendón sighed. "Fine. We'll bring in the big boat. Lieutenant, belay that last order. We'll stay aboard *Enterprise*. We should, however, drop our smaller boats in the harbor in case there's any trouble. Put a few good men on *Nimoy* in case they need to chase a rogue whaling vessel."

Gavin spun on his stool. "I love the names of these ships!"

∞

The USS *Enterprise* pulled into berth at the port of Victor Dagurson's whaling operation. Fortunately, the waters were deep enough for them to dock. They pulled in next to the largest whaling vessel.

As the crew established their boarding ramp, Rendón issued orders to the men lined up on the deck: "Secure the perimeter then tighten that perimeter until we have everyone contained. I want zero casualties and minimal injuries."

Abigail watched as Silas gripped the railing and peered down to the dock of the whaling facility. He tried one last time. "Please, can I be a part of the team that rounds up the whalers?"

Abigail didn't think that was a good idea, but Rendón responded before she could. "We have not trained you in any sort of hand-to-hand or firearm combat. You are not to engage with any of the hostiles."

Silas bit his lip.

Rendón stood at the top of the ramp. "Let's go, soldiers!"

Abigail stayed close to Silas as they watched the armed men descend the ramp and spread out around the facility, a massive warehouse that opened to the large wooden deck and a couple of smaller side buildings. There was some chaos as the whalers tried to flee, but the troops herded them onto the dock.

Silas walked to the top of the boarding ramp. "Now's our chance to get down there!"

"Wait, Silas, we don't have approval from the admiral. We're supposed to wait till he gives us permission."

Gavin leaned over the railing to watch the activity below. "Umm, I'll hold tight here."

Tkla added, "I will remain with Gavin. I am in a position where I must not cause harm to any humans for fear of creating increased hostility between our species. Believe me, I would like to help, but I would not like to cause more harm than good."

Abigail appreciated Tkla's reasoning and Gavin's common sense. Before she could convince Silas to hold tight just a bit longer, he headed down the ramp. She had no choice but to follow him.

They hurried down to the dock and spotted Victor Dagurson, a tall bear of a man with a graying beard and mustache.

Silas made haste to the large man. "I brought an army this time," he called as he approached Dagurson, who appeared to be much less cocky than when they'd met a few months earlier. Surely, the man thought he was going to receive a punch to the stomach to match the one he'd given Silas. Abigail didn't think Silas would resort to physical violence, but she knew he was savoring every moment. When they got closer, Dagurson abruptly pushed two of his workers into Silas's path and ran for his ship.

"Don't shoot!" yelled Admiral Rendón to his crew. "We want zero casualties. And he has no place to go."

Dagurson headed to his whaling ship with Silas hot on his trail. Abigail cursed and followed behind them.

They followed Dagurson onto the ship and through a maze of narrow walkways and staircases. Luckily, there were lights on in the ship, so as she ran, Abigail pulled some electricity into her body. After her genetic alteration, she had been able to draw power from sources like batteries. Her newest trick was to draw electricity from a distance without having to touch the source of electricity. She simply waved her hand over every light fixture she passed to draw a little more, which she stored in her body. It was good thing her hair was tied back, or it would have gotten pretty frizzy.

Unfortunately, by taking the time to "power up," as Gavin liked to call it, she had increased the distance between herself and Silas. She climbed the last stairway and was blinded by the bright morning light. Once she was able to focus, she saw Victor Dagurson at a harpoon station, pointing the swiveling harpoon gun right at Silas, who was holding a small handgun.

"Where in the world did you get a gun?"

Silas didn't answer but kept it pointed at the large man.

Dagurson aimed the harpoon at Silas's chest. "Stay back! Or else the young lad gets speared."

Abigail couldn't believe the situation they were in. "Okay, how about we make a deal? Silas, you lower the gun, and Victor, take your hands off the harpoon. It's the easiest way to get out of this with no one getting hurt."

"Fine." Silas lowered his weapon.

Abigail waited. Dagurson did not comply but continued to grip the handle of the harpoon launcher.

"Come on. I know you're smart enough to take this deal. No harm will come to you or your men."

"Fine. I cannot string two whales with one harpoon, anyway." Dagurson released his grip and put his hands in the air.

Abigail sighed with relief but saw a red flash in his aura, as she'd seen a few times before in other dangerous situations. He made a sudden movement to pull a gun from the back of his belt. Once she saw the gun, she shot every volt of electricity straight at him. Then she heard the gun fire.

Victor clutched his chest and fell back against the ship's railing. He tipped over the top bar and disappeared. She rushed to the edge to see his body sprawled on the dock below.

Abigail looked back at Silas, whose face was pale. He still held his handgun. *Did Silas shoot Dagurson, or was it the whaler's gun that fired?* She didn't see any evidence of Silas having been shot. She studied the ship's paneling behind him and found a small bullet hole. "Are you okay?"

"I-I think so." He flipped the gun in his hand and held it out for Abigail to take.

She relieved him of the weapon. "Do you even know how to shoot that thing?"

"I think I might have had the safety on."

She gave him a reassuring nod and a hug. By that point, they were surrounded by Rendón's men, who escorted them back to join the others.

Once they were back on the dock, Rendón shook his head. "Well, this is a mess. And that was quite a show you put on up there."

"Honestly, I didn't mean to kill him. I've shocked plenty of people before without that sort of consequence."

A man piped up from the crowd of whalers. "Victor was taking medication for his heart."

Rendón shook his head once more. "Great! You gave him a heart attack."

"He had a harpoon pointed at Silas, and then he pulled a gun."

"And Silas shouldn't have been there. You were supposed to stay on the big boat until everyone was contained. Also, I'll take that pistol off your hands."

She handed it over.

Tkla and Gavin came down onto the dock. Abigail hoped Gavin wouldn't open his mouth to say something about how she was such an awesome superhero with amazing powers, because she didn't feel awesome or amazing for killing the older man. Luckily, he kept quiet.

Tkla, however, commented, "I was beginning to believe your species' creativity and ingenuity compensated for your general lack of intelligence, but that man displayed an unbelievable level of stupidity when the odds of escape were so greatly against him."

Abigail nodded. "I have to agree with you, and now he's dead. But it's still my fault. I hit him with far too severe a shock." While she felt responsible, she agreed with Tkla, and an angry surge of electricity rippled through her body and out to her fingertips. If he had just complied, he would still be alive. Even though his poor judgment had led to his death, she was the one who'd killed him. She had killed another human being. It was a lot to process.

Rendón raised his eyebrows at her as if to say, "Yeah, you pretty much fried that old man." He then gestured to the group of whalers surrounded by his men. It was time for her to do her job.

With their boss dead, the whalers were compliant. Abigail walked toward them. She looked down at the pair of tall black boots she had purchased in anticipation of the trip—she thought they had a nice intimidating look to them. But by that point, she didn't think she needed any help to intimidate the men.

She studied the crowd of whalers. Their auras revealed that many were shaken, probably by Victor Dagurson's death. She felt like she was stuck in some sort of nightmare and just wanted to wake up to a reality where no one had died.

Abigail cleared her throat. "We can do this the hard way or the easy way. Your friend Victor chose the very-hard-and-now-he's-dead way, and I'm truly sorry for that. I promise no harm will come to any of you. We're certainly not going to shoot any of you with harpoons." She glanced up to where the incident had occurred and closed her eyes to see the indelible vision of the dying man.

"All of you have two options: you can receive a painless treatment from me, called Illumination, or you can be placed in the brig of our ship and be brought to trial. To be Illuminated is to be shown the harm of your ways and be enlightened to live a better life. It's hardly a punishment, but I can guarantee you will need to find a different line of work—you will no longer have the stomach to kill these magnificent creatures. If you wish to be placed in custody and face trial, follow the soldier up the ramp to our ship. If you choose Illumination, join hands in a circle, and I will complete the link with you."

Abigail had been putting some thought into how she would Illuminate them. She had a feeling that many of them were not bad or immoral but simply men looking for work. She had not slept well the night before because she felt that some of them maybe did not deserve to be treated like criminals.

She was surprised when every single whaler joined hands and two of them held out their hands for her to close the link. She saw concern in their auras, and another pang of guilt hit her because she had coerced them by giving them no other option besides prison.

She grasped the two men's hands and instantly transmitted a message to say that everything would be okay and she wasn't there to harm them. As she had experienced with the original Illuminating pulse, and as she had conveyed to the few people she had Illuminated so far, she sent out an image of the universe, the solar system, and the Earth, showing how everything was balanced and interconnected. She then showed the Earth falling out of balance with glaciers and permafrost melting, animals losing their habitats, cities clouded in smog, and the overall effect humans were having on the world.

She then shared an experience that Tkla had posted to his people's collective—of which Abigail had become a member—when he had met the whale and her calf off the coast of San Diego last year. Tkla had jumped into the ocean and swum with the whales and dolphins during a whale-watching tour when he and his people first arrived on Earth.

She placed that detailed memory into the minds of all of these men. Tkla had communicated with the mother of the young whale. The mother had felt concern for the future and for her calf. Abigail shared that concern with them.

She observed the men's thoughts. Many cared only about their paychecks and hadn't put much thought into the harm they were causing. Abigail made a note that she should work with Silas to set up some sort of foundation to help them find new work—work that might benefit the oceans and the world.

She remained standing with them for a minute longer, just to convey a sense of hope for their futures and to reassure them that they should move forward with their lives without guilt and make the world a better place. She then released the hold she had over them and opened her eyes. "Thank you for your cooperation. Iceland has not yet voted to join the Federation, but if it does, you may sign up to join the Federation Navy, and you may someday become part of a force that works to protect the whales instead of hunting them."

Her Illumination of the men somehow helped ease some of the guilt that weighed on her from having killed Victor Dagurson, but killing the whaler was not something she would soon forget.

The crowd of ex-whalers were free to leave. Many expressed their desire to see their families and children, whom they had not seen recently because of the busy whaling season. They appeared to be remorseful but retained an air of hopefulness.

The group was destined to become a catalyst for change in that part of the world. She thought back to how pessimistic she had been with the president about Illuminating the people on his list—*maybe it could be a solution to many of the world's problems.* She would find out once she Illuminated the ten subjects she had selected.

Abigail looked at Silas, who gave her a hopeful smile. The world was a slightly better place than it had been before their mission.

Before heading up the ramp to the aircraft carrier to depart, Admiral Rendón watched the crowd disperse. "I don't know what I've just witnessed, but it's nice to see that none of them are going to attempt to retaliate like Señor Dagurson."

Abigail nodded. "Thank you for your help. We couldn't have achieved this without you and your team."

Rendón gave Silas a stern pat on the shoulder. "If you could learn to follow orders, then perhaps we could train you to be part of the team. You're new to this, so I will give you a second chance, but if you blatantly disobey orders again, I'll send you rowing home on the smallest boat I can find." Rendón studied the pistol he'd confiscated. "You have the passion and the drive. You only need more skills and discipline to be a soldier. Once you prove yourself and are properly trained, you may have your gun back."

Silas's aura glowed with hope. Abigail could tell he was thrilled with the prospect of training aboard the ship. She could also see he was embarrassed about his blunder, the rosy color in his face matching the energy around him.

Rendón gestured to Abigail to lead the way up the ramp. "Although, with Abigail around, we might not need guns."

Chapter 7

Little Brother

Dr. Cynthia Roberts was trying to make sense of a letter Eliot had just delivered to her office. After reading it, she set it on her desk. "What the hell is this?"

Eliot was leaning against the doorway to her office, looking smug. "It's my lawyer's order for you to perform your procedure on me."

"This is a load of... A lawyer can't order me to do anything."

"You are withholding a cure to a disease, and we will inform the state of California about it."

"My treatment isn't even thoroughly tested. How can anyone demand an experimental treatment? And what if I refuse?"

"You know there's one well-documented case of the success of your treatment, and she's making headlines in the news every day with all of her exceptional acts of heroism. The world doesn't know exactly how she got her powers, though, which could be our little secret. If you don't comply, the state may become involved and revoke your license, and I might have to leak the story about how my sister got her powers to the press."

So far, no one had pieced together any connection between Roberts's work and Abigail's abilities. They had been seen together on a few occasions, like at the rocket launch and on visits to the White House, but that didn't prove anything. His attempt to blackmail her with the release of information to the public was despicable. She had to think of a way to buy some time. Silas and Abigail were on the other side of the world, and Evvie was in orbit aboard the *Harkin*. They were the first friends she could think of to help, especially because Abigail was his big sister, and Silas might have some advice or resources available to help. "I need to draw some blood and get your DNA charted. The results will take a couple of weeks."

Eliot crossed his arms and maintained his smug expression. "Isn't my DNA similar enough for you to repeat the procedure you performed on my sister?"

He was correct, but she said, "Not unless you're their long-lost identical female triplet? Every sibling has a different mix of genes from their parents." It wasn't a total lie, and it would buy her some time.

"I understand." Eliot rolled up his sleeve for Dr. Roberts to take a blood sample. She withdrew the blood and grudgingly put on a small round Band-Aid, and he left.

Cynthia couldn't believe the predicament she was in. She began making phone calls. She had Silas's cell number, and she finally got through to Abigail.

"Your little brother is proving to be a real pain in my ass. He came in, demanding to receive the same treatment as you, or he will go public with the true nature of your alteration."

Abigail huffed. "Yes, he's a real piece of work. I'm so sorry I'm not there. I'll get Silas to email you the name of a lawyer you should call. My brother is only driven by money and his own distorted idea of wealth. I don't think he's capable of real harm."

"I wish you were here to ensure that. Your Illumination ritual would be a comforting step in his or anyone else's transformation."

"I'm sure Eliot's only motive is to create some get-rich-quick scheme. If our lawyer sees no other option and you are forced to treat him, I don't think too much harm will come from it."

Cynthia gripped her forehead, feeling a headache igniting. "This is putting me in a very tough position. How long will it take for your return?"

Abigail's voice crackled though the poor connection. "We have really just begun our trip. It will be several weeks before we return.

If any crisis arises, I can jump in Silas's plane and come back, but there are lives at stake in some of the countries I'm visiting. We're just about to enter the Mediterranean, and from there, I'll start my more dangerous missions."

"Okay." Cynthia sighed, realizing she had to deal with this on her own. "You be safe and come back in one piece."

"Will do. I'm so sorry you have to deal with him. I know he can be a little shithead."

Cynthia hung up the phone then pressed her hand over her eyes, wishing it was just a bad dream.

She met with the lawyer. After reviewing the documents, he said, "This letter is nothing but blackmail written by an amateur lawyer. I don't think there is any danger of having your license revoked or anything, since I don't think he has actually contacted the state with any concerns... yet."

"Does that mean I can refuse to treat him?"

"That depends on how much trouble he could cause if you don't."

Cynthia realized that the boy had found a way to leverage her into treating him because she absolutely did not want to risk having her work revealed to the world. *Yep... what a little shithead.*

Chapter 8

England

Admiral Rendón, Silas, Abigail, and Gavin were on the bridge of *Enterprise,* heading away from Iceland. Abigail was relieved to see the strip of land diminish as they headed back out to sea.

"I'm so glad that's over and that our first mission has been accomplished," Silas said with a meek half smile. He still looked a little pale.

Abigail wasn't sure if it was appropriate to celebrate the success of their first mission, since she had accidentally killed a man, and they had bungled it so badly because they hadn't followed orders. She couldn't erase the image of his lifeless body being lifted onto a stretcher and hauled away.

Gavin patted Abigail on the back. "I think you handled that confrontation with Victor Dagurson in the only way possible. He had a gun that he could have used at any point. Things could have ended much worse. Also, Illuminating all those whalers at once was amazing. *You're* amazing, Abigail, or should I say *Master Illuminator?*"

"Just plain 'Abigail' will be fine. If I were a master, I would have better self-control and wouldn't have shocked an old man to death. Also, a master would have an apprentice or a whole academy of apprentices, wouldn't they? I'm far from having the skills to teach anyone anything."

It was easy to tell when Gavin's imagination started to run wild. Abigail could see the excitement in his aura. His eyes widened, and he spoke even louder. "That would be so awesome to have a bunch of Illuminators! When do you think Dr. Roberts will alter more people?"

Silas crossed his arms. "It's like the admiral said. With you around, who needs guns? Just imagine if we had more of you."

Abigail raised her eyebrows. "It's an interesting idea. I think Dr. Roberts is holding off until there's some sort of plan for how more advanced people would fit into society. Evvie and I are having a hard time fitting in, and I'm not sure the world is ready for more enhanced people."

Gavin said, "I'm definitely voting for more. Maybe you could join together to become some sort of Illuminator Army."

Abigail liked the sound of having more Illuminators—it would be nice to have extra people tackling the problems of the world. At the same time, she had to admit that she liked being special and unique. "We all agree that anyone who undergoes the treatment should be Illuminated so they use their advancement to help the world and not try to take it over with their superior brains." She thought of her brother and his wish to become advanced like her. She hoped Cynthia could find a way to avoid treating him.

Admiral Rendón listened quietly until he clapped his hands and leaned forward in his chair. "So, what's the next target for you meddling kids?"

Silas chuckled. "I would love to show up on England's doorstep with this ship to stop their bottom-trawling fishing practices. I still can't believe such a developed nation hasn't outlawed the use of destructive cages that strip so much life from the ocean floor."

Abigail couldn't believe England hadn't banned it yet either. The country apparently didn't want to put restrictions on the seafood industry, but the effects of dragging the trawling cages were devastating—they were like bulldozers stripping a path and leaving a cloud of muddy remains suspended in their wake. Some other countries known for their reckless trawling practices were Russia, China, and South Korea.

Gavin propped his chin in his palm. "Britain is a world superpower compared to the whaling operation we just shut down, so I think we should proceed more cautiously." He tapped a finger against his cheek. "Hmm…" His face lit up, and he shot that finger into the air. "I have a great idea!"

After he described his scheme for the next leg of their mission, everyone was excited to proceed—everyone except for Admiral Rendón, who shook his head. "How do you think this act of vandalism will convince them to change their laws? It sounds like it will just piss off everyone in charge. Also, we'll need to get the president to sign off on any such mission."

"I'll talk to him." Abigail thought of a way to leverage the British government. "We could leak the time of our stunt to the press so they can document it to raise awareness around their country and the world, and that will put pressure on the British government to make a change."

Rendón shook his head. "You kids better not get me into any more trouble. Make sure no one gets hurt and there's not too much damage, and I will support it."

"It's a deal." Abigail gave the young admiral a reassuring nod.

A week later, Abigail was flying the tandem-rotor heavy-lift CH-47 helicopter with a massive tangle of metal hanging beneath it above London. She hoped their plan would get the leaders of the country to open their eyes and that it wouldn't simply anger them. She wondered if perhaps they were going too far, but she reminded herself that if England hadn't yet banned the harmful practice of bottom trawling, drastic action was required to raise awareness.

She flew over downtown and hovered over Parliament. She was tempted to drop the load on the building itself but decided otherwise. Their stunt couldn't result in too much damage, and absolutely no one could get hurt. She was lowering her altitude and positioning the chopper, aiming to drop the mass of cages on the front steps, when she got a call from the *Big E*. "*Huey-1*, we're picking up two craft heading to intercept. They are coming in at high speed. We are identifying them as Eurofighter Typhoon FGR4s."

Abigail was a pretty well-trained pilot but not when it came to interacting with hostile aircraft. "Copy that. How should I proceed?"

"The admiral says to regain altitude and abort your mission."

"But I'm so close…"

"I repeat: regain altitude and abort your mission."

Abigail couldn't believe she thought of doing this—definitely something she'd seen in a movie—but she created some static sounds with her lips pressed close to her mouthpiece and said, "Sorry... you're cutting out." She was not going to hightail it out of there without finishing the mission.

She had only to position the chopper a little to the side to be over the front steps and not over the building so she could drop the cages. Before she made the adjustment, she spotted the jets coming in fast. They whipped by, and she realized that as they passed, the closer one had been shooting at her. Pings rang through her craft. *That's not good. Maybe Rendón is right, and I should abort.*

She was about to increase altitude when her chopper shuttered. A red light flashed on her control board. Her craft was losing fuel pressure. And the chopper dropped. She tried to maneuver, but it began spinning out of control.

She made one last attempt to stabilize the chopper, and her stomach shot up into her chest as it plummeted. She got a glimpse of where she was going to touch down as her craft fell—right on the building she had been planning to avoid.

She braced herself, and then her world became a loud storm of explosions and crunching sounds as her chopper crashed into the top of the building. All she could do was hang on tightly during the impact.

∽

Abigail awoke in a hospital bed. She attempted to rub the searing pain on her brow but found that her hand was handcuffed to the side rail. She conducted an inventory of her body. *Am I hurt?* She detected an aching in her back and neck, and her head pounded.

"All of the destruction was caused by your incompetent pilots," a man said. "Opening fire in the middle of London was the worst possible way to handle the situation. My pilot had strict instructions to drop the trawling cages where no one would be hurt and damage would be minimal. Now, the dumb fishing cages *and* a chopper are right in the middle of your parliament building."

Is that the president?

"You're just lucky she's okay." It sounded like he was haranguing an officer of the Royal Air Force outside her hospital curtain.

The curtain flashed open, and his flustered rosy face appeared. "Oh good, you're awake. How do you feel?"

"I think I'm fine. I'm so sorry that I crashed the chopper. No one got hurt, did they?"

The president inhaled deeply. "Parliament had been evacuated. You're the only one who got hurt. You have a couple cracked vertebrae and some bumps and bruises."

The gap in the curtains widened farther. A tan face peeked through. "I told you, not too much damage, and no one was to get hurt."

"Admiral. I'm so sorry. I—"

He frowned. "Someone, get in here and remove these restraints on the double!"

∞

Within hours, Abigail and Admiral Rendón boarded a small chopper to take them back to *Enterprise*. She sat back with relief to be a passenger instead of the pilot. Her head still pounded, and she wondered if maybe she had a slight concussion. She had been fitted with a back brace that prevented her from slouching in her seat.

During the flight, Rendón asked, "What is with you and Silas not wanting to follow orders?"

"I guess we're both just a little thickheaded. And maybe we care too much."

"Pipsqueak Gavin and the Jolly Green Taurian are the only ones who know how to listen. You do know that above all else, the safety of my crew is my highest priority."

Abigail liked that Fernando was talking to her more as a friend and not just her commanding officer. "I know. And I'm really sorry."

"You've got some special skills, and I think you can bring some positive change to the world, but not if you get yourself killed."

"I know. I'm sorry." Abigail gazed out the window to see the land disappear, replaced by the ocean.

"I don't want apologies. I want you to follow orders."

She looked him in the eye. "I'll try. I promise."

Chapter 9

The Transplant and the Primitives

Ringlow had been summoned back to report to the Overseer, but he felt pessimistic about the species into whom he had placed so much hope and bet the future of his career. He had spent thousands of years in their system, observing their blue planet and taking periodic cryogenic naps only to see that they were emerging as a hostile and warmongering species. He had also discovered alarming news about the planet on which the transplanted life forms flourished in a system hundreds of light-years away from their planet of origin.

With a pit in his stomach, he entered the Overseer's dark and warm chamber. With all of the planets available to inhabit in their system, Ringlow would have chosen a space with a natural source of light and a view of an exotically colored landscape or sky instead of the dark, cavernous lair lit primarily by an enormous screen and the slight glow of the purple floor, from which life forms grew to serve as furniture. The screen did at least give the Overseer a view of any of the landscapes he wished to see in their Ring of Worlds system.

"Ringlow, it's been quite some time since we last spoke."

If only it could have been longer, he might have had better news to report.

"How goes the progress of the barbarians into which you are investing your time?"

A purple-blue glob grew from the floor, and Ringlow sat on it. He chose to have it recline a bit and give him a neck massage, which he hoped the Overseer wouldn't notice. It was not a long trip home through the wormhole, but he was stiff from his travels. "I won't lie. They have a very long way to go. They are at a very crude stage in their development."

A smirk surfaced on the Overseer's face. "Do you still believe they will become an exceptional race?"

"I believe the potential is there. There are some unforeseen challenges. Their numbers are small, and they have unfortunately spread and separated into nomadic pockets, each not relating well with others. And they have not yet developed agriculture."

The Overseer tapped a pointy finger on his armrest. "It sounds like they do indeed have a long way to develop before they are a unified and cooperative species. I almost pity you for deciding to invest your time into observing their stunted species."

Ringlow nodded slowly. "I will continue with my task. I have made a more troubling discovery, however, with the help of some calculations from C-PU. The planet to which the life forms were transplanted—who are in truth a more encouraging species to study—is in a neighborhood of the galaxy that is seeing more violent stellar activity. C-PU has detected an imminent supernova explosion that may take place within their vicinity within the next hundred million years."

The Overseer had not morphed his appearance so far, but he let a reptilian tongue poke from his mouth, and scales grew on his lips and brow. "That is a distant event to worry about. Why are you concerning yourself with this now? Many civilizations rise and fall within a shorter period of time."

Ringlow willed his seat to raise him upright. "I have high hopes for the transplants but worry they will only be discovering space travel by the time a supernova strips all life from their world—and then they won't have time to escape."

More scales grew on the Overseer's face. "We don't have the ability to divert supernovas, so they may well be doomed. If I were you, I would be more troubled by the lack of development on your world of barbarians. I have heard enough. You may go."

Ringlow was relieved to be dismissed. He planned to brainstorm solutions to help the transplants. There had to be a way to assist them before it was too late. At least he had a huge stretch of time during which he could consider solutions. He did not want to waste any effort thinking about possible remedies for the primitives and their lack of development. Only time would help to solve their dissonant ways—he hoped.

Chapter 10

Space Force

Evvie reached for a pneumatic socket driver to connect another tow-cable assembly to the small Taurian ship that was parked in the hangar bay of the massive ship, the *Harkin*. She had used her new human hands for many tasks since meeting Abigail, but having a physical body was a novelty she was still getting used to. Grasping a tool had once been impossible. She missed nothing about her former self except maybe the way she could float around without needing to concentrate on balancing to walk, but she was getting used to standing and walking.

Evvie wanted to focus on her work but instead let herself be distracted by the sensation of holding the tool. It was heavy and cold to the touch, and the handle had a slight texture cast into it that made it a pleasure to grip. *Okay, instead of studying the intricacies of holding this tool with my new five-fingered hands, let's get to work.* Her job was to assist in retrofitting new parts onto a group of ships parked in one of the ship's many hangar bays. Her mega ship was serving as an orbiting station for the Space Force fleet.

The General barked orders. "Get those grappling-hook assemblies installed on each of these ships. We need everyone to be equipped for any mission that might come our way. Each ship should have a way to grab other ships or rocky bodies like asteroids and such. And each should be blast-jump ready with blast-jump reactors, shields, and projectors. Get it done, people."

Evvie knew that despite The General's apparent gruffness, he cared for the well-being of everyone on his team. Although he put on an air of impatience, she had seen him help astronauts who were struggling to adjust or who simply needed help to seal a space suit before going out into space. He was probably her favorite person to sit across from for a meal in the ship's mess hall, although she had to put some effort into not staring at his graying mustache, which she imagined as a furry caterpillar dancing on his face. In her mind, mustaches were perhaps the strangest human feature.

The General was one of three people the president had appointed to lead the new Space Force. Like in all the other departments of the New Federation, leaders were selected in groups of three, a Taurian practice that the president wished to implement universally. The General had worked with Abigail, Silas, and his team to launch the *Gemini-Infinity 1* mission and had a long history of service in the Air Force.

After her maintenance shift in the hangar bay, Evvie shed her work jumpsuit, washed the grease from her hands, and took a break with a cup of tea in the common room of the ship.

She peered out the large viewport to see the activity in space. A crew outside was performing repairs and modifications to her ship and others. Most of the figures were Taurians maneuvering proficiently in their space suits. The gathering of ships with the figures bustling about, all floating over a vast blue planet, was a sight to behold. As if each ship were a hive, the suited figures skittered like insects.

The Taurians were adept because of their size and strength, and their suits were designed to utilize their tails as handy extra limbs. On the end of the articulating encasing sleeve of each Taurian tail was a propulsion thruster that could be pointed then fired to direct their movement in space. There was also a multitude of tools added to the tail ends of their suits, including torches, cutters, and magnahold clamps that could anchor them to a ship's hull or grab objects to be carried. The result was the Taurians having their hands free for their work.

A man by the name of Ivanovich Korshunov walked over and greeted Evvie at her table as she gazed out the view port. He was shorter than the average human and had a lack of hair on his head.

He was a serious fellow, but when he smiled, his grin exposed teeth that were spaced more widely apart than the average human's.

Korshunov was the second leader of the Space Force and had been a Russian cosmonaut. He had set the record for the longest continuous stay in space and was overseeing the work done outside in the hard vacuum of space. Ivan was also a doctor who specialized in treating and monitoring the well-being of the astronauts, making sure they were healthy and safe.

He peered out the view port. "It is quite a sight to behold. I am very much happy to be alive to witness this new space age."

Evvie turned to greet him with a smile. "I am very happy to be alive right now too."

He remained standing near the view port. "This ship is a huge technological accomplishment. Your ancestors were amazing craftspeople. The structure has a geometric perfection that is both practical yet beautiful."

Evvie had been spending more time outside the ship, a huge feat for her—she still thought space suits were hardly adequate protection from the deadly conditions of space. That fear was something she was desperately trying to conquer. Although she was terrified every time she spacewalked away from the *Harkin*, she was mesmerized by its complex structure and design. The outer hull had an exposed network of beams and crossbars that gave it a sort of industrial look compared to the sleek paneling of the Taurian vessels. Working on the hull within the network of girders added a little security when she felt vulnerable to the dangers of space. During the occasions when she had dared to venture farther from the ship, she appreciated its elongated shape, which extended for miles. Ivan was right—her distant ancestors were amazing craftspeople.

He sat next to her, placing his cup of black coffee on the table after a small sip. "It was a childhood dream of mine to be part of a highly developed space age. I have frequently had to literally pinch myself to be reminded that this is real. Before your arrival, I thought I was destined to live in a flimsy space station, which had as much total space as a single storage closet in your large ship. Humanity owes you a debt of gratitude."

She laughed. The *Harkin* was almost too massive. It did, after all, transport thousands of colonists from Mars to Earth millions of years ago.

Ivan took another sip of his coffee. "And thank you for bringing the Taurians to Earth. Another childhood dream of mine has come to fruition. The Taurians have made it easier for humanity to inhabit space."

She watched him gulp the black liquid, for which she had not acquired a taste. She happily sipped her herbal tea. Having been part of rescuing the Taurians from their doomed planet was something she felt proud of. "They're an amazing people."

They both silently gazed out the massive view port for about twenty minutes, finishing their beverages. Then Ivan tapped his wristwatch. "Are you ready for some maneuver training out there?"

Evvie had signed up for that day's class but wished she could just stay aboard the *Harkin,* drink more hot tea, and maybe take a nap. She thought flying in a small vessel was safer than spacewalking— but not by much. She was prone to claustrophobia, and she couldn't help but remember how little material separated her from the cold vacuum of space. A huge goal of hers was to get over her space phobia so she could be of more help to her team on future missions. Still, she nodded and followed Ivan to a locker room.

Evvie and Ivan suited up, made their way to the hangar bay, and departed in two very small ships to join the group that was assembling for the training session. Evvie wished her craft was just a little larger. It was basically a cockpit capsule with rockets and adjustment thrusters. She fired her main thrusters to catch up with Ivan, and they departed from orbit.

The Taurians had swept Earth's space for inactive satellites, which over the last few decades had become a fair amount of space junk, and transported the material to much farther out in space to use as obstacles for training.

As Evvie approached the training grounds, she saw a ship weaving through the debris field. *Great! What in the world have I signed up for?* So far, she had practiced docking her ship to another small ship, and she had even landed on the debris heap when it was piled together into one large mass, but the spread-out field of debris looked dangerous.

She watched as the familiar ship crisscrossed through the field and circled each object like a planetary body pulling it into orbit, but it was really the use of the ship's thrusters that created the illusion, since the bodies of metal were not nearly massive enough to have that sort of gravitational pull. The ship belonged to Brklana, the only female Taurian Evvie had met. Brklana's ship shot to the next object and circled it as if drawing curlicues in space.

Female Taurians were a rarity in the refugee group because when the Taurians evacuated their home planet in the Kronos system, nearly all the females left with the generation ship to travel for hundreds of years to their new destination. She supposed, like the humans, the Taurians believed in the concept of saving women and children first.

Brklana stood out among the larger males because her coloring was different—she had more bluish-green patches splashed across the tile mosaic of soft scales that covered her body, face, and tail. She was also a little shorter and less bulky, but she still towered over the average human. Like with her obsession with The General's mustache, Evvie had to put considerable effort into not staring at Brklana's sleek, colorful body.

During the evacuation of their world, Brklana had piloted her own craft to serve as an escort to help larger ships connect to the convoy. Once the majority of the Taurians had departed on their voyage, she had been one of the pilots who refused to abandon the remnants of their population remaining on the planet. Now, she was putting her skills to work, training other pilots. She had been selected by the president to be the third Space Force leader because of her piloting and tactical skills.

Evvie set her headset to listen to Brklana's broadcast of instructions. The Taurian's deep but feminine voice came through her headset. "The trick is to maneuver your ship with its nose pointed at the obstacle during your rotation around it. Do not let the target out of your sight." Brklana's ship performed graceful loops around the clumps of metal.

Ivan called Evvie on a private channel. "Hey, are you excited to run this course?"

"Umm, probably not half as excited as I'm sure you are. Will you go first so you can walk me through it when it's my turn?"

"Certainly!"

Brklana's ship exited the course. "Any volunteers for the next run?"

Evvie was not surprised to hear Ivan volunteer. He set his small craft toward the first obstacle. He circled it three times then shot to the next clump of metal debris.

At the end of his run, he called to Evvie, "Now, it is your turn."

She felt reluctant to send her ship in. "You made it look so easy, but I'm sure it's more difficult than it appears."

"It is as easy as getting a fish out of a pond."

That didn't sound very easy to Evvie, and she thought his metaphor hardly applied. The more she considered it, though, the more she supposed figuring out the technique was the hard part. After that, completing the course might not be too difficult. Getting a fish out of a pond would be hard for someone who had no idea how to fish, but someone who had figured out a proper technique would find it easy.

Okay, so what's my technique? Brklana said the trick was to stay pointed at each obstacle. That's what I'll do.

She ignited her thrusters and headed into the course, feeling somewhat confident.

Ivan called in, "The trick is to shut off thrusters, rotate the ship with your adjustment jets, then fire main thrusters around each turn."

Sounds easy enough.

"I think you are coming in a little too hot. You need to slow down."

Evvie thought she could make the turn at her speed. She shut down the main drive and began turning the ship. She waited till the clump of metal was closer then fired the jets to keep her ship pointed at the mass.

"Still too fast," he called in.

She rotated her ship more and gave it some thrust to make the arcing turn around the first obstacle, but she was beginning to overshoot it. She gave the side jets more power then increased her main forward thrust.

Her target was slipping out of sight—or rather, she was shooting past it. *More rotation and more main thrusters.* Her body pressed back into her seat.

Ivan's voice rang in her headset. "You are off target, and you are traveling and spinning too rapidly. You need to reduce your spin and slow down."

She began feeling the effects of the g-forces. She closed her eyes and saw stars in her vision, which didn't make sense. *How is it possible to see stars inside my eyelids?*

She forced her eyes open to see real stars whirling across her cockpit viewport.

There was growing concern in Ivan's voice. "You need to counter your spin with your adjustment jets."

She couldn't make any sense of which thrusters she should use to counter the spin. The beginning of an all-too-familiar panic attack struck her. Her chest tightened, making it hard to breathe. It was probably the worst experience she'd had in her human body.

A new voice came through her comm. It was Brklana's. "You are heading toward a new mass of metal debris. You need to regain control of your ship, or you will collide with the debris." Brklana continued in a calm and steady voice, "Fire your forward port-side adjustment thrusters. Focus only on that task for now."

Evvie was well aware that her small ship had minimal protection and probably would not fare well in a collision. She did as Brklana instructed. The twirling stars gradually slowed. Her stomach didn't adjust so well, and she thought she might vomit. *Okay, throwing up was the most unpleasant experience I've had in my human body.* Once the view had stopped spinning, her ship began rotating in the opposite direction. She hadn't shut off the port-side thruster, and it was beginning to overcompensate.

Brklana's voice echoed into Evvie's ringing head. "You need to shut off the port-side thruster and initiate the stern-side thruster. And you are still heading straight toward the mass of metal. You need to stabilize and face away from the debris then fire your main rocket."

Another wave of nausea hit Evvie, and she felt clammy and light-headed. She had a hard time focusing. Blackness closed in around her vision, and she drifted away from consciousness. With a huge amount of effort, she managed to shut off the port-side adjustment thrusters. Her next task was to initiate the stern side, but the blackness continued to close in, and she couldn't focus. Everything went black.

A jolt brought her back to wakefulness. Something struck her small ship with a thud. A tug jostled her back into her seat. The thud had been the heavy magna-clamp at the end of a tow cable that she could see was attached to the nose of her ship. Another tug jolted her.

"I've got you, Lapochka," Ivan called through her comm. "I'll take you home."

Through her viewport, she saw his rocket glowing in the distance as he towed her to safety. She couldn't wait to get out of the death-capsule and back aboard the *Harkin*—her home in space, where a cup of tea might settle her stomach and her nerves.

Disappointment sank in. She was now further from conquering her fears. She really wanted to be someone who was useful on future missions rather than being left behind to cower on the ship. Abigail had been understanding in the past when Evvie was unable to help recover the *Harkin* from the asteroid field. At this point, she was pretty sure she would never voluntarily leave her ship to pilot one of these flying coffin contraptions ever again, but she still vowed to be braver.

Chapter 11

New Little Brother

After a couple of weeks of debating possible options, Cynthia came to the conclusion that treating Eliot was her only choice.

He returned to her lab to receive his gene treatment, but she would have preferred slapping the smug expression off his face over enhancing his genes. She had contacted his parents, who'd agreed with Abigail's assessment that yes, while they thought he was a real piece of work, they didn't think any harm would come of it. They admitted that the only power they had over him was to cut off his allowance. Basically, they weren't responsible for any of his actions since he had graduated high school and turned eighteen.

Cynthia gritted her teeth and laid her syringes on a rolling tray table. "Are you sure you don't want to wait until Abigail returns so she can assistance you through your transformation?"

His smug expression remained. "I'm sure I would like for you to begin the procedure. I'll be fine without my sister here to hold my hand."

"Fine. I've prepared your modified blood sample with the newly unblocked cells that I can inject into your blood stream. It will start a chain reaction, affecting every cell in your body. I have no idea how it would feel to be awake during the process, so I have a dose of anesthesia to knock you out. Will you be okay with this?"

"Sure, if that's what you did to my sister."

She gestured to the cot and rolled her chair and the tray table with the syringes and the few other supplies next to it. He lay down with his sleeve rolled up and didn't flinch when she gave him one shot after the other.

Cynthia couldn't believe she had been forced into performing the genetic alteration to this boy, who was surely faking his condition of severe depression. For one, he just wasn't very convincing about it, and two, all of the family members she spoke to thought his claim was fake. Her first hope was that Abigail was right and no harm would come from his advancement. Her second hope was that if he did get into trouble using his new abilities, Abigail would soon be there to stop him.

"How do you feel?" asked Roberts as Eliot woke up. She had come in from her office when she saw him stirring in his cot.

"I feel great!" He blinked and looked around. "It's amazing to think the average person is stuck with their limited brains, and very few will experience this sort of superiority!"

"So I take it your state of 'depression' has cleared and you feel cured? Can you report any changes, like to your vision?"

"Yes, I see what Abigail refers to as your aura." Eliot squinted his eyes at her. "Very interesting. What is it that you're feeling?"

"I'm pretty sure you can guess what I'm feeling." Cynthia generally had a hard time concealing her emotions, and by that point, she was pissed at the little twerp who had leveraged her into this.

The young man sat up. He peered at her more fixedly. "What a disadvantage the rest of the world has for their feelings and intentions to be so evident."

"Yes, I suppose that's true. I believe Abigail has used her ability to detect people with deceitful or harmful intentions, and I don't think she has misused her abilities. I have a sinking feeling you're going to go clean out a poker game or something."

"Wow, that's not a bad idea. Thanks! Before today, I would dream of how to strike it rich. Now, I have so many opportunities. The only hard part is deciding where to begin. Do you require anything more of me, or am I free to go?"

Great. Not only had she enhanced his genes, she had accidentally encouraged him to abuse his powers by cheating at poker. "Ideally, I'd like to test you and make sure your results match your sister's. I would recommend you stay to be observed, which I know you will not agree to, but could I at least have you come back in a few days for a checkup?"

"I'll think about it, but if I feel fine, I may skip the checkups. Goodbye, Dr. Roberts."

She glared at him, looking for any sign of physical changes, but it was too early for any to be evident. She thought maybe his eyes had lightened a little. Not being able to study or document the results of her second procedure stung almost as badly as his underhanded coercion. She would be unable to obtain any useful information about the effects of his alteration. "You're welcome... and have a nice life."

Cynthia felt conflicted, to say the least. She imagined many of the possible ways Eliot could misuse his new advancements. She realized how lucky she had been to find Abigail, who had proven herself to be caring and thoughtful and showed concern for the well-being of others. It was obvious there was only one person Eliot cared about—himself. Cynthia had a sinking feeling that she had created a monster.

Chapter 12

Paleontologist

Eliot's first stop after his treatment was to a larger lab in San Diego, where he met with Dr. JJ Hornwell, who was a large rugged-looking man in denim who had stubble and a ponytail of light gray. Eliot had seen the world-renowned paleontologist on talk shows, describing his desire to bring about dinosaur features in chickens, calling them dino-chickens. Eliot had concocted a plan to share samples of his blood with JJ's team in the hopes that he might someday have access to exotic animals that resembled dinosaurs.

Jane Grant, a slim woman with dark-brown hair cut into a shoulder-length bob, had drawn some of Eliot's blood and treated it in a centrifuge, and was studying it with an electron microscope.

He studied her aura and didn't know what to make of the purplish-blue colors. He supposed she was probably concentrating on her work. Eliot thought that maybe cataloging colors of auras with people's feelings might have been something Dr. Roberts could have helped him with, but he would just have to figure it out on his own. That was the story of his life. No one had helped him or showed any interest, so he had figured everything out by himself.

Jane spoke while she was viewing the sample. "The procedure appears simple enough. It looks like she removed some blocks in your DNA and replaced them with artificial links."

"So you're saying she didn't change my DNA?"

Jane spun on her lab stool to face Eliot and Dr. Hornwell. "That's right. Your DNA samples from before and after the procedure are matching up. The only difference is the manner in which your cells are reproducing."

"So can you repeat the procedure Dr. Roberts performed on me?"

Dr. Hornwell looked to Jane for an answer. She tapped her fingernails on the desk. "At this point, no. I would have to experiment quite a bit in the hopes of accidentally achieving what she has. It would be a revolutionary accomplishment to use the same procedure to bring back ancestral traits in birds to make dinosaurs, though. We will, however, have to go through a whole new process of elimination to determine which genes to repair with artificial strands."

JJ asked, "So do you think we might be able to use this technique to make dino-chickens using the bird's DNA then altering it?"

Jane shrugged. "I'm not sure, but this *is* hopeful because we may be able to block genes that produce modern traits in birds, and then we can reactivate the ones that produce ancestral traits. This procedure might assist in tapping into the ancestral genes of living birds, making them more dinosaur-like."

Eliot liked the sound of those advancements, but he was thinking of dinosaurs larger than chickens. "What if we had a specimen who had evolved from an actual dinosaur? Could you alter that animal to become a real dinosaur?"

Dr. Hornwell adjusted himself in his chair with a slight jiggle. "That's precisely what we want to do. Birds have evolved from dinosaurs and have many characteristics of dinosaurs except they have wings instead of clawed hands and a few missing features like snouts, teeth, and tails."

Eliot cut in. "But I was referring to the Taurians. Aren't they super-evolved dinosaurs? As I understand, they evolved from ornithopods, whereas birds are evolved from therapods. We see birds that evolved from small coelurosaurian theropods every day. Wouldn't a real duckbill dinosaur be way more amazing?" Eliot was astonished at how well he could retain information since his transformation. He had been on the internet, studying everything he could about Dr. Hornwell's research.

"I see you've done your homework." JJ repositioned himself yet again in his chair. "I suppose any technology we develop for the dino-chickens could be applied. But Taurians are not animals. Regressing a being like a Taurian has ethical issues. It would be like turning a human into a monkey. It's an interesting possibility to imagine, but we're going to stick with chickens and hopefully someday, something larger like ostriches."

Eliot smirked and leaned back in his chair, crossing his arms. "I'm sure the sixth-graders of the world will be excited to see chickens with dinosaur features running around and pecking the ground, but don't you think kids deserve to see a *real* dinosaur?"

Dr. Hornwell glared at Eliot. "If devolving Taurians was the only way to accomplish that, then I absolutely forbid any such plan from getting developed. I appreciate your willingness to offer yourself for study, and our work is already heading in a new direction because of your contribution, but you need to understand that there are some lines that cannot be crossed."

Eliot nodded. "I understand. Perhaps there will be ways to make your dino-chickens profitable. If nothing else, I'm sure KFC could sell a new line of fried chicken. They could add a tailpiece to every bucket. Don't forget about our agreement—I receive fifty percent of any profits made from your—I mean *our*—advancements."

Dr. Hornwell let out a deep breath and rubbed his temples. "Why did you offer to help us? Do you really think this is the easiest way to get rich? Because it's not."

"Let's just say that *Jurassic Park* is my all-time favorite movie. And I do have other ventures in mind for wealth building. Maybe I want to get rich *and* have some pet dinosaurs."

Eliot could see a flash of red in JJ's aura and wondered if the paleontologist was regretting the agreement he had made. Too bad if he was.

Chapter 13

Operation Illumination

Abigail kept her activities minimal during their uneventful trip into the Mediterranean Sea. Once they were in the majestic waters, their plans were to join the scientific team on the *Orca* to sightsee before her first Illumination mission in Algeria. She felt like she had already made too many mistakes and that she wasn't experienced enough or properly trained to be taking on the position as some sort of world Illuminator. She wondered if she was in way over her head, but the desire to bring about change kept her focused.

Admiral Rendón had taken some time to train Silas and Gavin on some mats in the ship's gym facilities, while all she could do was walk laps around the gym with her back brace on. The worst time for injury, besides missing the training drills, had been sleeping—she was required to sleep on her back with pillows under her knees, so no rolling over in the night to find a more comfortable position.

Abigail studied the admiral during his daily training sessions with Silas and Gavin. Even as a high-ranking officer, he displayed some youthful traits. On the mats, he was able to horse around like he was their peer, and he almost appeared to be a normal friend, but he got serious as they began the drills. Fernando's aura confirmed what she saw in his face—he felt a sincere protective concern for her and her friends, as he did for everyone in his crew.

After some sightseeing off the coast of Spain in a smaller ship, they returned to *Enterprise*, and she and Silas prepared to fly to Algeria.

As they loaded their packs into the plane, Gavin, Tkla, and Rendón came to see them off.

The admiral had his usual serious look. "Remember that your safety is more important than anything. If something isn't right, do whatever it takes to get out of there. No mission is worth taking unnecessary risks."

Gavin nodded. "Mind what you have learned. Save you, it can." Luckily, he said it without trying to do his Yoda impersonation, which was worse than Abigail's.

She gave Gavin a hug, faced the admiral, and wasn't sure what was appropriate—*a salute?*—so she held out her hand. He took it into his with a hint of a smile. *Okay, that was a little awkward.*

He stepped back to study *Little Dipper* "Let's see if your plane has what it takes to get you into the air before falling into the sea."

Silas patted the plane's smooth paneling. "Just wait and see the extra boosters fire!"

Rendón saluted them. "Good luck on your mission and be safe. Come back in one piece. That's an order."

Abigail wasn't sure if she should salute back. She opted for an affirming nod then climbed aboard and closed the hatch.

The seat wasn't as comfortable with her back brace. She wasn't supposed to slouch when seated, a habit her mom had hassled her about during her teen years. The sharp pins-and-needles pain had dulled a bit, and she couldn't wait to lose the brace. After strapping in and checking the gauges, she turned to Silas. "You ready to do this?"

"Yes, ma'am!"

She punched it, and the acceleration pressed her into her seat—she loved that feeling of extra g-forces. The end of the aircraft carrier vanished beneath them in an instant, and they took to the sky. She banked the plane and gained more altitude, smirking to herself that Rendón's concern for their falling into the ocean had proven to be needless.

As planned, Silas had reached out to the president of Algeria, who agreed to meet with them. Silas claimed that he might want to find a new home for some of his ventures and would trade some of the technology he had developed in exchange for some "help setting up shop." He'd left his offer intentionally vague, saying that they should discuss the details in person. It worked, and they received clearance to land in the capital, Algiers. From the air, she noted the Sahara meeting the sea with a pristine but rocky coastline.

Abigail landed *Little Dipper* smoothly, and after parking the plane in their assigned space, they were met with a driver in an SUV who looked a little shocked to see her face. She wished she had heeded the internet's advice to wear a face scarf when visiting the country. The driver, still wearing a curious expression, loaded their luggage, periodically glancing in her direction.

During the drive, Silas kept his composure, but Abigail could see in his aura that he was feeling doubtful. She felt vulnerable, too, and wondered whether they were heading into a potentially risky situation. Having no idea where the driver was taking them gave her an unsettled feeling, despite the city's welcoming feel with its French colonial architecture and Ottoman-style mosques. She would never forget their fateful trip to Texas when their Uber driver took a detour to the remote location where they were abducted and nearly electrocuted.

Through her research, she'd discovered that the Algerian government was responsible for imprisoning and torturing protesters and organizers who wrote blogs. She read stories of massacres of civilians protesting and of families unsure of the whereabouts of thousands of disappeared persons. The country required compulsory military service of its men, and women were suffering from inadequate rights, sometimes lost in legal limbo because they were neither granted nor denied citizenship. Stories of strife among people in many neighboring countries were common, but this was a place where she thought her intervention was urgent.

She knew many of the struggles the citizens faced were because of a bottomed-out economy and harsh mandates from a president who they demanded step down from his fifth term in office. The rioting there was worse than in almost all other African countries.

Abigail hoped the president could pull the country together with a little bit of enlightenment from her.

Although Silas had claimed the president sounded friendly over the phone, Abigail was somewhat worried they would become two of the many disappeared.

The sun was close to setting over an unexpectedly lush landscape when their vehicle entered through the gate of an estate. Once parked, they stepped foot onto a cobblestone driveway with stairs leading to the entrance of a mansion. Standing to greet them was a seventy-something year-old heavyset pear-shaped man who had only a ring of silver hair around his bald head.

He raised his bushy dark eyebrows and gestured toward the house. "Welcome. I have been anticipating your arrival. We have some prepared refreshments so you may relax after your travels."

Abigail thought he seemed pleasant enough for a man whose position in office had been widely protested by his citizens. His aura, however, showed the warning signs of a power-hungry tyrant. She had seen similar violent swirls of red in their own president before she had Illuminated him.

She nodded to the man. "Thank you, Mr. President, for having us. It is a pleasure to visit your fine country."

He shook Silas's hand but made no attempt to shake hers and led the way into the mansion. "If only this country could become more settled, it would be a fine place indeed. We have had turbulent times, but we will talk more about our issues after a meal. And you may call me Abdel."

She took in the ornate tapestries, art, fine furniture, and everything else made of beautifully laid stone. "Thank you for your hospitality, Abdel."

Silas added, "Yes, thank you for agreeing to see us. We are traveling on our honeymoon, and I promised the wife that I would show her some beautiful parts of the world but only if I could squeeze in a little business."

A woman entered the hall and said, "Welcome to our home. It is a pleasure to meet the both of you. Did I hear you were on your honeymoon?"

Abigail shook the woman's hand. "I suppose we are." It had been totally unscripted, but it was a perfect cover.

The woman's aura flashed an alarming mix of colors, which gave Abigail the impression that she was living in fear. The woman revealed nothing concerning in her face or body language. She held Abigail's hand firmly and looked her in eye. "It is a pleasure to have guests. I will assist you in any way that you may need."

"Perhaps you can show me to the women's restroom?"

The president burst out. "Of course! Our guests must wash before we sit."

Once safe in a secluded bathroom, Abigail gave the woman a reassuring squeeze of her arm. "We are here to help you. Have you heard of the way our president changed his ways and is now a more compassionate person? I can perform the same treatment on your husband."

"I'm not allowed to view any world news, so no, I have not heard of such a story from your country." She paused for a moment then took Abigail by the hands. "Do you really think you can reform my husband? Is it some sort of magic? I've been wanting to leave this place but have dared not try. Perhaps this will be the start of a new, better life."

Abigail wanted more than anything to help the woman and the country. "It's not exactly magic, but yes, I think it will improve things for you. All you have to do is collect me once he's fallen asleep tonight."

The woman nodded. "If there is any hope that you may set my husband on a new path, then I will assist in any way I can. Perhaps I can keep his wine glass filled tonight, and he will drink more than usual."

During the meal, Silas performed sensationally, asking questions about possible locations for facilities and talking about some of his company's innovations. He put on an air of confidence that she appreciated, but she could see underlying fear in his aura.

For his part, Abdel displayed an interest in the conversation, and he definitely tried to steer it toward rockets. All the while, his wife kept his glass full of wine.

The meal was amazing and included a couscous meat stew, flatbread, and a dish called Tajne Zitoun, a mixture of mushrooms, potatoes, meat, and lots of olives in white sauce. Abigail detected onions, ginger, and a hint of cloves. All the food was hearty and delicious, and eating it melted away much of her worry.

They finished eating at a late hour, and the woman gently touched her husband's arm. "Surely, our guests would like to retire. After all, it is their honeymoon." She turned to Abigail. "Let me show you to your room."

The president gave Abigail a scrutinizing glare. "Yes. The husband and wife must wish to retire to their room." He narrowed his eyes at her. "I've been rude, though, only wanting to talk about business. Tell me first, how did you both meet?"

Abigail could see suspicion swirling in his aura. She realized she hadn't been acting much like Silas's wife. She grabbed Silas by the hand. "We met at an electric vehicle show—isn't that right, sweetie? I was a model, posing with the cars."

Abdel's suspicion turned to disbelief as he looked Abigail up and down like he was trying to detect a model's body underneath her T-shirt and jeans. He wasn't buying it.

"I'll never forget the first time I laid eyes on him. It was love at first sight." She laid a kiss right on Silas's lips.

His face turned instantly red. "Um... yep. Love at first sight for me too."

Abdel gave Silas a firm pat on the shoulder, his suspicion dissipating. "Enjoy your room, my friend."

They bid their host goodnight and followed his wife. As they left the dining area, Abigail thought, *Oh man, do we really have to share a room? And after we kissed?*

They followed the woman up the stairs and through a wide corridor to enter a room that was the fanciest suite Abigail had ever seen. The bathroom alone was basically a spa, although it was open to the main bedroom.

The woman gave Abigail a nod. "I will collect you once he is fast asleep." She winked then departed, closing the door behind her.

Abigail dropped her bag. "Um, so I guess we have to share this room..."

"Oh yeah, sorry about the honeymoon thing." He coughed. "And the kiss."

"Uh, yeah. Well, I'm the one who kissed you. Sorry. I could tell he wasn't buying our cover story, so I had to take drastic action. It's a good cover story, but the problem is, I have to pee… and there's no door to the bathroom."

Silas fished into his pocket then pulled out his phone and ear buds. "Go ahead and tinkle away."

∞

They settled into bed, staying as far apart as possible, a task made easier because the bed was enormous. Neither of them slept but just lay there, waiting. At last, a gentle knock on the door came. Having gotten into bed fully clothed, Abigail was ready to go.

"Good luck," Silas whispered.

Abigail walked with the woman to another wing of the mansion. She watched as the woman's nervousness transformed into hope.

The scene was much the same as when Abigail had Illuminated their own president as his wife looked on in a dark bedroom, the only light coming from the hallway.

The man stirred, and Abigail waited a few moments before placing a hand on his head. She began by transmitting a soothing message that everything was fine and that she was going to take him on a journey. She next gave him a view of the universe, the galaxy, then the solar system, as if she was presenting a galactic tour. She focused on the Earth and showed all the intricate ways in which it was alive and fell into balance—the procedure was becoming routine for her.

Then she showed a kind of faster-paced slideshow highlighting all of the trouble in the world. She sent Abdel a message that he could make a difference by bringing his country back to prosperity with some fundamental changes. At dinner, they had talked about some ideas he could implement to make it a better place, especially focusing on ways to power the country that would add economic prosperity to its people while doing less harm to the environment. She ended the Illumination with an image of his wife and instructions to treat her with care and respect.

Abigail came back to the present and stood from her kneel. The woman guided her back to their suite, where Silas waited wide-eyed.

"So you did it?"

"Yes. He'll be a new man in the morning. Try to get some sleep."

She lay in bed, fully awake, restless, and not sure if she would ever fall asleep, but was then pleasantly surprised to wake with the sun shining in.

They changed into fresh clothes and found their way to the dining area, where the husband and wife were enjoying breakfast, his hand clasping hers. Abigail sighed.

"Join us for breakfast!" Abdel called to them.

Abigail and Silas sat and heaped some fruit and yogurt into their bowls.

Abdel grinned. "I have reconsidered some of my future plans, and while you are welcome to set up facilities in my country, I will not be pursuing any sort of missile rocket technology to solve my problems. I am outlining a new plan as we speak."

A wave of relief washed over Abigail. She enjoyed the breakfast perhaps more than the previous night's dinner.

After the meal, Abdel and his wife wished them well and sent them with a driver to be taken to wherever they would like to visit before leaving the country.

After some sightseeing, their driver took them to the hangar, where *Little Dipper* safely waited. Abigail sighed with relief at the sight of their small plane.

Chapter 14

Tripoli

As Abigail strapped in and checked for all systems go, Silas said, "That was almost too easy. I don't know why I couldn't shake an uneasy feeling I had the whole time we were there."

His underlying worry had been evident, but he'd hidden it well. She thought about how things had gone badly for them in Texas and knew he was dealing with persisting trauma. "It *was* pretty easy. I couldn't shake an uneasy feeling either." She tapped the fuel gauge out of habit. "So our next stop is the capitol of Libya, Tripoli. Do you want to contact the chairman and see if he would like to meet with us?" She performed the math in her head. "It's six hundred thirty-four miles away, so we can get there in just under two hours."

Silas had contacted the leader in advance, so he had a direct number that he dialed. "Hi, this is Silas Rutherford of Sky Fire Rockets and Energon Motors. Yes, we spoke a few days ago. I'm sorry for the short notice, but I can be there in a couple of hours if you'd like to meet." He paused. "Um, well, it'll just be my new wife and me. We're traveling on our honeymoon."

Abigail rolled her eyes. *Great, now we have to keep up that charade.*

Silas ended the call. "We're all set. They'll meet us at the airport. It seemed a little strange that he asked me who I'll be bringing along. Don't you think that seems a little suspicious?"

"Hmm. I wouldn't think so, but I'll pay extra close attention to their auras."

She pulled the plane out of the hangar and called into flight control to get clearance.

Silas relaxed in his chair. "It sure is good for you to have that ability."

Their takeoff was uneventful and the flight picturesque as they traveled along the northern coast of Africa, weaving over the Mediterranean and Tunisia. Tripoli was a coastal city, so their approach was scenic.

Flight control gave her clearance to land and a hangar bay number to park in. When she and Silas stepped out of the plane, about ten or twelve men, all in dark suits, waited. She watched one man speak into his phone and could have sworn he said, "It's her," though she was too far away to have heard him with certainty.

Silas started to ask, "So what are everyone's auras looking like—"

The men pulled out guns—and not just small handguns but military-grade rifles.

She put her hands in the air. "I don't think it matters what their auras are hinting. Their intentions seem pretty evident."

Two more vehicles squealed to a stop outside the hangar building. Additional men filed out with more guns.

Abigail studied her surroundings. Light fixtures were far up in the rafters, higher than any she had ever pulled electricity from. She followed the conduit network, which led to a few outlets. The hangar bay was so large that every source of electricity was pretty far out of reach.

A bearded man stepped forward. Abigail recognized him as the Chairman of the Presidential Council. He called out, "I know what you did to your own president, and I'm not going to let you interfere with my mind."

"Great. I guess they've heard about you," Silas muttered.

The man continued, "The world is actually a better place when there is war and conflict because there is more money to be made than if there is peace. Your president is making a mockery of the most powerful position on Earth—not that I mind a weakened America, but we can't have you interfering elsewhere."

In a quiet voice, Silas said, "Do their auras show the same hostile intent that their guns do?"

"Yes. When I say so, get down on the ground."

"Men, keep your aim on Mr. Rutherford. We want to ensure that Miss Abigail Montrose doesn't try anything foolish."

A lot of guns were pointed at them. Abigail had a bad feeling that the group wasn't going to risk trying to capture her. Their intent was to kill her. And yes, she saw it in their auras.

"Mr. Rutherford, step away from the girl."

She nodded to indicate that he should do as he was told. He stepped away with his hands still in the air.

She knew she couldn't give Silas any warning to get down without tipping off the men, and she was pretty sure she didn't have much longer to make a move. Time seemed to slow as she watched the men turn their guns toward her. Each man took a firing stance and placed a finger on each trigger. Unlike the situation she'd escaped from in Texas, no one here was reciting any speeches to give her time to think of a way out of her predicament.

A feeling of desperation and anger welled up in her. It was not the way she wanted to go out, and yet again, she didn't want this to be the end for Silas. She didn't think she could conjure enough electricity from her body to send a powerful enough shock—the men were too spread out and too far away. She needed an external source of electricity.

The chairman began his next order. "Men—"

With her hands held high, she reached up and pulled electricity from every outlet and socket in the airplane hangar. It danced through the air, passing through the men as she collected it into her body then instantly sent a shock wave of electricity in every direction. The inside of the dingy metal building became dazzling as electricity shot out of her hands and into everyone in the area, including Silas.

The men were jolted off their feet. She took a moment for her vision to return to normal—producing such a shock blinded her. She ran to where Silas lay, grabbed him under his arms, and hoisted his limp body. He was heavier than she anticipated. She managed to lift him onto her shoulder. Every step required extra effort, but she finally came to within reach of their plane's fold-down stairs. Getting him up the boarding steps and through the hatch was an even bigger challenge.

Once she had him strapped into his chair, she plopped into the pilot's seat and started the engines. She got the plane rolling, but something obstructed one of her wheels and caused a bumping stop, as if she had nudged the plane onto a large speed bump.

She got up and opened the plane's hatch to see the obstruction. A man's body blocked one of the wheels. She was tempted to get back in the plane and punch the extra booster, but that would have hurt or possibly killed many of the men in the hangar because of the fiery rockets.

"Oh, jeez," she muttered. She didn't know how long the men would stay knocked out even after shocking them with every volt of electricity she could draw. She still felt lightheaded and depleted. As she jumped down from the plane and moved the body that was wedged, she noticed a few more in the way. Feeling grateful for Rendón's rigorous training, she quickly dragged them out of the way.

As she was dragging the last man by his ankles, he awoke, focused his eyes on her, and kicked her away. He reached for his gun, which was on the ground, just out of reach, when she pulled another bolt from an outlet and jolted him. Perhaps he had been shielded by another so he hadn't received the full initial shock. She looked around to see if anyone else was stirring then darted to the plane. Abigail sealed the hatch, sat, and pulled the throttle without taking the time to buckle in.

She realized she needed to call for clearance to take off. In as calm a voice as she could muster, she called into flight control. "This is *Little Dipper* requesting clearance to depart."

The time she had to wait for a response was excruciating. While she waited, she reached over and placed her hand on Silas's head. He was still knocked out. He had been the closest to her when she fired the bolts, and she hadn't held back.

If any of those men awoke and alerted the authorities, she might find herself in another entanglement with military jets—jets with more firepower than those two little Eurofighters that had engaged her in England. She was also hoping the chairman had been so confident in detaining or killing them that he had not instructed flight control to restrict her takeoff.

Finally the clearance came through. Silas was beginning to stir in his seat, which was comforting but simultaneously disconcerting. If he was waking up, the men in the hangar building could be doing the same.

Okay, fly casual. She was tempted to hit all the plane's extra boosters to get the hell out of there, but instead, she took off in a standard manner.

She kept her eyes peeled for other aircraft, but none arrived. She got to a good cruising altitude then reached over to nudge Silas. "You doing okay there, big guy? I am so sorry I shocked you. How do you feel?"

"Oh man, what happened?"

She raised her eyebrows. "I decided it wasn't a good destination for our honeymoon and got us out of there."

Abigail followed the coordinates to where *Enterprise* was located in the Mediterranean, and after flying over the sea for some time, she saw the ship, a sight for sore eyes. Of course, she still had to manage her landing on its short runway.

She came to a stop with a couple feet to spare. She emerged, supporting Silas, to see Gavin, Tkla, and Admiral Rendón all looking concerned. Silas leaned against her as they walked.

Gavin came to Silas's other side to help hold him up. "What happened to you? Did you get clocked in the head again?"

Abigail shook her head sheepishly. "He actually got caught in a little bit of the crossfire when I shocked a group of men who were trying to kill us."

Gavin's jaw dropped. "Whoa, how did it feel to get shocked by *The Illuminator*? Do you feel enlightened now?"

"I don't suppose I feel any different in that regard. But I do feel like I was hit by a bus."

Gavin grinned. "Maybe, if you're already a good person, her shock treatment won't really change you."

Abigail shot Silas a concerned glance. "Well, we encountered an airplane hangar full of some pretty bad people who I hope did get Illuminated, but I don't want to go back to find out."

Rendón approached her. "I'm glad you managed to follow orders this time and come back in one piece. It was a very impressive take-off when you left, although your rocket boosters left scorch marks on the runway, and that was a very clean landing this time."

"Thanks! I'm glad I didn't let you down, El Capitan."

Tkla gave Abigail a wink, another human expression he hadn't quite mastered. "He's actually an admiral and a very high-ranking one."

"Yes, Tkla, thanks for filling me in. You want to help me find Silas an ice pack and a soft bed to recover in?"

Chapter 15

Big Trouble in the China Seas

At breakfast in the ship's mess hall, Gavin sat beside Silas, poking him in the arm while they ate. "Okay, if you were truly Illuminated, you'll be patient with me bugging you, right? Are you feeling like I can keep doing this without getting irritated?" He kept poking.

Silas gave Gavin a soft punch in the shoulder. "Why, was I irritable before? Honestly, I'm just so glad to be here that I don't care about anything else—even your incessant questioning and poking. Yes, I'm happy to see you, and for some strange reason, I don't mind what you're doing." He gave Gavin a sideways hug from his chair.

Abigail sat with her breakfast and tea. "Wow. I must have really Illuminated you in that shock. I *am* sorry about that. Are you sure you're okay?"

"I'm fine. You didn't have much choice, and the alternative was to be filled with bullets. I'm just amazed that you single-handedly got us out of there."

Abigail smiled at the sight of Silas and Gavin getting along, but it faded. While Silas's reassurance helped, she still felt guilty for shocking him. She also felt terrible for having put him in such a dangerous situation in the first place. "Listen. I'm calling off the rest of my Illumination missions. For one, I want to wait and see if the work I did in Algeria and Libya will change anything for anyone. I do kind of wish I had stuck around to finish the job with the leader of Libya and his goons instead of hightailing it out of there."

While she hoped she had encoded some sort of message of enlightenment into the burst she sent through the hangar, she was concerned by the man who had awoken to cause more trouble before she shocked him again. Then again, the first time she had accidentally shocked a group of people, on the beach, they had shown signs of being Illuminated by not wanting to press charges and expressing regret for having intimidated Evvie and her.

With a mouth full of cereal, Gavin said, "I think it worked! Based on the testing I've done, I think Silas is a new man."

Silas took a bite of his scrambled eggs. "Um, having a dozen guns pointed at you can change your life too."

Admiral Rendón walked over to the table with a tray of food then sat. "Speaking of hightailing it, we traveled through the Suez Canal last night and are heading toward the Philippines. I think it could be a nice stretch to experience from a smaller boat. We could even get a few hours of shore leave then catch up with the *Big E* before we tackle China's bottom-trawling issues. You still want to engage with China?"

Abigail had been considering it. "Well, doesn't the president want us to at least finish *that* mission?" She felt bad that she was pulling the plug on completing her list of Illuminations, but the president would have to understand.

Rendón speared a lump of his scrambled eggs. "The president gave his consent for us to proceed with the operation but asked that we use caution. I feel confident that we can safely engage a few fishing boats." He looked directly at Abigail. "I will say that during the next operation, all of you will need stay aboard the big ship. No more flying into trouble, and that's an order."

"Yes, sir!" Abigail said a little too enthusiastically. Then she saluted him with a quick smile and added a wink, hoping she didn't come across as mocking.

∞

After a leisurely trip through the Philippines, they entered the waters south of China. Before the *Big E* intercepted any fishing vessels, the admiral ordered a chopper into the air to report any boats' whereabouts and to keep an eye out for bigger ships that might have been coming to interfere.

On the first raid, Abigail wished she could have boarded the fishing boat, but as ordered, she stayed on the bridge of *Enterprise*. She watched as a cage contraption was hoisted onto their ship's deck. If she had been allowed, she would have liked to connect with the fisherman to show them a glimpse of the harm they were causing. The effects she had on the whalers and on Abdel in Algeria had encouraged her to believe that maybe Illumination wasn't a harmful option.

The crew of the next boat they intercepted put up more of a fight. Rendón's troops had their guns drawn and were using excessive force to try to herd the fishermen together on the boat's deck. She hated seeing anyone being treated that way. "Please let me go down there. I can remedy the situation."

Rendón kept a stern expression. "My men have it under control."

"What about what you said after we shut down the whalers? That with me around, we wouldn't need guns. I'm part of the team, and I'm here to help."

Just as Rendón opened his mouth to say something, they heard a gunshot. One of the Chinese fishermen collapsed on the deck of the fishing boat.

"What the hell!" Abigail pressed her fists against the window. "Who gave the order to shoot an unarmed fisherman? I should have been down there."

Rendón frowned as he got on the radio. "Lieutenant, please report."

"The man pulled a knife, sir."

Abigail watched from the control room tower as one of the crewmen tended to the man who'd been shot. She glanced at Gavin and Silas, who appeared as shocked as she felt.

The lieutenant's voice crackled through. "I'm sorry, sir. We lost him."

Tears welled in her eyes. "If I had been down there—"

"If you had been down there, you could have been attacked."

She shook her head furiously. "I would have seen his intentions well before he pulled the knife, and I'm actually pretty good at incapacitating someone who's wielding a weapon."

The admiral picked up the radio. "Get back aboard and let's depart." He dropped the radio and closed his eyes with his chin down, his lips moving as he whispered a silent prayer.

Anger welled up in Abigail. "If we stop another fishing boat, I'm going to assist."

"There won't be another—"

"Sir, I've lost radio contact with the chopper," a man called out from his station. "The pilot's last report said there were multiple warships approaching."

Rendón turned to his helmsman. "Get us to the last known location of the chopper. Our pilot is down in the water."

The man at the radar station replied, "Sir, there may be a problem with that. Enemy ships are closing in on that location."

Abigail watched as Rendón processed. She knew he was weighing his options and pleaded with him. "We can't leave a pilot out there."

"I know." He let out a deep breath.

"We could surrender?" She thought it wasn't a bad idea. "We could explain to the Chinese that shooting the fisherman was unintentional. Our president might have some diplomatic issues to clear up, but it's an option. We need to apologize for killing the fisherman."

"I wasn't raised to surrender. I'm sorry, Abigail. I have a mission to get all of the crew home… and to get you home."

His stubbornness infuriated her. "Why couldn't you let me do my job? A life could have been saved. And now you just want to hightail it out of here?"

"Abigail, you're too important to risk losing. It's too dangerous. And now, getting you to safety is my highest priority."

"So you think I'm important, but you won't let me do my job? Instead of trying to protect me, you should encourage me and help prepare me for challenges. I could have handled the situation. We've drilled disarming each other countless times on the mat. Besides, I've been in way more dangerous situations." She held up her scarred wrists as proof.

"I'm sorry. I perhaps became overprotective. But I didn't keep you out of harm's way simply because I've grown fond of you. You're important to the world. You have a gift, but you can't use it if you're dead."

"Well, I can't use my gift if I'm cooped up here either." She realized they were wasting time, and there was a more pressing matter at hand. "There's got to be some way to get our pilot back."

She watched Rendón's aura turn a tragically sad color of blue with red swirls. "Helmsman, set a course away from the mainland… and the enemy ships." He whispered another prayer. "Please, Lord, protect those who I was meant to protect."

More tears shot down her cheeks. "But we've got to do something." She looked at her friends, who stayed silent. Gavin and Silas were pale, while Tkla showed his sadness with his big dinosaur puppy dog eyes.

That's it! "Tkla! Go! Swim! Find the pilot!"

Gavin's eyes went wide. "That… is the best idea ever! Tkla, you can swim as fast a boat."

Tkla stood then walked to the top of the stairs that led down to the deck. "I will find him, and we will catch up to you. Travel to a safe location due south and wait." Then he was gone. Abigail and her friends peered down to the main deck, where he disappeared off the edge and into the water.

The ship accelerated and turned as the *Big E* made its move to depart from the China Sea.

After over an hour at full speed, the blips on the radar were far behind.

"Full stop. Drop anchor," Admiral Rendón ordered. Abigail wanted to reassure him that his pilot would be all right, but she was still overcome with rage, sadness, and regret. If he had been less clouded by his feelings of protectiveness, she could have helped prevent some of the trouble they were in. She decided to say nothing.

One hour passed, then another. The sun was low on the horizon, marking the end of a depressing day.

Gavin voiced uncharacteristic pessimism. "How would Tkla even be able to swim if he was carrying another person?"

They sat in silence with little hope. After another twenty minutes, a crewman at the radar station called, "Sir, I have two small blips coming toward us."

"What are they?" Rendón asked.

"Well, they're not big, whatever they are, and they're moving somewhat quickly."

Abigail jumped from her seat. "I'm going down to the deck to see."

Rendón started to object, but she glared at him, causing him to close his mouth before getting a word out.

Everyone rushed down the stairs. Standing on the edge of the deck, they peered over the water, searching for a sign of Tkla.

In the distance, two forms broke the water then disappeared. They repeatedly popped up then submerged until they were close.

Rendón's jaw dropped. "Now, I've seen it all."

His chopper pilot was riding astride one dolphin, and Tkla's large form was on the other. The dolphins swam to where the rope ladder was dangling into the water. The pilot and Tkla climbed up it and were assisted onto the deck. The pilot's jumpsuit was sopping wet.

Gavin was the first to speak. "That was the coolest rescue operation ever!"

Abigail hugged Tkla. "Thank you so much for doing this. Leaving a man behind was the worst." Although that wasn't true. Killing the fisherman was worse.

Rendón walked up to Tkla and saluted. "This is the greatest miracle I have witnessed. Thank you, señor!"

Tkla held out his hand to shake the admiral's, but Rendón brushed it away and went in for a hug.

The pilot spoke up. "Permission to change into some dry clothes, sir?"

Rendón hugged him next. "Yes, pilot, go get changed. Perhaps you can someday be part of a program that uses dolphins and whales for missions."

A smile broke from the serious crew member who brushed the water from his buzz-cut hair. "If I may be allowed to speak freely, sir—that was the best experience of my life! With more appropriate swimming gear, it could be very useful for recon missions."

Gavin looked like he could burst, raising his hands into the air. "That's what I said at the beginning of this mission! Navy SEALs on dolphins would be so cool!"

As everyone headed back into the ship, Rendón announced, "That wouldn't be the craziest thing I've seen. Now, it's time to get all of us home."

Chapter 16

Money

Eliot had big plans, but they depended on capital investments—he needed money. He drove his Honda Civic out to Las Vegas to use Dr. Roberts's unintentional advice of cleaning out some poker games. His plan was to end up in Manhattan, so Vegas was his first step east from California.

He was adjusting nicely to his transformation, which had given him more than the ability to see people's auras. His train of thought felt so expansive, as if he could calculate many thoughts at once. He wondered if maybe he would have benefited from staying with Dr. Roberts to be tested. Her tests might have helped him harness his new abilities. But he would just have to adjust on his own.

He wondered, too, if perhaps his sister could help him. After all, she had figured out how to do some pretty amazing things after her transformation.

It was nighttime when Elliot drove into the bustling city, awestruck by the bright lights and activity. Vegas was very much alive and awake—"the city that never sleeps." He checked in to a hotel, watched a few tutorials on poker and blackjack, then made the rounds to a few casinos. Sleep could wait.

He started with blackjack, which was easy for him because he could keep track of the cards with zero effort. He was aware that casinos frowned upon card-counters and would kick him out if it was obvious that he was keeping track of cards, so he tried to look like he was distracted by every person who walked by. After winning a good chunk of change, Eliot moved on to poker, which he preferred. Instead of playing against the house, he was playing against other people, people whose feelings and intentions were evident through their auras. He quickly learned to identify whether someone had a good hand or if they were bluffing.

Eliot also quickly learned which were good cards to keep and which to discard. He learned that a strong opening hand was the best way to win the pot. He also learned never to be afraid to fold. People who were playing poker for the excitement tended to stay in, just to see what would happen, but those who were there to make money were folding most of the time. He also adopted a strategy of constantly raising the bets. If he didn't have a good enough hand to raise the bet, he didn't have a good enough hand to stay in.

He started with his savings of five hundred dollars—money he had saved from his childhood allowances and every birthday and Christmas card—and quadrupled his money on the first day. He was smart enough to not succumb to greed and draw attention to himself. He allowed himself to lose often enough that he seemed like a regular player. Losing also showed him what other people's auras looked like when they had a good hand.

On his second day, he visited five casinos and turned two thousand dollars into twelve thousand. It was more money than he had ever held in his hands, but it was nothing compared to how much more he wanted to amass. Every day, he went to a few different casinos and kept a mental account of where he'd been and how much he had won. He didn't want to raise suspicion by winning too much at any one casino. He kept up that routine, and within a week, he had a few hundred thousand dollars. He spread it out on his hotel bed and was tempted to lie in it but instead made stacks on the room's small table and counted it all over again.

He used ten thousand dollars of his winnings to enter the World Series of Poker Tournament, anticipated by everyone in the poker world every year. Eliot started out as one of thousands of entrants, but it was easy to advance through the masses of contestants. Once he was in the quarterfinals, he had to step up his skill level. Clues from the players' auras weren't enough to win without skill and strategy of his own.

During a break from playing, he talked to a skinny guy with dark curly hair and dark glasses, Tony. His clothes looked kind of vintage—a V-cut satin shirt and leather pants. Eliot couldn't figure out if he was trying to look like he was from the seventies or the eighties. That fine gold chain around his neck made it harder to tell.

Tony asked, "What's your game, man?"

"We're playing no-limit Texas hold 'em. Isn't that your game if you're here at this tournament?"

"Nah, man, *why* you playin?"

"For the money, duh. What other reason could there be?"

Tony smiled. "Money comes and goes. The title lasts forever. I want to be in the history books."

Eliot was puzzled again, realizing that even with his super intelligence, he had a lot to learn. "They teach kids about winners of poker in history class?"

"Jeez, where you from, and how you play so good for being such a dummy?"

"Luck," he lied. "I've really only started playing recently, so this is kind of new to me. Do you have any tips?"

"All I can say is the table can turn very quickly, man. You can have twice as many chips as anyone else, blink an eye, and they're gone. It goes the other way too. If you get down to a short stack, don't give up. The table can turn on that guy too."

"Thanks. Good luck to you. I hope you make it into that history book."

"I'll see you in the finals, my man. We're friends, but that don't mean I won't take your pile of chips every chance I get."

Eliot cleared his throat. "I guess I should warn you, too, that my strategy is to bet high and win." Eliot wasn't sure why he felt compelled to share that with his new acquaintance. Maybe he was trying to intimidate him, which surely didn't work.

Tony chuckled. "That's right. You're here for the money. I'll be seeing you at the final table."

∾

Eliot kept winning and advancing. His new acquaintance, Tony, stayed in too. The two hadn't played at the same table until they were among the six finalists.

Eliot felt confident he could win quickly and ruthlessly, but he was worried about drawing too much attention to himself and raising suspicion. He decided to make a few mistakes—to stay in a round instead of folding when he knew he didn't have the best hand. He let his supply of chips dwindle, but he still won the pot every once in a while. The first player to go out didn't last long.

The next player, named Melvin, melted down. "I'm in," he said, but it was obvious to Eliot, even without seeing his aura, that he should have folded. Eliot raised his bets but not by much. He wanted Melvin to stay in and keep adding to the pot. It would be Eliot's comeback. His chips were low so that if he didn't get a large win soon, he would be out.

Melvin lost it all to Eliot, and they were down to four players at the table. The crowd in the darkened arena remained utterly silent. The only light was on the center table. After two more rounds, another player went out.

Eliot, Tony, and a guy named Tristan, who had red hair and freckles and had made rude remarks to the other players, remained. Eliot saw that for the next round, Tony's aura revealed a very good hand, and he saw that Tristan was bluffing. Eliot didn't have the best cards, so he decided to fold and sit back to watch Tony clean Tristan out. Tristan was out of the game.

Tony smirked. "That's poker, baby. You know what I mean? Look who's not so cocky now?" Their rival stood and left, kicking the carpet as he trudged away.

Tony had two-thirds of the chips on the table, so Eliot went into the final round as the underdog. They both knew tables could turn.

Eliot didn't see a reason to prolong any hope Tony might be feeling. He placed a small bet for the next round and watched Tony's aura closely. Tony had a good hand. Eliot's cards weren't bad, but they also weren't great. He decided to fold.

Tony took the chips and asked, "Oh, so now you're being cautious? Doesn't matter. I can do this till the sun comes up."

Again, cards were dealt. Eliot studied Tony, bet small once, then folded.

Tony narrowed his eyes with a scrutinizing stare.

Finally, Eliot had a great hand—a straight flush. He studied Tony, whose face hadn't changed from the last two rounds, but his aura flashed with what Eliot thought was alarm. It was time to bet high, time to bet it all.

Tony's face continued to remain unchanged, but his aura flashed with more turbulence and brighter reds.

Finally, Tony's aura and the look on his face showed that he knew it was over before the final cards were laid on the table.

Tony put on a forced smile, but the suspicion in his aura remained. "That's poker, baby!" he said as he shook hands with Eliot and gave him a hard pat on the shoulder. He leaned in and quietly said, "I know you cheated somehow. I ain't no snitch, but you should probably leave town and never come back."

This shook Eliot, but he was ushered away to receive his prize money, 1.5 million dollars, available in cash or check. Eliot chose cash. The World Series of Poker winner also won a bracelet that looked like a miniature version of a wrestler's prize belt, made of gems and gold. An attractive blond woman clasped it to his wrist. He also received an additional prize, a duffel bag just big enough to hold his cash.

The next day, Eliot traded in his rusty Honda for a Chrysler LeBaron convertible. It wasn't the fanciest or most expensive car, but it was a convertible, and it had a custom paint job that sparkled. Even though he had won big, he didn't want to waste his money on something too expensive. He switched his personal belongings into the duffel bag and bought a larger suitcase to carry his prize money and his previous winnings of over a million. He would not let that suitcase out of his sight. He was glad he chose cash because he wanted to stack it up in his next hotel room so he could see how big a pile 2.5 million dollars would make.

As he left town the following morning, he took a moment to appreciate his new bracelet, which glittered like his new car's paint job as he drove with the top down into the sunrise of a new day. He planned to wear the bracelet everywhere he went. His next destination was Manhattan. He hadn't made any friends in Vegas and was almost discovered for cheating, but that didn't matter. He had made some money, but it was small change next to how much he wanted to make on Wall Street.

Chapter 17

Coalition

When Silas, Gavin, and Abigail arrived at port in Los Angeles, an agent in a black suit asked them to accompany him. He led their group away from the docks and to a parked limousine. Abigail studied the man to be sure he didn't have any harmful intentions. He appeared to be fine. He opened the limo door for them to enter.

Inside sat the president, Russell Randolph. "I'm glad you all made it. Welcome home! I thought I could give you a ride."

Gavin jumped in. "This sure beats a cab or an Uber."

Russell smiled his tight-lipped smile. "Come on in. We have a lot to talk about."

Abigail studied his face and aura, trying to determine just how displeased he was. She was still upset over some of what happened on their trip.

As they climbed in and settled into the leather seats, Russell said, "I have some good news and some bad news."

Gavin asked, "Mr. President, are you going to make us choose which we want to hear first?"

He shuffled some papers in the briefcase resting in his lap, flashing a quick, slightly pained smile. "I'll start with the good news. First of all, good job on your mission and for making it home in one piece. That's the most important thing. You produced positive results in many parts of the world. The UK has finally banned bottom trawling. I guess crashing a chopper into their building was very effective. Plenty of news outlets captured the incident on camera. That was clever to inform the press. The fact that it was well televised put extra pressure on their leaders. Also, it's good no one else got hurt, so well done! How did you recover from your helicopter crash, Abigail?"

"I was fine. Thanks for traveling over there to help clear up the mess." The way he commended her was puzzling because she had been sure there would be dire consequences for how badly their trip had gone.

"It was my pleasure. As you know, the whaling operation in Iceland is history, and Iceland is putting Federation membership to a vote. They will make a fine addition to our coalition. I think plenty of the men you sent home from the whaling operation may end up serving in the Federation Navy. Also, the leader of Algeria is already turning that country in a new direction. It's amazing the good that can come from a little enlightenment!"

Abigail sank into her seat with relief. Gavin and Silas visibly relaxed too. "So what about Libya?"

The president let out a deep breath. "Well, the chairman, whom you apparently Illuminated, got deposed and replaced by someone else—and not in a very peaceful way. He was assassinated. And to be honest, the replacement is probably just as bad or worse than their former leader."

Silas, who had remained quiet, gave Abigail an apologetic look. "That's a tough part of the world. There was never any guarantee that trying to help them would produce the best results."

Disappointment settled in. More people had died because of her efforts.

Gavin squeaked, "Okay, so is that the bad news?"

Abigail could see a shift in the president's mood. His lips tightened into a narrow line. "Well, it's no surprise that China is not happy. There are other countries, some of which you didn't interfere with, who want to side with China. Countries like Russia, Japan, North Korea, as well as a few smaller ones are starting their own coalition to unite against the Federation. I guess they believe we have no right to interfere in affairs that don't concern us directly. The death of the Chinese fisherman was unfortunately the perfect catalyst to get them to rally against us. Now, we appear to be the bullies."

Abigail was devastated. She held some animosity toward Rendón for keeping her off the front line. She had been unable to help or do her job because of him, and the situation had worsened.

"Great, we just started World War Three," Gavin said.

"It's not a war yet." The president stayed calm. "We *should* stay out of China's waters, but we have many other tasks at hand. We will focus on helping other countries so we may have more allies."

Abigail's stomach dropped into a pit. It sounded like all they had caused was harm.

Silas reached over and put a hand on her knee. As if he could read her thoughts, he said, "Just think of the good you did. No more whaling operation. An entire country is in better shape because of you. Even that president's wife in Algeria is probably living a better life now."

The president nodded. "It's true. And as you told me before the trip, change takes time and hard work." He tapped on his briefcase. "So back to business: China has been aggressively buying land in South America to grow crops to add to their food supply. They're bringing industrialized farming methods to pristine areas that will be damaged. We could interfere in those countries to help the local people preserve their way of life and protect the rainforest."

Abigail crossed her arms. "That just sounds like it will aggravate China even more."

"Yes, but it will also put pressure on them because they're counting on the food they can produce in those countries, and those are countries we could recruit to join as member-states to the Federation."

Silas sat up straight and frowned with a look of resolve. "I think helping in South America sounds like a great start, and if it upsets China, so be it! When can we go?"

Abigail wasn't so sure she thought stirring up more trouble with China would help, although she was equally unsettled by the thought of uprooting rainforests for farming.

A glimmer of a smile broke through the president's stern facade. "Well, I have another destination in mind for you, and we have army bases full of soldiers who are back from the Middle East who can be deployed to Brazil, Ecuador, Bolivia, and Peru to put a stop to the Chinese. China is starting construction of a railway to haul lumber across Brazil to the west coast of the continent, where they will ship lumber across the Pacific. We are going to stop that too. I don't want any of you in harm's way, because it may be dangerous. This is a job for our troops."

Wanting to keep Abigail out of harm's way had been Rendón's big mistake in China. She thought sending troops with guns could be necessary, like when they needed to round up the whalers, but she saw herself as someone who could prevent an escalation and thought she could help in South America. "So what new mission do you have in mind for us? Stopping Japan's whaling in the Antarctic?"

"Actually, I'm sending Admiral Rendón with an armada to stop the Japanese whaling vessels, which I'm sure is going to make Japan wonderfully unhappy. I've reached out to their prime minister, and they won't consider any alternative but to continue hunting for whale meat. It's a tradition that runs deeply in their country."

Abigail hoped Rendón was the right person for the job. She still harbored some animosity toward him. The remainder of their trip home from China had been awkward, as had their final farewell.

The president's face and aura continued to brighten. "Evvie and our Space Force team report that they are ready to travel to the Polaris system to scout for the future colony world. I think you three are needed aboard the *Harkin*, if you're willing to leave Earth and make the trip to a new system? I actually think that might be the safest place for you, Abigail, because it sounds like you're gaining a reputation around the world."

Gavin shook his head. "I can't wait to get into space and leave the never-ending ocean behind us."

Abigail knew Gavin had had a rough time being stuck at sea for so long, even though he'd never complained. She was struck by the irony that getting around the Earth in a boat was more difficult than traveling to a new star system in a ship.

It was great news for her because she missed Evvie dearly and couldn't wait to see her again. She studied the president, wondering if he could endure the challenges the future might throw at him. She felt guilty that she would be leaving him with such a huge mess and once again pondered whether her Illumination of him was eventually going to cause more harm than good. Ultimately, she thought her Illumination was a force for good, but there could be unforeseen consequences. Since she had altered the president's mind, he had shifted his priorities in a positive way, but as result, imminent war loomed.

Chapter 18

More Money

Eliot arrived in Manhattan, found a hotel, and spent a couple of days apartment hunting. The process of signing a lease was made easier when he paid for a full year's rent with cash. He found a large loft apartment a few blocks away from Wall Street. His first order of business was to get a high-speed fiber-optic connection and set up his server. His close proximity to Wall Street meant for a fast exchange of information.

He was tempted to drop a message to his family to update them on his whereabouts, but he really saw no need to have them meddling in his life. They probably wouldn't be very supportive of his choices, anyway, but they never had been.

He contacted brokerage companies, pretending to be a potential client. He spent two days meeting with investment professionals then wrote a list of the ones who had made good impressions and seemed the most knowledgeable. He was surprised by how most brushed him off with disregard because of his young age. Too bad for them. He was slightly discouraged—he would have a hard time finding anyone who would want to work with him.

On his third day, he met with a hedge fund manager, Tom Morris, whose name was at the top of his list. Tom looked and dressed like he belonged in the 1980s, with a mustache, sideburns, and tinted wire-framed sunglasses that he wore indoors. His aura flashed differently than anyone else's, with a strange orange swirl that Eliot wished he could more accurately interpret. He guessed that maybe Tom was more compassionate than the average stockbroker, partially because of his warm smile and friendly handshake.

Tom rose from his desk to greet Eliot. "It's good to see you back, Mr. Montrose. Were there any more questions I could help you with?"

Eliot liked the way he treated him with respect, even though he was only an eighteen-year-old kid. "I have just one more question: would you like to start your own brokerage company as my partner? I'll provide all the start-up costs if you'll share your knowledge and experience."

Tom raised his eyebrows. "Okay, which of the partners put you up to this?"

Eliot shook his head. "I don't know what you're talking about. I'm not here to trick you. I'm here to start a company and make some money. I'm certain that I can help you get rich too. I've been studying trading since I was a kid, but I'm lacking hands-on experience."

"You still look like a kid to me. How old are you?"

"I just turned eighteen. Is that a problem?"

"No. Not at all." Tom cleared his throat. "But I'm pretty busy this morning, and I can't just drop everything for a school project."

"I'm not in school, and I'm serious about trading. I have some money—"

Before he could brag about his millions of dollars, Tom said, "Sorry, kid. I'd love to help you, but if I don't show some progress with some clients today, I'll have to answer to my boss."

"But I *am* a potential client."

Eliot saw conflicting colors in the man's aura. He was sure there was something about him that stood out—maybe discontentment with his job.

"Sorry, kid. I've got a ten o'clock who'll be here any minute."

It was the same story as ever before, the story of his life. No one took him seriously and just brushed him off. "Fine! Enjoy working for the man instead of being your own man." Eliot stormed out.

He rushed back to his apartment and opened the safe that had been his first purchase since arriving. He filled his backpack with money.

Eliot watched from the seating area of the office until Tom Morris stood from his meeting, shook hands, and said farewell to the well-dressed client. As soon as Tom sat again, Eliot rushed in and dropped his backpack on his desk. "Fifty thousand. It's your retainer if you'll join me to start a brokerage company."

Tom eyed Eliot and reluctantly opened the backpack. Just watching his eyebrows rise above his wireframe glasses was priceless. Eliot was a little disheartened that it took a bribe to get anyone to take him seriously, but he knew that money talked louder than words.

Tom cleared his throat. "I have to admit, I'm interested. I would rather work with a young gun than continue to slave away for rich old men."

Eliot had a feeling that might have been the case. "Great. I'll pay you this advance so you can feel secure in quitting your job right now and coming with me to buy some computer equipment."

Eliot pulled the bundled stacks of bills from his backpack and laid them on Tom's desk, catching Tom glancing at the World Series Poker bracelet. He raised his eyebrows again as if thinking, "Who the heck is this kid?" He asked, "What'd you do? Rob a bank?"

"No, I earned it fair and square." It wasn't totally the truth, but whatever.

"So you're serious about this? You really want me to drop all of my other commitments?"

"That's right."

Without another word, Tom pulled a briefcase from beneath his desk and set it beside the pile of money. He placed his belongings from his desk into it, along with his new bundles of cash. As they left, he told his secretary, "Nancy, I'm going out for an early lunch. I'm not sure when I'll be back, so you may want to cancel my afternoon appointments… Actually, cancel all of my appointments."

Within two days, they were up and running in Eliot's large apartment, which had become their trading headquarters. It still needed some furniture, but they had desks and computers. He didn't see the point in buying furniture to make it more comfortable. He only wanted to invest time and money into things that would yield a high return. He also didn't want to rent a separate office space if he could live and work in a single space.

They began their task at a new computer station.

Tom typed away. "Okay, let's start with a few safe bets first, just to get your capital rolling. I have a pretty basic algorithm my friend helped me out with that will not make huge amounts of money but will trade somewhat aggressively. so that a tenth of a penny here and there will add up pretty quickly."

Eliot sat beside him at the computer. "I dabbled in writing code in high school. May I see the program for your algorithm?"

"Sure, but it's really too complicated for an average computer programmer to understand. We're dealing with non-linear equations here."

Eliot scrolled down the screen. "Hmmm. So it basically evaluates the input, looks for patterns and correlations, then acts with certain assumptions about the defaults."

Tom's jaw dropped.

Eliot continued, "I think I can add more derivatives that will consider a wider range of possible probabilities. Is it okay if I make modifications to this program?"

"Sure. It's a pretty basic program. Any chance of improving it would be fantastic."

After customizing the algorithm, they sat and watched the results of the improvements. After an hour, Tom turned to Eliot. "Congratulations. You just made a million dollars."

Eliot was thrilled, but it was small change next to the goal he had in mind. He had his sights on billions. His goal was not only to get rich—he wanted to use large amounts of money to accomplish something huge in the tech industry that would perpetually generate even more money, a money-making empire.

He set to work writing an even more advanced trading algorithm. He couldn't believe how his new brain had been able to comprehend the complexity of the program and make improvements. *This is the moment I've spent my whole life dreaming of.* He had Tom order pizza so he could work through the night.

Chapter 19

Reunion in Space

Abigail, Silas, Gavin, and Tkla traveled to the airport, where a new area had been designated as a launch pad for spaceships. Abigail thought it seemed futuristic that LA International had become a spaceport. A Taurian unlike any Abigail had seen was waiting at the entry hatch to a small ship.

The Taurian was shorter and slimmer than Tkla and had more greenish-blue striping. Upon introducing themselves, Abigail realized she was a female. Tkla greeted her with a sideways pecking of their snouts on each side.

The female Taurian spoke in clear English and in a deep but feminine voice. "My name is Brklana. It is an honor to meet all of you and to accompany you on this mission."

Abigail nodded. "We would have a challenging time even getting up to the *Harkin* without your assistance, so thank you."

The ship was typically Taurian, with a rounded nose and curved features. Abigail thought all their ships had a slightly amphibious look, as if they could be used underwater as well as in space. They boarded, and Tkla took the seat next to Brklana as Abigail, Gavin, and Silas sat in the row of seats behind them.

They strapped in, and Abigail watched as Brklana maneuvered the ship into the air in a very smooth takeoff, even by Abigail's standards. Leaving Earth felt more like an airplane flight and less like blasting off in a dangerously combustible rocket. Abigail was mystified to watch the clouds drop below them and the blue sky gradually darken to reveal stars in their view port. She looked down to see the continent patched with clouds, and on the horizon, the atmosphere layers glowed in the morning light.

She listened as Tkla carried on a conversation with Brklana, who he apparently had never met before. They spoke in their native language, so only Abigail could understand them, and she worked hard to pretend she wasn't eavesdropping as the two became acquainted. He asked what clan she'd belonged to back on their home world and if she had family on the mother ship that was heading for the colony.

In their native language, she said, "I was raised in the clan of the Nishtrra, and yes, my parents and younger sister are aboard the mother ship. I miss them terribly and wonder if I might ever see them again."

Tkla replied, "If we have a chance of reuniting with them, I think it will be made possible with the help of these humans."

Abigail realized that reuniting with that colony ship would be a challenge simply because of the incredible vastness of space. The Taurians' trip to their new world sounded like it would take a couple hundred years to complete because, while they had very fast ships, they didn't have blast-jump technology.

Before attempting to locate the Taurian colony ship, the Space Force's first mission would be to explore the system to which they were heading, the Polaris system. The humans and Taurians on Earth were eager to determine the viability of any of the planets there—the scouting mission was the first step in establishing a colony.

Abigail felt a sudden pang, as if she had forgotten something at home. She realized she had never checked up on her brother to make sure he wasn't getting into trouble. Her parents and twin sister, Eileen, had no idea where he was. She could have tried to track him down, but space was calling, and she didn't want to hold up their departure because of family issues. She supposed Eliot was on his own for the time being.

So far, Tkla and Brklana appeared to be getting along well. Abigail even detected some of his attempted humor and put a lot of effort into not chuckling from her seat.

Traveling to space was an experience Abigail thought would never lose its magic. The pure blackness with the glowing planet below was a sight to behold. She was thrilled to see the massive ship, the *Harkin*, surrounded by other smaller ships as Brklana brought the ship into dock.

∞

Evvie was standing at the airlock, where Abigail, Silas, Gavin, Tkla, and Brklana boarded. Abigail ran ahead of her crewmates at the sight of her friend then grabbed her in a long hug.

While walking, Evvie asked, "Where's Max Fambozi?"

Abigail cracked a grin. "He's coming up in a later shuttle. He had some final exams to grade."

Evvie nodded. "Oh yeah, he's a college professor."

"And a very handsome one," Abigail teased.

Silas and Gavin both snickered as the group walked through the corridor toward their bunk rooms to unload their belongings.

Maxwell Fambozi was the astrophysicist with whom Evvie had been enamored when they'd met—he had determined the location of the Taurian colony world with only a handful of clues. Everyone agreed that having a knowledgeable astrophysicist on board was a great idea. Abigail thought he was a sweet, kind, and intelligent man.

After a winding walk through the ship's corridors, Evvie opened three consecutive doors along the passageway. "Here are your bunks. Come to the control room when you've unpacked."

For being on such a massive ship, the bunks were pretty small and minimal. Each would serve as a private place to sleep and maybe relax and read.

Once they regrouped in the control room, they sat in newly in-stalled captains' chairs, which Gavin couldn't stop swiveling around in as he gazed up into the massive clear dome. Because of the grav-plates in that section, the nose of ship felt like "up," and the clear dome gave an expansive panoramic view. The gravity in the rest of the ship was toward the outer hull, so any view ports that revealed outer space seemed as if they were in the floor.

Evvie turned to Silas and asked, "So, you've all been busy comb-ing the oceans for no-gooders, huh?"

Silas chuckled. "I guess that's a good term for people who are causing harm to the ocean. Yes, we stopped a lot of 'no-gooders,' but there are still plenty of them out there. In fact, whole countries are standing in the way of the do-gooders."

Abigail appreciated the way he oversimplified the situation and left out any mention of the mistakes they had made and the people who were killed.

Evvie asked, "How are your other ventures coming along? Are the electric vehicles becoming popular?"

Silas shook his head. "That's been a little discouraging too. I mean, we're doing well in terms of sales, but in terms of percentage of cars on the road that are electric, we still have a long way to go."

Evvie winked and flashed a supportive smile. "Silas, don't be discouraged. From what I've heard, you have accomplished many amazing deeds. Even saving one whale's life is huge, much less shutting down an entire whaling operation. I have missed the ocean."

Abigail appreciated Evvie's outlook. She needed to focus on the good they had brought about, but the prospect of future conflict weighed heavily on her. Traveling into space helped to make all of Earth's problems fade away.

At that moment, a voice came from the doorway. "And the ocean misses you, Evvie!" Max Fambozi walked into the control room at precisely the perfect moment.

Abigail watched as Evvie melted at the sight of him. Silas and Gavin rolled their eyes. Evvie's smile eclipsed the moon, which was now growing smaller in their rearview screens. Max had curly, sandy-colored hair and blue eyes that sparkled almost as much as his smile. "This is quite an impressive ship. You'll have to give me a tour."

"That could take about an entire year," Silas pointed out. "This ship is massive!"

Max walked over to Evvie. "Well, maybe we could start with the mess hall and get a table for two."

She blushed.

Silas elbowed Gavin. "He's probably hungry after repeatedly losing his lunch all the way out of Earth's atmosphere."

"Thank you for your concern, Silas. Yes, I am feeling much better now. I'm an astrophysicist, *not* a trained astronaut, although there is no place I'd rather be than aboard this ship."

Abigail wondered if Silas's supposed Illumination had already worn off because he was not being the kindest to Max. When they had met, Silas didn't respond well to Max's enamoring traits and personality.

Evvie looked smitten with the doctor, and Abigail hid a smile behind her hand and pretended to cough.

Gavin cleared his throat. "Um, we're glad to have you aboard, Doctor. I just wanted to offer my services if we get to name any new planets."

"Sounds great. I'll keep you in mind. Naming celestial bodies will be exciting indeed. Evvie tells me you're a fan of comic books. I have a little collection—nothing amazing, just kid's stuff from my childhood."

Abigail held in a gasp. *Had they been writing to each other? When did Evvie get a chance to brief Fambozi on the interests of her friends?*

Gavin gave a quick nod. "I'd love to see any old comics! Not to say that you're old—um. I'm actually working on some of my own. I did have a lot of spare time out at sea while these two were crushing evil without me."

Silas gave Gavin a sideways hug. "Hey, don't forget that you were the mastermind behind the greatest stunt of the trip. It actually worked, too, because England changed their laws. Tell us more about your comic books."

Gavin's volume increased. "Well, my main hero can manipulate super-dense material to distort gravity and cause destruction."

Dr. Fambozi scratched his chin. "Super-dense material, huh? Like perhaps from a neutron star?"

Gavin raised his arms. "*Exactly!* That's his name—*Neutron!*"

Fambozi grinned. "You know that a piece of a neutron star the size of a stone that could fit in your hand would weigh one hundred million metric tons. The mass of Mount Everest could fit into a sugar cube." He was full of such facts.

Gavin nodded. "Yes, that's why Neutron has the most amazing superpowers."

"I'm impressed," the doctor said. "I can't wait to read how he'll use his powers responsibly. He could cause a person to literally shred apart into a stream of atoms."

"Yes, you get it! Would you be the first person to read them when they're done?"

Silas looked offended. "Hey, I want to be your test reader!"

Gavin shook his head. "You can read them after the doctor has substantiated the science and given me his feedback."

Abigail gave Gavin a mock punch. "I want to read it too!" So far, he had been reluctant to let her read any of his work. She had seen his drawings, though. Maybe she could have spent more time with him aboard *Enterprise*. He really had been left alone for the majority of that trip. "You get it polished so we can all read it." She gave him a wink.

Gavin glowed. "I hope it's okay, but you're in it too. Her name is The Illuminator, and she basically has all your superpowers, plus she can take away other people's superpowers."

"That's so awesome. I'm honored. I hope she kicks ass in your story. If I ever meet an evil supervillain, I'll have to try to remove their superpowers when I Illuminate them."

"Yeah, my villains are actually way more afraid of her than they are of Neutron. She *is* a badass. She also helps Neutron keep his powers in check and teaches him self-control."

Abigail tried her best Yoda impersonation. "Control. You must learn control."

Everyone laughed.

Silas said, "Hey, what's my superpower? I want to be in your comic book!"

Gavin shrugged. "Well, being rich is *almost* a superpower if you were more like Tony Stark or Bruce Wayne. You just gotta make a suit and some cool gadgets and actually learn to throw some punches."

Everyone chuckled some more.

Still in her Yoda voice, Abigail said to Max, "Chaperone, we must. At a table of five, we must sit."

While Evvie was smitten with the professor, and Abigail was sure some alone time with him was something she'd been hoping for, Abigail wasn't going to let her out of her sight any time soon.

As the ship traveled away from Earth, they had a week to catch up with Evvie and get to know the other crew members before they were far enough to initiate a blast jump to the Polaris system. Abigail was glad that the troubles of Earth would soon be light-years away and couldn't wait to see what novel sights waited to be discovered in the new system.

Chapter 20

A Crap Load of Money

Eliot was reviewing his new trading program and resisting the urge to give himself a literal pat on the back—his work was a masterpiece of computer programming. He sat in his suite, which still lacked comfortable furniture or even a lamp. Furnishing hadn't been a priority. "Okay, I'm ready to get it going," he said to Tom. "Do we have all the cooling fans switched on? This may be a lot for our processors to handle."

Tom turned on the last cooling fan. "Yes, press the start button." He had a hopeful look on his face.

Within two seconds, each processor popped and let out a puff of smoke. The monitor went black.

"I think we're going to need more computing power to run your program. I'm going to phone a friend."

They would need to spend money, and even though they had acquired truckloads of it, Eliot winced at the thought of spending more.

∞

One day later and after hours of upgrades, Eliot reloaded his program. "Okay, here goes round two. Keep your fingers crossed." He pushed enter. *It has to work this time.*

Tom's face glowed by the light of the computer screen. "It seems to be working!" But after a few moments, he noticed something wrong. "Oh, shit. The screen's locked up."

Eliot saw that all the computer screens were indeed frozen. He tried typing in commands with no effect. "Jeez!" Eliot typed furiously onto his keyboard until he was jolted by electric sparks.

Tom flinched. "What the... Are you okay? We must have faulty wires or something."

Eliot realized that *he* must have created the sparks—maybe he had the same skill his sister had. He had been so consumed by the prospect of making money that he'd forgotten about the possibility that he could develop other abilities. Eliot got up and rushed to the bathroom.

Tom called after him, "Hey, man, are you okay?"

Eliot didn't answer as he closed the bathroom door. He looked closely in the mirror. Sure enough, the corneas of his eyes were bright white with flecks of blue that almost glowed. He studied his hair, and, yep, he had quarter-inch roots of pure white. He couldn't believe he hadn't taken the time to notice these changes and supposed he'd maybe been spending too much time in front of a computer.

He came out to see Tom unplugging all the equipment. "I guess the third time will be a charm. You okay there, buddy?"

"Yeah, I'm fine. I think I did receive a little bit of a shock."

Luckily, Tom remained focused on his task. Their work space was not well lit, and they both spent most their time peering at computer screens and not scrutinizing each other's appearances.

Eliot noted that he should buy a hat and sunglasses if he was to go out in public. He would go to the corner store at night.

The next day, with a New York Mets cap on and a little effort to avoid eye contact with Tom, they assembled their third computing station, which they hoped would have the processing power and cooling fans strong enough to run the program.

With everything set up, Eliot started the program. He quickly removed his finger from the keyboard for fear of shocking it and ruining an even more expensive setup. He held his breath and watched it get to work without freezing or going up in smoke.

He was afraid to blink as he watched his program start slowly—it began by trading cautiously but gradually increased its activity. After thirty minutes, it hit its stride, and they sat there, watching their money multiply. "Phew," Tom said with a grin.

After about a week, Eliot grew impatient. "We're making a mediocre amount of money," he said to Tom, "but how can we improve what we're doing? I have some big plans that are going to require even larger amounts. How can we more efficiently make progressively larger and larger amounts of money?"

Tom raised his eyebrows. "You want even more money?" He paused and regained his composure. "Well… your algorithm is outstanding, but we're faced with limitations placed on us by how quickly information can be transferred. Every millisecond makes a difference. If other traders are getting their information even two milliseconds before we do, they have an advantage." He paused, resting his stubbly chin on his knuckles. "Well, you can further enhance your algorithm to do a couple tricks. One is quote stuffing, which is sending out thousands of small insignificant offers just to keep other systems busy and deceive them into considering useless offers. They basically have to sort through all the offers to find the interesting ones."

"Okay, I'll start on that. Very clever. What's the other trick?"

"It's called spoofing. The idea is to send out overpriced phantom offers that we cancel as soon as they're seen. This will artificially raise prices. I should warn you that anyone illegally spoofing can face penalties of up to ten thousand dollars."

"That's a risk I'm willing to take to increase our profits."

Tom pulled his sunglasses down to study Eliot and had a slight reaction, seeming to have noticed the change in his appearance. Tom's aura flashed briefly, as if he was startled to look Eliot in the eyes and see them glowing.

Eliot held his gaze.

"Listen, Eliot. This is a business of taking risks, but risks need to be calculated. If you get too greedy and disregard all caution, you could lose it all. Also, there are some lines that shouldn't be crossed. Venturing too far into questionable activities could take a toll on you. I'm fine with cutting it a little close, but we shouldn't get too carried away."

Eliot didn't need his business partner acting like his parent. "I brought you on to help make as much money as possible. If you have a problem with that, there's the door."

Tom removed his tinted glasses and glared at Eliot. "Don't you think you're getting a little big for your britches? If you really don't want any more of my help, just let me know. It's sounding like you're wanting to manage all this money on your own."

Eliot realized that losing Tom would hurt. He still couldn't interpret auras very reliably, but he thought there was something more to Tom than just a love of money. Perhaps he really cared. "Hey. I'm sorry. You're right. Maybe I don't need to get too reckless."

Tom studied Eliot once more. He shrugged, and the alarm in his aura dissipated.

Despite the fact that his eyes were probably glowing, Eliot continued to hold the other man's gaze. "I guess I have a history of being headstrong. Sorry... So, um... how can we get an even faster connection to the incoming feed of information?"

Tom cleared his throat. "Well, we're close to the New York Stock Exchange and NASDAQ, but we're actually dealing with longer distances to data warehouses and other stock exchanges. The big problem is that information has to travel to many different locations, taking different amounts of time. The traders with the biggest advantage get information before everyone else then trade against them before everyone has that information. We want to be the ones who know something, like a price drop, sooner than the other traders."

"I see. There's nothing I can do in the algorithm to change that. I'll put some thought into how to get a jump on the information that's coming in. I want to keep developing a program so it can take larger leaps on its own. I want it to learn and change its own code so it can evolve."

Tom scratched his chin. "That sounds kind of like artificial intelligence. I would love to see what the future possibilities are for that."

Eliot nodded. "As a matter of fact, developing AI is a part of my master plan. I have some ideas I want to pursue outside of trading, like robotics and AI. Since you're my partner, I'd like to get your opinion on pulling some of the company funds to start a few new ventures."

Tom leaned back in his chair. "We have amassed more wealth than most people can hardly conceive of. You've turned millions into billions. I think now is a great time to invest in any ventures you can think of. Also, you should take a percentage of the money you're earning and put it someplace less risky, like a money market account. You won't be generating more wealth, but it will be there in case you need it." Tom eyed him again. "My grandpa had a saying: 'Don't bet the ranch.' There's also the common saying, 'Don't put all your eggs in one basket.' Both pieces of advice apply to trading."

Eliot tried to not roll his eyes. He thought highly of Tom but still didn't want to miss opportunities to generate wealth by being overly cautious. "Great. Thanks for your feedback." He actually had no intention of putting any money into an account that didn't generate more wealth. "I'm going to leave town for a few days. I'll work on a way to get information even more quickly from the exchanges, and I'll keep working on the master algorithm. All you have to do is keep an eye on the trading and count our money. I think we've accomplished enough that it's now time to buy some furniture for the place too. We no longer need to sleep on foam pads on the floor."

Eliot decided to trust his partner. He knew there was a chance Tom could someday betray him and skip town with all of the money, but Eliot couldn't detect any signs in his aura. In fact, he was beginning to think that the man actually cared.

Chapter 21

New System

With the smaller ships connected to the *Harkin* and enough distance between them and Earth, they made the jump. As with the previous blast jumps they'd made, Gavin had to initiate their ritual of chanting, "Best friends forever, blast jump, go!" Abigail thought his cheesy saying was sweet and was glad he had come on the mission to explore a truly new system.

Bright light shot through the view ports, replaced by a moment of pure darkness then the return of stars.

They had reached the new star system. As they approached the outermost bodies, the *Harkin's* sensors took measurements, and Evvie announced the results. "Their sun is slightly larger than ours—one-point-two-six-five times larger. There are four inner rocky planets, a debris belt that's much denser and wider than our asteroid belt, and a single gas giant that's huge, about eight times the size of Jupiter. Outside of its orbit is another debris field. This is where the ice giants in our solar system would be. Just a guess—there could be a lot of ice in those asteroid belts."

Abigail was no astrobiologist, but she knew that any sign of water was good when it came to supporting life.

"Hmm." Fambozi tapped his fingers on the console of his workstation. "I like how this system is sounding. That single large gas giant—or maybe we should say 'gas supergiant'—probably prevented the formation of planets in its neighborhood with its massive gravitational pull. If it were much larger, it could even be a brown dwarf, which would make this system even more interesting. Gavin, that's the first body we should name."

Gavin didn't take long to make a suggestion. "How about Colossus? He's one of the most underrated members of the X-Men."

"Perfect! We have officially named our first planet in the Polaris system."

Abigail sat upright in her chair, studying the main view screen, but there wasn't much to see beyond a few bright dots in the distance. She squinted to look for any sign of a blue dot that could be a habitable world like Earth. She couldn't see one.

The smaller ships were getting ready to depart from the *Harkin* to scout different regions of the new system. Brklana was saying goodbye to Tkla, since she had her own ship to pilot, and he would stay aboard the *Harkin*. Apparently, the two had grown close.

Silas teased, "Parting is such sweet sorrow."

Tkla responded, "Sweet sorrow? That makes no sense. What is the term for when two words contradict each other with their meanings?"

Abigail answered, "Oxymoron."

Tkla continued, "Here, let me try one. Silas, you are a handsome ugly person. Not to make you humans feel badly, but you are somewhat strange-looking, with a lack of texture on your skin, but among you, Silas might perhaps be a little less ugly."

Abigail laughed. "That's a good one. You nailed it."

"You still said I'm handsome, so I'll take the compliment."

Taurian emotions were still difficult to judge, and they didn't have auras—at least ones that were visible to Abigail—but Tkla looked like a sad puppy dog—but with scales—to see Brklana go. "Be safe," he said as she boarded her ship.

The smaller ships dispersed across the system. One stayed in the outer belt beyond Colossus to take samples. Another traveled to the inner debris belt. The three remaining scout ships, including Brklana's, headed toward the four inner rocky planets. The scouting ships' purpose was to document the region and look for any sign of danger.

Abigail tried to imagine what kinds of danger could await them in a new system. She hadn't considered that there could be any hostile alien life present. For some reason, she'd assumed the system would be uninhabited. So far, they hadn't detected any other ship activity.

The Taurian crafts were much faster than the *Harkin,* so they scouted ahead—although the Taurians had helped to upgrade the *Harkin's* propulsion system so it could travel vast distances in a relatively short time, it was still slow in comparison.

Fambozi suggested they should head toward the outermost rocky planet, where the planet's distance from the sun was not too close and not too far away to be habitable. "To the Goldilocks zone," he said. "Not too hot and not too cold."

After over a week of traveling, their view out the domed view port showed a glittery field of asteroids. They had arrived at the edge of the asteroid belt.

Reports were coming in from the scout ships. Fambozi studied them and announced their findings from his station on the control deck. "Evvie, you were right. News is coming in saying the outer debris ring does indeed consist of considerable amounts of frozen methane and water ice. Next is the gas supergiant, Colossus." He winked at Gavin. "It's similar in composition to Jupiter, only way more massive. Lots of hydrogen and helium. By the way, I've warned our expedition to keep a safe distance, since it's probably emitting huge amounts of radiation. This rules out colonizing any of its moons. Not to worry, though—it's not affecting the inner rocky planets. Scouts are counting up to one hundred twenty moons around the supergiant, compared to Jupiter's seventy-nine."

He scrolled down on his readout. "Next is the inner asteroid debris belt, which we are now entering. Brklana conducted an analysis as she passed through, reporting similar findings to the outer belt but with more rocky bodies. She says that about half the bodies are rocky and the rest are mostly pure water ice. This is exciting!"

Evvie nodded. "Yes, I'm very glad you're here to help sort out these discoveries."

Abigail couldn't help but crack a grin. She loved watching the two interact. She had eased up and finally allowed them to eat a meal together without an entourage of friends to chaperone.

Fambozi shook in his seat. "I can't wait to see what the inner planets have in store for us!" He appeared to be the only one who was patiently enjoying the time-consuming trip into the system. Silas, Gavin, and Tkla had periodically voiced their impatience to find out if there were indeed habitable planets. Tkla had good reason for his apprehension—the Taurians were heading to this system in their convoy of ships and needed a home. If no world was habitable, they would have to head to another system. Fambozi had talked about the very low odds of finding habitable conditions in any system, which didn't ease Abigail's pessimism.

As they passed through the inner asteroid belt, Abigail was awestruck by the sparkling icy bodies. It was like a field of gems.

"I'm going to have to name this asteroid belt myself," proclaimed Dr. Fambozi. "It shall henceforth be called the Evvie Belt because it sparkles like her eyes."

Evvie blushed and blinked.

Abigail said, "Awww, that is so romantic! No one ever named a celestial body after me!"

Silas spoke up. "I wanted to name that gas supergiant after you, but Gavin beat me to it with 'Colossus.'"

Gavin scrunched his face. "We haven't named this system's star yet. Can we name it Abigail because it shines so brightly like she does?"

"Hmmm… *Abigail Montrose* isn't really a good name for a star," Fambozi said seriously. "Technically, our sun is called Sol—how about adding the word 'rose' from your last name to make *Solrose*? It will then share a little bit of your name. The star does have a slightly rose-colored tint to it. Its scientific name could be *Solroseus*."

"That's a great name for the star! Very sweet, you guys." She turned to Silas and punched her fist into her cupped hand. "So were you saying I'm really big or just gaseous?"

"Both." Silas chuckled. "It's actually that you have a bunch of moons orbiting your big fat head."

Abigail filled her cheeks with air to make her face look bigger. Then she pantomimed orbits of a couple of pretend moons circling her head. Everyone laughed.

"You know, Gavin," Fambozi said, "*Colossus* is a Latin word, so you may have started a trend of naming planets with Latin root words."

Gavin started typing away at his station. "Okay, I'll bring up an English-to-Latin translator on my terminal and start looking up more."

Fambozi continued through the reports. "It looks like the inner planets run the gamut of inhospitable conditions. We have the hot innermost one like Mercury. In fact, it's so small that is does not meet one of the requirements for a planet in that it's not entirely round. It does meet two other requirements, though: it circles the star, and it has cleared its orbital path of other objects. Even though it's not like Pluto, which is a body among others in the Kuiper Belt, some might say this is also a planetoid or dwarf planet and not a real planet."

Gavin huffed. "Screw that. We're the ones who get to decide, and if it's circling around with other planets, then we'll call it a planet."

Abigail was glad to see Gavin taking an active role in the mission. She thought he had a tendency to be immature when he didn't have anything else to contribute.

Fambozi grinned. "I'm glad we agree on planet designations."

Gavin kept typing. "I'll look up the word 'lump.' How about *Glaeba*?"

"Sounds great. The next planet out from Glaeba is sounding very hot. It has an atmosphere with a large percentage of sulfides. It's probably volcanic."

Gavin said, "Oooh, *Calidus* is 'hot.' That sounds like a good name for the second planet."

Fambozi nodded. "Okay the two inner planets have names—Glaeba and Calidus. The third is our first candidate for life, but it's a bit close to the inner edge of what I would consider the habitable zone. Reports say its atmosphere is very reflective. Seventy percent reflectivity. Sounds similar to Venus. Whoa! The estimate is coming in that it's about three times the size of Earth. It's like a mega-Venus."

Gavin grumbled but kept his eyes locked on his screen. "Okay, I'm not having much luck finding anything that fits this one."

"Let's skip it until later," Fambozi suggested. "It's probably even less habitable than Venus—huge atmospheric pressure on the surface and probably a runaway greenhouse effect, so it's too hot. The last rocky planet gets my vote for being the best candidate for habitability. Actually, it's our only hope."

Abigail crossed her fingers. This had to be the one. Fambozi magnified an image on their main view screen. Abigail was disappointed to see a solid brown ball of a planet. There were no greens or blues. It was not a lush oasis like Earth.

After further studying his readout, Fambozi continued, "Reports are saying it's one-point-one-two-five times the size of Earth and similar in mass. We're detecting a magnetic field. That's very important—it's what protects planets from all kinds of nasty rays. There's an atmosphere with nitrogen and trace amounts of oxygen. Oxygen is a byproduct of plant life, so this is very hopeful, although there's not enough oxygen present for us to breathe. The single biggest concern, though, is a lack of water. There's no surface water, and the atmosphere is devoid of moisture. That can create a red-tinted sky. Evvie, you might feel right at home here—it's sounding a bit like Mars."

"At least it has its magnetic field intact," Evvie said. "Mars lost its magnetic field a hundred million years ago, so it's reassuring to hear this planet has one."

Abigail tried to assure herself that all of this was sounding hopeful, but she couldn't shake her pessimism that living on the planet would not be pleasant or even possible.

Silas waved an arm in Gavin's direction. "Hey, Gavin, aren't you going to rush in and name *this* world?"

Gavin bit his lower lip. "This is more than just Planet Lumpy. I think we need to discuss this among all of us, especially the Taurians. Tkla, what do you think?"

"Thank you, Gavin, for your thoughtfulness. What does your Latin translator say for the word 'home'?"

"Well, there's *Domum*, but that's more like a house. Here's one: *Nidus*, which is 'nest or abode.'"

"Perfect," said Tkla. "If there is a planet we will call home, it will be Nidus."

Abigail liked the sound of that. She only hoped that it would indeed become a home for the Taurians. As Fambozi had mentioned, that single planet was their only hope. They would have to land to find out just how far from habitable it might be.

Chapter 22

Venture

Having donned his Mets cap and sunglasses, Eliot traveled to New Jersey to look at warehouse spaces for setting up a research-and-technology-innovation facility. He found a gem on Dayton Avenue. As he walked the property, he visualized how it could serve as a production complex.

The lot contained one large four-story industrial building and a dozen smaller buildings, all old-style brick structures, on a lot that took up an entire city block. The compound reminded him of Hollywood studios, where all the buildings housed different crews that offered services for the central studio. He wanted to copy that model but develop new technologies.

He bought the lot with cash and decided to name it Tech Venture Industries. As had happened many times before, no one took him seriously until he pulled out the cash. He was thrilled to actually own something so substantial as an entire city block of property.

After his purchase, Eliot traveled to recruit people to work at the new facility. He poached JJ Hornwell's assistant, Jane Grant, the paleogeneticist. He asked her to assemble a team and acquire the equipment to continue the work to alter DNA to construct real living dinosaurs. Eliot wanted to continue the work that JJ Hornwell had started, but he was thinking much larger than dino-chickens. He could see that Jane had some moral objections, but money cured that pretty quickly. Offering to pay off her entire student loan swayed her. JJ wouldn't be happy to lose his staff, but it was survival of the fittest, and JJ hadn't been making the most of his team's skills, anyway.

He also appropriated robotic engineers from top companies, gave them massive budgets, and assembled a team to focus solely on the advancement of artificial intelligence. Eliot knew that AI was going to be the future of business, and its development was integral to robotics.

A couple of the scientists he pursued worked in fringe areas that were way outside of mainstream science, like time travel. He invited one such doctor, Dr. Baylon, who worked with lasers, and gave him a small building of his own and a good-sized budget. When he met the white-haired man, he almost reconsidered housing him at the facility because he seemed to have a loose screw or two.

But with huge amounts of money at his disposal, he decided to throw caution to the wind. Like every other facet of his venture, time travel could be a huge moneymaker—he just wasn't sure how yet. He thought investing in Dr. Baylon's work was worth the risk of it not panning out. Eliot had to admit that he would probably work more closely with the rest of his team and let Baylon tinker away until he made any advancements.

Each group who was coming to work at Eliot's new facility was asked to give feedback for the renovation of the buildings. A design company received their feedback and began work, remodeling the interior. Eliot gave the design firm some parameters as well but detected reluctance from the designers. He was, after all, just an eighteen-year-old kid in a baseball cap and sunglasses, but once he slapped some cash on the table, all their concerns faded. Watching their auras as they adjusted their attitudes was entertaining.

Within weeks, the result was a super-modern facility hidden by a rustic brick facade. The grounds were exquisitely landscaped with engaging outdoor spaces for the staff to enjoy. His idea was to offer an inspirational environment for his employees, people who would be making revolutionary innovations, so he installed a park space with fountains, a creek bridged with pathways, and relaxing spaces to sit and eat or drink a cup of tea or coffee, or a smoothie.

Some of the outer buildings were retrofitted to offer services to employees, including a diner and bistro, a coffee and smoothie bar, a yoga studio, a fitness gym, and a small grocery and drug store. It was almost like a small town, and it was his.

The only problem with developing the property was that Eliot was investing huge amounts of money, and the facility was far from producing any profits. He tried to reassure himself that the venture would soon become profitable. He just had to be patient.

Eliot was most excited to sit down with the head of his AI team, not forgetting that Tom, his business partner, had commented that Eliot's direction with his algorithm sounded like it could lead to artificial intelligence, a program that could learn, alter itself, and evolve. Some of the people he had hired had made steps toward self-improving robots, but he wanted to take it to a level that would make a robot self-improve to the point of becoming a unique individual. While he was most excited to create robots for himself, he also wanted to market them and sell them with huge price tags.

Eliot sat in the newly completed research center's main conference room, speaking with a forty-something programmer named Greg, who was tall and lanky with a hawkish nose and short salt-and-pepper hair.

Greg had explained some of the challenges to making progress with artificial intelligence.

Eliot fidgeted with the straw in his smoothie. He brought smoothies to every meeting. At some point, he wanted to lose the hat and glasses, but until he got to know all of his staff, he wouldn't reveal his new appearance to anyone. "So you're saying our biggest limitation to programming artificial intelligence is ourselves?"

"Yes. We're like overprotective parents—we want to write code so that our AI is prepared for every encounter or decision it will have to make. We've been struggling to create a truly autonomous program because code writers are, by their very nature, control freaks. The leap we need to make is giving control to a new intelligence to improve itself."

Eliot thought for a moment. "It sounds like we should aim to start an intelligence that begins its own process of learning, development, and self-improvement. Then we can leave it up to the program to self-improve."

Greg sipped his smoothie. "The only problem with that—and the reason I think this hasn't been successfully developed to a high level—is because it's too random. The initial program needs some parameters. The issue is that once we start setting up those parameters, we end up back where we started, micromanaging every detail. I'd say we've made huge advancements to get programs to imitate intelligence and personality, but they're ultimately the result of their programming. I would love to see an AI develop its own identity with its own personality."

A robot with its own personality was exactly what Eliot wanted. "What if we gave the program an underlying purpose, and *it* chose how to proceed? Like, for example, if you had a nanny-bot, it would be given the description of the job then develop for that task."

The programmer replied, "Yes, that sounds great, but there's still a feedback loop, like the hole-in-the-bucket syndrome, where you need the tool to make a plug to fix the hole in the bucket, but you need water in the bucket to whet the grinding stone to grind the plug. In this case, we need a program to come up with solutions to a problem, but the only way to make it aware is by programming it."

Eliot slurped the last of his smoothie. He thought they were getting closer to a good idea. "What if we gave the program an underlying goal and a self-building starter program that was asked to evaluate itself and look for improvements? Part of its starter program could be to study its surroundings and look for patterns. It could be like an infant human baby, who knows very little but is programmed to study everything in its surroundings."

The programmer smirked. "That sounds wonderful. I'm not exactly sure how to do it, but I would love to help develop a program that does exactly what you're describing."

"Well, you're going to have to figure it out soon because I want some products to test and get onto the market within months."

The programmer choked on his smoothie, and his aura swirled with new colors. "Months? I think we're looking at years."

Eliot rolled his eyes under his sunglasses. "I'm paying your hefty salary, and I sank a lot of dough into this facility filled with expensive equipment. If you don't want to work hard to meet our goals, and you don't want to produce results quickly, there's the door."

Eliot loved putting the man in his place. While Greg was at the top of his field, Eliot needed to remind him who was in charge.

The clouds in Greg's aura calmed, and he let out a deep breath. "Okay. We'll get to work on this immediately and begin drafting a finished model that will be our first robot to present to the public."

Of all the projects Eliot had in mind, he was the most excited about making robots. He was eager for the facility to begin generating an income, and he thought selling them could be profitable. He was glad to get the message through to the head of the department, and he would oversee his staff closely to make sure they were productive.

But mostly, he really wanted a robot for himself, even more than he wanted a pet dinosaur. He wanted to make something that would assist him, was able to carry on a conversation and maybe even show some support and care for his well-being. He'd struggled while growing up with a lack of caring and support because his priorities had differed from those of everyone else in the household. He would put his new super brain to work with the task of making a truly autonomous robot that would have its own personality and might care.

Chapter 23

Nidus

As the *Harkin* traveled to within visual range of Nidus, Abigail peered at it through the view port. She tried to remain optimistic, but all she saw was a big brown ball of dirt.

Fambozi was hunched at his terminal. "Everything about the planet sounds desirable except for its lack of water. We are detecting some water in frozen layers at the poles, but it's not a huge amount of ice—probably the remnants of polar ice caps. Vestiges of river- and lake beds also show that water once existed on the planet."

Abigail supposed all of that was good news.

Fambozi continued to study his screen. "This is interesting—the computer has been studying its spin as we've been approaching for the last few days, and it's detecting a slight wobble to the planet. Does anyone have any idea as to a possible cause?"

Silas pursed his lips. "Could there be an irregularity in the planet's core? Like that it's not perfectly round?"

Fambozi shook his head. "Gravity tends to pull everything evenly, so that seems unlikely. I think something must be happening closer to the surface."

Abigail watched Silas's smile fade with his aura. He was no astrophysicist, and she knew he wanted to contribute more to the mission than he had so far.

"Maybe there's a cavernous pocket in the crust where the locals are holed up, like Evvie's relatives on Mars?" Gavin suggested.

Abigail watched from the copilot's station, where Evvie was giving her tips on how to fly the massive ship. Silas shrank away from the conversation.

Fambozi scratched his chin. "That could account for the wobble, if it was a large enough empty space, but the dirt would have to be piled up somewhere. I'm going to have the computer study the wobble and determine where the less dense side of the planet is."

After some time letting the computer work, Fambozi proclaimed, "I have it! I don't think it's air. The difference in density must be a cavernous supply of water." He transferred the image to the main screen and zoomed in on a map of the surface. "I think we need to land at this site." He highlighted a region of the map, showing a large flat sunken area with what looked like a network of river valleys surrounding it.

Abigail nodded. "I suppose that could have been a lake." She tried to add some optimism to her voice, but a dried-up ancient lake bed wasn't necessarily a sign of habitability.

Fambozi agreed. "It does looks like a lake bed, where I think we will find underground water. We should drill through and retrieve a sample. Do we have that capability?"

"Yes," Evvie responded. "Brklana's ship has a boring device that can drill into the crust. Then we can drop a probe."

Tkla shook his head. "If there is life on the planet, then it is my responsibility to make initial contact. My people wish to live here, and I am their ambassador. We will not use a probe for first contact."

Abigail wasn't sure she liked what he was proposing. "Don't you think jumping into alien water sounds a little dangerous? We don't know what's down there."

Fambozi agreed with Abigail. "I'm no microbiologist, but I would say we should at least study a sample of the water to make sure there are no deadly pathogens. I second the vote for a probe."

Abigail had never seen a Taurian become angry, since they were a patient and reasonable people, but Tkla stood extra tall, extended his arms outward, and puffed his chest. *Is he trying to become more intimidating than the seven-foot-tall alien he already is?*

He made a huffing sound through his beaked lips. "I will have to insist that on this matter, there will be no committee discussion. I will make first contact."

Damn, I don't think we can disagree with him on this. Abigail looked to Dr. Fambozi with raised eyebrows. She supposed they had no choice but to let him plunge himself into an underground cavern of water on an alien planet, although she still thought it was a terrible idea.

The group boarded Brklana's ship to descend from orbit and to the new world, Nidus. Although it should have been exciting, palpable tension filled the air. She couldn't see Taurian auras, but she thought she detected concern from Brklana. Tkla remained as bullheaded as ever.

As they dropped, Abigail thought the planet looked an awful lot like Mars but less colorful. Instead of monochromatic red, it was nothing but brown.

Silas gripped his armrests, his face pale. "Are you sure we'll be okay without space suits?"

"All we need is oxygen," Evvie replied. "The conditions are suitable for us. The temperature is reasonable, and the surface is protected from solar and cosmic radiation thanks to the planet's magnetic field."

Abigail thought that sounded somewhat better than Mars, where a person would be frozen and crispified within seconds, but she worried about what could be lurking in the water in the underground reservoir. She wished she could talk some sense into Tkla.

Brklana landed the ship smoothly on the surface of the lakebed. Tkla was wearing a wet suit, an oxygen tank, and a mask. The rest of the crew placed oxygen masks over their faces. The hatch opened to a barren landscape, and pink light from the system's star, Solrose, glowed through the opening.

"Who wants to take the first step out there?" Silas asked, still buckled in.

Everyone stayed glued to their seats. Abigail hadn't thought about that. Who would make history for all of humanity by stepping foot on a planet in a new star system? Abigail wanted to, but she looked around to study her crew. Gavin's aura was glowing particularly brightly with pinks and oranges. He had unstrapped and was clearly eager to go out there. Silas looked terrified. Dr. Fambozi looked excited but a little intimidated. She couldn't decide. "Do you guys want to play rock, paper, scissors to choose?"

Tkla unbuckled and stood.

"Wait! Are you sure you want to be the first one out there? It will be documented in our history books, like Neil Armstrong taking the very first step on the moon."

Tkla blinked. "We have landed in this ship together. What difference does it make who among us takes the first step onto the surface?"

"Trust me, it's kind of an important human ritual."

Tkla let out a sigh—a newly acquired human gesture. "Any of you may be the first footstep-makers on this planet if it pleases you, but I would like to step foot on it myself at some point in the near future."

Abigail was wondering what had gotten into him. He seemed impatient. She looked to Brklana for a clue but found none. Her neutral face was impossible to read, compared to Tkla, who maybe tried excessively to emulate human expressions.

They stood, their oxygen puffing with each breath. Abigail tapped Gavin as if playing duck, duck, goose and nudged him toward the hatch. "Go put your footprints into some alien soil!" She chose him because he appeared to be the most excited. If Tkla had cared, she would have thought it appropriate to send him and Brklana out first to make history. After all, it was going to be their new home—if it proved to be habitable.

With uncharacteristic seriousness, Gavin nodded and walked down the steps from the hatch. He set one foot onto the brown dirt then another. Everyone cheered while Tkla rolled his eyes—another adopted human gesture.

Abigail tapped the doctor. "Next is you, Max."

He raised his eyebrows.

Before he could argue, she gave him a nudge. He wasted no time in joining Gavin, standing in the brown soil, and patting the younger man on the back. Seeing how ecstatic they both were made it worth all the fuss she'd made over the silly ritual.

Abigail eyed the two Taurians. "Now, it's your turn. Silas, Evvie, and I will take up the rear. You both should go out and walk on what will hopefully become your new world."

Tkla nodded, and he and Brklana departed from the ship.

She followed with Silas and Evvie. The surface didn't feel all that alien. It was simply dirt, and the gravity felt identical to Earth's. She hopped in place to test it. The sky, however, was nothing like home. The sun glared through the pinkish-red sky and shimmered off the hilly landscape.

As the ship's boring device set to work, the group explored. Everyone had experienced landing on a foreign world except for the doctor, although they hadn't walked on Mars or Kronos. Fambozi jiggled with excitement as he set to work collecting soil samples and taking photos. Abigail thought it was funny to watch him because he was searching under every rock as if he expected to find some sort of alien centipede hiding underneath.

The drill was about three meters deep and had created a large pile, from which Fambozi periodically collected soil samples. Pessimism persisted in Abigail's head. *What if there's no water, or what if it's too deep to get to?* But then mud slopped onto the pile, and Brklana raised the boring device to reveal a hole barely large enough for Tkla to be lowered down into.

Abigail peered down the hole. "Are you sure about this?"

"Yes. I would not leave this task to any other or to a probe. It is my responsibility to make first contact."

Before he put his mask on, Brklana gave him a firm hug with a nudge on the side of his neck with her snout. This elicited some movement from his tail, which patted the dusty ground.

Brklana worked the winch controls to lower Tkla into the hole like a worm on a fishing line.

They watched a feed on a portable screen, but Tkla's camera revealed nothing but darkness. They waited for twenty long minutes—Abigail hated it. Her friend was down there, dangling in some unknown body of water like bait waiting to be eaten. She doubted friendly dolphins or whales waited below, eager to become his friends.

Suddenly, a flash of something fish-like streaked across the screen. Abigail saw a fin. The line shook, Tkla's signal to be raised.

Brklana hit the controls to reel him up, but it pulled hard like a huge fish on a line. Tkla called through the comm, "Stop the winch! This thing has my leg and won't fit through the hole with me."

Brklana disengaged the motor. Abigail imagined the terror she would feel in his position, stuck in the narrow shaft with a large animal clasped to her leg, preventing her ascent. *What can I do to save him? I could shock the monster to get it to release his leg, but Tkla is basically plugging the hole between it and me.* She had an idea. She wanted to warn Tkla to brace himself but didn't feel like she had a moment to lose. She grabbed the metal cable and sent a jolt of electricity down it. Her idea was that if she electrified Tkla, whatever was holding onto him would get a shock too. She worried that it was perhaps too much electricity, but Tkla was a big guy, and whatever was holding onto him must have been even larger.

"Hurry, reel him in!" she shouted, feeling slightly faint after expending a shock without powering up from another source of electricity.

The winch came to life, now unhindered by any sort of fish monster. Tkla's limp form rose from the hole. Everyone pulled him to one side while Brklana released some cable. They laid him on the dirt and freed him from his harness.

Abigail removed his face mask and gave him an oxygen mask. He was unconscious. She put her hand on his head to try to sense if he was alive. "Come on, Tkla, wake up."

After a moment, he stirred. "Something grabbed my leg…"

"We noticed." Abigail saw a trickle of red blood coming from the calf section of his wet suit. There was a rip in his suit and puncture wounds in his leg. "You're safe now. Sorry I had to shock you."

It was the second time she'd had to electrify one of her friends. She looked at Silas, who had taken much longer to return to consciousness after she shocked him in Libya. Silas furrowed his brow at Tkla as Gavin stared at the hole in the ground as if expecting something to come slithering out. The joy that had been evident in his aura had been replaced with fear.

Abigail kneeled next to Tkla and patted his shoulder. "We should get off this planet and get everyone to a safer place. Can you stand up, big guy?"

With Brklana and Abigail's help, he did. He limped for a couple steps then collapsed. "I am not feeling well."

Abigail had a hunch he wasn't fainting because of the shock she had given him or the injury to his leg. She had a strong feeling there was some other cause.

It took all of them to drag Tkla into the ship. Brklana stayed by his side the whole time. Before sealing the hatch, Evvie ran back outside and connected a beaker to the tether line on the ship's winch and lowered it to get a water sample. She brought the sample aboard and studied it with her pocket microscope. "Umm, I'm seeing some very foreign-looking microbes."

Abigail cursed under her breath. *Would it have been so hard to detect dangerous microbes before Tkla subjected himself to them?*

They sealed the ship's hatch, removed his suit, and treated his wound.

Upon studying a sample of his blood, Evvie announced, "The same microbes are in his bloodstream."

Silas patted Tkla, who lay on a foldout cot. "I suppose you've made first contact. Would it be xenophobic to give you some anti-biotics to kill them?"

Tkla briefly came back to consciousness. "Under no circum-stances will I want to take such measures. Although they are only microscopic, they are connected to the rest of the life under the sur-face of the planet. They have a collective link like my people do, but theirs connects all levels of life within their entire ecosystem."

"How do you know this?" Abigail asked.

"I was able to hear the thoughts of the one that bit me, and I can hear the thoughts of the microbes within me. Their goal is to protect their home and their planet's precious resource—the water."

He tried to sit up but collapsed onto the cot. "Let my body adjust to these visitors. If it's their intention to kill me, I would prefer to die rather than harm them."

Silas shook his head. "Taurians have the strangest sense of logic."

Abigail understood Tkla's reasoning. "They are a species who rely on logic and thoughtfulness. Harming the life on a new planet could have severe consequences. Like on Earth, the Taurians wish to stay in good relations with the local life because they wish to live here."

"Yes, Abigail is correct. I would rather die than receive any anti-biotics."

"That's heroic, but what do we do now?" Dr. Fambozi asked. "We can't let you die. Also, our whole mission and the two-hundred-year-long-trip of the Taurian convoy will be a waste if they come to a planet where the local life is out to kill anyone who makes contact with the water. We need to do something to improve relations with the natives."

Chapter 24

Space Water

The mood was somber aboard the *Harkin* as they orbited Nidus. None of the crew had been able to come up with any ideas about what to do to help their sick Taurian friend. They sat looking out the medical facility's view port, gazing at the pinkish-brown planet below.

Abigail pressed her hand onto Tkla's head. She'd never been able to communicate with other forms of life in the way Tkla communicated with dolphins, but she tried with all her focus to reach out to the life forms inside his body. *Please, don't kill my friend. We mean you no harm.*

All she heard back was the same message he had spoken of: *Protect our water. Protect our home.*

It gave Abigail an idea. "Evvie. Tell me more about the water sample you collected from Nidus. Is there anything peculiar about it?"

Evvie shrugged. "Besides the microbes, it's just water—like the water on Earth. It's a little saltier than Earth's bodies of fresh water but not as salty as the ocean."

"Fambozi, can you see how Evvie's analysis compares to the ice samples we obtained from the inner asteroid belt?"

"You mean the *Evvie* Belt?" He winked at Evvie. "I will make a comparison." He began typing at the med bay's computer terminal.

Gavin spoke up. "Wait! Are you thinking we could bring ice from the asteroid belt and deliver it to the planet? That's genius! I wish I had thought of that."

Fambozi studied the results on his screen. "We wouldn't want to bring them water that has a different chemical makeup than their own. Even a slight difference in acidity could cause harm. But fortunately, they match pretty closely. There's more nitrogen and phosphorus in the sample from the underground lake, but more mineral content is a natural byproduct of past erosion. I think they look like a close match in every other way."

Silas tapped his finger on his chin. "Bringing water sounds like a great idea for helping to colonize the planet, but why do you think that will help Tkla?"

Abigail stood from her seat but kept a hand on Tkla's shoulder. "I'm not sure it will help him, but their water is all they seem to care about, and the river- and lake beds are clues that there used to be more water on their planet. If all of the life is interconnected through some sort of collective, maybe once we show our helpful intentions, like by bringing more water back to the planet's surface, the microbes in Tkla's body will get the message that we're not a threat."

Evvie jumped from her seat. "Sounds like a great idea. We'll have to figure out how to haul large amounts of ice. I'll go set a course back to the asteroid belt."

Brklana laid a hand on Tlka's forehead. "I will remain with Tkla. All of you should assist Evvie in the control room. Go."

Abigail hated leaving Tkla but knew he was in good hands, and she would come back to the ship's med bay soon to visit him. They had work to do.

Once they regrouped on the bridge and settled into their workstations, Abigail wondered how in the world they were going to haul such large quantities of ice.

Silas pursed his lips. "So... how much water would we need to haul to make a difference on the planet?"

Gavin started typing away at his station. "Let's see... Earth has three hundred twenty-six million cubic miles of water—"

"Yes, that's right," Fambozi said. "If the Earth were the size of a basketball, all the water could fit inside a Ping-Pong ball."

Silas grimaced. "So if we could haul one cubic mile of water, that would be three hundred and twenty-six million round trips to the asteroid belt and back. Count me in!"

Fambozi's lips curved into an amused smile. "We don't need to aim at such a huge volume of water, and I think we can haul much more than one cubic mile of water, since it is in the form of ice. Let's make one trip and see how much we can haul. The *Harkin* is an impressively large ship. Even filling a few lakebeds would make a difference. Beyond that, the most essential aspect of our operation will be to dispense water vapor into the atmosphere to help regulate the temperature and form rain."

Gavin raised a finger. "If we can use the hull's grav-plates to attract chunks of ice, then we can turn the ship into a flying space Popsicle."

Evvie winked at Gavin. "Hopefully, more like a large space snowball. If we can pack ice into a sphere that matches the length of the ship, we could haul… let's see… The volume of a sphere with a six-mile radius equals nine hundred four cubic miles, minus the volume of the ship, and we're looking at over nine hundred cubic miles of ice. Of course, it won't be solid ice because we can't possibly pack it without gaps. Even if the volume of ice turns out to be half, we'd be looking at around four hundred fifty cubic miles of ice per trip."

Dr. Fambozi added, "As a reference, Lake Tahoe is thirty-six cubic miles of water, so I think delivering over ten times that amount sounds like a good start. Can we figure out a way to deliver water to some of the lake beds without turning it all into vapor when we enter the atmosphere? We'll want to add moisture to the atmosphere as well, but I am eager to see those lake beds filled with water, especially if it might help save Tkla from the microbe attack."

Abigail thought about it. "We can use our blast-jump shield as we enter the atmosphere. Then we'll land on the edge of a lake bed"—she paused, realizing a flaw in her plan—"but then we'll have to wait for the ice to melt off the ship."

Gavin added, "If we park the ship and keep the shield up and use some of the ship's thrusters, even just the auxiliary maneuvering thrusters, we can melt it off quickly."

The team had their plan. On the way to the asteroid belt, Evvie started her work to modify the hull's grav-plates. She had removed an access panel to get to the heart of the system.

Abigail thought she was beginning to grasp the concept of how it worked—the main component was a pump that sent ionized plasma through conduits like arteries throughout the ship's hulls. Different levels of protons versus electrons in the mixture of super-heated gases and its magnetic polarization could create different effects, causing the hull either to attract or repel outside objects.

After tinkering for a while, Evvie dropped her wrench in defeat. "It's hard to come up with a way to attract the icy asteroids and not the rocky ones. Gravity affects them all equally. I can't figure out a way to tune it to accomplish that."

Silas suggested, "If there's iron in the rocky ones, couldn't there be some other way to repel them and use the grav-plates to attract the non-rocky ones?"

Evvie picked up her wrench. "Perfect! We'll have to build a magnetic-field generator, but that should work, providing that there is enough iron present in the asteroids to be repelled."

A smile shone though Silas's serious demeanor. "I could help build one. I've tinkered with making smaller ones before. This one will have to be much more powerful."

Evvie nodded. "I'd like the help."

Abigail gave Silas a sideways hug. "Wow! You finally came up with a good idea!" She was teasing, but she could tell he was happy to finally contribute. His face and aura glowed.

By the time they completed the trip to the asteroid belt, Evvie and Silas had finished their task. Rocks would be repelled like the way matching poles of two magnets repel each other, while non-rocky bodies would be attracted to the hull's grav-plates.

Evvie stood at the grav-plate controls. "Time to see if our contraption works. Do you want to be the one to activate the hull plates or the asteroid repeller?"

Silas grinned. "I'll start with magnetic-field generator to repel the rocky ones. Let's see if it works before we turn on the hull plates."

Abigail loved watching them work together. She sat in the pilot's chair. "Should I go ahead and fly the ship in?"

Evvie nodded. "Yes, take her in."

"I'll bring up a better view on the screen," Fambozi announced.

The screen showed a section of the hull and a view of space from the nose of the ship. Abigail thought seeing any of the rocky bodies move away from the ship would be a comforting sight before she headed deeper into the debris belt.

Fambozi was studying the screen. "It's hard to tell if it's working. You need to go ahead and fly into the more densely packed debris field."

"If you say so." Abigail pushed the thrusters, keeping her eyes on the forward view port. Some rocky bodies came into view. "Here goes nothing." She kept the thrusters firing. The asteroids came close enough so she could see their jagged forms. She was sure they were going to collide with the nose of the ship, but they bounced away as if an invisible force field rolled them out of the way.

"Yes! It's working!" Silas raised his fists and flexed. "Now, you can turn on the hull's grav-plates."

Evvie did so, and within moments, Abigail heard clanks on the hull. Then a few more. Then a barrage. Ice started covering their domed view port.

"Okay," Abigail said, "who's going to go out there and clean off the viewport so I can see where I'm flying?"

Unsurprisingly, Gavin volunteered. Silas accompanied him, and they were entertaining to watch as they cleared the view port. Some of the frost remained on the clear surface, but Abigail could see well enough. The two floated farther away from the ship then verified via their comms that it had been covered to the point of being spherical in shape.

Once her two friends were safely aboard once more, Abigail set a course back to Nidus. She noticed it took more time to get to speed with the extra ice mass.

∞

Abigail couldn't wait to get to the lake bed where they had drilled. She hoped it would remedy Tkla's condition, and they could maybe make second contact with the native life forms. He had been unconscious during the trip to the Evvie Belt. His condition was worsening, and Brklana would not leave his side.

Once they were in orbit, Abigail set their descent at a very slight angle and relied on the friction of the atmosphere against their blast-jump shield to slow the ship. She had a feeling there was some ice beyond the diameter of their shields that had vaporized into the atmosphere, something Fambozi had hoped for.

She thought that with so much mass, a gradual descent was prudent—the ship's thrusters could only counter so much weight. She definitely would not try a vertical drop, a maneuver for which the ship would normally have had enough thrust.

She studied her scopes. "I think we're going to be coming in hot. Or as hot as a snowball can come in. I can't get the ship to slow down. It's too massive. I've already circled the planet a few times."

Gavin spoke up. "Maybe you should lower the blast-jump shield and let the ice make contact with atmosphere. That would offer more resistance, and we could shed some of the ice to reduce our weight."

"Great idea. Everyone, brace yourselves." Sure enough, the ship shuddered as if she had put on the brakes. Abigail wondered what it must look like from the ground because they were probably creating a trailing cloud of vapor.

"It's working, but I think my thrusters are still not up to keeping this much weight from pulling us down." Abigail was watching her map, which showed where they wanted to land. It was still a good distance around the globe, so she hoped they would lose more ice by then. She maneuvered as best she could and lowered their altitude. "We're getting closer to the landing site, but we're still coming in a little too fast."

Gavin bit his lip. "If you just keep the nose up, we can do a skid landing, using the ice-coated belly of the ship to protect us and grind into the ground."

"Sounds like a bumpy ride, but I'll do it. Everyone, brace yourselves again." Abigail punched the forward-adjustment thrusters with everything she had, and it felt as if it helped slow the ship a bit more. She saw the ground approaching quickly. "I'm going to touch down!" She didn't want to overshoot the landing site like she had on her first attempt to land on the aircraft carrier. It was time to set her down.

She was jostled in her seat, and there was an exploding crashing sound then a loud scraping noise, but she kept firing the forward thrusters to keep the nose up. The last thing she wanted was to crash nose first into the ground then flip the ship.

After a long, bumpy stretch, the ship settled to a stop.

They disembarked in their oxygen masks to see that the dried lake bed wasn't far downhill from the nose of the *Harkin*. Abigail thought the position of the ship couldn't be better. "Okay, do you guys want to watch from a distance as I melt off some ice? Let me know when the lake bed is full."

Fambozi, Silas, and Gavin turned to hike across a ridge while she climbed aboard to activate the shield and ignite the thrusters to melt some of the ice off the hull.

After some time, Fambozi called in on the comm, "I think the lake is looking good. If you fill it much further, we'll need a boat to get back to the ship. We also noticed churning in the middle of the lake, where we drilled. I think some of the ground around there might have broken away to connect this body of water to the depths below."

That sounded like a desirable thing, since they'd brought the water for the planet's inhabitants. She got out of the ship to see that the lake's edge was just a couple hundred feet from the ship. What was more, Abigail looked up to see that the ship still had quite a bit of ice packed onto it, but it was much slimmer than when they'd landed. That was good—she needed the ship to be less encumbered to take off again and fly to a new lake bed.

It was time to see whether all of their effort and the risky landing would help Tkla. The crew carried his moribund body toward the water's edge. He stirred and mumbled about the mother ship being in trouble. Abigail was slightly spooked, since she had recently started to wonder if the massive colony ship was in danger and thought that locating it should be their very next priority.

They lay Tkla on the shore with most of his body submerged. He was breathing raggedly through an oxygen mask. The blue-green stripes of color in his scales didn't look as vibrant, and when he opened his eyes, they appeared cloudy and dull. For ten long minutes, there was no activity. Abigail felt that they were being silly. *What are we expecting—a miracle?*

Nothing happened.

The group watched. Abigail felt helpless and wondered whether the mission was going to end with his death. She imagined going home to report that the planet was a deadly place. The Taurians on Earth would be devastated. *And what about the huge population of Taurians who are heading here from Kronos?* Abigail never supposed there would be that sort of obstacle in the way of colonizing a new world.

His breaths became even shorter and weaker. Then he stopped breathing. Abigail knelt and put her ear to his chest. He was still. *Why hadn't this worked? Hadn't the interconnected network of life witnessed their kind act? Why hadn't they ceased with the microbe attack on her friend?*

She wasn't prepared to see him die. She placed both hands on his chest and gave him a shock with every ounce of electricity she could muster. His body jolted. As she kept her hands on him, his chest rose and fell with new breaths. She stood to watch him lie in the water, still expecting some sort of miracle but worrying nothing would come of their efforts.

Then, the water began to swirl around Tkla with a luminescent glow. He became conscious, rolled onto his stomach, then disappeared into the lake. After a few long moments under the surface, he popped his head up, shot air and water out of his n'shta, swam to shore, then walked in the shallow water toward shore.

Abigail wanted to rush out to greet him, but part of her was afraid of the water. She and the others stayed firmly planted on dry land and watched with relief.

As he walked, the water started to churn around him, and more streaks of glittery luminescent particles swirled in the dark water. Tkla stopped.

The water surged above the surface. A watery form rose up, filled with small life forms. There was a slightly larger life form in the middle that resembled a spiked glowing jellyfish. The liquid form rose up to face Tkla, matched his height, and became more defined. The shape formed itself into a mirror-image version of Tkla, but instead of skin and soft scales, it was made of water with the luminescent swirls of the life forms within.

Tkla raised his left hand. The form mimicked his movement. Tkla moved his hand closer to the form as he took two steps deeper into the water. The form responded by moving toward Tkla.

They touched hands. After a few moments, the watery form melted back into the lake.

Tkla announced, "They thank us for the gift we have brought, and they welcome us to their home. Taurians and humans are welcome to live on this world with no more harm from them. They have also removed the microbes from my body."

Abigail sighed deeply. It was everything they had hoped for.

Off in the middle of the lake, a few dolphin-like forms that had wing-like fins and pointier snouts broke the surface of the water, glided through the air, then dived back into the lake.

Tkla walked to shore. Everyone was overjoyed to see him cured, and they rushed to meet him. Brklana embraced him. She removed her oxygen mask to whisper into his reptilian earhole. Abigail was either getting better at reading Taurian emotions or Tkla was improving his emulation of human expressions, because he showed surprise and happiness. As if it had a life of its own, his tail patted the beach.

"We are going to be parents!" he called. "I fertilized her egg shortly before I fell ill."

Abigail and her friends cheered and hugged them both. Brklana mimicked a human smile as well.

She remembered Tkla having explained the details of Taurian reproduction to Dr. Hornwell during their museum visit and asked, "So how long until she lays her egg?"

"I will be the caretaker of the egg in about three months, and the baby will emerge a couple months after that."

Abigail clapped her hands. "Hopefully, we'll be back to Earth by then. I'm so excited to be an auntie!"

As they prepared to board the ship, Silas patted Tkla on the shoulder. "Okay, that was first contact with *real* aliens. No offense, Tkla, but your people are just over-evolved trans-galactic dinosaurs. These are real aliens."

Abigail folded her arms. "As I recall, Silas, you were so worried about meeting the Taurians that you needed us to hold your hand and reassure you that they wouldn't eat you."

"Ha, ha. I was a little nervous, and I let my imagination get the best of me."

Gavin practically vibrated with excitement. "Okay, my mind is blown. The life forms here are like water-bending-fish beings that are linked together in an ecological community. Actually, I think since all the life forms share one consciousness, it's like a single being lives here and manifests itself throughout the entire underwater population."

Tkla smiled. "That is the sense I have gathered as well. I believe there may be even larger and more complex animals lurking in the depths. You're very perceptive, Gavin, for a human."

Abigail thought so too.

Once Tkla was seated in the control room, he gripped the armrests of his chair, and his smile faded. "When I was close to dying, I kept having hallucinations about the large colony convoy that is heading to this system. I kept seeing the same vision of ships disappearing into darkness. Brklana, have you had any such visions?"

"I have not. Perhaps you were more open to a call from our people when you were unconscious?"

"Whatever it was, I am certain that they are in trouble, and they may not make it to this place if we don't find them."

Abigail grimaced. "I've been thinking about them, too, and imagining the worst. We need to figure out how to pinpoint your convoy's location. That's going to be a very small needle in a very large galactic haystack. Max, what do you think will be required to make that sort of calculation?"

Dr. Fambozi scratched his head. "There are so many variables— I wouldn't even know where to begin. I imagine it will require a fair amount of computing power to make those kinds of calculations. The main problem is that the smallest error in our calculations would result in missing them by a huge distance. For starters, do you know their mass and acceleration?"

"I can make reasonable guesses," Tkla replied.

Fambozi shook his head. "We'll have to come up with a creative way to locate them. The good news is that we at least know what path they're taking, so our main challenge is to find where they are on that path. We're still talking about massive distances."

"I'm sure we will use every available resource to locate the convoy," Abigail said in an attempt to reassure Tkla, "and we'll go find them and rescue them from whatever trouble they're in. I promise."

Tkla nodded. "I feel conflicted because I want to depart immediately from this mission, but this world would benefit from the delivery of more water. Would it be irresponsible to leave our task unfinished?"

"Let's deliver a couple more loads then be on our way," Silas suggested.

Abigail thought that sounded like a reasonable compromise. "Who knows? Maybe there are seeds hiding near the surface that could be germinated so some plant life could grow and add oxygen to the atmosphere. If we provide the water, maybe that natural process could help make the planet more habitable while we search for the convoy."

Fambozi nodded. "I like the sound of that. Let's bring more loads of water. But next time, I think you should spend more time in the atmosphere, shedding water, so we have a less risky landing."

Abigail thought that sounded sensible. And it would help to make clouds and rain.

∞

They spent the next few weeks hauling ice from the asteroid belt to Nidus. As Fambozi recommended, Abigail revised her landing strategy to melt off more ice in the lower atmosphere so that she could touch down with less weight.

Fambozi expressed his approval of the plan because adding moisture to the atmosphere would benefit all regions of the planet. Abigail was excited to make clouds that could send rain down onto the land.

∞

The crew was boarding the *Harkin* for their final departure from the planet after delivering the last load.

As they were about to enter the ship, Gavin paused to look up into the sky, and Abigail joined him.

Solrose had set. A super-bright dot above the horizon shone through a gap in the newly formed clouds, making for the most colorful sunset she had ever seen, full of purples, pinks, and oranges.

Gavin pointed. "That's the Venus-like planet we've had a hard time naming. Maybe we should name it *Lumos*."

Dr Fambozi, who was at the base of the ramp, looked up. "It does produce—or I should say, reflect—a lot of light. It is very *luminous*. Well done. Many times brighter than Venus viewed from Earth. In a way, Gavin, I think it could be named after you because you are so very bright. Every time you have a good idea, it's like you literally incandesce like a light bulb."

Abigail rolled her eyes. "You're telling me. I sometimes think I need sunglasses just to look at his aura." She gave him a sideways hug and announced, "Awww, Gavin is now part of the new solar system too!"

Gavin beamed. Abigail thought she saw a shimmer of the man he might become shine through his boyish facade.

The team boarded the massive ship, ready to head home to Earth.

Chapter 25

Eliot

Abigail made checking up on her brother her first priority when they arrived back on Earth. When she tracked him down and called him, he sounded more than happy to have her come for a visit.

She brought Silas, Gavin, Dr. Fambozi, and Tkla along to visit him at his new facility, and as they entered the fancy lobby of his Tech Venture Industries, she couldn't believe it was his.

She introduced her friends to her brother. Silas and Gavin had briefly met him at their first space launch, which felt like a lifetime before. Gavin had also hung out with Eliot at the White House dinner to celebrate their arrival home after the first space mission. He greeted Silas and Gavin with handshakes then shook Tkla's hand. It was a custom Tkla took seriously, and it looked like he squeezed perhaps a little too firmly.

Eliot massaged his hand after the handshake. "It's nice to meet you, and welcome to Tech Venture Industries and back home to Earth."

"Thank you." Tkla appeared more uninterested than Abigail had ever seen him. She wondered why he had requested to come along.

Studying Eliot was intriguing. He was the same little twerp, but he had a new air of confidence, as if he had become... a successful grown-up. Abigail had known him to be smug, but his new confidence was different—she saw it in his aura. She wondered whether the apparent success of his business and wealth had changed him or if it had been the genetic enhancement.

Eliot looked at Max. "And I've never met an astrophysicist before. Welcome, Dr. Fambozi."

Fambozi shook Eliot's hand. "Thank you, Mr. Montrose. I am eager to see what you're working on here."

Abigail took stock of the lobby of the large building, an impressive space with nicely designed furniture, a glass elevator, sculptures, artwork, and a fountain that caught the morning light to create a sparkly effect. "I was worried you were up to no good with your new abilities, but this looks pretty legitimate." Deep down, she still wondered what he was up to behind closed doors.

Eliot smirked. "I'm not a saint like you, trying to save the world, but I have made some pretty decent accomplishments. How was your trip to the new colony world?"

"It was a long time to be away, but it was a productive trip—some terraforming and first contact with an alien species that can manipulate the shape of water—just another routine trip. It's good to be back. Your hair looks good." Eliot's hair had white roots, but instead of buzz-cutting it like Abigail had chosen to do, he kept the brown tips, so his hair was variegated pure white to brown.

"Yours looks good, too, now that it's grown out." Eliot started walking. "Follow me, I've got a lot to show you."

Abigail brushed her fingers through her hair, which wisped down to her shoulders. She noticed a gold bracelet jingling at his wrist as they started walking. "Nice bracelet! Super blingy!"

Eliot held it up to show it off. "Yeah, it's pretty sparkly. I won it in Vegas."

"You always did love shiny sparkly things. Ever since you were a baby."

"Well, nothing sparkles nicer than gold and diamonds. I get a lot of funny reactions when I wear it. Winning the World Series of Poker is a pretty big deal, I guess."

"Especially if a regular human were to win it." Abigail couldn't resist the jab at her younger brother. She thought she had always used her powers to help others and never for her own personal gain. She was more than a little concerned about how ethically Eliot had used his new abilities. She imagined him abusing his powers to the point at which she would be forced to Illuminate him to set him straight.

Eliot led Abigail and her friends through the grounds of his Tech Venture Industries. Silas, who had experience running Edison Motors and Rocket Corp, kept nodding as he studied the robotics machine shop full of parts and equipment. "It looks like you're working on some advanced stuff here. Maybe we can work together on a few projects?"

Eliot replied, "I'm not trying to save the world. I'm just focusing on ventures that might pan out in the future."

"I don't see why you can't do both," Silas replied.

Eliot smiled. "Well, maybe it's possible to do both, but having your vision clouded by wanting to do good might reduce profitability. I see that some innovations may help people in the future. For example, robots could go into dangerous places to be heroes, but it's who's paying for those robots that interests me."

Silas winced. "I guess it's good to look at all the angles, and there's no harm in considering the marketability of your innovations."

Abigail liked how Silas's goals were based on his values—the money was secondary. She hoped maybe Silas's good intentions would rub off on her little brother. She could see, however, that Silas was already a little annoyed with Eliot's attitude.

They arrived at a door, for which Eliot typed a code into a keypad to gain admittance. "Do you want to meet IRIS? She's the product of a collaboration between a couple of the teams working here, but I set up the parameters myself. The one thing no one has gotten right yet is the size of a robot. They are either seven feet tall and lumbering or little four-foot-tall weaklings. I'm going with five feet six inches. Not too big, not too small, but just right."

When they entered the room where IRIS was charging, the guests oohed and aahed—mostly Gavin and Silas.

The robot's eyes glowed green.

"Oh good, she's fully charged. Her eyes are red when she's still charging." Eliot unplugged her.

IRIS had been built to have a humanoid appearance, except she was constructed of panels of white molded plastic instead of skin, and her joints were exposed, revealing machined metal connections.

Eliot pushed a button on a remote, and IRIS stood upright. "She needs to reboot and wake up. She was hibernating after we installed some upgrades. Once the green lights in her eyes stop flashing, you can introduce yourselves."

They waited a few moments for the blinking to cease. It was replaced by a soft white glow.

Silas stepped closer to the robot. "Hello, IRIS. I'm Silas. What is it that you're programmed to do?"

"Hello, Silas. I am programmed to safeguard the best interests of my maker."

Silas raised his eyebrows. "Wow. Eliot, are you her maker?"

"Well, yeah. I customized her program with a recursive algorithm, so she learns on her own. It's a system of deep machine learning and self-improvement. The more she learns and improves, the more efficient she gets at improving herself. Most of her technology came from my robotics team, but I created her 'brain.' Instead of a neural network of microchips and a circuit-control board relaying signals, her head has a spherical chamber that houses a pressurized neural cloud. It turns out that the magnesium silicate you used for your spaceship was the perfect material out of which to construct the cranial chamber. In fact, much of her frame is fabricated from that metal. Thank you for making the material publicly available."

"I felt very strongly about sharing it with the world," Silas said. "Besides, if aliens sent the knowledge to Earth, it should be everyone on Earth who benefits."

Abigail hoped Silas's altruism would inspire her brother, who still sounded pretty profit driven.

Eliot added, "No other metal could retain all the fast-moving neurons while at the same time acting as a neural conductor. In fact, synthetic neurons are traveling so fast in her brain, they are present in multiple locations at one moment in time. That's how she got her name: Intermittent Random Integral Synapses."

Silas raised his eyebrows at the robot. "Wow, you sound pretty sophisticated."

IRIS mimicked blinking eyes by flashing her eyes off then back on again. "I am pleased with how I was designed. I still have much to learn. I am connected to the internet and am studying every detail I can. I engage in many activities in the cyber world—with humans and other artificial intelligences. In fact, while we are speaking, I am currently competing in an online tournament game of chess."

Abigail crossed her arms as she studied the robot. She would never have thought of using her enhanced intelligence to create something like it. She tried to see any potential benefits of his creation, but she couldn't help but feel like it was a wasteful use of her brother's abilities.

Gavin excitedly asked if he could engage with IRIS.

"Yes, ask her anything." Eliot replied.

"Okay, IRIS, please tell me a joke."

She responded, "What do you call four humans at thirteen thousand feet above the Earth who forgot their parachutes?"

IRIS waited until Gavin asked, "What?"

She replied, "Dead."

Eliot chuckled. "She's been learning about mortality. I would say she's a little obsessed with the idea of death."

Silas crossed his arms over. "That's a little creepy, but it's a huge leap for a machine to even begin to grasp the concept of death."

Abigail spoke up, still not sure if she liked IRIS but was trying to warm up to her. She thought that creating sophisticated toys wasn't really something that could help the world. "I have a riddle for you: if Eliot is your maker, then what does that make me?"

"You are my maker's sister, and as I understand, you protected him when he was younger, so I feel gratitude toward you."

"Wow, impressive. I didn't even introduce myself to her." Abigail felt a pang of guilt, though, because she didn't exactly look out for him when they were younger. It was more like she'd tormented him—or rather, they tormented each other.

Eliot shook his head. "It doesn't take super-complex facial recognition software to recognize *your* face."

"Um, thanks? It does sound like she has your best interest in mind."

Eliot nodded. "The thing I've learned by being able to see people's emotions and intentions is that most people are really just looking out for themselves, and I can admit I'm no different. My main goal was to have a friend who genuinely cares. It is at the very core of her programming, and it's what will set my robots apart from any others."

"Wow, it sounds like you made yourself a new best friend!" She sounded more sarcastic than she intended. She still wasn't sure if she liked the robot.

Eliot crossed his arms and narrowed his eyes at her. "Well, I initiated her program to have more of a maternal instinct. Even though I am kind of like her parent, she has an underlying goal to protect me."

Gavin spoke up. "My mom is my protector, too, and she's almost as cool as you are, IRIS, and she cooks amazing food."

Abigail hadn't heard Gavin talk about his mom before. She supposed there was more she could learn about him, but it had been a little challenging because he only talked about comics.

The robot's eyes flashed again. "I am studying culinary arts as a hobby. Perhaps you will all stay for a meal prepared by me?"

"That sounds... enticing," Abigail said, "but we need to get back to the West Coast." She was a little disappointed that Eliot had chosen to use his special abilities to cheat in a poker tournament, amass wealth, and build a faithful toy robot. She had seen enough.

"Why do you need to leave so soon?" Eliot asked. "You just got here."

"We just do," she said as she walked to the doorway.

∞

Eliot couldn't believe Abigail's abruptness. He wished that he hadn't admitted that he had created a robot to care. It made him sound desperate for friends. He turned to Tkla and Dr. Fambozi, who had been silent the whole time. "Do either of you want to ask IRIS anything?"

Dr. Fambozi answered, "Not unless she has any knowledge about the expansion of the universe." The doctor shuffled a couple steps toward the doorway, where Abigail was waiting.

The robot replied, "I do not have enough information to form an opinion about whether the universe is expanding or not."

Eliot looked at Tkla.

The seven-foot-tall alien said, "I'm not particularly interested. My people never developed artificial intelligence or robots. We never saw the need for such innovation." Tkla had a baby carrier containing a round object hidden from view attached to his torso.

Eliot was trying to figure out what was in the chest pack. "If humans were as smart and as strong as you, we'd be content to do everything ourselves too." He focused his sight and noticed the object had a small glowing aura of its own. It was alive. "Congratulations on your egg. The first Taurian born—I mean hatched—on Earth will be very exciting."

"Yes," said Tkla. "My partner and I are very excited to have a young one. I apologize for being so preoccupied."

Eliot winked. "Fatherhood is a legitimate reason to be preoccupied."

Tkla shook his head. "That is only part of my concern, and I do worry about what the future may hold for my child, but my main concern is for the colony convoy, which we cannot locate."

"I wish I could help," replied Eliot. "But that sounds like a monumental challenge. I don't know too much about all the space stuff, but I do know there are astronomical distances involved."

Dr. Fambozi spoke up. "Astronomical indeed! One small inaccuracy in the data plugged into our calculations could lead us light years away from where the convoy might be."

"If there is anything I can do to help, let me know." His offer to help only came from his desire for Abigail to be a little nicer to him. She remained standing in the doorway with her arms crossed. He studied her aura to see that her disapproving state produced a swirl of oranges and reds.

"We could use some processing power," the doctor said. "Maybe one of your robots—"

"We don't need any of Eliot's help," Abigail interrupted. "We'll figure it out on our own."

Eliot tried to ignore Abigail's disdain. Instead, he focused on Silas, who he could tell didn't want to leave just yet, as he continued to study IRIS. Silas reached out to touch her arm. "So... I like the size and design of your prototype. The molded facial features look very neutral and just human enough without being creepy. Overall, I think it looks very marketable, not too big and intimidating but large enough to help out. What kind of price tag are you estimating?"

Eliot put some effort into ignoring his sister, who still stood in the doorway. He tried to remove any shakiness from his voice. "Yeah, I didn't want any poorly done latex masks to creep anyone out, although we're working toward a line of more realistic models. Um, my goal is to get the price down to around the price of one of your high-end sports cars, but we still have a long way to go to get there. As you know, it's more than just the design of the product— it's designing the production of the product."

"Good job, Eliot, with everything you've accomplished," Abigail cut in, "but it's time for us to go." She headed down the corridor, away from his robotics lab. Silas and Gavin gave Eliot apologetic glances then followed.

Eliot still didn't understand why his sister was in such a hurry to leave. It had been typical of his childhood: everyone was too busy to spend time with him. His family made up for it by buying him toys and video games. He had accomplished so much, and Abigail was not interested.

As soon as the group left, Eliot picked up his phone to call an acquaintance who was known for tackling odd jobs and finding people. "I've got a job that I need done discreetly. Can you travel to Los Angeles? The target is about to head there from here, so you have a few hours."

Chapter 26

Overseers Motivate the Taurians

Ringlow had traveled back to his native system to visit his superior. A longer-than-average amount of time had passed since their last meeting. He had spent thousands of years on his recent sabbatical, traveling between the barbaric X-47892 planet and the system where the transplanted animals had made tremendous progress on their new world. Both civilizations were at prime levels of development for his study because neither had the means to detect his ship in space, which meant he could orbit each planet and study them at close range and even land in remote locations. It was a characteristic Ringlow knew would not last long, since both races were on the cusp of rapid development.

Since returning home, Ringlow had visited C-PU's moon to feed updated information into its system and verify the earlier prediction of a supernova destroying the planet of the transplants. He was hoping that since a considerable amount of time had passed since the original prediction, things might have changed, and maybe they would have more time, or maybe the star had shed enough mass so that its imminent death would not be so violent.

Neither had been the case. In fact, the supernova was predicted for explosion even sooner—within the next million years.

He walked into the Overseer's chamber, where the screen typically showed a scene from one of the worlds in their Ring of Worlds system. They provided habitats for their collections of life forms, but it had all been transplanted—none were indigenous. Most of the specimens had lived and died on their native worlds then had been reanimated here, yet another function C-PU performed that required its huge processing power—reassembling life forms from sometimes the tiniest tissue samples was no easy task.

Their people preferred the concept of giving life a second chance rather than abducting specimens from their natural habitats. They did, after all, adhere to a policy of non-interference, for the most part, which was why Ringlow was nervous about the outcome of this meeting.

The massive screen didn't show much activity—only a horned animal grazing in the forested hills of a planet that was circling somewhere among the hundreds of worlds, moons, dust, and debris that composed the Ring. Many of the worlds were kept pristine with no advanced life to muck them up.

Ringlow cleared his throat. "Greetings, Overseer. I have returned."

The Overseer broke his attention from the screen, and his seat rotated to face Ringlow. He took on their species' most natural form, a large pale face with beady dark eyes and a thin mouth, and their basic body structure with two arms and two legs. He had, however, added sharp protrusions at his cheekbones. The Overseer seemed to like the use of horns to accentuate his appearance.

Ringlow continued, "I have reconfirmed with C-PU that the planet of the transplants will indeed be faced with an imminent supernova. I have come to ask permission to intervene. If they are ultimately going to survive to reach further development, they need to find a new home."

The Overseer's voice boomed. "We have witnessed the premature ends of many civilizations due to external catastrophes without interfering. Why should this case be any different?"

Ringlow knew his hunch wouldn't carry much weight with the Overseer. "I have a deep-rooted feeling that they are bound to be an exceptional species because of the planet from which they originated. I still believe that their planet has special characteristics that spawned life that will eventually exceed our expectations."

"Oh yes, the watery blue planet that holds your obsession. How goes the advancement of the barbaric primitives?"

"Truthfully, their technological advancements have been slow, but their civilization is making large strides with agriculture and slightly larger community pockets. I believe they are at the cusp of a technical revolution, but honestly, at this point, a wheeled contraption pulled by an animal is about their most impressive accomplishment, although fermented foods and beverages show a level of ingenuity that is on the rise."

Against all protocol, Ringlow had assimilated some of the local beings' DNA and used it to blend in while visiting the planet's surface. If such excursions were not such blatant violations of their regulations, he would have loved to share his documentation of his encounters. Consuming the fermented beverages with the locals was an experience he would not soon forget. He would also love to report that the people on the blue planet were some of the friendliest he'd ever encountered, but he could not reveal that detail without revealing his jaunt outside of their strict policy.

The Overseer rolled his eyes that had become larger than their natural beads of black onyx. "Fermented beverages sound as crude as the rest of the civilization on that planet. How are the more civilized transplanted life forms faring on their new world?"

"They have exceeded the technological advancements of the primitives on their native blue planet while living harmoniously within their ecosystem. They have much further to progress with their technologies, but they are a much more cooperative species, so I think they will make advancements quickly. The transplants do basically have a deadline to reach a level at which they are capable of evacuating their world before the supernova occurs in their more densely congested arm of the galaxy. The problem is that they will remain unaware of any such supernova until it's too late. I would like to cause an earlier disruption to give them warning."

"How do you propose to intervene?" asked the Overseer, his face morphing with more of a whiskered snout to show what Ringlow thought might be inquisitiveness.

Ringlow reminded himself to avoid optimism, since it was very unlikely that the Overseer would approve his plan. "We need a way to motivate them to leave their system without causing excessive harm. It needs to be an interference that motivates yet allows time for them to develop into a spacefaring species."

"I see. That does sound like a challenge."

Ringlow had put much thought into the problem as he traveled through the wormhole tunnel that made insurmountable distances travelable within days rather than the millions of years it would otherwise take to travel across the galaxy. "I would like to disrupt the orbits of the planets in their system without causing any cataclysmic collisions so that the planets will be put on paths that will eventually and predictably spiral into their star."

The Overseer added longer teeth to his whiskery snout. "That is a creative solution. Something to give them time to evacuate but that would spell imminent destruction for them if they stayed. How do you propose to create this sort of disruption?"

"Perhaps C-PU can run some simulations then make the calculations and plot a course for a stellar neutron remnant to cause the required disruption. Although neutron stars are super dense and may contain more mass than an average star, they are small enough to send though our wormholes. C-PU can create a route to transport a super-dense body into their system."

The Overseer drummed his long fingernails against his armrest. "I still don't see what difference it would make if we allowed the supernova to wipe their world clean and life could start over? It will be a breach of protocol to intervene. In fact, allowing the eradication would be a desirable scenario because we could then collect a multitude of samples before such an event."

Ringlow shook his head. "The development of beings who are living in such a responsible balance within their ecosystem is such a rarity that I think it is worth saving. The standard for most species, even our own, is to hoard wealth and resources with little concern for others and a lack of foresight for the future. Wouldn't you like to witness a species that expands in an undisruptive way?"

After an unbearable full minute of continuing to tap his talonlike fingers into his armrest, the Overseer nodded. "I will authorize the intervention in their system. Take time to make the proper calculations before performing the procedure. It sounds like you may want to wait perhaps a few centuries before intervening so that they may further develop their spacefaring technologies and can make preparations to evacuate."

Ringlow tried to hide his relief. He stood to leave.

The Overseer clasped his boney fingers together. "I have one additional task for you. At the point at which their planet is close to its doom, you should collect samples of their life. If any of the beings or animals are left on the planet when all hope is lost for them, you may collect an assortment. If any die, collect tissue samples, and we can reanimate them for our specimen collections. In the meantime, you have some calculating to do to ensure that events are timed properly. If you intervene too soon, the transplants may not develop the necessary technologies in time. If you wait too long, they may not have time to evacuate."

Ringlow nodded. That was precisely the time crunch the transplants would be faced with. They would need to develop spacefaring technology to a level where they could abandon their planet before it spiraled to its fiery death. He hoped disrupting the planets in their system would give them enough warning to make those developments and evacuate.

Chapter 27

Egg

Tkla rushed out of his quarters. "Does one of you have my hshrta—I mean my egg?"

Abigail looked up from her morning tea. She couldn't understand why he was asking about his egg when he hadn't let it out of his sight since it came into his care. She noticed something poking out of the side of Tkla's neck. "Oh my God, you've got a dart sticking out of your neck!"

Tkla yanked the dart from his neck and searched frantically from one room to the next. He shook as he came out of the last room, and Abigail knew it was gone.

Tkla flipped open a comm screen, swiped, and tapped with a shaky finger. Within moments, Brklana's face appeared. In their native language, he said, "I have failed. I have lost our egg."

Abigail stood behind Tkla to see Bklana's concerned face on the screen. Abigail gripped him by his shoulders. "We'll get it back. I promise."

Brklana nodded. "I will fly down to the Los Angeles port."

Abigail liked the sound of that. "Perfect—we can get across the country faster with you." That would save them hours of flying in an airplane back to New Jersey.

Not many people knew of the egg's existence, so Abigail had no doubt who was behind the eggnapping.

∞

At the Venture Industries paleogenetics lab, Eliot was discussing plans for moving forward with the dinosaur project with the senior geneticist, Jane Grant. "Okay, our goal is to figure out how to add blocks within a subject's DNA like the blocks Dr. Roberts was able to remove. I want to reduce the evolutionary advancement of the creature in this egg."

Jane raised her eyebrows. "Are you sure you want to test our procedure on a Taurian?" She was peering at the egg, which was the size of an ostrich egg.

"I want to test on chicken eggs, and then I want to turn this one into a dinosaur."

He paid close attention to her reaction and her intentions through her aura. He could see her reluctance in sharp violet streaks, but there was also a red tint that suggested deceitfulness.

Jane sighed. "I'll pull a blood sample and get to work right away."

Her face showed she was very good at hiding her feelings. Eliot couldn't wait to see what actions she would take. He would be watching.

∞

Within a couple hours, Abigail, Silas, Gavin, Brklana, and Tkla barged into Eliot's facility. Eliot had been monitoring the surveillance cameras, saw their vehicle screech to a stop in the parking lot, and was waiting for them in the lobby. He gulped when he saw two aliens enter the building with them.

Abigail got right in his face and pressed her finger into his chest. "Where is it? Where's the egg? And what the hell? We just flew across the country and back again."

"That's a good question." Eliot tried to not shrink from her poking. "I've got a pretty good hunch, but perhaps you should ask Jane."

Tkla brushed Abigail out of the way. "You will hand over the egg, or I will break every bone in your body with my bare hands."

Brklana added, "And then I will mop up your human tears with your freshly removed scalp."

Oh, man. It was up to his sister to prevent these beasts from tearing him apart.

Instead, Abigail raised her fists, and bolts of electricity bridged between them. "Stop playing games and hand it over!"

"I don't have it! Honest. You can tell if I'm lying, right? I let my assistant, Jane, smuggle it out of the lab. It's safe, so call off the scalping. She didn't do anything to the embryo or even take a blood sample."

Before anyone had a chance to pummel or scalp Eliot, Silas's phone rang. Eliot thanked his lucky stars for the interruption.

Silas answered then listened for a moment. "Thank goodness. Where are you? Okay, we're on our way." He hung up. "The egg is safe, although it's no longer an egg."

"What do you mean?" Abigail's felt a slight sense of relief, but angry electricity still tingled in her fingertips. "And who has it?"

"Dr. Hornwell has it, and the egg has hatched. He's at a nearby park."

Abigail glared at her brother as they left.

Eliot realized he was lucky that his sister and the Taurians had been called away in that moment. He knew he would still have to face her wrath. He had crossed a line, but it was worth it. He wouldn't be ignored by his big sister any longer.

Abigail was relieved to see JJ Hornwell sitting on a park bench, holding a bundled flannel shirt close to his chest. He looked up from the bench. "I'm guessing I've made an impression on your baby. He or she seems very content. Jane called me and had me bring an ostrich egg to swap out with yours. How do you tell if the baby is a girl or boy?"

Tkla ran a finger along the infant's face. "Those extra blue-green markings around her eyes show she is a girl. I can also tell by her scent. And yes, the first person a new hatchling sees is the person the baby latches onto or imprints with."

Abigail saw the resemblance between the baby's coloring and her mother's.

Brklana stood over the man holding her baby, and JJ raised it to her.

She shook her head. "If she is content with you, she can remain."

Abigail couldn't believe Brklana didn't want to snatch her own baby from a man she had never met.

JJ nestled her back into his arms. "I'm so sorry she didn't see either of you first. I hope that doesn't cause concern for you. Does this mean I have imprinted myself upon her?"

Tkla let out a snort, and Abigail watched as he put visible effort into calming himself. Abigail was furious that Tkla had missed his child's hatching but reminded herself that the baby was safe.

"We raise our young in a more communal way than do humans. In fact, Brklana and I were concerned that our roles and responsibilities on this planet would interfere with parenthood. She is a pilot, and I am a diplomat. How would you like to study Taurian development firsthand by being—what's the word—our nanny?"

Abigail knew JJ had made a good impression with Tkla when they first met and shared his extensive knowledge of their dinosaur ancestors, but that was unbelievable. For them to want help to look after their young one from someone who was essentially an alien was shocking.

JJ patted the bundle. "Nothing would make me happier. The first of many questions I have in caring for a non-mammalian infant is what do you feed her? And what's her name?"

Tkla finally reached down to pick up his daughter. He gave her a quick smile, moved his head and neck in a wavelike motion to regurgitate some food, then fed it by mouth to the infant, whose beaklike mouth opened and closed. "We've decided on Tlana for her name."

Although the feeding process didn't look too enticing, Abigail thought the wide eyes and little duck-billed mouth pouting to receive it was the most adorable thing she had ever seen.

JJ chuckled. "Okay, I should have guessed that a parent dinosaur would feed a baby in that manner. Like a papa bird. I'll probably need a blender, some ingredients, and a dropper bottle to feed her. It's very nice to meet you, Tlana."

"Thank you for rescuing her," Tkla said. "I have been studying human customs for raising infants, and the idea of godparents is interesting. I would appreciate guidance from you. If anything should happen to Brklana and me, would you consider being Tlana's godparent?"

Tkla placed Tlana back into JJ Hornwell's arms. JJ peered into the infant's large hazel-colored eyes. "I would be honored. And I will protect you from that bad kid who wants to devolve you into a duckbilled dinosaur."

Electric current sizzled inside Abigail's fists. "What? Is that why he abducted the egg? I'm going to have to go set my brother straight. He really crossed a line."

Tkla patted Abigail on the shoulder. "No harm was done, and your brother inadvertently united our daughter with a caregiver who Brklana and I need. She is in very good hands."

Abigail agreed that the baby appeared to be comfortable in JJ's arms, but she couldn't believe that Tkla showed no resentment about his egg getting abducted or that he was willing to entrust his baby to someone he barely knew. While everything had turned out fine with an adorable baby nestled safely into the paleontologist's arms, Abigail still shook with anger at her brother having stooped so low. She wanted to get back to his facility immediately to confront him. She wouldn't be so forgiving.

Chapter 28

Detected

Ringlow came into the Overseer's chamber, feeling a burning heat radiating from his face. He'd known the day was bound to come when a species reached the level of advancement that would make it possible to detect the presence of his ship, but he had not been cautious enough, and he had made a grievous mistake.

He forced himself to sit in the molded seat that grew from the floor and composed himself before he began. "The inhabitants of the blue planet in the X-47892 system, which I have learned call themselves *humans*, have made huge advancements in a very short period of time. In fact, they've become so advanced that they are monitoring their system with vigilance. I am now witnessing an exponential growth in their technology." Ringlow thought focusing on the positive aspects first would soften the blow of reporting his mistake.

"As always, I look forward to your full report."

Ringlow took a deep breath. "The most impressive news is they have developed instantaneous star travel."

A frown creased the Overseer's giant face. "They haven't discovered our network of wormholes, have they?"

"No, they have not. It was actually a member from the mostly abandoned fourth planet, called Mars, who initiated their first interstellar jump. It's a crude way to travel, but they have bypassed the constraints of traveling vast interstellar distances."

The frown disappeared, and the features on the Overseer's face morphed into those of a horned animal with white fur and a long golden beard. "I suppose we should celebrate. This is a huge development. It is extremely rare for a species to advance in interstellar space travel before they cause their own extinction."

Ringlow had never seen the Overseer show anything but disdain or impatience, so his benevolent appearance was a sight to behold. "Yes, I have been concerned for the species' survival. They are in the precarious position that any civilization with advanced technology has to face. Acquiring the ability to travel among the stars also gives them the ability to utterly destroy themselves and their world."

The Overseer's straight white horns curled and darkened, but his fur remained white. "Are you certain they have not made this advancement prematurely? If they retain their barbaric tendencies and are permitted to spread across the galaxy, they could become a problem."

Ringlow had considered that. "I will keep an eye on their possible spread to other systems and keep you informed before they do so." The humans did indeed need to remedy many fundamental flaws within their civilization before they should begin colonizing. He hoped he would never be forced to take drastic action to prevent the humans' expansion. If that ever became the case, the only sure way to do so would be to eradicate their species.

The Overseer reclined in his chair. "Yes. Do keep a vigilant eye on the humans. And what of the transplants you had planned to motivate to leave their system?"

Ringlow was relieved to report more good news before he would confess his mistake. "Our interference worked perfectly. The neutron remnant performed its task flawlessly. Ninety-five percent of their population successfully evacuated on their own, and the remnants were rescued by the humans. That group of Taurians is back on Earth. The Taurians' ancient ancestors, who were rescued from Earth before the distant meteor impact, were called dinosaurs, and they once dominated the planet. It is exciting to see their return to their world of origin."

"And how did you learn all of this if you haven't made contact?"

"They have been broadcasting all of their information in ways that are easy to intercept."

The Overseer leaned farther back in his chair. "Everything sounds as if it is unfolding perfectly. Do you have anything else to report?"

Ringlow let out a deep breath. "Well, they are closely observing the space within their own star system, which now requires the use of a porthole farther from their sun. I came through their system and was detected by a human from an island observatory. They have named my ship *Oumaumua,* in a language native to the island. The term translates as 'the scout' or 'messenger from the distant past,' which I thought was rather insightful."

The golden beard turned black, and the white fur turned gray. So much for a benevolent Overseer. "I find it interesting that you were so surprised by their sudden advancements and that you were detected. Where were you while the humans made their rapid leaps?"

Ringlow hated to admit that he had taken a cryo-nap in the outskirts of their system. He'd never seen any species make such huge advancements in a period as short as a hundred revolutions. "Their development took place within the blink of an eye."

The Overseer raised his furry eyebrows in obvious disbelief.

Ringlow cleared his throat. He had slightly worse news to report. "I will take precautions to prevent future sightings. I did make one glaring mistake, though. After I orbited their sun, as the humans call their star, I accelerated so that I could connect with the outer wormhole's entrance without changing course. I thought the acceleration would be less noticeable than a course correction. They did, however, detect my increase in speed. They have postulated that my acceleration could have been due to the rays of the sun striking my vessel when I did indeed have it turned to collect more energy."

"That is unfortunate. You know that your full report will be posted, and your rank among Observers will plummet for this infraction. I have not seen such an irresponsible mistake made by any Observer within the last millennia." The Overseer shook his head. "Is it possible they will retrace your steps and discover the porthole?"

"I am aware of the consequences." Ringlow knew that unless he performed some miraculous achievement, he would remain lower in rank than his peers, and he would watch all of them advance to higher positions while he would not. He would also never be able to father an offspring with a mate if he remained posted as an Observer. He cleared his throat. "Most of the humans seem to believe that my vessel was a natural phenomenon and not a ship. At this point, they do not have fast enough means to travel to the wormhole entrance."

"That is not reassurance enough. You will have to close that entrance to ensure that they do not accidentally travel to our system."

That would delay his next trip because C-PU would have to create a new entrance leading to the human's system, but he would make it so. He hoped he wouldn't miss any unfolding progress because of a delay. He had been putting some thought into where an entrance could be located and thought maybe close to their sun could work well to keep him hidden.

"And how go some of the barriers to unifying the planet of barbaric humans who have now traveled across the stars?"

"The humans are still a warring species, and the early separation of groups in their tribal days still affects their society. They are not very close to becoming a truly unified race, and they are also causing harm to their planet and wiping out other species, which is an indication that they are far from meeting our classification of *advanced*. I wonder if they will ever reach that designation so we may make contact with them."

The Overseer replied, "It will be interesting to document and study their reaction on the day when we can make ourselves known to the humans of Earth, although I agree that day may not come very soon."

Ringlow kept a stern expression as he tried to move forward from the embarrassment of his mishap. "I am also doubtful that day will come soon."

The Overseer willed his seat more upright. "So there are no more Taurians left on their world, which is spiraling into its star?"

"That is correct. The disruption caused by the super-dense neutron body gave them centuries to prepare for their evacuation, although their numbers were so large that not all were able to depart from their planet until the humans arrived and rescued the remnants of their population. This means none of their kind will be available to collect for reanimation as their planet approaches its star."

The Overseer made a brushing gesture with his hand as if sweeping the topic away. "That is only slightly unfortunate. These humans do sound intriguing. For being a barbaric race, it is a surprising turn for them to perform such a heroic act."

"Yes, their culture is unlike any I have encountered. They are without a doubt the least rational species I've studied. They have admirable traits, like their willingness to take risks. I think that characteristic alone has enabled them to make rapid advancements where other species lack the courage to push boundaries."

The Overseer turned his morphing chair toward the screen in his chamber. "I suppose you will want to return as quickly as possible to resume your work. Update C-PU with your new information, fix your blunder by creating a new porthole, then keep an eye on them."

"Thank you, Overseer. That is my plan exactly."

Chapter 29

Crash

Abigail burst into the lobby where Eliot stood as if he had been expecting her arrival. She had asked her friends to stay in the car because she wanted to deal with him on her own. "Okay, you need to explain yourself. The baby Taurian is fine, so you're not in super-hot water, but what the hell?"

Eliot gestured to some comfy-looking couches in the lobby. "Let's sit."

"I don't need to sit. I need answers." The idea of behaving like it was some sort of business meeting was preposterous.

Eliot went ahead and sat. "Well, there are a few reasons I insti-gated the eggnapping. Most importantly, I hated to see you go back home. Why couldn't you have stayed longer? You came to check up on me then left in such a hurry. You know… I wanted to hang out with you."

Abigail couldn't keep the sarcasm from her voice. "That's heart-warming, but that's not a good enough reason to do what you did. Were you really going to try to devolve the baby Taurian into a di-nosaur?"

Eliot sank into the plush couch. "That was really only a test. I knew the instant that I asked Jane to alter the baby, she had no in-tention of doing so. I also knew it was way too developed within its egg to make the genetic alterations. I would need an embryo in its early stages of development to pull that off. Also, we're still stumped about what the actual process would be." He scratched his chin. "Anyway, part of the test was to see how Jane would react. I thought she would stand her moral ground against me. I was pleasantly surprised that she chose a sneakier route. I think she proved herself to be very resourceful."

Still sarcastic, Abigail said, "I'm glad you tested your employee and she passed, but that still doesn't justify what you did."

Eliot sighed. "The third reason I stooped to eggnapping was to study a theory I have that everyone is only looking out for themselves. No one is truly altruistic. Jane made a selfless choice, and you and your friends proved you cared about something beyond yourselves. I guess I just wanted to witness it firsthand. In fact, you're proving you care by even coming back to ask for an explanation. If you didn't care, you'd have written me off and disowned me as your brother."

"Maybe I'm here because I'm angry and want to set you straight. You're this close"—she measured a centimeter between her thumb and forefinger and sent an electric shock across them—"to getting Illuminated."

Eliot crossed his arms. "You know, you have proven another point that I'm realizing is a lifelong issue for me: people only take interest in me when I'm getting into trouble. Once you saw I wasn't getting into too much trouble, you bailed and went back home. If the only way I can get any attention from you is to behave badly, what do you expect me to do? Of everyone in the family, Eileen was the nicest, and she's pretty self-absorbed. Did you ever notice that I didn't give her as much grief?"

Abigail thought back to their childhoods and realized he was right. "I never considered why you have been such a brat your whole life." She thought she should still be angry about what he had done, but it all made sense. He had been deprived of positive attention, so he resorted to attracting negative attention by whatever means possible. She sighed, letting her anger dissipate. "I'm sorry. You're right. How about I stick around this time? Does IRIS's invitation for a robot-prepared meal still stand?" She hugged him then added, "Just don't ever try to pull anything like that again, or I will seriously shock you into next week."

∞

The next morning, Abigail awoke to a strange text on her phone. She didn't recognize the sender's number. *Come quickly,* it said. *I have caused harm to your brother.* She supposed it was from his robot, IRIS.

Abigail rushed to the door of Eliot's suite and knocked. He had purchased an entire complex of apartments and had them renovated for his and his employees' living quarters. Like the research facility, the building had been built with a pretty average exterior, but the interior spaces had been updated to luxury standards. He kept a few suites unoccupied and well-furnished for visiting guests. Abigail had come from next door wearing a bathrobe and fuzzy slippers

Eliot, in his pajamas, hair disheveled, opened the door.

Abigail burst in. "IRIS sent a strange message. Is everything all right?"

Eliot's face lost all color. In a meek voice, he said, "Actually, something terrible has happened. It's not IRIS's fault, though—it's mine."

"Did you do something worse than eggnapping an alien baby?" Abigail couldn't think of what he could have done that could be worse.

Eliot shuffled back to his couch and sat down and stared into space like it was his own private abyss. His aura showed some black swirls of despair. "Not intentionally, but it's not good to be me right now."

"Oh my god. What happened?" Abigail couldn't make the faintest guess as to what kind of trouble Eliot was in now.

He finally explained. "I developed IRIS to do more than cook meals and look out for me. One of her main designations was to trade on the stock market. I had developed other algorithms that took in data and bought and sold stock, but I wanted IRIS to incorporate a mathematical approach along with some intuition and creativity when it came to trading. Her output for trading was off the charts too. She could make more deals in a millisecond than our previous program could make in a day."

Abigail crossed the room and sat next to Eliot on the leather couch. "That doesn't sound so bad. Where's the harm in having a super-efficient high-speed trading robot?"

"Well, she was too efficient, and she did make a lot of money in the first three seconds of her trading career, but in the fourth second, the whole market crashed. It did worse than crash—it vanished. She placed an uncommonly large number of orders totaling hundreds of billion dollars in just three seconds. After the fourth second, it all ceased, as if the entire stock market had a heart attack." Eliot made a poofing gesture in the air. "Over eight hundred and sixty-two billion dollars just vanished. I'm ruined. A lot of other people lost a lot of money too. I didn't even take my business partner's advice to sock some money away into safer and less risky investments like money market accounts. The only good news is that nobody is pointing any fingers at me because I used an encrypted URL. If word got out that it was me, the authorities and a giant mob would be tracking me down." He pantomimed a throat-slitting gesture.

Abigail wondered if it was dishonest for him to avoid responsibility for the trouble he had caused. She did see him as just a reckless eighteen-year-old who didn't mean any harm, even though he'd been greedy. "I'm sorry that you lost all your money. What are you going to do now?" She put a comforting hand on his shoulder.

Eliot covered his face with his hands. "I don't know. Have a garage sale to raise some funds so I can start all over again. I'll have to sell all of my properties."

Abigail wished there was something she could do. She had a decent-sized savings account, but she figured her twelve thousand dollars was pretty small potatoes compared to the billions he'd lost. "Maybe Silas could help you somehow. He's pretty well situated financially."

As Abigail finished her sentence, a mustached man wearing sunglasses knocked on the door that Abigail had left ajar. He came into the apartment and inspected Abigail over his glasses, which hung low on his face. "Your robot called me and told me what happened. I'm sorry to hear about your losses. You okay, man?"

Abigail studied him. She'd never met him, but his aura showed that he was concerned about Eliot. Could it be that her brother had made a friend who wasn't a robot?

Eliot looked up. "I lost it all. Everything was going so great, and then poof—it all vanished. I can't feel my limbs, and my stomach is a pit of despair. Oh, Abi, this is—or was—my business partner, Tom. He helped me make all the money I just lost. Sorry, Tom. I lost it all."

Tom smiled. "You know that I've been socking away some of my shares, right? I've got a billion or two in a safe place. It's a good-sized nest egg."

For having lost a lot of money, Tom seemed pretty chipper. Abigail wondered where in the world Eliot had found him.

Tom pushed his tinted glasses back up. "I have a business proposal for you. How would you like to go into business with me? I'll kick in some funds, but I'll need help understanding what the heck you're working on. But this time around, you really need to take *every* piece of advice I give you."

Eliot nodded. "Putting money in a safe, less risky place sounds like great advice. I -got greedy and wanted more. I accept your business proposal."

"This is a business of making and losing money. The trick is to make more than you lose and to take very calculated risks."

Eliot nodded.

Abigail was amazed to study Tom's aura and see that he was genuine in his offer—he really did appear to have good intentions. It sounded like Eliot would keep his company running. "If you want a customer, Silas hasn't shut up about wanting his own robot. The General has also authorized me to put in an order for you to make half a dozen robots to put to work in the Space Force. They'll need propulsion systems so they can get around in space. Silas could help you with some of the rocket science. I have to admit that it took a while to warm up to IRIS when I first met her, but now, I'm in love with her... and her cooking."

As if summoned by name, the robot walked humbly into the room. She wore an apron like hired help. She took small steps and approached slowly with her head bowed. "I have caused irreparable harm to my maker. There seems to be a terrible feeling coursing throughout my synapses that I believe to be guilt and regret. Is everything going to be okay?"

Apparently, the robot did experience something resembling remorse, not that it displayed an aura for Abigail to see.

Her brother gave the robot a pained smile. "Yes, IRIS. Your concern for my well-being is greatly appreciated, and your response to the market crash has really helped. Please don't feel responsible. If anything, you should know that you only did your job a little too well. Thank you."

"Will your sister and your business partner be able to help you?"

"Yes. Thank you for contacting them. That was very thoughtful and resourceful. I am doing much better now because of the action you took. I'll be okay. A government contract could really help." He squinted at Abigail. "Tell your general that I'll get to work on a prototype Space Force robot, but it's not going to be cheap. And thank you, Tom. Your help will keep me in business."

The robot straightened her posture. "I am pleased to hear that. Would you like to try a new experimental omelet recipe I have developed?" IRIS wiped her robotic hands on the front of her apron. Abigail suspected the robot had studied human behavior closely and had watched more than a few cooking shows.

Eliot groaned. "I think my stomach is still feeling too unsettled for eggs right now, but thank you. Maybe Abi and Tom are hungry for an experimental omelet."

Chapter 30

Lasers

After recovering from the shock of losing all of his wealth, Eliot resumed his work at the research facility. Even though Tom had transferred funds to keep the facility afloat, Eliot realized that he needed to tighten the company's budget and manage some of the excessive spending he had allowed in the past. He had achieved much to reach his goal of creating a super-tech empire, but he had spent a lot of money to get there. He vowed to move forward in a more sustainable manner. In reviewing their costs, he discovered a massive electricity bill for building D that he wanted to investigate.

He walked to the farthest corner of his compound, to the unit where Professor Baylon, one of the more fringe-science members of his staff, was working on developing time travel. Eliot liked the eccentric old man and was feeling guilty because he was pretty sure he was going to have to cut his funding and kick him out. He had hired the professor on a whim, when there was no limit to what he could spend.

Dr. Baylon met him at the door with a jittery handshake and turned to lead the way into the building. His aura appeared to be on fire with bright swirls of orange and red, showing that he was excited about something and accentuating his frizzy white hair.

Eliot walked into the cluttered building. He figured he might as well see what the man was working on before delivering the bad news. He struggled to keep up with the professor. "I'm sorry I haven't had time to see what you've been working on. I've been busy, and now I'm trying to get back on my feet after a major setback."

The older man led the way through the maze of parts and junk that littered his small building. "I quite understand, and I've been busy at work too. Sometimes, a little time and space are all a person needs."

Eliot thought that sounded like a nice nugget of wisdom. "I'm excited to see what you're working on. Would you bring me up to speed on your progress?" Eliot wondered how the professor had been able to fill the space so full of junk and machine parts. It would take a lot of work to clear it out when it was time to send him packing.

They stepped into a back room, where there was a large table that was surprisingly clear of any junk or debris. The professor gestured to the object sitting on the table. "Here's my first working device."

The contraption resembled an enormous steel doughnut, about two feet across, standing on four thin legs to float it off the table. It looked like a flying saucer on stilts. It wasn't steel, though—it was made of magnesium silicate.

Professor Baylon tapped the hull of the contraption. "The use of this new metal has changed everything for me. And your fabricators who formed this chamber did so with exceptional precision!"

Eliot nodded. "I'm glad to know my crew did their jobs well." He remembered footing the bill for the materials and fabrication. It hadn't been cheap. He wondered if it could be repurposed or recycled once he'd determined that this project was a failure.

The professor gazed wistfully at the device. "Yes, without this material, I would have dawdled with no results for the rest of my life."

Eliot ran his hand over the smooth metal contraption. It was exceptionally well formed. "Yes, it's been an invaluable material for many purposes. Silas Rutherford was thoughtful to make it available for public use instead of patenting it for himself. Can you explain more about your machine?"

"First, let me explain time! You know how in quantum physics, it's possible for a particle to exist in many locations at a single moment in time? Well, that's because it's moving so quickly that strange things begin to happen. What I have managed to do is speed up time itself instead of merely speeding up particles. This is a time turbine that alters time."

Eliot nodded, but he was pretty sure he was going to have to pull the plug on the project. He humored the old man, though. "I like the sound of that. What powers the turbine?"

"I'm using lasers to generate a circling beam of light. The space inside this ring becomes twisted. It's like a laser-powered vortex."

"There're lasers inside this metal doughnut? That explains the huge electricity bills." The usage for the one small building had exceeded the total power consumption of the entire compound.

The doctor scratched his head. "Yes, I suppose it does take a considerable amount of power. Anyway, back to the way time works. You've probably heard space-time referred to as a fabric. I believe when your sister makes her blast jumps in space, they actually begin the jump by punching a hole in the space-time-fabric. What I am attempting to do is bend that fabric to bring two different points close together. Do you remember the charting of x- and y-coordinates on graph paper in geometry class?" The doctor studied Eliot with a squint. "It looks like tenth grade wasn't so long ago for you."

"Yes, I remember it like it was yesterday. Now, I'm in Algebra II," he said jokingly, even though he had just recently graduated high school and had completed both classes in the ninth and tenth grades.

The professor nodded. "Well, points in time are like coordinates on graph paper. My goal is to bend space-time so two different co-ordinates are in contact with one another. The machine utilizes two planes of existence. To use the doughnut analogy, if you placed the contraption on a cookie sheet then placed another cookie sheet on top, the upper cookie sheet represents here and now, and the lower cookie sheet can be set to a different point in time. Anything that goes through the hole in the center will travel to that designated point in time."

Eliot rose onto his tiptoes to try to look inside the doughnut hole. "I'm following you so far. This is amazing progress, and I'm super impressed. Does it actually work?" He wanted the project to succeed but wasn't keeping his hopes up.

The doctor pointed a finger into the air. "Before I go any further, I need to make advanced preparations for the demonstration." He gathered a ceramic plate, which Eliot recognized from the café, and set it on the far end of the table. The professor glanced at his watch and stepped back, and a penny appeared from nowhere and pinged onto the plate. "2:03 p.m. is the time I will have to send it back to."

"Would you check the date on that penny, Eliot?"

Eliot wasn't sure what he'd just witnessed, but he complied. He was trying to figure out where the penny had come from. "Um, 1993, and it's pretty beat up. I guess because it's older than I am."

"Great! Go ahead and put it into your pocket. Now, it's time to turn on the machine!"

The professor flipped a switch, and the machine started to hum. "I have only figured out how to travel through time and not space, so we have to move this machine to the other side of the table. Will you help?"

They carried the contraption across the table to stand directly over the café plate. The professor punched numbers into the attached keypad. He mumbled, "Two-oh-three, two-oh-three." He then reached into his pocket and pulled out a penny.

"Check the date on *this* penny."

"1993." Eliot squinted at the penny. "That's a good magic trick! What a coincidence!" Eliot reached into his pocket to be sure his penny was still there. It was. He wondered if the professor had dug through his piggy bank to find two matching pennies.

"It is not magic—it's time travel," the professor said sternly.

Professor Baylon pushed one more button on the machine then dropped the penny through the doughnut hole. Instead of hearing the penny land on the plate, nothing happened. The penny vanished. "You see, for a brief period, the penny was in two places at one time, but now, it's back to being the only one."

For his enhanced superintelligence, Eliot felt embarrassed that it took so long to comprehended what he had just witnessed. He fished into his pocket and retrieved the penny. It was the same penny. It even had the same scratch mark across Lincoln's nose. There was no doubt. Baylon sent the penny back in time to a point before he had even turned on the machine.

"This is amazing!" Eliot smiled then took a second glance at the penny. He pushed a button on his wristwatch. "IRIS, could you bring us a bottle of champagne?"

Professor Baylon shook his head. "I don't drink alcohol. And aren't you still in high school?"

Eliot rolled his eyes then spoke into his watch. "IRIS, make that some sparkling grape soda. I'm in building nine."

Her voice echoed out of his watch. "I am aware of your present location. I will be there in four minutes and thirty-three seconds."

All his plans to cut the funding for Baylon's department had vanished. He began thinking of the implications. "We need to start designing a larger device that we can send people through. Also, if someone traveled back in time, how could they travel forward to the present?"

"It's much easier to travel forward in time. In fact, we are doing it as we speak!"

Eliot shook his head. "Yes, but if I were to go back a few million years, how would I travel back to the present?"

"This device can do the job. I have sent pennies to the future, but it would be hard to test on people, because I wouldn't want to get stuck—or cause anyone else to be stuck—in the future. I like living in the here and now."

"It sounds like we have our work cut out for us." Eliot had an idea about the limitations they were experiencing when receiving information for their stock trading. "Is there a way that we can retrofit this device so that instead of dropping a coin through, we can plug in an Ethernet cable that's delivering information, like… let's say stock exchange information, so we could get the information before it was even sent from its source?"

The professor scratched his head. "I believe so."

"Could you make that your highest priority?" Eliot realized he was throwing his planned budget cuts out the window. "I can allocate the funds, and my staff can fabricate all the parts you need."

The man nodded excitedly.

∞

A week later, Eliot and Tom were back at their trading headquarters in Manhattan. They had hefted the metal doughnut contraption up to their second-level suite apartment.

Eliot was pretty confident that it would work. He had, however, spent a considerable amount of Tom's money to retrofit the time machine. It would be a big waste of his money if it was a failure. "Okay, are you ready to make back some of the money I lost?"

Tom was studying the device over the top of his sunglasses. "As long as it doesn't crash the market again. You know there were some pretty big repercussions from that? I lost a lot too. The only reason I didn't come for your head on a plate is that I know money comes and goes and that there're a lot more important things in this world."

That sentiment sounded familiar. Tony, whom he'd beaten at the poker tournament, had said he thought the title was more important than the money. Eliot settled back into his chair, pondering how anyone could make that claim. "I'm sure everyone is recovering just fine from the crash." He thought he should feel more guilty about causing everyone to lose their money, but he didn't. He did appreciate Tom's lighthearted attitude about losing so much. Eliot would pay him back, counting on the success of this device that he was fairly certain wouldn't crash the market again. "No, I've designed a reasonable algorithm that won't trade too aggressively, but this new device is going to give us a real leg up!"

Eliot plugged in the device then paused before switching it on. He really hoped it would work—it just had to. He flipped the switch, and suddenly, the lights shut off with a pop. They must have blown an electrical breaker. They fumbled in the dark. He located his phone to provide some light so he could locate the breaker box and flip the switch.

"Man, it drew too much power. I guess we need to call an electrician and get some work done."

∞

They had an electrician install a larger fifty-amp 240-volt receptacle with its own designated breaker fuse. That required an alteration to the device, because he had asked the professor to wire it for 110 volts so that he could plug it in anywhere, which had proven to be a mistake. They traveled back to New Jersey so Professor Baylon could make the upgrade.

The next day, Eliot asked, "Okay, ready for round two?" He hoped it would work without any further complications. Once he plugged it in and switched it on, the device produced a humming sound. That was a relief. He then plugged one Ethernet cable into the top and another into the underside, which led to their computer.

Eliot started typing away. "Okay, let's set up trading like usual."

He sat and watched in amazement.

Tom gazed at the screen. "How is this possible?"

Eliot grinned. "I told you, it's a time machine. We're trading based on information that is generated in the near future. One whole second to be exact. Instead of just a fast connection to the market, we are getting a sneak peek at the future and are trading based on that information!" Eliot was pretty sure word of this would incite an angry mob of traders wanting to smash his door and probably his skull with baseball bats. "Um, this is our little secret, too, okay?"

Tom's jaw dropped. "So you invented time travel just to make more money? Now, I've seen it all! Tell me how it works."

"I didn't invent it. Professor Baylon did. It's a laser-powered time turbine."

Tom watched the screen with his mouth hanging open. "Amazing! So you're going to put some of this money aside, right, so you have a safe nest egg?"

"Yep, right after I pay a massive electricity bill. There's also another real estate investment I'd like to make when we've amassed enough wealth. I have my eye on an island that's for sale."

Tom nodded with the glare of the computer screen lighting up his glasses, still looking dumbstruck by the advancement. "An island sounds good to me. I need a vacation."

Eliot thought expanding to a location where they had space for more expansive projects would be a nice next step.

Chapter 31

Big Sister

Abigail and Eliot were seated at a patio table outside the bistro in his compound. It was a nice change to actually get to know and become friends with her little brother. It was also a relief to feel somewhat sheltered from the outside world while being a guest in the isolated new world that he had created, although guilt was creeping in that she wasn't doing anything to improve life for anyone.

She rationalized that maybe some of her brother's work could make a difference, so by supporting him, she was helping the world. She occasionally checked in on the news to confirm that the country was as divided as ever. The latest news was that the president was about to face an impeachment trial for his unconstitutional grab for more emergency powers.

Abigail thought that technically, by declaring a state of emergency because of the ecological disasters connected to carbon emissions and global warming, like fires and droughts, not to mention the need to save forests that by their very nature counteracted carbon levels in the atmosphere, the president *was* using his constitutionally granted powers. The problem was that not everyone agreed that it was indeed a state of emergency. Abigail kept herself updated on the ongoing news and emailed Russell, offering to help in any way she could.

In the meantime, her main focus was her brother, and she was keeping in touch with Dr. Fambozi, who was on the other side of the country with her friends, working on calculations to locate the Taurian colony convoy. To her, that was the most pressing task, and once they had an idea of where to look, they would be departing on the *Harkin* to search for the convoy. She thought helping Eliot get back on his feet was a nice, sisterly thing to do. She had been considering that maybe he could contribute to the search for the convoy with his robot's impressive computing power.

After slurping the last of his soda through a reusable metal straw—Abigail had convinced him to stop using plastic ones—Eliot proclaimed, "I still want some Taurian DNA, by the way. I think the Taurians would like to see the development of animals from their evolutionary family tree. Also, when are you going to teach me to harness electricity? I just can't get the hang of it."

Abigail was used to hearing Eliot's "I-want" proclamations ever since he had learned the term, which had been among his very first words. "I want!" she remembered him saying as he pointed with his infant fingers at a toy or shiny object that was out of his reach.

"Maybe you just aren't as naturally gifted as I am." She snapped her fingers, creating a spark. "And what would you do with the dinosaurs you brought to life from Taurian DNA?"

"Put them on a tropical island, of course! Duh! I don't think dinosaurs would appreciate having to adjust to such a cold climate. It seems reasonable here now, but winter gets pretty frigid."

It was nice outside, and the outdoor patio area was a relaxing space that Eliot must have hired a landscape architect to design. Flowers were in bloom, and his artificial creek sparkled. She imagined what he was proposing—dinosaurs on a tropical island. "I know both with and without seeing your aura that you just want yet another way to make money, although that does sound like it would be an amazing place to visit."

Eliot grinned. "Once I'm back on my feet financially, which is happening as we speak, I will be purchasing my very own island to be a preserve for dinosaurs, and yes, if people really want to pay money to visit the island, why not? Setting up a tourist destination with nice hotels is not a despicable way to make money."

Abigail ate a bean sprout off the top of her salad. "You know, if the only DNA you have available is Taurian, then the only dinosaurs you would have on your island would be duck-billed hadrosaurs.

That's not a lot of variety." She thought Tkla might like to see some of their ancient ancestors come to life but wasn't sure how he'd feel about experimenting with his DNA. "If Tkla does not wish to voluntarily donate a DNA sample, will you promise to avoid any more nefarious schemes to get some?"

"Sure. And I do realize the Taurians are descended from harmless herbivores and not from the *T. rex*, which will make my island safer but boring. The *Hadrosaurus* is like the dinosaur equivalent to a cow—not that cows aren't somewhat smart. I was wondering, though, did the Taurians save any other animal life when they left their planet?"

"That's a good question. Maybe they have some domesticated pets that are descended from *Velociraptor*s, like how our dogs are descended from wolves. That would make your island more interesting."

Eliot clapped his hands. "Now we're talking! Only they're on a two-hundred-year-long voyage to Nidus in the Polaris system—"

"Are you proposing we try to find their convoy and steal some of their pets' eggs?"

"It's just an idea. I've been putting some thought into the challenging problem of locating their convoy of ships. I'm working on the first Space Force robot, and I decided to assign it the task of locating the convoy. Her name is IRENE—Internal Random Engineered Navigation Entity—and I think she'll have the navigational processing power to help find the missing ship. Also, don't you think it's neat that she has Mom's middle name?"

"Yes, I like the name. Very sweet." Abigail was thrilled he'd taken the initiative to help, but she knew his motives weren't purely altruistic. "You're just doing this for the chance to get some of their pet dinosaur eggs, aren't you?"

Eliot raised a palm into the air in a confessional manner. "I want to contribute to the success of your mission for a number of reasons, but yes, I really want some dinosaur eggs. I think there are a lot of reasons why we need to bring dinosaurs back to be part of the animal kingdom on this planet. They were tragically wiped out, and *we* could bring them back from extinction. Also, I need you to test out the space-model robot before I make more for the Federation Space

Force… And yes, they're going to pay a lot of money for their order of robots."

She knew he had too many bills to pay to be giving away any robots, but she thought he could have donated it to help make up with Tkla for stealing his egg. "I'll see what I can do to get the Taurians to agree to donate some DNA. Tkla has had some horrible premonitions about the fate of their colony convoy, so I'm sure he'll be grateful to hear that you're working on a way to find them. Taurians don't seem to hold grudges, so maybe they'll volunteer some DNA, but seriously, no more abducting eggs."

"Thank you, Abi. I promise—no more eggnapping."

∞

Abigail contacted Tkla, wanting to meet and talk. He quickly arrived at her apartment suite with Tlana, his baby.

As Abigail opened her door to let them in, she squealed. "Aw, I think she's grown since I saw her last. Can I hold her?"

"Certainly." Tkla handed over the infant. "She seems to like you very much."

"Well, I like her too!" Abigail jiggled the baby in her arms then touched noses with the infant, who had her big eyes fixed on her human auntie—as Abigail considered herself.

Abigail took some time to interact with the baby Taurian. Once the little one had fully melted into her arms, she began explaining, "My brother, who I know you must be furious with, has expressed interest in connecting with the Taurian convoy of ships heading to your colony world. To be honest, he's only interested in having dinosaurs he can exploit for money, but he's working on a robot that may be able to help locate the convoy."

"Yes, my people who are traveling in the convoy have consumed my thoughts lately. I can't get the image of them disappearing into darkness out of my mind. Separating from many friends and family was a painful experience when they left our world because we knew we would never be reunited. Your rescue of the remnants of our people on our doomed planet was a miracle, and it improved the chances of our ever reuniting, but two hundred years is a very long time for them to travel. My child may have a child of her own who may someday meet her distant relatives, but I may not. And any reunion will only happen if they survive their journey, which, according to my visions, they may not."

Abigail looked up from the baby, whose big round hazel eyes were still fixed on hers. "If we can calculate their location, Evvie and I would volunteer to take the *Harkin* to go find them."

Tkla's eyes widened to match his daughter's. "If that were possible, it would be a gift beyond measure. I feel distressed that something has gone terribly wrong for them."

Abigail imagined his heartache. "I joined the Taurian social network when I met your people, and I'm used to being part of your collective consciousness, but I never experienced it with the full population of your world. It must feel empty to have so many of them gone from that connection."

"Yes, you are correct. I think in the absence of that connection, I have imagined the worst. I would love to see a mission depart from Earth as soon as possible."

Abigail got up and walked to the center of the room to sit on her yoga ball then began bouncing with the baby. "Well, I know this is silly, but did your people bring any animals along on the colony ship? And if so, could we bring some back for my brother? I'm sure Dr. Hornwell would be excited too. I have to admit, I've also always wanted to see a dinosaur."

"Yes, we have saved specimens of our animal life, and I do see the value of bringing them back to Earth. I would be relieved to locate the convoy to see that they are safe and that my worry for them was only a product of my imagination. I am certain that parting with animal eggs will be a reasonable way to repay you for your help."

Abigail realized she would volunteer to help without bargaining for some animal samples and wondered if Eliot's business savvy was rubbing off on her. She was probably just as excited as he was to see real dinosaurs—or at least the descendants of dinosaurs. "We can also speed up the colonization of Nidus by getting the colony convoy there sooner," she added. "They could continue the work we started to make it habitable, like by planting vegetation and trees. Silas is impatient about getting people to the colony world too. He doesn't want humanity to have to wait any longer to inhabit another planet because he's worried something could happen to Earth, like an asteroid impact."

Tkla nodded. "Establishing the colony on Nidus sooner would be wonderful for my people as well. We are feeling that we are wearing out our welcome here."

"Just because the humans of Earth can't comprehend that this is your world, too, doesn't mean you're not welcome here and that you don't have a right to be here."

"My people would still like the choice to leave Earth or remain. At this point we are truly refugees with no other option. Finding the colony convoy and expediting their arrival to our new world would be a gift beyond measure."

Abigail bounced the baby a little higher. "Great! We have a new mission. You'll have to reserve some babysitting time with your nanny paleontologist, JJ, because I'm assuming Mama Brklana will want to bring her squadron along."

Tkla retrieved his infant and gave her a gentle pat on her bum. "I am sure Dr. Hornwell will love the opportunity to measure the cranial development of our child."

"Before you leave, there's another favor I wanted to ask. Some of the dinosaurs Eliot would like to bring back from extinction are your distant ancestors, the duck-billed hadrosaurs. He and his team are working on retrieving ancestral traits from bird DNA, and he's expressed interest in studying your genes but only from samples that are voluntarily donated. I know it's asking a lot, but is donating a blood sample something you'd be willing to do?"

"This is yet another advancement my people would like to see. If I could be assured that his plans are only to bring back the hadrosaurs, I would agree to this."

Abigail knew she was making a huge request and wondered how she would feel if aliens were asking her to donate her DNA for study. "Perhaps you can select a Taurian to join his research team, to be part of their work and ensure their research only leads to ethical advancements?" She trusted her brother but still thought he might need someone to keep an eye on him, especially once she was heading back out into the galaxy to find the Taurian convoy.

Tkla nodded. "I will allocate a Taurian babysitter for your brother."

∽

After her visit with Tkla, Abigail came back to Eliot's robotics lab to report the good news. As always, he was in the lobby to great her. She wondered if he had a surveillance feed patched into his wrist-watch.

"Tkla would be very grateful for your assistance. I guess you're playing your cards right because he and Brklana will donate their DNA for study, *and* he says that the colony convoy is loaded with animal life."

"That's great news! I'm making progress on the purchase of a small tropical island, so it feels like all my cards are falling into place nicely, and I will have a home for any animals you bring back." He flashed his phone at her to show some pictures of the island.

Abigail studied the images. "Nice! So do you want to come along on the space mission?" She was pretty sure his answer would be no, but she wanted to include him.

"No, thanks. I've got way too much going on here to pick up and leave. The robot industry is taking off, and I'm receiving orders every day. Your space model is ready and has a propulsion system that Silas helped design. You can let me know how she performs before I move forward with the entire order." They walked from the lobby of his building though the corridor to the vault room, where Eliot kept his most valuable projects locked up. "Do you want to meet her?"

"You bet. Does she cook too?"

"Yes, and she plays chess." Eliot punched his code into the door keypad and swung the heavy metal door open. "This is IRENE."

The robot bore a resemblance to IRIS, with white molded plastic panels and silver metal joints, but she had a slightly more robust look, with protruding compartments on her forearms and calves. Maybe that was where her propulsion jets were concealed. It made her look less dainty than her counterpart. "Hello, IRENE. It's nice to meet you."

"Hello, Abigail. It is a pleasure to meet you as well." The robot must have identified her with facial-recognition software.

"Are you ready to travel into space?" Abigail asked. "Do robots get nervous like humans do when we're about to take a long trip?"

Abigail wasn't exactly nervous, but she was uncertain about what they would encounter on their new mission.

The robot flashed her eyes to simulate blinking. "I am not nervous, but I am working diligently to be prepared. I have been assigned to improve myself to better assist you and your crew."

Abigail turned to Eliot. "I'm so excited! Thank you!"

Eliot gave her a lopsided smile. "IRENE is not a gift. I've already dropped an invoice to your Federation Space Force, so I'll be well compensated by the Empire—I mean your Federation government. As she mentioned, I have helped to customize her to be helpful on your mission—although technically, she's mostly improving herself. She's been studying her astrophysics, and her computing power is even greater than IRIS's. I'm sure she has many skills that will come in handy."

"Great! I'm so excited! IRENE, are you ready to travel into space?"

The robot nodded with another artificial blink of her glowing eyes. "It is the primary purpose of my programming."

Chapter 32

Mission to Intercept

Abigail and IRENE boarded the *Harkin* after shuttling up from Earth in Brklana's small amphibious-looking ship. Silas, Gavin, and Fambozi had taken a separate shuttle from California.

Abigail found her way to the control room with the robot, whom she couldn't wait to introduce to the crew. Gavin and Silas were studying a screen together, debating over some detail or another. She looked forward to spending time with them after having been with her brother for so long.

Evvie came hustling in. "Abi! I'm sorry I didn't meet you as your shuttle boarded. I had some last-minute repairs to tend to before we set off."

Abigail hadn't realized how much she missed Evvie until she was standing in front of her. She took her in with a long hug until the robot beside them produced an artificial coughing sound.

"Oh, yeah," Abigail announced. "Everyone, we have a new crew member on board. This is IRENE."

"Hi, IRENE!" the crew said in unison. Then Gavin added, "It's nice to have you on board."

"It's nice to be aboard. Thank you."

Silas looked at the robot. "So, what is the underlying purpose of *your* programming?"

"I am here to assist in locating the colony convoy and to provide extra assurance that all of you make it home safely. I've downloaded all the information I could find related to astronomy, astrophysics, and cosmology. The origins and development of the universe are my greatest interests. I've also put together a galactic map, just in case we get lost."

Gavin gaped. "Wow, it's awesome to have a robot watching our backs!"

Abigail rubbed her palms together and smacked her lips. "Our galley is extra stocked with ingredients if you would like to practice your culinary skills. Your sister, IRIS, won me over with her cooking."

The robot nodded. "I plan to add sustenance to your diets as well."

Abigail thought she might drool, remembering the meal IRIS had prepared for them. It had been a bizarre mix of ingredients and flavors but was delicious. The robot had used cinnamon and nutmeg in dishes that didn't typically require those flavors, but it worked well. It still baffled her that a being who couldn't taste food was responsible for creating such deliciousness. "We will be grateful for your culinary and astrophysical expertise. Thank you!"

Dr. Fambozi spoke up. "Hello, IRENE. How are you coming along with the calculations for the location of the colony convoy we're searching for?"

"I have had to improvise because of insufficient data. Since the ship is actually a conglomeration of a few massive ships with smaller ones attached, there seems to be a bit of uncertainty about their actual mass and acceleration. Brklana has helped me to make the best guess as to their mass and combined thrust. If those figures are inaccurate, then the convoy may not be present in the location I have calculated."

Abigail nodded. "Sounds like a needle in galactic haystack. I'm sure we'll have to do some searching once you've made your best guess."

∞

The *Harkin* traveled away from Earth so they could initiate the blast jump. The smaller vessels, mostly piloted by Taurians, connected to the titanic ship to travel under its blast shield.

One human pilot called in to confirm his connection. "Ivanovich here," he said in heavily accented English. "I am the last of the group to connect to the *Harkin,* so we are clear for the blast jump."

Evvie smiled as she pushed the comm button. "It's great to hear your voice, Ivan." She looked around the control room. "Is everyone ready?"

The crew voiced affirmation from their seats. Gavin's grin eclipsed the sun shining through the viewport. Silas held tightly to his armrests. Abigail nodded. Evvie hit the large red button.

"Best friends forever, blast-jump, go," they said in unison.

Bright light glared through the view-port dome then was replaced by two seconds of solid darkness before a backdrop of stars popped into view. It was the first time they had jumped into an area of deep space where there weren't any stars or planets close by.

"That was the most dazzling experience of my life!" Ivan said through the comm.

Brklana, who was in her own ship, called in. "Scout team, depart from the *Harkin* and assume formation to expand our search radius."

"Are we picking up anything?" Dr. Fambozi asked.

Evvie was monitoring the ship's sensor reports. She let out a disappointed sigh. "I can't detect the convoy, and I've got long-range scanners that should be able to pick them up if they were anywhere close."

Abigail had kept her fingers crossed. She knew finding the Taurians right away was probably too much of a miracle to hope for, but disappointment sank in. "What do we do now?"

IRENE's normally upright posture slumped. "I apologize that my calculations have proven to be faulty."

Abigail wasn't sure if her instinct to reassure the robot was silly. "You tried your best, and that's all we can ask of anyone."

Traveling to this location in space gave Abigail an eerie feeling because of its isolation. Sure, there was the glow of the starscape out the view port, but there were no anchoring central stars or planets to use as a reference points. She felt like they were truly adrift and wondered if they would ever find the convoy. It was perhaps overly optimistic to have thought that they would be able to guess the convoy's location, make the blast jump, and instantly find them. She also realized that she couldn't really comprehend the vastness of space.

She looked to Tkla, who bit his scaly lip. She realized that she had given him a false sense of hope about finding his people.

Dr. Fambozi studied his screen. "This is interesting. The ship's sensors are detecting a body that is exerting a gravitational pull. The odd thing is that it's not producing any light, so it's not a star, but by these numbers, it may be fairly massive. Since we can't see it, it's impossible to determine its size or distance from us. In fact, its pull is altering our course. I would say that if we don't adjust our heading, it will pull our ship into a new path."

Abigail was relieved to hear that there was something out there. The question was whether to investigate. She was no astrophysicist, but a dark object with a massive gravitational pull sounded pretty ominous. Anyone with any sense of self-preservation would probably want to avoid the mysterious body that was pulling them in, not go toward it.

"Should we break away, or should we go see what it is?" Fambozi asked.

Abigail's gut said that the gravitational pull could have something to do with the fate of the colony vessel they were in search of. "Does anyone else want to see what it is?" She didn't want to coerce any of her friends to travel headfirst into danger if they didn't feel one hundred percent committed.

"I believe this is the source of the convoy's troubles," Tkla said. "It is the dark force from my visions. I feel an urgency to travel toward it."

Brklana called in. "My pilots confirm their willingness to scout toward the anomaly."

To Abigail's surprise, the consensus among her crew and friends was to travel toward whatever was out there. She herself felt drawn to the mysterious mass and wished to follow its pull.

Chapter 33

Stellar Remnant

After about six hours of high-speed travel, Fambozi made an announcement from his station, where he was closely monitoring his screen. "I've been studying our increased velocity and trajectory, and I've determined that the mystery body that's exerting its pull on us is *massive*. I still can't see it, but I think we are dealing with something comparable in mass to a star or even several stars."

Gavin spoke up. "Do you think it could be a neutron star?"

Abigail eyed Gavin. "What exactly *is* a neutron star?" She knew he had created a comic book character named Neutron, but she didn't see the connection.

Gavin straightened in his chair. "A neutron star is a star that lost its fuel and collapsed. Since it's not burning any fuel, it's gone dark. They're so dense that the subatomic electrons and protons have combined to produce neutrons, and it's because of the neutrons' ability to resist further collapse that the star doesn't become a black hole."

Fambozi gleamed at Gavin. "That's right. The mass of a super massive star can collapse to the size of a small planet. I do believe that as neutron stars go, the one we are following may be fairly massive. Also—and this is interesting—it's traveling at a very fast rate. Our velocity is increasing to match its speed."

Abigail had been feeling the acceleration for the last six hours. "Can you tell if the convoy is close to this neutron star?"

"No," Fambozi said. "There's no sign of them."

IRENE produced her artificial throat-clearing sound. "I have been analyzing the space within the wake of the neutron body, and there *is* a faint exhaust trail that matches the Taurian drive engines. The trail is spiraling around the source of the massive gravity pull. I have not yet determined whether it ends with a deadly collision or if they are still circling the body."

Abigail took a deep breath, relieved to have finally found evidence of the Taurians, but she realized that she and her friends might be too late. It was possible the Taurians had spiraled to their deaths, as Tkla had seen in his visions.

Evvie punched the controls for the thrusters. "I'm going to lay in course so we can catch up."

For three more hours, the acceleration pushed Abigail into her seat. She could see a faint glowing blue disc that gradually grew larger in their viewport.

"I have visual contact with the convoy," Fambozi announced. "They are actually a good distance away from the stellar remnant and are orbiting it in a somewhat stable but high-speed elliptical trajectory. As Gavin points out in his comic books, dense neutron material is dangerous stuff. That convoy of ships is lucky they haven't been pulled apart into a stream of atoms. Once we connect with them, we shouldn't be in danger of being spaghettified, but we will be faced with the challenge of escaping the pull of the massive body."

"When can we have audio contact?" Abigail asked.

"There will be a delay in their response because of the distance, but we can send a transmission and wait for a reply." Fambozi was readying the comm system when they got a ping of an incoming message. He patched it through to the speakers.

Abigail understood the Taurian language, but Tkla translated for everyone else. "They say they are trapped in the gravity well of the neutron remnant, and it is too dangerous for us to come any closer. They say to stay away." His winced as if relaying the message was causing him physical pain.

Abigail gasped. "What are we going to do, just leave them stuck orbiting the giant meteor?"

Dr. Fambozi shook his head. "Um, that's much denser than your average meteor or even planet. We're talking about many solar masses packed into that remnant of a star. They're lucky to have a stable orbit around it, although their path is super elliptical. And they're right—getting any closer would be dangerous."

Abigail hated the idea of abandoning them. "But we need to help them escape. Does anyone have any ideas?"

Silas pursed his lips. "If we were to connect with them, couldn't we just make a blast jump to get us all out of there?"

Evvie shook her head. "That body's distorting space-time. The basic requirement for our blast jumps is to have a smooth section of space-time from which to take off. Blast jumping from anywhere near there could send us to who knows where, maybe even another plane of existence. We could try, but we might end up lost in space."

IRENE spoke up. "I am confident I can navigate our way back to Earth if we are to get lost. It is the primary purpose of my programming."

Abigail studied the crew. "Okay, I have no doubt we should attempt this rescue. It might be dangerous, and we could end up in some far-off place—or worse, pulled into that thing. If anyone feels reluctant, we can designate our largest scout ship as a return ship to Earth. Does anyone wish to separate from this mission?"

Brklana called in from her ship. "My team is reporting their desire to continue with the rescue mission. We are fully committed." She was connected to the members of her squadron through their collective network, so they didn't have to radio in—except for Ivanovich, who, through the comm, voiced his willingness to proceed. "Let us pay a visit to our lost friends."

Silas and Gavin studied each other as if wondering what the other was thinking. They didn't have a connection to an alien collective consciousness, nor could they see auras to get a hint of each other's intentions. Instead, they nodded and simultaneously said, "We're in."

Evvie gave Dr. Fambozi a concerned look. "Are *you* sure you want to risk going in closer to that neutron star-comet?"

"I wouldn't miss this opportunity for the world." He tapped a finger on his armrest. "But before we proceed, we should periodically drop probes with synchronized clocks to keep track of time so they may serve as markers in our trail. I have a feeling we may experience a slowing of time because of the extreme mass and density of the neutron star. It's distorting the space-time fabric and will cause a time dilation."

"Okay, I'll drop one now and one every hour till we join them," Evvie said. "I will engage each probe's thrusters so they will hopefully keep their position and not follow us in."

Fambozi gave Evvie a wink. "Great. They may serve as bread crumbs."

∞

Twelve minutes away from dropping their third space buoy, Abigail finally saw the convoy through the viewport. From their distance, it looked like a massive cluster of lumpy forms stuck together, with almost a hundred points of light—their rockets firing in an effort to keep them from spiraling toward the anomaly. The faintly glowing blue sphere of the stellar remnant had grown larger in the viewport.

The doctor took a moment to appreciate the faintly glowing celestial body. "No one has ever actually seen a neutron star, so we're making history."

Silas winced. "I just hope we live long enough to get home and tell the world about it."

Abigail thought that the beauty of the star didn't look so foreboding, but the sight of the Taurian convoy desperately and futilely firing its rockets reminded her that they, too, were in a precarious position.

Fambozi broke his gaze from the neutron star. "Go ahead and drop our third buoy. It will represent when we first saw them, almost three hours from when we made contact."

Evvie complied.

As they got closer to the convoy of ships, Dr. Fambozi asked, "Evvie, would you check in and get a report from the first buoy? What time does it say?"

"I think a better question is what day does it say? It's reporting that three days have passed since we dropped it."

The doctor nodded. "Yes, time is moving slower for us as we get closer because of the distortion the neutron star is creating in space-time."

Silas crossed his arms. "I guess that's better than for us to age super rapidly."

Fambozi nodded. "Yes, but if we get stuck here, time will be moving rapidly for everyone we know outside of this time ripple. I don't have kids, but Tkla and Brklana would go back to Earth to reunite with their elderly daughter."

Tkla raised his scaled eyebrows in an adopted gesture of concern.

Abigail thought the prospect of remaining stuck for very long and having everyone they know back home age rapidly age sounded terrible. She considered her parents. They weren't too old, but it would be horrible for them never to see her again because she spent the rest of their lives orbiting the remnant of a neutron star.

"Here's the plan," Evvie began. "We are going to match velocities with the convoy, join our ship to theirs, erect our shield, and blast jump out of there. Anyone have any questions?"

Dr. Fambozi raised his hand. "I can't explain how I got this insight, but we should link to their ship and delay the blast jump for perhaps an hour."

"I don't see any harm in that." Evvie smiled at Max. "Are you sure it's not because you want to take some time to study this monster meteor?"

"Yes. It is a sight to behold, but there is another good reason to delay—I just can't think of it now. And yes, we should take the time to study this neutron star. I would like to make measurements of its size and mass and try to determine if it has some sort of core."

Abigail maneuvered the ship as they approached the Taurian convoy. Evvie became too nervous to perform the docking procedure. Abigail was fine with taking the helm. She could see that it wasn't just one massive ship but consisted of hundreds of smaller ships connected to a few larger ships, each dwarfing the *Harkin*.

Brklana called in. "Scout team, connect to the convoy and assist with additional thrust."

Ivan called in. "Let's go help our lost friends! Pilots, follow my lead."

Abigail watched their ten scout ships connect to the conglomeration. She hit her thruster controls. "I'm taking us in too."

As she docked, she positioned the *Harkin* so that its main thrusters would help to keep the massive cluster of ships from falling closer to the super-dense body.

She eased the ship in then locked on with the docking clamps. It made a clunking sound, so she didn't really need to announce it, but she wanted to note the accomplishment. "We're now connected." She checked her wristwatch. "Okay, be ready for a blast jump in one hour." She couldn't wait to blast jump away from the deadly star.

She, Evvie, and Fambozi walked to the airlock to meet three Taurians who came aboard through the hatch.

In their own language, one of them said, "You should have heeded our warning. We thought we would use the star to catapult us on our journey, but instead of accelerating us outward, it has trapped us, and we have been unable to separate our ship from the path of the celestial body."

Tkla replied, "We made a unanimous decision to come. This is Evvie, owner of this ship, who rescued the remainder of our people, who were destined to perish on our home planet. Her ship has the technology to blast jump us away from this massive body."

The Taurians nodded.

Tkla added, "We are going to make the jump shortly. In the meantime, you should link with Abigail, Evvie, and me so you can understand their language and can see where we've been and what we've experienced. We've been to the Mother World and to the colony world, where we will make a new home."

Abigail appreciated his optimism, although making a new home on Nidus wouldn't happen if they never managed to escape from this predicament. She reached out and clasped hands with two of the tall beings as they closed the circle. She remembered the first time she had connected with the Taurians, their hands soft and warm—not scaly and cold as she had imagined they would be, proving they were not truly reptilian, but warm-blooded.

She focused on their connection, conjuring images to share with them, showing them Earth and the colony world. She also connected to their collective, shared by the population aboard the convoy. Unlike the group of refugees they had rescued on their doomed planet, there were women, children, and elderly Taurians, and they were all fearful of dying in the massive gravity trap. Abigail sent a message that she and her friends were there to help.

After they released their hands from the connection, the three Taurians didn't reveal much, but Abigail could tell they were thrilled about all they had just witnessed in the connection. And they were perhaps a little more hopeful about escaping. Knowing that many of their kind had traveled to the Mother World was surely a relief for them.

After the full hour had passed, Abigail set the controls for their jump. "We've got a scheduled blast jump to initiate. It's not usually a bumpy ride, but I think we should strap in due to the extra force the neutron star is exerting." The three Taurian guests found extra seats and secured their straps.

Abigail tightened her harness. "Okay, is everyone ready?"

She and her friends recited their ritual phrase. "Best friends forever, blast jump, go!" Abigail hoped more than anything that it would work and they could depart from the gravitational forces that were pulling them relentlessly toward the massive neutron star that had all of them trapped in a precarious orbit. She pressed the button.

Chapter 34

Dinolab

Standing before his staff of geneticists, Eliot drew a crude picture of a chicken on the dry-erase board then an arrow pointing to his best attempt at a dino-chicken, which had a long pointy tail, and hands studded with pointy claws. He even drew little teeth in its mouth, which was an important differentiation between a chicken and what he wanted to create. Of all the projects he had overseen, the dino-genetics department had shown the least advancement. He wanted to change that.

Eliot had convinced JJ Hornwell to travel to the lab to review their work. All it had taken was a description of Eliot's plans to populate an island with their genetically altered birds and the animals from the Taurian convoy—who like the Taurians, were descended from dinosaurs—to get him to agree, albeit reluctantly.

JJ held the baby, Tlana, on his lap while she gnawed on a toy Brontosaurus. JJ examined the expensive lab and the team of scientists Eliot had assembled. The paleontologist narrowed his eyes at Jane Grant.

Eliot knew JJ would have issues with her because she'd abandoned their work together. He also knew that JJ was uncomfortable bringing the baby back to the lab. Eliot provided a daycare for the children of his employees, but JJ had only responded to the invitation by saying, "No offense, but I'm not going to let Tlana out of my sight."

Eliot began the meeting. "I think we're approaching the problem from the wrong angle. Instead of adding, let's say, genes for a snout and teeth, maybe we just need to block the genes that are responsible for the toothless beak."

JJ let out a deep breath. "Blocking current genes to let ancestral ones prevail makes sense, but how do you think we can create those blocks?"

Eliot tried to draw a double helix strand of DNA on the board, but unlike his sister, he was a terrible artist. "The treatment Dr. Roberts performed on my sister and me was to remove blocks that were somehow placed within our DNA. I think what we need to do is recreate the process of inserting those blocks into bird DNA."

JJ tapped his fingers on the table. "So we have a new objective: instead of turning the teeth gene on, we just need to turn the beak gene off. Any ideas how to do that?"

Jane Grant, who gave JJ an awkward glance, spoke up. "I'll have to put some thought into that, but in the meantime, I will keep charting chicken DNA so we know which genes to block. There is one problem with this theory: tails have not been replaced by another feature. There is nothing to block."

Eliot watched JJ cross his arms. He could see that the paleontologist was withholding an idea. It was strange to see the normally jubilant man holding a grudge.

Eliot thought he should finally address the woolly mammoth in the room. "Would you like to say anything to one another?"

JJ shook his head. "I don't have anything to say to her."

She added, "Nothing to say here."

"Listen, we all want the same thing, right? Real living dinosaurs. I'm sorry I already stooped to immoral levels to make that happen, but let's turn a new page. JJ, it's my fault Jane left. Can you blame her? Unlimited funding at an advanced facility with an on-site coffee and smoothie bar."

"You bribed her with money, and she took it."

Jane pursed her lips. "Um, I did have student loans to repay."

"Fine. I understand why you made your choice, but you didn't even let me know. You just cleared out your work space and left. Not even a goodbye."

She winced. "I'm sorry about that. It just happened so fast, and I was excited."

Eliot added. "That was my fault. I tend to be pushy."

JJ huffed. "Your apology is accepted. Well... when it comes to chickens, they do have tails in their embryonic stages. Their wings also look more like hands before certain genes kick in to fuse the bones together. There must be a gene that's instructing the tail to regress. Let's find the genes that are responsible and block them."

"Sounds good." Eliot was happy to have a plan and to see JJ and Jane cooperating. "But how are we going to place artificial blocks into the genes once we locate them?"

Jane raised her eyebrows. "Maybe the person who discovered the blocks might have an idea for how to recreate them?"

He realized he might have burned a bridge with that person. "Yeah, it's too bad, though. I don't think I made a very good first impression with Dr. Roberts. I guess it's true: you never get a second chance to make a first impression, but I'll try."

Eliot had traveled to Los Angeles and sat in Dr. Roberts's sterile office across the desk from her. He had explained the dead end they'd reached in altering bird DNA to make birds into dinosaurs. He waited for her response.

Dr. Roberts closed her laptop and glared at him. "I can't think of any reason why I should help you. I'm not able see your aura, but I can guess you probably don't have the best intentions."

"I can understand why you wouldn't trust me, but I *am* helping other people's dreams come true, and I could argue that the whole world will benefit by bringing dinosaurs back from extinction." He paused to compose an even better argument. "Dr. Hornwell would say, 'Just think of the sixth-graders.'"

"Yes, I do see that the youth of today needs something to spark their imaginations and encourage them to do more than post selfies. I still don't trust you. You can probably see that in my aura."

He could indeed see her aura flashing with reds and purples, but the cold look on her face was enough to see that she didn't think too highly of him. He had to think of something he could do to show his goodwill. "I understand. How about I stay for my overdue checkup appointment? You can conduct all the tests you like."

Elliot saw the reds in her aura lighten to pinks and oranges. Examining him was a priority for her. Walking out right after his treatment without giving her a chance to study the results had been a crappy thing for him to do.

Her frown lightened too. "That would be helpful because I need to verify that the results of your gene treatment match your sister's."

"Great! Then will you'll come to review our work and help us come up with a way to create these artificial blocks in bird DNA? We really are stumped."

"How can you assure me that you won't take any process I help develop and use it for something besides making dino-chickens? Like, what's to stop you from devolving all of humanity into primates?" He saw her aura darken once again with distrust.

"I guess you just have to take my word that I won't. I'm sure that once you meet some of the people who are working to make this dream a reality, you'll see that we have good intentions."

She huffed a deep breath and pulled out a kit of medical instruments to begin documenting his vitals. He rolled up his sleeve for her to measure his blood pressure. He hoped his cooperation was enough to persuade her to make the trip to his research facility.

Chapter 35

Space Ghosts

Their blast jump didn't feel like any other blast jump she'd experienced before. It lodged Abigail's stomach up into her throat, as if the floor had fallen out from under her. There was a moment of weightlessness, instantly replaced by a force so gut-wrenching it was as if they'd hit a brick wall.

After the jump, Fambozi steadied himself at his station. "Is everyone okay? IRENE, can you determine our location in space?" He held one hand on his stomach and pressed his eyelids closed for a moment. Abigail felt discombobulated after the jump too.

The robot reported, "We have successfully moved in the reverse direction and away from the neutron star. We are closer to the Taurians' native system of Kronos."

A moment of relief gave Abigail a chance to forget about her nausea. It was good to know that they had escaped the massive body and were still in a recognizable region of space. She steadied herself and began studying her scopes to see if the Taurian convoy was close by. She didn't see any sign of them.

"The neutron star is nowhere in sight, but neither is the Taurian convoy," Dr Fambozi reported.

Abigail looked to the three Taurians who had been strapped in. Their seats were empty. *How could they have vanished?*

Fambozi noted their disappearance with a glance and shook his head. "Something isn't quite right. Evvie, can you get a signal from our first buoy? I want to know *when* we are."

Evvie shook her head. "There's no signal coming in from any of the buoys."

Fambozi turned to the robot. "IRENE, how far away are we from where we dropped the first time buoy?"

"At our current speed, we will be at its location in 8.9 hours."

"That's interesting. It took us about that much time to locate the convoy and drop that buoy. IRENE, how close are we to our original coordinates?"

"We are at those coordinates now."

"What the…" Silas and Gavin said in unison.

Abigail knew something was wrong. While she was checking her screen for any sign of the Taurian convoy, she felt like her fingers weren't making contact with the keypad even though she was watching them work. She stood from her chair to stretch her legs and walk around the control room because they had gone numb too. Her body wasn't recovering from the blast jump. When she completed her loop around the deck, she returned to see someone sitting in her chair. That someone was her… in her flight jumpsuit, eyes so light they almost glowed, and pure white hair that she kept trimmed to shoulder length. "Um, hey, everyone, do you see that there is another me sitting in my seat?"

Gavin rubbed his eyes. "Yeah, I'm seeing two of you."

The Abigail who was seated made no indication that she had seen or heard anyone.

The numbness in her hands and legs spread through her body. "Something's wrong! What's going on here?" She tried to take some deep breaths to settle the panic rising in her chest, but breathing didn't help.

Gavin jumped from his station to approach the other Abigail. "She looks just like you." He reached out to touch her, but his hand passed though the other Abigail's shoulder. "Is she a ghost?"

Abigail looked around. Everyone's eyes were wide with shock, and there was another Gavin sitting at his station, paying no attention to the commotion.

Dr. Fambozi wiggled his fingers. "I had a feeling something fishy was going to happen when we attempted that blast jump. I think *we* might be the ghosts."

Evvie frowned at her own hands. "Do you know why this is happening? And where are the Taurians who were on our ship?"

The doctor scratched his head. "The problem with the neutron star is that it's massive and ultra-dense, so it's distorting gravity to the point that time becomes space and space becomes time. By attempting to travel away from it, we have traveled back in time. I believe we are back to when we first arrived in this region of space. Our three Taurian guests are not with us because at this point in time, they're on their own ship."

"But how does that explain our seeing doubles of ourselves?" Abigail tried to keep her voice calm, but she was silently freaking out.

"I'm not a quantum physicist, but I do know that two physical bodies cannot occupy the same space at the same time. By coming back in time, we are technically inhabiting the same space as we did when we first arrived. I think something has changed to make that possible." Fambozi held his hand in front of his computer screen. Abigail could see the glow of the monitor though his hand. He continued, "I think we have undergone some strange shift where our physical particles are now displaying bosonic behavior."

"What does 'bosonic behavior' mean?" she asked.

"Well… at the quantum level, physical bodies consist of fermions, which are associated with matter, whereas bosons are a kind of particle that are generally force carriers, so they are more like bundles of energy. Photons, like in light waves, exhibit bosonic behavior and they have no mass." Fambozi tried rubbing his hands together. "It is a very strange sensation indeed to be in this state."

Abigail was amazed that he didn't appear to be as freaked out as she was. Her hands and body felt numb. She could rub her hands together and feel them, but it wasn't the firm contact it should have been. It felt more nebulous, like attempting to run in a dream. She wondered if it *was* a dream. Pinching herself had no effect—she didn't wake up.

Fambozi gave her a consoling half smile. "We still have some residual properties of physical matter, so that's good, but there's definitely something more photonic about us now."

Silas shook his head. "So you're saying we are now made up of photons? Are you sure we haven't died?"

IRENE let out her synthetic cough. "How can you explain my presence? I was not alive to begin with."

Dr. Fambozi nodded. "I think we're still maintaining a little connection to our physical selves—we're just closer to the less-substantial realm. Even though you are made of plastic and metal, you do have neural material that uses energy. Maybe you are more alive than you think."

IRENE cocked her head. "I would like to think that I am alive."

Fambozi added, "In some ways, this is a relief because if we had come back to this space and time with full physical bodies, we would have been occupying the same space as our previous selves. I have a feeling we would have become splattered stains on the inside of this control room."

While Abigail was happy to be alive, she wasn't dealing very well with her new ghostlike quality. "So how do we get back to our normal physical bodies?"

Fambozi tried supporting his chin on his knuckles only to have his hand slip away. "I think we have created a time loop, and unless we do something to break the loop, we will watch ourselves continually travel to the neutron star then make the jump back to this point, over and over again."

"And what of Brklana and the other scouts?" Tkla asked. "I cannot feel their connection through our collective network."

Abigail studied her screen, which showed the smaller ships in formation. "Their ships are still with us, so I'm sure they're fine—I mean just as fine as we are without actual physical bodies." She supposed it must be a terrifying experience to be stuck in a smaller ship with no control and with no one to help explain the strange phenomenon. She was grateful for Dr. Fambozi's explanation, even if he hadn't yet thought of a way to remedy the disturbing state they were in. "What do we do now?"

Fambozi shrugged. "I don't think there is anything we can do except hitch a ride back to the neutron star with our other selves."

They watched as their counterparts did and said everything they had done as they traveled toward the neutron star. Abigail felt helpless that they couldn't change their course even if they wanted to.

They sat by and watched events unfold. As they approached the convoy, Abigail realized that during their first approach, Dr. Fambozi had suggested an extra hour before the attempted blast jump. "Hey, Max. Why did you suggest the extra hour? You said you had a good reason but couldn't think of it at the time."

The doctor scratched his head. "I still don't know."

Abigail gestured for Max to accompany her to face the non-photonic doctor. "We need to somehow send the message to the other you to give us that hour."

"How do you propose we do that?"

"I don't know. Maybe if you occupy the same space and chant, we can get a message through?"

He complied, standing in the same place as his other self. Abigail stood facing both doctors and reached out to grasp them by their shoulders. "Say it with me, Max. Give us an extra hour before the blast jump!" He joined in to repeat the request over and over. Abigail moved her hands to his temples and concentrated on the message.

To her astonishment, Max stepped forward through her and said, "I can't explain how I got this insight, but we should delay the blast jump for perhaps an hour."

The real Evvie smiled. "I don't see any harm in that. Are you sure it's not because you want to take some time to study this monster meteor?"

They'd done it. A new sense of hope surged though her. Maybe they could change their fate, though the same event had happened on their first trip in, so technically, they hadn't changed anything. She was a little baffled, though, about who exactly had the original idea to allow an extra hour. She decided to stop trying to wrap her head around the conundrum and just be grateful for the extra hour.

As before, the *Harkin* docked, met with the three Taurians. Then the ship made the jarring jump.

After the jump, Abigail stood from her seat with the same numbness that had prompted her to get up and walk around after the first jump. Sure enough, her other self sat at her station, looking for a sign of the Taurian colony ship, making no indication that she had been there and performed the same actions twice before. Abigail could barely feel her fingers as she tried rubbing her hands together, her hands passing through one another.

She tried unsuccessfully to keep the panic from her voice. "Um, I think our condition has worsened, and this is already feeling like an eternal cycle. I have a feeling that if we make that jump one more time, we'll lose whatever physical qualities we have now."

Fambozi tapped a finger on his chin. "I'm not sure what we can do to change the events that keep leading us back to this point."

Gavin spoke up. "What will it take to get the Taurians away from the neutron star if what we've tried hasn't worked?"

Evvie stood from her station. "Maybe if they had their own blast-jump projector, they could perform the jump on their own."

Abigail thought that helping to rescue the Taurian convoy was important, even if their own situation was dire. For the next few hours, as they traveled on their third approach toward the neutron star, she pondered how they could manage to install a projector onto the convoy. She was stumped because she couldn't even manage to lift a screwdriver off the table.

They reached the point at which the convoy had been detected but was still a few hours away. She thought that maybe if they could only get the Taurian convoy out of there, it wouldn't matter what happened to her and the crew aboard the *Harkin*. After all, they were not quite living in physical bodies. It was good to focus instead on how they could help the Taurians.

She watched the real version of Evvie working away at her station. She was the person who could actually do something to help. Evvie had recommended earlier that the Taurians might be able to escape with the use of their own projector. Maybe Abigail could convince the other Evvie to do exactly that. As with sending the message to the other Max, she thought the photonic Evvie should occupy the same space as her counterpart and help convey the message.

She had photonic Evvie sit in the same space at the real-bodied Evvie. Abigail raised her hands to her friend's temples. "Evvie, you need to install a blast-jump projector on the Taurian ship. It's the only way to help them. They won't make it out by attaching to our ship. The blast jump will happen exactly one hour after you dock to the colony ship, so that's all the time you'll have. There's no way to give you more time. You're our only hope."

Abigail removed her hands and studied her friend, who kept working at her station. Frustration welled up in her. She needed to get through to Evvie. Since their photonic transition, she hadn't tried to conduct electricity. She attempted to shoot a spark between her fingers but didn't see any light. She did, however, feel some tingling and regain some feeling in her fingers.

Abigail reached out once again to touch Evvie's temples and tried to send the message about helping the Taurians make their own jump in an Illuminating shock. For a brief moment, the contact she made with Evvie felt like she was really touching her with real hands. She removed her translucent hands from Evvie's temples. "I hope I got through to her."

Evvie departed from her other self, looking discouraged that they had made no progress. After a gloomy moment, though, the other Evvie stood abruptly. "I need some assistance. We need to get to work converting some spare parts. I want to install a blast-jump projector and shield generator onto the convoy ship so they can make the jump independently."

The other Fambozi looked up from his station. "What gave you that idea? Won't it be the same as if they were connected to us to make the blast jump?" That version of Dr. Fambozi hadn't seen their multiple failed attempts.

Evvie replied, "I don't think we can save them that way. They need to depart on their own."

Abigail felt a wave a relief that something in the potentially never-ending cycle had been changed. It was up to her friend Evvie to free the Taurians from the neutron star.

Chapter 36

Unfortunate Report

Ringlow set up a holo-meeting with his master. He was relieved to remain on his ship, although the projection of the Overseer was almost too lifelike. It appeared to Ringlow that he was really standing in the chamber where an oversized viewing screen glowed within the dark space. The Overseer held a beverage in a cup that was molded out of the same morphing purplish-blue material as the chairs.

"I have a bit of tragedy to report," Ringlow, who would appear to be standing in the chamber, said. He had followed the large ship from Earth as they traveled to locate the Taurian convoy of ships that was en route to their new colony world, a tricky task because C-PU had to create a wormhole to the remote location. He cleared his throat. "The majority of the Taurian population on their two-hundred-dred-year-long voyage to their new world is doomed. They are stuck in a spiraling orbit around a remnant neutron star that is destined to become a black hole."

It was terrible news for Ringlow to have to report because he had invested so much time and energy into studying and trying to motivate the species to evacuate their system that would soon be irradiated by a nearby supernova. He would also have to admit that the predicament was entirely his fault.

The Overseer carefully placed his beverage onto the armrest of his chair, which molded itself to secure the cup. His face morphed only slightly when sharp teeth emerged. "You can't be serious! How in the Galaxy's Spiral Arms did this happen?"

The Overseer's reaction didn't help. Even though Ringlow was safely aboard his ship, the holo-projection of the displeased Overseer was unsettling. "I am disturbed by this as well, but it won't be a total loss, since there are substantial numbers of Taurians who were rescued from their planet by the Martian and her band of Earthlings. The Taurians will be able to continue to breed and evolve, and they now have a new world to inhabit. I do feel solely responsible, though, because it is the neutron star I sent to disrupt the Kronos system in the first place that has now trapped the convoy. They caught up to it and became captured by its massive gravity well."

The Overseer had reduced the sharpness of his menacing teeth. Perhaps Ringlow admitting fault had helped to diffuse the Overseer's anger. His green eyes grew larger on his pale face. "But how will it become a black hole?"

Ringlow let out a deep breath. "They're experiencing a bit of a time loop right now, but once they've exhausted all of their possible options, the neutron star will collapse into a black hole. The humans initiated—or I should say they *will initiate* their blast jump, which caused or will cause the already super-dense matter to further collapse in on itself."

"For being a semi-advanced race, that seems to be a pretty unintelligent thing for them to do. Have you considered any possible rescue attempts for the colony convoy?"

That surprised Ringlow, who would have thought the Overseer would press for non-interference and to let the convoy meet their fate. "I have considered a rescue. I've analyzed their situation and sent the parameters to C-PU, and there is nothing we can do. It will be all but impossible for us to provide enough additional acceleration to break their ship free of the stellar remnant. Trying to do so would risk the lives of whoever was attempting the rescue. It is a risk none of us are willing to take."

The Overseer sighed. "I understand. I see we are not in a position to help the convoy. Continue your observation and document their demise for our records. It will be a rare occurrence to witness a large ship stream apart as it enters a black hole."

"I will do as you say."

"This is unfortunate, but as you have pointed out, their species will not go extinct."

"Yes, Overseer." Ringlow had plummeted to the lowest point in his career. It was an oversight for which he would never forgive himself. He should have disposed of the stellar remnant properly by sending it through a wormhole to the center of the galaxy, where its mass would have caused little impact. Millions of beings who would have gone on to continue their species' legacy were to perish because he did not dispose of the stellar remnant properly. He had the urge to try to rescue them himself, but his sense of self-preservation over-rode his heroic impulse.

Chapter 37

One Hour

The *Harkin* docked onto the Taurian convoy as it had done twice before. Abigail followed the other Abigail and Fambozi as they walked with Evvie out to the airlock that connected their ship to the Taurian ship. Even after so many hours of watching herself from outside herself, Abigail couldn't get used to the experience.

Evvie had packed some tools and the spare parts into a large canvas bag. "Give me an hour to install the shield and the projector. If I don't make it back, continue with the blast jump, and I will find you."

The other Abigail quirked an eyebrow. "Are you sure you don't need help installing the new parts?"

It was weird for Abigail to watch herself do and say things she had never said before but wanted to say now. The thought of sending Evvie off on her own was disconcerting. She wanted to follow her onto the Taurian ship but felt she was needed on the *Harkin* with the rest of her crew. She needed to find a way to regain control of her body and the ship.

Evvie hoisted her duffel bag. "There's really only room for one person to work at the junction box where I will be connecting the projector and the shield emitter. I'll have to deal with my claustrophobia on my own. I've got it."

The other Abigail checked her watch. "Be careful. We're counting down one hour that you've given yourself to accomplish this. I don't understand why we can't have more time, but I know you can do it."

Evvie headed for the airlock. "If I don't make it back, initiate the jump at the scheduled time. I can't explain how I know that we have only one hour, but I believe there will be an unstoppable blast at that time, no matter what."

Fambozi nodded. "Please come back."

Abigail sensed he wanted to say more, but he left it at that.

As the airlock opened, the three Taurian elders stood waiting to board the *Harkin*, and Evvie boarded their ship.

Abigail followed the group back to the bridge and watched yet another Taurian connection with the three elders. All they could do was sit back and observe. Fortunately, things were proceeding differently than they had for the last two cycles. Evvie was on board the Taurian vessel, attempting to give them the means to escape on their own.

After forty-five minutes, Evvie called in. "I've got the blast-shield generator installed, so they'll be safe no matter what happens, although they might survive the blast only to be stuck orbiting a black hole since it's likely we'll destabilize the neutron star with our blast jump. I'm patching in the new projector now."

Abigail hadn't thought about the possible consequence of creating a black hole by attempting their blast jump.

Fambozi glanced at his watch. "You've spent three-quarters of your time on the shields. Please hurry!"

"Copy that."

Fifteen minutes later, Fambozi called her through the comm. "Evvie, come in. We are just one minute away from the blast jump. Are you going to make it?"

"I'm having some trouble patching in the projector. I need more time."

Abigail knew there was no delaying the explosion, since it was predetermined to ignite. She wished they had allowed for more time, but time had run out.

Fambozi announced, "We have a blast jump in three, two, one, go."

The view port went dark.

Chapter 38

Evvie

The stars came back into existence through their view port.

As if taking a moment to recompose himself following the jump, Fambozi rubbed his stomach and his head, and he looked even more ghostly. He leaned forward, separating from his other self, to study his terminal screen. "Okay, IRENE, can you confirm that we are once again at our original coordinates?"

The robot replied, "Yes. Your assumption is correct. We have yet again come back to when and where we were when we first began the search for the Taurian convoy."

The blast jump hadn't rattled Abigail's organs as much as the previous ones, but she also felt more numb than ever. The continuing lack of physical sensations worried her. She looked around, hoping Evvie had somehow miraculously made it back on board the *Harkin*. "Has anyone seen Evvie?"

There was no sign of the her.

The robot shook her head slowly. "She is not aboard this ship."

The only strong physical sensation Abigail had was a pit in her stomach. She knew it would be too good to be true for Evvie to appear back on board after the blast jump, but if the three Taurians kept vanishing from this ship to rejoin theirs, she didn't see why Evvie hadn't appeared on this ship. Abigail tried clasping her hands, but she could barely feel a tingle as they passed through each other. She thought that if they sat idly for one more cycle of the recurring loop, they would turn fully photonic and never inhabit their physical bodies again.

It was time to try to alter their course and take control of the ship before they were nothing more than ghosts made of light.

Abigail tried to imagine the most positive outcome. "Maybe the Taurian colony ship made their escape, and Evvie's with them. Tkla, has anything changed for you and your link to the Taurian collective?" She hadn't felt any change but hoped he could somehow detect their presence.

He shook his head in despair. "No, I detect nothing. Not even from my mate."

She stood over her other self, who was sitting at her station, performing the same tasks as she had a few times before. "I've got to get through to her—or me—and take control of the ship. We can't go back to the neutron remnant."

Fambozi's eyes went wide. "But what if Evvie is still stuck there?"

"We don't know that she is. I think we are at a point now where we can still change our fate, but if we don't make a change now, we'll be doomed to repeat this cycle and forever lose the ability to change anything."

Fambozi remained wide-eyed. "Can't we go back one more time to make sure Evvie is safe?"

"I honestly don't think we can do anything to change what happens to her." It broke Abigail's heart to say. "We need to escape now, no matter what. It's what Evvie would want us to do."

The doctor crossed his arms and shook his head. "I can't do it. I can't abandon her."

Abigail's heart felt like it was coming apart. "We have to. We can't help her or anyone else until we help ourselves. We have to break the cycle, and now is the time, while we are still far away from the massive pull of the neutron star. We have to turn this ship in a new direction."

He resigned with a solemn nod.

Abigail sat in the same space as her other self and reached out to take control of the ship. She closed her eyes and stated firmly, "Abigail, we cannot go back to the stellar neutron remnant. We have to turn the ship around."

After a full minute, nothing had happened. She felt her other self resisting, determined to save the convoy. "Come on. Why does my other self have to be so thickheaded and determined?"

Silas smiled. "Because she's you."

"It's true," Gavin added. "You've got to figure out a way to convince your other self to change her mind."

She nodded then tightened her grip on the controls, only to feel the same nebulous feeling in her fingers. She tried to send some electricity out to her hands to increase the feeling in them. "Okay, Abigail, you have to trust that everything will be all right. The best way to save your friends is to turn this ship around. We can't save anyone unless we save ourselves first. You have to let me steer the ship." Abigail's hands made contact with the controls of the ship. "Hey, everyone, do what I'm doing and try to take control of your bodies. I think I'm getting feeling back in my fingers."

Her friends hustled to sit with their other selves. Abigail continued to repeat her mantra: "Abigail, you have to trust that everything will be all right. The best way to save your friends is to turn the ship around. You have to let me steer the ship." Her grip tightened on the yoke controls. She began turning the ship.

Once the ship had turned, she hit full thrusters and was pushed into her seat, a feeling she welcomed more than anything. She was back in her body. "Is everyone else back?"

Dr. Fambozi clapped and rubbed his hands together. "I think once you maneuvered the ship into a new direction, it was easier to inhabit my body. You broke the cycle we were stuck in and set us on a new course, so we are in a new space and time."

"I, too, have control of my body," replied Tkla. He flexed his fingers then punched the button to open a comm to the scout team. "Brklana, if you can hear me, resume control of your body and ship and join the *Harkin*. Do not pursue a course toward the neutron star. Gather your squad and retreat. Our colony convoy may no longer be in that direction."

Abigail worried that Brklana was perhaps even more stubborn than she herself had been. Tkla repeated his call over and over, concern growing in his voice.

Abigail watched the blips continue, not changing direction.

Tkla looked at her with desperation. "You have to do something. They're not changing course."

Abigail pushed the comm button. "Squad, listen to me. Focus all of your effort on regaining control of your ships. Tell your other selves that we can't help anyone unless we change direction and set a new course. Just focus on conveying that message and on grasping your ship's controls. You can do it!"

After a long moment of continuing on their course, the blips of the scout ships changed direction on her screen and headed toward the *Harkin*. She designated hangar bays for them to dock in and let out a deep breath that felt like the first real breath she'd taken in days.

∞

Abigail blasted the *Harkin* away from the massive anomaly with the squadron of scout pilots safely aboard. Tkla was holding onto Brklana and nuzzling his snout into her neck.

Ivanovich, the older Russian cosmonaut, was clutching a cup of coffee and had an emergency blanket draped over his shoulders. "So, we don't know where Evvie is?"

Dr. Fambozi shook his head. "I think she's still at the neutron star. Now that we have regained control of the ship, I would like to go back and save her. I know she's still there, just like I knew we needed that extra hour before blast jumping away from the neutron remnant—although I am regretting that I didn't give her more time."

Abigail had to admit that she was considering the same thing, but she forced herself to remain on course, heading away from the super-dense body.

Ivan gulped coffee as if it was a lifesaving remedy. "I second the vote to go back and save her."

Before Abigail could say anything, Gavin asked, "How do we know Evvie is still there? And isn't the neutron star probably a black hole, now that we've disrupted it with our blast jump?"

Fambozi raised a finger into the air. "Actually, it will be a black hole in about thirteen hours. There's time to save her. I don't think she got the projector online in time. If she didn't, then she's still there, and we have to go save her. And there are millions of Taurians we need to rescue too."

Tkla bowed his head. "If my people have not escaped, I will not permit any of you to risk your lives to go back."

Abigail could tell that while he was joyful to have Brklana back, the prospect that the convoy had not escaped was heartbreaking for him too.

Gavin raised an eyebrow. "If Evvie *did* complete her task, where would she and the convoy be now?"

Fambozi's face and aura brightened. "That's a good question. If we kept getting pushed back to now, which is when we began our trip toward the neutron remnant, they probably also got sent back to the point in time when they started following it. How could we determine that?"

Tkla said, "We engaged in a link with their collective. I know they spent three weeks in the wake of the comet."

"Perfect!" Fambozi typed hastily. "IRENE, can you determine where the comet was three weeks ago, based on its velocity and direction of travel?"

IRENE's eyes flickered. "Yes, I have those coordinates now."

"Okay, I guess we have a few options to consider." Fambozi let out a deep breath. "Do we go to where the comet was three weeks ago and where the ship could be traveling from, or do we head to where the neutron comet will collapse into a black hole in thirteen hours?"

Abigail was debating the two options herself, but her gut told her that going back to the massive stellar object was no longer an option. She couldn't subject her friends to that danger again. She kept the ship's thrusters firing away from the neutron star.

"The problem," interjected Silas, "is that if they went back three weeks in time, they won't be at that location now. They will have had time to travel. And if Evvie's with them, they will travel to this location."

"Hey, IRENE," Gavin spouted, "can you calculate their location if you subtract three weeks from the comet's trip then add a trip to this location?"

"Yes, if I knew what their velocity was."

"What if they traveled at two percent of the speed of light?" Tkla asked. "That's only a rough guess of the point at which they were accelerating in their trip."

IRENE replied, "At six thousand kilometers per second, their convoy will get to this location in approximately nine point five days."

Gavin raised his finger into the air. "I have an idea. Why don't we travel in that direction, and we'll intercept them? It shouldn't take longer than four days, and we'll be traveling *away* from the newly forming black hole."

That sounded like a good plan to Abigail, who kept her grip firm on the firing controls of the ship's thrusters. She was realizing that she was possibly abandoning her friend in a black hole but wanted to allow for the possibility that Evvie had succeeded and was out there, heading their way. "IRENE, give me the coordinates so I can adjust our course to intercept them."

Fambozi's frown deepened. "I think we need to go back to the neutron star one more time. Evvie is there, fixing the projector. I just know it. If anyone wants to stay here, I'll go by myself in a smaller ship if need be."

Abigail shook her head. "Max, you don't even know how to fly a ship."

Ivan stood and let his emergency blanket fall to the floor. "I will go. We can take my ship." He raised his mug to get the last few drops of coffee then slammed it onto the workstation. "I am ready!"

Abigail wanted to go find Evvie, probably more desperately than anyone, but she was no longer willing to risk the lives of her friends. "I'm sorry, Max, Ivan, but I can't allow anyone to go back. We wouldn't last ten minutes until we decided to follow you, and then we would all be in the same predicament we just escaped from."

Ivan looked her in the eye. "Are you proposing that you will stop me from flying my own ship to save her?"

Instead of answering him, Abigail pushed the comm button. "Brklana, could you detain any scout ship that breaks formation and attempts to return to the neutron star remnant?"

"I will do so if you make the request."

Ivan bit his lip. "I carry the same rank as Brklana, and I will order all scout ships to stand down. Let's go, doctor. We have our little Lapochka to rescue."

Abigail intentionally left the comm channel open. Brklana's voice came through. "I will perform the duty as a personal request of Abigail's and not as an order. I am sorry, Ivan."

Abigail wished there was something she could say or do to remedy their discontent. "I'm sorry too, but we need to stay firm in our decision to get away."

Max glared at her. "You mean *your* decision."

Abigail had her doubts about whether it was the right thing to do, but she held firm. "Maybe you both should go get some food or rest in your bunks."

She watched Max's anger turn into sadness as he walked toward the exit. Ivan shook his head and narrowed his eyes at Abigail then turned to leave. Abigail's main goal was to get the crew and her friends home safely, but she wasn't sure she had any friends left. Gavin and Silas looked upset, but she couldn't tell if they supported her decision.

Both Ivan and Fambozi were out into the corridor when Silas called out from his station. "Hold on, everyone! We have an incoming transmission." He flipped a switch to patch the transmission through the ship's comm speakers.

A woman's voice came through. "Hold your position! I repeat, hold your position. We are coming in on your port side. We will shoot past you because we don't have enough reverse thrust needed to slow down from a higher velocity to meet you."

Fambozi ran back into the control room. "Evvie, is that you?"

"Yes. We didn't want to keep you waiting, so I modified their thrusters. It's slowing down that's proving to be the real trick."

Abigail couldn't believe her ears. The sound of her friend's voice had turned a moment of despair into one of joy. It took hours for the ships to match speeds. Abigail gave the *Harkin* every ounce of thrust to catch up, while the convoy had made a 180 and was burning to reduce their velocity.

Once the ships finally matched speeds, Evvie met them at the airlock. Abigail rushed to grab onto her, a flood of tears streaming down her cheeks.

Gavin smiled from ear to ear. "It's a good thing you showed up! Fambozi and Ivan were determined to go jump into that black hole for you!"

Abigail let out one more sob. "I'm so glad you made it out of there. How did you do it?"

"I followed my other self onto the convoy and helped her with the installation of the blast-jump projector. I think getting off the *Harkin* allowed for me to have a little more feeling in my hands. At the last moment, I completed the last wire connection and activated the projector for the blast jump. Once we made the jump, my other self and I combined back into a single me. It was almost like we were jolted back together."

Abigail wiped her eyes. "You're so amazing! And now we can all stay away from that stellar monster."

Ivan pinched Evvie's cheek then pulled her in for a hug. "My little Lapochka did it! You saved so many people, and now you're safe!"

Fambozi was next to hug Evvie. He was quite a bit taller than she was, so he had to drop his chin to look into her sparkly eyes as he held her close. "I'm so happy you made it back to us." He cleared his throat as they released their hug. "Um, doesn't anyone want to go study a newly forming black hole? I know precisely when and where it will come into existence."

IRENE flashed her robotic eyes off then on again. "Your attempt at humor is unsuccessful. Let me try. What do you call a ship full of people who go sightseeing at a black hole?"

"I give up. What?" replied Fambozi.

"Dead!"

Silas patted IRENE on her shoulder. "I love a robot with a sense of humor. Let's go home!"

Tkla nodded. "Yes, IRENE, that humor was well executed. You will have to coach me to improve my jokes." He gave the robot a scrunched Taurian attempt at a smile with an eye-wink then turned to Evvie. "Thank you for yet again saving my people. You are a true hero. And thank you, Abigail, for regaining control of the ship and sending us on a new course. I am very happy to be reunited with Brklana and my people."

Abigail didn't want to let Evvie out of her grasp. They held hands as they walked back to the bridge with their friends. She couldn't imagine the pain she would have felt if Evvie had been lost inside a black hole. She knew she would never have forgiven herself if she had abandoned Evvie to save herself and the others. All that mattered was Evvie was safely aboard the ship, and they were ready to head home.

Chapter 39

Observed Rescue

Ringlow entered the chamber, skipped all formalities, and announced, "The convoy managed to escape the imminent black hole!" He did not want to rely on a holo-meeting to present this news.

The Overseer cocked his eyebrows. "What do you mean?"

Ringlow continued into the chamber, where his seat was growing out of the floor. He was not in the mood for the cradling comfort of the globular chair. He wanted to pace the chamber but instead opted to stand and face the Overseer. He paused to catch his breath. "On their third attempt to escape, they managed to free themselves and the colony convoy from the gravitational pull of the neutron core."

The Overseer's eyebrows remained fixed high on his head. "If we could not figure out a way to save them, then how could the humans have done it?"

Ringlow forced himself to take another deep breath. "They somehow broke the cycle after giving the convoy the means to escape on their own, at which point they decided to no longer follow the neutron star. In their previous cycles, making the decision to pursue it was the point of no return. Each vessel had to go back to the point at which following the massive comet was a choice. When each ship made the choice to follow the body, there were no other possible paths but imminent collision with the neutron star."

"But how did they manage to travel back to the point at which they could make the decision not to follow the fragment?" It was rare for the Overseer to be perplexed by anything.

Ringlow explained, "Their first attempt accidentally revealed the nature of a time-space reversal. It was only luck that their crude method for interstellar space travel would convert a space leap into a time leap when they attempted to blast away from the neutron fragment. Their first attempt did not pull the convoy from their path because the convoy had made their choice to follow the comet at a different point in time."

The Overseer tapped his claws on his armrest. "How did they overcome the barrier for both ships to escape?"

"They gave the convoy the means to make their own blast jump to the point at which they could make the decision to follow a different path. Any lesser species would have given up on the convoy to save their own lives. These humans have proven themselves to be resourceful and selfless."

"Yes. Well done! I am glad you are keeping an eye on these humans. They are proving themselves to be an intriguing species."

Ringlow nodded. "Their future is going to be an interesting one to follow." He felt that he personally owed the humans a debt of gratitude for the rescue. He had recently begun to lose hope for humanity because in the last hundred revolutions around their sun, they had proven themselves to be a destructive and warring species, but this was an encouraging turn of events.

There had been many occasions for Ringlow to doubt their survival or the survival of the ecosystems they disrupted. In the back of his mind lurked the possibility that such a barbaric civilization, one who had recently achieved interstellar travel, might need to be prevented from spreading. As invested as he was in their development, he was rational enough to know that if it became necessary, drastic action might be required to avert their expansion into the galaxy. He hoped they would remedy their harmful ways before they attempted to migrate.

Never before had a lesser species performed a feat that would affect galactic history in such an impacting way. And by saving the Taurians, they'd saved his career as an Observer. He wondered if he would ever meet the humans or if, as the Overseer had warned, their expansion into the galaxy would need to be halted.

Chapter 40

Dinosaurs in Space

Once the ships were connected and traveling farther from the neutron star to make their blast jump, Abigail met with the three Taurian leaders who had come aboard the *Harkin*. They met in the common room, which provided comfortable seating, tables, and an expansive view of the million points of starlight that lit up the vastness of space. Through the Taurian collective network, Abigail heard and felt an overwhelming sense of joy and relief at having been saved from the neutron star.

She looked up to the eldest Taurian, who was even taller than Tkla. "Are you sure you don't want to come with us to Earth to see the mother world?"

"Yes, we are sure, Abigail. While it would be tempting to travel to our people's distant planet of origin, we have a new home awaiting us in the Polaris system. We are eager to continue the work you began to make it habitable. We will seed Nidus with plant life then watch it turn green as we orbit the planet in our convoy."

Abigail sighed. "That would be an amazing sight to see." She tried to imagine the new world covered in green. "I understand some families were split up during the evacuation of your home world. If there are any women and children who have family on Earth and would like to join us to travel there, we have room."

"Yes. I will make that offer known to everyone within our convoy."

Abigail nodded. "Also, the animal life that was rescued from Earth before the meteor strike is of great interest to my people. We call them dinosaurs. They have captured humans' imaginations since their fossils were discovered. I remember the very best thing about my first day of kindergarten—the first level of schooling for our young children—was discovering the classroom's collection of plastic toy dinosaurs. It's not uncommon for our young to become experts on their names and to have a favorite one. I know you need animal life for your new world, but would you part with some to be reintroduced into Earth's animal kingdom?"

The Taurian nodded. "This sounds like a noble cause. So yes, we will send a few samples of each species we have brought. We have many extra eggs in cryo-stasis, as well, so we have an abundant supply of animal life."

Abigail hugged the Taurian, which she realized might have surprised the large being. "Thank you! Once Evvie is done showing your people how to operate the projector on your ship and we get any of your crew who wish to travel to Earth, we'll initiate another simultaneous blast jump to send you on your way."

The Taurian took a sideways bow. "We are indebted to you for your assistance. You have proven yourselves to be a heroic people."

"Our assistance isn't done yet. We'll transport your Taurian refugees from Earth to Nidus, once it is habitable."

"We will be indebted for that service as well."

Abigail realized she and all of humanity were counting on sending humans to the colony world, but they hadn't technically been invited by the Taurians. "Will it be okay for humans to settle on your new world, once it's inhabitable?"

The central Taurian lowered his head to Abigail's level, his neck curving. "I have to be honest with you, Abigail. Tkla has shared many details about the humans of Earth, and it should be of no surprise that some of your people's activities are alarming to us."

Abigail felt a pang as if she had just gotten a report card with low grades on it. The Taurian didn't have to list the specific atrocities humans were responsible for: pollution, global warming, the extinction of countless species, the dwindling supply of natural resources, not to mention war, hunger, and suffering. She was very aware of humanity's shortcomings when it came to caring for their world and one another. "Are you saying that you don't want humans on your new world?"

"As you are aware, my people are a very rational race. In light of all of your great deeds, we would feel no regret in making the decision to keep our new world pristine by barring your kind from making it a home."

While it shocked her, she also understood their concern. She had been counting on sending people to Nidus, though, and the thought of informing Silas, the president, and all the people of Earth that humans would not be welcome on the new world broke her heart. She tried to reassure herself that there was time to turn things around on Earth, and Nidus was still far from habitable. "Perhaps we can continue to prove ourselves to you. And then we can earn a place on your new world."

"You have already proven yourselves to be an exemplary and heroic people. We accept your request to be considered co-inhabitants of Nidus, which will be habitable solely because of your efforts to bring water and make peace with the local life. All we require is proof that your reckless and irresponsible stewardship of Earth will be reformed into something more sustainable."

That was exactly what Abigail wanted to accomplish. "I'll personally work hard to make the change our world needs."

"I believe you will. And I do not enjoy portraying my people as ungrateful or selfish, but we have the health of a new planet to consider, and there is the previously established life dwelling in the water that will require our consideration and protection."

"I understand, and I don't blame you for your concerns."

The Taurian gave one more bow. "We thank you, Abigail, for what you have done, and we look forward to the day we meet again."

Abigail imagined the day when Nidus was lush with life and inhabited by the Taurians. She sincerely hoped humans would have a place there too.

∞

With some new Taurian passengers on board, a storage room filled with eggs, and a cargo bay converted into animal pens housing a unique assortment of actual dinosaurs, Abigail initiated the blast jump home. Once they were back in the solar system, she excitedly contacted Eliot so he could begin making arrangements for the new animals. They had a couple weeks of travel left to approach Earth, so he had time to prepare.

While everything had turned out well, her heart was heavy with the prospect of dealing with the blundering humans of Earth. She couldn't help but feel pessimistic in proving that they could be a worthwhile people to invite to the new colony world. But she would try.

Chapter 41

Teamwork

Dr. Cynthia Roberts traveled to Eliot's dino-chicken lab at the Venture Industries compound in New Jersey. Eliot had paid for her plane ticket and had a car waiting for her at the airport.

Once she arrived at the fancy-looking facility and was led into the state-of-the-art lab, she sat and listened to Jane Grant describe their team's progress and what they were still unable to accomplish with the project.

She thought it sounded like an interesting challenge, and she began to understand Eliot's enthusiasm for reintroducing dinosaur qualities into birds. Everyone in the lab looked to her after Jane had finished her presentation. Cynthia composed herself and looked down at her notes, mostly in an effort to avoid the staring eyes. "Okay, so you know which genes are responsible for producing a beak, which you want to replace with genes that produce teeth and a snout, but you haven't altered the genes to produce the proteins on their own. So the next step will be to block the beak gene in the DNA."

Dr. Hornwell, a sturdy, stubbled man with a graying ponytail, nodded. "Yes, teeth are the next big hurdle."

Cynthia had never met such a rugged man. She looked back at her notes to focus again. "What are birds' closest relatives that do have teeth?"

"The crocodile," replied three different people at once.

"Great. Can I see some crocodile DNA to compare it to the chickens'?"

"Certainly." Jane Grant typed on her laptop. "We have a comparison already on file, but it's the actual procedure that's challenging us. Every attempt just produces a jumbled mess."

"Okay." Cynthia wrote a quick note on her pad. "How about instead of Frankensteining a monster, let's first try altering the proteins that those genes produce. That might give us some clues about to how to splice the genes."

Cynthia set herself to work. She quickly learned each team member's strengths so she could ask for help to fill in the gaps in her own knowledge. She had never worked as part of a team before and found their variety of specialties, skills, and perspectives valuable. They attentively listened to all her ideas. Maybe they appreciated her fresh outlook on solving the problem. Although she couldn't see auras, she thought Eliot glowed with excitement to see some progress. JJ looked luminous, as well, and he kept smiling at her.

At lunchtime, she walked out of the building and toward the garden patio area with her lunch bag. JJ intercepted her and asked to join her.

Truthfully, Cynthia had been looking forward to eating by herself to gather some of the energy she had expended by interacting with so many people, but she agreed. She felt her face grow warm.

They sauntered to the courtyard, JJ pushing the sleeping infant in a stroller. Cynthia had watched the baby play during their initial meeting and admired the way the man cared for her. She wondered what it would be like to hold and play with the wide-eyed, adorable bundle. Perhaps if the infant woke, she would ask to hold her.

It was a pleasant day, and the water flowing in the artificial stream sparkled in the sun as they walked over an arching bridge. Cynthia tried to make small talk. "This is a nice facility."

He glanced around. "Yeah, they did a good job of making it pleasant enough. I still prefer the wide-open spaces of Montana."

She selected a seat at a table. "Is that where the best dinosaur fossils are found too?"

JJ parked the stroller and sat down, too, placing his crumpled brown paper bag onto the table. "Yeah, some very important finds have been made in Montana. In fact, the first dinosaur found in all of North America was found there."

"It must be exciting to make that sort of discovery."

He pulled an apple from his lunch sack and bit into it. "Yes. It's probably similar to some of the discoveries you've made. Abigail and Eliot are two of the most interesting people I've ever met."

Cynthia unpacked all the items from her insulated lunch bag then arranged them carefully. "I didn't have anything to do with creating their personalities. I just bypassed some limiting blocks in their DNA." She did suppose her discovery was somewhat similar to finding the fossilized remains of dinosaurs because it was a gene structure that existed in the ancient past. The alien body at Edmund's Air Force base was proof of that.

"How do you think the blocks were placed there, anyway?" JJ asked.

"That's a good question. My work since then has been to find blocks in other people. I'm finding that we all have blocks in our DNA. The only difference between some people, like Abigail when I first met her, and others, like her twin sister, is that some people have proteins that are trying to bridge the blocks. Those proteins are how I discovered the blocks in the first place."

He narrowed his eyes. "Maybe aliens put them there? Sorry, I'm not usually a conspiracy theorist."

Cynthia played along, "Or maybe it's a top-secret government conspiracy? They want to keep humanity from evolving so we don't rise up against our oppressors."

They both laughed. His was a deep chuckle.

She smiled. "I think the blocks were probably introduced at some point in ancient human history, but I think their existence will probably remain an unsolved mystery."

"Hey, that rhymes!"

She felt her face heat another ten degrees. She tried to sit back and relax. "I guess I'm a poet, and I didn't know it." *Oh my god, this is a nightmare. Where did the rhyming come from? Maybe I could turn the conversation back toward his interests.* She cleared her throat. "Why do you like dinosaurs so much?"

He repositioned himself in his chair. "I think there's something youthful about feeling the wonder and imagining dinosaurs having once roamed the Earth. That magic gets pummeled out of us when we're forced to grow up. What were you interested in as a child?"

She winced at the thought of admitting it. "I was really into horses. It's all I would draw, and I would concoct plans to sell our apartment and move to the country, where I could own a horse. My parents had careers that kept us in the city, so I grew up as a horse-less city girl."

"I'm intrigued by horses too. In fact, the fossil record of their evolution is more complete than most any other species. Their evolutionary family tree is displayed at many museums. Horses are *almost* as amazing as dinosaurs."

She laughed, her face cooling a little. She really liked how knowledgeable and passionate he was about his career.

"But seriously," JJ continued, "they're powerful animals. When a horse turns its head, it can literally knock a person over. I have to admit, I'm a little afraid of them."

"Scared of horses? What's there to be scared of?"

"Well, they can step on you, for one. And if you're riding way up on one and it bucks you off, that's a long distance to fall. Horseback riding is more dangerous than people realize."

"Well, I've put off riding one, because there was always something more pressing, like school, studies, and now my research."

JJ pulled out his phone and typed away. Cynthia hadn't pegged him for the type to check his texts or social media in the middle of a conversation. She was a little disappointed that he had been so personable yet had become distracted by his phone.

"Here!" He held up the screen to show her. "There's a stable with riding lessons and some trails. And it's only sixty-eight minutes away."

"Don't you think we're a little too busy to take a field trip?" Actually, it sounded like a date.

He winked at her. "You know, Eliot has a strict policy that all his employees take one day off per week to prevent burnout. He sees it as way to increase productivity. He's implemented the policy for his own selfish reasons, not for our benefit."

"That kid rubbed me the wrong way when I first met him, but at least he doesn't try to hide the fact that he's only interested in his own personal gain."

JJ laughed. "You really created a monster with that one."

She grimaced, remembering how terrible he'd been. "He was already a monster. I just helped to turn him into a super-monster. Yes, count me in." Cynthia hadn't been on a date in ages.

She realized Eliot was solely responsible for bringing her to this new place and meeting this man who wanted to hang out with her. She teased the handsome paleontologist: "We'll request the most docile horse for you, since you're scared, and if there is a horse that has 'princess' in her name, that's the one I want."

Chapter 42

Staff Meeting

Eliot hosted a staff meeting in the lobby of his research center. He planned to begin by announcing their huge advancements before he had to deal with one item of unpleasant business. So far, all the progress they'd made at the facility had been kept secret, at least before a staff leak was aired on every news channel the previous night. Eliot had had to cross a line of protestors on his way in that morning.

He tried to forget about those issues as he made a toast with some sparkling grape soda in a coffee mug. "This is a momentous day!" He stood on the landing of the stairs, which had been built on widely spaced concrete pillars to look as if they were floating. It gave him a view to overlook his staff. "We are all new mamas and papas to some baby chicks that are no longer chickens!"

The crowd applauded. He saw his partner, Tom, in the group. While not a geneticist, he was just as responsible for the milestone, since he'd kept Venture Industries afloat through Eliot's economic hardships. Tom wasn't usually a smiley person, but his grin stood out among the crowd.

Eliot kept his mug raised. "Our six new dino-chickens have everything we wanted: snouts with teeth, hands with claws, and tails!"

The group hooted and hollered.

Eliot grinned while waiting for them to quiet. "This would not have been possible without the work of all of you, but I want to specifically commend Dr. JJ Hornwell, Jane Grant, and most importantly, Dr. Cynthia Roberts. You three are amazing! And you're fertilizing more eggs every day, right?"

Jane nodded and smiled.

"We also have two other breakthroughs to celebrate. The first is that my sister contacted me from their ship because they are back in the solar system, and they have a cargo bay full of animals from the Taurian world, plus extra eggs. They'll be arriving home in about a week. She says the animals look and act just how she imagined dinosaurs would. And... we have a place to put them. With the help of my business partner, Tom, who manages to save money instead of losing it, we have acquired an entire island! Thank you, Tom."

Everyone cheered. Tom's smile eclipsed those of the others in the crowd. "The sales of a few of your high-end robots have helped too."

Tom was right. Eliot had produced a handful of robots, whose sales added up to a decent revenue. He'd started a line of more masculine robots that he considered his butler line. They weren't quite as complex as IRIS and IRENE, but they served their purpose well. The money that came in from their sales certainly helped. He planned on keeping the New Jersey location as a factory for commercial robots while developing larger and more experimental projects on the island.

Eliot announced, "It's called Windermere Island, and it's only two hundred miles off the coast of Florida, in the Bahamas. Fortunately, there's already been some building development, so we won't have to start from scratch. It has an airstrip and some infrastructure, like roads and building sites. We're going to start construction of a new research facility. So the big question is: who wants to go live on a tropical island?"

Everyone in the group raised their hands and cheered. One smart-ass said, "But I want to stay here in New Jersey!"

Eliot shook his head. "Hmmm, New Jersey or a tropical island—tough choice. So the island, which is over five hundred acres, is linked to a larger island with a gated bridge. We might have to reinforce that gate, depending on how big our dinosaurs get!"

The group laughed.

"The beautiful thing about the new location is that all of the creatures Abigail will be bringing will be free to roam across the entire island. They'll be free-range dinosaurs." Eliot glanced around at his staff. He tried not to pay too much attention to the only person there whose aura showed a nervousness that stood out among the other employees. He would soon have to deal with that staff member.

He wanted to stay focused on how awesome his island was going to be. "Even though there is a fair amount of work that needs to be done, there's a town on the larger island with hotels, shops, and housing. This means we don't have to rough it on Windermere during construction. I suppose we could rename the island. Any suggestions?"

"Dinosaur Island!" an intern hollered.

"That's a possibility... I guess. It's not super original. Maybe I'll start a post for entries in a contest on our social media."

Eliot could not have been happier with his team's progress. It was like all the fantasies he could have ever dreamed up as a kid were coming true.

He noticed the one troubled aura in the crowd again and sighed, realizing that the morning wasn't going to be all celebration. "So... did anyone see the news last night or notice the protestors at our front gate this morning?"

The crowd instantly quieted. Eliot was referring to the leak someone had made to the press about their new creations, complete with cell-phone photos of the newly hatched dino-chickens. One person among his staff had betrayed him and his company, and that man's aura stood out.

Eliot's smile faded. "I've had to triple our security team because I'm worried some of the protestors are capable of vandalism or arson. We've identified members of an eco-terrorist group called Earth Liberation Force, who have claimed responsibility for burning genetically modified trees in an Oregon lab because they think it's 'unacceptable to be tampering with nature.' There are other protestors out there from PETA who are worried that we're causing harm and suffering to our lab creations. And there're even some religious protestors who think we shouldn't be 'playing God.'"

Eliot had flown a drone to photograph each face in the crowd then performed background checks on each protestor. Some of their signs branded slogans like "Who died and made you God?"

"Stop tampering with nature!" and "Animals are not ours to experiment on."

The guilty face among his staff went white with shock.

"Haven't I taken good care of you? You're all very well paid, I've eliminated your student debt, and each of you owns stock in the company—so this is your company too. What benefit could any of you have by leaking this?"

The guilty lab technician sank into his chair.

"Not only that, but all of you have signed nondisclosure agreements."

Every member of his staff, including Tom, looked around as if trying to detect the culprit.

It was time to send the lab tech packing. "Jared Weaver, it's time to gather your belongings. You'll be escorted off the property. As detailed in the NDA, by disclosing classified intel to the press, you've forfeited your severance package and the stock you owned in Venture Industries. I thought I had more intelligent people working here, but you've made a poor decision. I won't pursue any legal action unless you continue to violate your nondisclosure agreement. That means no interviews with the press."

Two of his security guards walked to each side of Jared, who stood then left.

Eliot almost felt sorry for the young man, but then he thought about how inconvenient the whole thing was. He had big plans to unveil his accomplishments when the time was right, which would have been closer to the opening day of his dinosaur resort. He knew his sister had dealt with a public relations disaster when she'd accidentally shocked a crowd of people at the beach, and he was grateful this wasn't worse. He realized he might need to hire a PR team to manage his public image. Perhaps his sister could help.

Eliot wasn't happy to put a damper on an otherwise festive event. He raised his mug one more time. "To everyone else, thank you for your hard work and dedication. Let's not let one bad apple spoil this special occasion!"

Luckily, they were going to relocate to a new location for their work. It was time to move, and a secluded tropical island would be perfect. He couldn't wait to see their new dino-chickens roam there alongside the dinosaur-like animals his sister had stowed aboard her ship that was heading home.

Chapter 43

Arrival

Once in orbit, Abigail, Silas, and Gavin boarded a shuttle so they could travel to meet with the president. Evvie remained aboard the *Harkin* to oversee the unloading of their cargo—the animals from the Taurian world—and to coordinate the departure of the Taurian passengers who had come to be reunited with fellow refugees. Brklana piloted the shuttle to the Washington National Airport, where a driver collected them and transported them to the White House.

As they entered his office, the president gave them all handshakes. They sat across from him at his large mahogany desk. Abigail was happy to be home, but the Taurians' reluctance to allow humans to occupy their new world weighed heavily on her. She hoped she could help advance humanity into a future where they could become responsible stewards of Earth.

"Welcome home," he said, letting a smile shine on his otherwise haggard face. "I'm so glad you made it safely. It sounds like you really risked your necks out there."

Abigail nodded. "It was a pretty dangerous situation, but we survived. The Taurians are now at Nidus to seed their world with plant life. It feels good to have helped them arrive at their new home, and we saved so many lives."

He shuffled a pile of papers on his desk. "You are true heroes. I'm sorry you're not coming home to a more unified and peaceful Earth."

"Is it really much worse than when we left?" She had a bad feeling that global conflict was on the rise. Gavin and Silas sat stiffly upright in their chairs.

"Unfortunately, it is." He leaned into his chair and crossed his arms. "The world is more divided than ever, and so is America. We succeeded in getting China out of South America, but they're not happy about it. Admiral Rendón also accomplished his task in sending the Japanese whaling ships home from Antarctica empty-handed with no whale meat, so they're not happy. We haven't even messed with Russia, but they're pledging support to the China-Japan coalition. Russia is demanding we give back their cosmonaut Ivanovich Korshunov, but Ivan wants to continue to serve in the Federation Space Force, so Russia is not happy. A few other countries have joined their coalition. Together, they're blocking us from their waters and airspace."

Abigail pursed her lips. "That's unsettling. It's frustrating that I can't think of a way to unify the world." She decided to wait to tell everyone about the Taurians' reluctance to allow humans onto the colony world. Global conflict on Earth wasn't going to help their case.

"It gets worse," the president continued. "Many states in this country have united as a Confederation. We call them the oil states, because they don't want to give up their oil drilling. They claim they are protecting capitalism and the Constitution. We have the armed forces on our side, but they've put together a considerable citizen militia."

Abigail thought of her brother, who at a very young age had learned the word "capitalism" and claimed he was a capitalist.

Abigail's favorite word at a similar age had been "paleontologist." She thought it was funny how young children latched onto big words as if they were badges they could wear to prove how grown-up they were. She and her brother had agreed to disagree about politics, because even with his transformation, he thought everyone should simply pull themselves up by their bootstraps and work harder to make their lives better.

Abigail thought everyone's basic needs should be met, no matter what, and knew that sometimes, people had no bootstraps to begin with. It was disconcerting to hear that half the country was banding together, thinking that capitalism was something they needed to protect.

Gavin gripped the armrests of his chair. "I would hate to see violence escalate among American citizens. Any bloodshed would ignite a civil war that would be unstoppable."

The president nodded solemnly. "Yes, the American Civil War was a perpetual nightmare for the same reason. Once any Americans die on either side, they have fuel to keep fighting, and the only way to end it would be to fight until one side has exhausted its resources. It would be tragic for everyone. Even though no violence has occurred yet, the country is literally divided, with borders being drawn to separate the oil states from the Federation. At this point, the Confederation has seceded from the nation and is blocking travel between their states and ours."

Silas and Gavin both winced. It was terrible news. Abigail had a sinking feeling that unity among the human species was becoming increasingly unattainable.

Silas furrowed his brows. "Are there any ways to leverage them without violence, like sanctions where we don't allow goods to enter their boarders?"

"Well, many states, like California, are providing food for us, but the oil states have enough food-producing states to be okay on their own, and they're trading with other countries with whom we are not. I'm trying to get Mexico into the Federation, which would help. A lot of food is imported from there to many of the oil states, which, in turn, sell oil to Mexico. We're actually the ones suffering because of trade sanctions."

Silas shook his head. "It sounds like the oil states have something valuable to offer in trade with other countries, which makes an embargo between them and the Federation less effective."

The president sighed. "Yes, they're continuing to trade with China. Many of our states are beginning to run out of inventory of manufactured goods because of our trade embargo with China."

Abigail's excitement about their recent trip evaporated as the grim prospect of continued division and confrontation threatened the world.

Gavin scrunched his face as if trying hard to think of a solution. "This is terrible. Why's the world got to be so divided?" He rested his chin on his hand. "The only thing I can think of that could unite the world would be for a giant meteorite to head straight toward Earth. That would end the pettiness pretty quickly."

Abigail agreed that humanity needed a new perspective. She didn't necessarily want to see widespread peril bring about that unity, but she knew something had to change. Before her genetic treatment, which felt like a lifetime ago, she had felt helpless to affect change in the world. She hated that she felt that way now and couldn't imagine what one person could do to bring about change. "Maybe you can send me as a diplomat to speak with members of the oil states and to other countries like China and Japan?"

The president frowned. "I suppose that's something we can consider. In the meantime, I've got a speech planned that I'm going to deliver outside in an hour, and I would love to thank you in front of the cameras and the press. I think your presence could help. Would all of you accompany me onstage?"

"Of course," she replied. She thought appearing before the world after accomplishing their daring rescue and paving the way for a new world to be colonized could perhaps help unite people in a cause. She hated thinking about a future in which humans couldn't stop bickering and fighting long enough to focus on advancements like colonizing another world.

Abigail was surprised to see her family and friends seated in the front row below the stage. She ran and hugged her parents and sister. Ives was there, too, his chest and arms causing his suit jacket to bulge almost to splitting. She hadn't seen their faces for what felt like a lifetime. She noted Eliot's absence and wondered what he was up to.

She held on to each of her parents. "I had no idea you'd be here. I wish we had more time to catch up." She glanced at her watch.

"He's going to begin soon, but I'll catch up with you afterwards." She wanted to ask about her brother too.

They nodded as she left to rush onto the stage then took her seat.

The president wore a stern expression as he began his speech. "As many of you already know, these are tough times. No one ever said that change was easy. We've made some major accomplishments, but we've faced some major setbacks as well."

His face and aura brightened. "I'd like to talk about some of those endeavors, and maybe we can get excited about the future. Let me describe the new planet our Space Force team visited. It sounds similar to Mars, but it's closer to being habitable. Abigail, would you like to let the world know what your team accomplished?"

Abigail was in no way prepared to address the crowd or the world. She did, however, see an opportunity to convey a message of unity. She stood and joined him at the podium.

"Um, greetings, everyone." She had no idea how to begin her speech. "It's good to be back. I have to be honest, though… I wish I was returning to a more unified world. If anyone hasn't heard, the world we visited could be a potential new home for humanity.

"Our team dropped water to the surface and into the atmosphere, so it's on its way to becoming a planet we can live on. By doing so, we made peace with the local aquatic life that nearly killed one of our crew in an effort to protect their world. Without the water we delivered and the alliance we made with the beings, no one would be able to live there. But the alien life on the planet has now welcomed colonists. The huge Taurian convoy of ships is there now, seeding the entire planet so that it may someday be habitable."

The audience applauded.

She continued, "We're not ready to take that step, though, because we need to get our own house in order before we can move to a new one. What I mean is that we need to stand together to take care of our planet and of each other. Only then will the Taurians welcome us to join them on their new world." She looked at Silas and Gavin, who both wore determined expressions. She hadn't mentioned the Taurians' reluctance to either of them yet.

The president, who remained standing beside her, cut in. "We do have a lot of work ahead of us. I think maybe we can all be inspired by the selfless bravery of our heroes, who risked everything by rescuing the Taurian convoy, who would not have arrived safely to their new world and instead would have perished in a newly forming black hole. I think it would be pretty hard for any of us to imagine the danger they were in. As I understand, black holes are not to be trifled with. I would like to personally commend our Space Force team for a job well done!"

Abigail nodded and smiled. Her parents beamed from their seats. Members of the crowd smiled and clapped. Maybe her accomplishments could inspire the rest of the world to unite.

The president gave her a sideways hug then continued his speech. "Thank you, Abigail. I too wish you had come home to a more united world too. There are bigger rifts than ever between the countries of this world, and there's division within this one. I have to admit that I have had some very discouraging days. I would like to take a moment to ask the rest of the world: don't you want to be part of something bigger, like sending humanity to the stars? Or do you really want to be stuck on this planet, bickering and fighting over resources?"

Boos erupted from the audience.

Abigail nodded. She wondered how anyone could disagree with what he was working toward—a unified world.

He nodded. "I get discouraged by the state of our world, but then I get a ray of hope from people like Abigail Montrose, who puts her life on the line every time she goes into space to advance humanity. She and her friends Silas, Gavin, and Evvie are taking humanity to a new frontier. And you, too, Dr. Fambozi—I heard you were quite the heroic leader on the last mission."

Max Fambozi flashed a smile and waved from his seat next to Tkla and Brklana.

"You are also turning this planet around and are working tirelessly to make it a better place. Even if the progress seems slow, you are making a difference. Abigail, you are a true superhero."

Abigail remained standing next to the president but motioned for her friends to join her onstage. Silas, Gavin, Dr, Fambozi, and their friend Ives—even though he hadn't been part of the space mission—gathered around. Abigail felt that maybe there was hope. She smiled and waved to the crowd and cameras.

Then, gunshots rang out in quick succession.

Abigail had never seen Ives move more quickly. He bolted past her and onto the president, tackling him to the stage and covering him with his body.

After two shots rang through the air, Abigail waited, anticipating more, but none came. She lifted her head from the stage to peer into the seating area below the stage to see her family and friends scurrying. Gavin and Silas had jumped down to join her parents, and they huddled low to the ground. Abigail studied the crowd to look for who could have fired the shots. She thought she might spot them by their aura, but she saw no one displaying anything other than fear and alarm.

The president remained lying with Ives, who pressed a hand to the other man's chest. "Let me speak to Abigail," the president called.

Abigail knelt beside the president, Russell, her friend. Ives pressed her hand onto his chest then sat back against the podium and held his left hand over his own shoulder. He'd been shot too.

She looked into the his eyes with a reassuring nod. "We've got paramedics coming. You're going to be okay." Blood seeped between her fingers though. "Russell, I have something I need to tell you. The effects of your Illumination wore off within just a few months. You have been who you are by your own choice. When we returned from our first space mission from Mars and Kronos, I noticed the difference in you. You were back to normal, whatever that means." She let out a laugh that choked her as it turned into a sob. "You are who you chose to be. I didn't change that. Stay with me. We'll get you patched up." She continued to hold pressure on his chest.

Despite the pain he must have been in, he let a hint of a smile shine through. "My friends call me Russ… Thank you for all you have done. I am relieved to be leaving the world in your hands. I'm sorry about Ives. I hope he recovers."

"Ives will be fine. Don't worry about him." A security agent had laid Ives down and was tending to him.

The president said, "That's wonderful news…"

Abigail watched as his aura faded until it disappeared.

Chapter 44

Shooter

Uniformed police and Secret Service agents ushered Abigail's friends and family away from the stage. Abigail joined Ives, who was receiving treatment from a paramedic.

"We've caught the perpetrator," a male voice reported over an officer's radio. The officer stood over the president's body, vigilantly peering out at the dispersing crowd as if danger still lurked.

Abigail wanted to stand but remained with Ives. She called up to the officer, "I want to interrogate him and find out who's responsible for this." She gave Ives, who looked to be in good hands with the paramedic, a pat then stood to face the officer. "I am personally going to make sure whoever did this is held accountable."

The uniformed woman raised her eyebrows. "Once the perpetrator is booked, you'll have to get clearance through the appropriate channels. The feds are in charge of the investigation."

Abigail dug into the chest pocket of her jacket hoping to find... *Yes! I still have it.* "Is this clearance enough?" She handed over her laminated badge she had been issued when she was living on the Air Force base. It had an FBI stamp on it.

"Um," the woman said, "it says 'guest advisor,' not 'federal agent.'" She looked Abigail up and down then studied the photo on the badge—Abigail with her pure-white buzz cut hair. She returned the badge to Abigail. "I'll see what I can do."

Abigail must have made a good impression with the officer because after she saw Ives off in an ambulance, the woman offered to drive Abigail to the federal building, where the perpetrator was detained.

∞

Abigail flashed her badge to a doughy uniformed guard, who shrugged and led her to the door of a holding cell.

"Who did it?" Abigail asked. "What kind of person could have shot the president?" She was still in shock. Yes, she had lost a friend, but more than feeling the sadness of the loss, anger overtook her. He had been killed while earnestly trying to help the world.

"Actually, the shooter isn't exactly a person." The ginger-haired officer opened the door to the holding cell. "This is IOTA."

A robot that had the same molded white panels as the others her brother had made was chained to the stainless-steel table in the cell. Abigail was stunned, feeling electricity surge through her body and out to her fingertips. "Bring in my brother, Eliot Montrose."

During interrogation, the robot denied shooting the president and claimed to have been inactive during the entire morning when the shooting took place. Dealing with a machine with no emotions or aura to read was frustrating, its denial infuriating. Maybe she would be able to get more information out of her brother.

∞

Eliot had never felt so shaken as when two federal agents and ten uniformed officers arrived at his facility to arrest him. All of his employees watched as he was escorted out of the building. It was humiliating, and he had no idea why he was being apprehended.

After being fingerprinted and forced to change into an orange jumpsuit, he was placed in an interrogation room and handcuffed to a table. Moments after the guard left, his sister burst in.

"What the hell, Eliot! I gave you a second chance. I don't even want to hear any explanations or excuses. It's over. Dr. Roberts was worried about you misusing your abilities, and I defended you. Now, my friend is dead, and the world is in danger without him."

"Wait, what are you talking about? Do you think I killed the president?" His stomach dropped to think that his arrest was related to the assassination. "I wasn't anywhere close to the White House when it happened."

"Well, a robot named IOTA was caught red-handed."

That was not good. "I'm sorry about the president. I really am. But IOTA was not designed to kill anyone." Eliot winced at the thought that maybe he had been negligent in the sale of the robot. "I guess I never thought of performing background checks on my customers. It was just a rich guy who said he wanted an assistant for household duties. He mentioned he didn't trust hired help. I figured he had valuables in his home that he didn't want to go missing. You have to believe me." Eliot couldn't believe his life had taken such a turn from epic success and accomplishment to locked-up criminal.

Abigail stood over him with her knuckles on the table. "Can we track down the buyer? Surely you filed some contact information."

"He paid in cash and told me if he had any problems with the robot, like warranty stuff, he'd contact me. I don't have any information on the buyer."

"Great. That's just great. Someone comes in flashing cash, and you lose all integrity when it comes to the safety of others."

"I'm sorry. After the stock market crash, I felt desperate to make some sales. I'll perform background checks in the future."

"There's not going to be a future… for you or your robots."

Eliot began to apologize again, but his sister cut him off.

"I don't care one iota about anything you have to say. Sorry, you set me up for that. This is much worse than abducting an egg then returning it, Eliot. Somebody's dead."

"You have to believe that I had no intention of creating a robot that could kill anyone. This is impossible because helping and protecting humans is the underlying core of their programming." The fact that she wouldn't believe him was almost worse than the knowledge that someone was dead because of his robot.

"Mister Montrose," interjected the officer who had been watching from the door, "you are under arrest. Anything you say and do can and will be held against you in a court of law. You can make one phone call."

Eliot had no plans to call a lawyer. He considered calling his partner, Tom, but he thought of someone who might be more adept to help with legal matters, although technically, she wasn't really a lawyer or a person.

A few hours after Eliot's arrest, a slim woman walked into his holding cell, wearing a skirt suit, high heels, and deep-red lipstick. She was accompanied by a guard who held the door open as she entered. She was explaining, "I am functioning as my maker's—I mean Eliot Montrose's lawyer. It is necessary that I speak to him. I would also like to question the perpetrator."

Eliot could see a pink glow in the guard's aura, revealing the man to be smitten with the well-dressed and made-up woman who lacked any sort of aura of her own.

Eliot had been working on artificial skin for his robot, modeled with realistic human features, but it was an upgrade his staff had to install in his absence. "IRIS!" He eyed the guard, waiting for him to leave before saying anything more. The guard gave her one last scrutinizing glance then left them alone.

"Wow, your face turned out amazing! Very believable!"

IRIS smiled. "I've been practicing facial expressions in the mirror. I am pleased with my upgrades."

Despite his dire situation, Eliot was thrilled with how the robot's enhancements had turned out. His team had replaced her molded plastic panels with realistic cast latex. "I'm glad we produced some realistic features for you before I got locked up. I'm sorry I wasn't there to help install them. Nice eyes! Let's see how your hands turned out?"

She blinked her new eyes, which still had a faint glow to them but were otherwise a natural-looking amber-brown, then held out her hands. They looked just like a woman's, detailed with nicely manicured nails. "I am very pleased. Your staff did a fine job of installing my new features."

Eliot had planned on her upgrades long before the incident, and as he had been escorted out, he'd asked his team leader to finish the work. The excitement of seeing her upgrades nearly eclipsed the terror of being accused and incarcerated for a crime he didn't commit. Yet the heavy cuffs chained to the table reminded him of the trouble he was in. "I'm pretty sure they won't be giving robots access to any public buildings, so it's fortunate that we had your parts ready."

She blinked again. "Luckily, I did not have to go through any metal detectors."

"That's a good one." Eliot chuckled, but it faded into more of a groan. "Silas would appreciate your humor. In fact, we could really use his help. Could you contact him? Maybe he'll be more receptive than my sister."

"It is not pleasant to see you in this state of incarceration, although I am pleased to be here to assist. I have contacted Silas, who is on his way. I may be of service to help clear your name, but I do not think I can do it alone."

Eliot couldn't help but think of the marketability of robots with more realistic human features, but as his sister had pointed out, he might not have a future in making robots. He raised his cuffed hands to rub his face. While he was devastated at the thought that the president had been killed at the hands of one of his creations, he knew there had to be some sort of mistake and that it was impossible for one of his robots to have done this.

For twenty minutes, he and IRIS debated possible causes or defects that could have led to IOTA's actions. Neither could come up with a plausible scenario. Eliot began to wonder if perhaps he had overlooked some sort of glitch. "IRIS, would you be capable of shooting a gun at a human with the intent to kill?"

"It is challenging to imagine a scenario in which I would consider such an action to have any benefit, but if a human was threatening harm to other humans, I could see the rationale for killing one human to save many."

That didn't help.

After some clanking outside Eliot's cell, a guard opened the door and allowed Silas in.

Eliot wanted to stand to greet him, but his chained handcuffs wouldn't allow it. "Thanks for coming, Silas!"

Silas looked IRIS over with raised eyebrows, like the guard had done earlier, then focused on Eliot. "Man, did one of your robots really shoot the president? And why isn't Abigail here?"

"You could say she's disowned me. I swear that I don't think it's possible for IOTA to have shot anyone. I tried to explain that to her, but she didn't want to hear it."

Silas took a seat across from Eliot. "She must be very upset. I didn't get a chance to see her after the incident. I was just giving my statement to the feds. She's probably making her statement too. Maybe we should include her in figuring this out."

"I don't think she wants to be in the same room as me right now."

Silas shook his head. "She's definitely having a hard time with this. Let's give her some space and see what we can figure out on our own. We can fill her in once we discover anything. What's your plan?"

"Well, you know IRIS. She has access to IOTA, but she's pretending to be a lawyer, not a robotics specialist. Could you go examine IOTA to see how he was tampered with?"

Silas studied IRIS. "Wow, IRIS, I fell in love with you when you were just metal and plastic. You look amazing! You had me fooled that you were some hotshot lawyer."

"Thank you, Silas. And thank you for coming to the aid of Eliot. As you know, seeing him in this predicament is unsettling to my programming."

Silas scrunched his face. "You know, I bet if IRIS and I can talk to the right person, we can bring IOTA into this cell, so you can help study him to find evidence of any tampering. IRIS, you've probably downloaded some lawyer knowledge, right?"

"I have downloaded a sizeable amount, but unfortunately, there is not much precedent in a case like this."

"I'm sure you'll do the best you can." Silas tapped on the steel door for the guard to allow IRIS and him to leave.

∽

After a long twenty minutes—although Eliot was having a hard time keeping track of time—Silas, IRIS, and IOTA were escorted into his cell. He was amazed by how IRIS presented herself as a confident lawyer.

Silas grinned. "Man, she really held her ground to make this happen."

The guard took a seat in the corner and pulled out his phone. His interest was instantly diverted by the small glowing screen.

Silas added in a low voice, "Maybe you should create a new line of lawyer-bots. She quoted all kinds of statures and legal terminology."

A ray of hope sliced though his despair. "Thank you, IRIS. I knew you'd be the most helpful person to me right now." He realized that he'd just referred to her as a *person*.

"May I begin my interrogation of IOTA?" IRIS asked to the police officer who was sitting by the door.

The officer grunted in response. "Be my guest, lady. We haven't gotten anything useful out of him."

"Good afternoon, IOTA. How are you?"

The robot looked at her then flicked its eyes off then on, mimicking blinking. Eliot studied IOTA, who stood motionless with his hands cuffed together. He had seen IRIS show remorse for crashing the stock market and thought that if the robot had killed someone, it would be showing some sign of regret, but it remained standing tall and unconcerned. "I am functioning within acceptable parameters."

IRIS asked, "How long has it been since you were purchased and were no longer the property of Venture Industries?"

"It's been thirteen days, four hours, eighteen minutes, and fourteen seconds."

"And in that time, how long were you operational and serving the function for which you were purchased?"

"I was operational for less than a third of my time away from Venture Industries."

IRIS paused as if considering, although Eliot knew she didn't need any extra time to process information. Maybe she was trying to mimic humans' delayed response times. "Are you aware of anything that happened in your time of inoperativeness?"

"I am not. My power switch was turned off manually."

IRIS continued with a more rapid stream of questions. "Are you aware of any additional components that were added to your system?"

"I am not."

"Who is you new owner?"

"I cannot access that information. I am detecting corruption in my files."

"Have you ever pointed and fired a handgun?"

"I have not."

"Have you been told to lie in response to any of these questions?"

"I have not."

Silas interjected, "Maybe he was instructed to lie when asked *that* question?"

"I believe I would be able to detect if he were lying." IRIS gave Silas a wink and lowered her voice. "I am studying him as I ask questions leading to the most important one. IOTA, did you shoot the president?"

"I did not."

"If you were commanded to kill the president, would it be within your abilities to do so?"

"It would go against my fundamental programming. I believe it would cause irreparable harm to my coding if I were placed in a situation where killing a human was considered an act of least harm."

IRIS tapped her new fingernails against the metal table. "You mentioned your power was switched off during much of the time since you were purchased. Were you functioning this morning at 10:25 am?"

"I was not. My last period of operation ended yesterday at 6:05 pm."

IRIS scrunched her face in a very human gesture. "I think it's time to look inside. Can we remove some panels?"

Eliot wanted to get up to help remove them, but he couldn't. Being cuffed to the table was infuriating and humiliating. "There are some release levers on each side. They should just pop off."

Silas jumped from his seat to remove the robot's chest and back plates.

Eliot immediately saw something that was not part of the original construction of the robot. "What's that box at the base of his neck?" He gritted his teeth at the thought of someone tampering with his robot, but he realized that it was evidence that might help.

IRIS pointed at the box, which had been wired directly into its spinal neural harness. "A foreign component was added to your system. Can you run a diagnostic to detect its presence?"

"I cannot detect it. It has no connection to my system."

Silas scratched his temple. "Maybe it's been disconnected? Maybe a fuse was blown via remote control. Should we go ahead and remove it?"

IRIS shook her head. "I think it would be better to leave it in its place, as we don't want to tamper with evidence."

Eliot lowered his voice, not that the officer was paying much attention. "We're all thinking that this is some sort of overriding remote-control device, right? We just need to find who installed it and operated it." He looked up at IOTA. "You had a problem identifying your new owner. Can you tell us where you have been for the last couple of weeks?"

"I am unable to access that information, as well, but there may be a way to connect directly to my GPS to find my past whereabouts."

Eliot whispered, "IRIS, go ahead. Plug into it." He then gestured with a tug on his wrist to hint that she should remove one of her hands.

IRIS raised her new eyebrows then looked at the officer.

Eliot glanced between Silas and the officer then gestured for Silas to move over and block the view.

Silas nodded and took a sideways step to position himself between IRIS and the officer. She removed her hand to expose wires in her wrist, reeled out a cable, and plugged it into a box located in IOTA's lower back.

After a moment, she said, "I have it. I have the location where IOTA spent the last thirteen days."

"Great!" Silas clapped his hands together. "I guess we'd better get a warrant and go raid some warehouse in the industrial part of town."

"How did you make such an accurate deduction as to its location?" asked IRIS, her eyes blinking in rapid succession.

"It's because humans are so predictable." Silas turned to the officer sitting in the corner. "Hey!" The large man stirred from his waking slumber. "Where do we go to get a search warrant? We've got the location of a warehouse we need to raid."

Chapter 45

Raid

Abigail had just finished giving her statement in the federal office building where her brother and his robot were being held. She was furious that she had made no progress getting any information out of either of them. She wished she had more helpful information to offer to aid with the investigation. As she stepped out of the office, she received a call from Silas.

"We have a lead," he said without a greeting. "The vice president has authorized us to join a SWAT team's raid on the warehouse where IOTA was altered. We're suiting up in the basement level. Are you still in the building?"

"Yes, I'll join you." Abigail felt electricity tingle through her fingers, and a bright light flashed across her vision. If Gavin had been there, he probably would've commented on her glowing eyes. She wondered if he was in the basement with Silas.

She entered a stairway and leapt down the stairs to get to the basement level where she'd meet Silas. She wanted nothing more than to find out who was responsible for killing her friend.

Silas greeted her with a long hug. She declined the SWAT protective gear but thought Silas looked pretty intimidating in his. They loaded into one of four armored trucks with other SWAT team members.

As it rumbled out of the basement parking lot and into the afternoon light of the city, Abigail sat beside Silas. "You remember some of the skills we worked on aboard *Enterprise* with Admiral Rendón, right?"

"I think I still have some moves." He sounded confident, but she could tell he was nervous.

Their time aboard the aircraft carrier felt like a lifetime ago. She elbowed him. "Remember to duck first or move aside then counter-attack. You don't want to be blocking punches with your face this time."

He nodded, a look of determination on his face.

Sitting with Silas and heading out in search of answers helped ease the pain she'd had in her chest. She felt like reality had been distorted into a waking nightmare since the shooting—she had been clouded by intense grief, pain, and anger. Seeing Silas gave her a glimmer of hope that she would get through the dark tunnel. She still had what felt like a dark chasm in her chest, though, and worried about the future. She realized, however, that her friends would help get her through. She looked around at the other SWAT team members. "Where's Gavin?"

Silas tightened the strap on his helmet. "After the shooting, he accompanied your family to their hotel. He'll meet us at the warehouse, but he's on the other side of town, so we'll get there first."

"How did you even arrange to have us included in this raid?"

"IRIS helped to discover the past whereabouts of IOTA. We talked to someone who happened to be in touch with the vice president, who authorized that every asset be used to find out who was behind this. I guess the time we served with the Federation Navy probably helped."

Whatever the reason, Abigail was truly grateful to be included. "Wait, IRIS came to question IOTA?" She lowered her voice. "They let another robot into the building?"

"Well, she's had some work done to her face and body, so nobody knows she's a robot. She's keeping an eye on Eliot."

Abigail wasn't sure how she felt about trusting another robot, although she was grateful IRIS had made progress. She didn't want to think about her brother or his robots at the moment, although she was realizing that she might have reacted too harshly with him. She just wanted to get to the warehouse and get answers.

The SWAT commander called out from the front of the vehicle, "We'll be at the target building in one minute. Enter the building and neutralize the threat with no casualties."

The truck came to an abrupt halt, causing the team within to lean into each another. The rear doors swung open, and they filed out. Abigail was swept along and had to focus on her footing out the back door. She and the team sprinted to the warehouse entrance as SWAT vehicles surrounded the warehouse, and guards spilled out to form a perimeter. Her team was the first to approach the building.

The lead guard made quick work of the locked door, wielding a heavy battering ram with his brawny arms. All it took was a single strike against the door handle. Luckily, there was no dead bolt or padlock to slow them down. The agent who had breached the door held it open as they filed in.

Upon entering, the four guards ahead of Abigail rushed to apprehend two figures who had their hands in the air. "Don't shoot. We're unarmed."

Abigail almost felt guilty for how forcibly they were thrown to the ground, pinned, and handcuffed.

At the room's center was a table, surrounded by shelves filled with parts and equipment. Silas began rummaging. "So, we're looking for some sort of remote-control device, right?"

All Abigail saw were parts, wires, and tools—nothing resembling a remote device. She studied the two men. Their auras showed that they were nervous, but there was something more suspicious hidden in their swirls of concerned oranges and reds. They were hiding something.

Silas shook his head. "There's nothing here."

Abigail knocked some junk off a shelf. "Where is it? What have you been working on in here?"

The two men, a tall one with a ponytail and a short and round one, didn't make a peep.

Silas walked over to a cabinet. "We'll keep looking."

Abigail saw an increase in the alarm of the two men as Silas reached to open the large metal cabinet. The words "Hold on. Don't open that!" got stuck in her throat as he turned the handle. The door sprung open, and a large man burst forth, brandishing a screwdriver.

Silas parried the screwdriver away and grabbed the wrist of the hand wielding it. He then pressed into the back of the man's elbow and locked his arm straight, causing him to fall past him. The man, who was larger than the other two, fell to the ground with a thud. Silas disarmed him and sent the screwdriver skidding across the floor. He then pinned the man's hand behind his back and pressed down.

The man sputtered from the ground. "What the hell? You nearly broke my arm."

It had happened so quickly that Abigail didn't have a chance to help. She had been startled but felt proud of Silas for defending himself. Once the man stopped resisting, she called to the two other men, "Are there any more goons hiding in here?"

"There's only three of us," one replied.

"Where's the device—the remote control? We know you worked on the robot that shot the president."

None of the men spoke.

Electricity surged through Abigail's fingertips, and her vision started to flash blindingly white. "I don't have time for this." She knelt beside the large man, who Silas still had pinned. "I've got ways to get information out of you." Sparks bridged across her fingertips only inches from his face.

Silas raised his eyebrows. Maybe she was going too far.

The man held his ground. "You're welcome to search our workspace."

She could tell by his aura that he was confident in the fact that they wouldn't find anything incriminating. She wanted to shock him with every volt of electricity she could muster.

She remembered how she had accidentally witnessed Silas's childhood memory while standing in the candy aisle of the convenience store. Maybe she could probe the man's memory. She reached to grab hold of the back of his neck and put her other hand on his forehead then closed her eyes and concentrated. She wanted to do more than Illuminate the man—she wanted to enter his mind and see his memories. At first, nothing happened, so she relaxed and focused on her breathing. After a moment, she realized she was outside of her body, sharing the man's thoughts and feelings. "Silas, lighten up on his arm. You're hurting him." She felt his pain dissipate.

That reduced the man's resistance as she co-inhabited his mind. She became even more oblivious to her own body. *Show me your work. Show me the robot.* She had no idea whether she had said the words out loud or had spoken directly into his mind.

She saw the robot as if she were standing over it at the table. Its chest panel had been removed. She saw what felt like her own hands but larger, digging into the compartment of the robot, working with needle-nosed pliers to pull some wires.

Show me the remote device.

The image resolved into a new one of the robot standing, and in her hands—or rather, his bulky ones—was a remote. The robot walked around, stopped, and bent over to pick up a cardboard box. She felt the man's pleasure as he controlled the robot to perform its tasks by manipulating the controls on the handheld device.

Where is the remote now?

The image shifted, and she saw a compartment in the floor. He placed the remote into the hole, covered it with a square metal panel, then had his associates slide the cabinet into place.

She broke the connection. "Hey! Can I get a couple men over here to move this cabinet?"

"What did you do to me? First, your boyfriend nearly breaks my arm, and then you're somehow in my head. I didn't give you permission to violate me like that. I'm sure the world would love to hear about this. You're that girl who goes around shocking people, and now this?"

Abigail knew he was right. She had forced her way into his mind. "You do know the President of the United States was assassinated with your device? I think you could be locked away in a place where no one will be able to hear your story." She kept a hand on the man and gestured the SWAT team toward the metal cabinet.

Two men slid the cabinet aside, revealing the sunken compartment in the floor. Silas raised his eyebrows.

Before they pried open the panel, the large man said, "Fine. You win, but that's not the device we sent off with the robot. It's just a prototype. Read my mind again if you don't believe me."

As the team led the captives out to the van, Gavin showed up. "What are you doing in SWAT gear? What did I miss?"

Silas grinned and patted his chest armor. "*We* caught the bad guys."

Abigail gave Gavin a hug then tapped Silas on his chest armor. "Great job apprehending that man and not getting stabbed with a screwdriver."

Silas kept smirking. "Yep, I apprehended that guy." He remained puffed up in his SWAT gear. "And we found out that IOTA had been remote controlled to shoot the president."

Gavin gripped Silas by his shoulder. "Sorry I missed out on the action, but I'm glad you're all right."

"Yeah, we needed to get in there as quickly as possible. It looked like they were packing up to leave."

Abigail crossed her arms. "I'm just glad we're not heading to the hospital yet again." She remembered that they did need to visit Ives. But first, she wanted to interrogate the men. She also realized she owed Eliot an apology. He had been correct that his robot hadn't acted of its own volition. Still, the fact that he hadn't collected any information on the buyer was infuriating. If he had a future in selling robots, background checks would be crucial to prevent them from falling into the wrong hands and being misused by people with malevolent plans. If she could see harmful intentions in others' auras, it shouldn't be hard for Eliot to use his new skills to see them too.

∾

At the FBI headquarters, once the men were booked and placed in a holding cell, Abigail was allowed to further question them. She looked down at her tall black boots and pulled her hair tightly into a ponytail. She knew she didn't have to put any more effort into intimidating them, but she wanted answers without playing games.

"You three are in a heap of trouble. Conspiring to kill the president is going to carry a heavy sentence."

The big man Silas had apprehended spoke first. He had unruly curly brown hair and a stubbly beard. "We were just hired to work on the robot, I swear."

"Yes, but one of you pulled the trigger, and now, the president's dead."

The scruffy man shook his head. "Like I said, the remote control you found is just a prototype. It's not the one used to assassinate the president. None of us pulled the trigger."

She could see in his aura that he was telling the truth. "But you knew what you were doing when you installed the bypass control into the robot's system."

"We didn't know what purpose it was going to serve until we heard the news that a robot had been apprehended in the attack. You've got to believe us. Lots of robots have bypass features so they can be remote controlled instead of autonomous. Just look up any robotics competition."

Abigail studied the man and his aura. "You're lucky I can tell when someone is telling the truth. I would like to hear it from the rest of you. Did any of you know the robot was going to be used to assassinate the president?"

The tall ponytail guy shook his head. "No."

The smaller one shook in his chair. "No, we had no idea. I promise."

Abigail could tell he was the most nervous, but they were all telling the truth. She asked, "How do we find the person who hired you?"

The ponytail guy said, "His phone seems to be deactivated. We tried calling him once we saw the news."

"Great. Is there any way we can locate the remote device? Like tracking it somehow?" Abigail placed both fists on the metal table.

"Not that I can think of. I would think that whoever used it would destroy it." The scruffy man seemed to be sincerely trying to help.

Abigail let out a deep huff. "Can you give me any information at all that can help? Like was the person who hired you affiliated with any political group? Anything?"

"All I know is he took the robot away in a black Sprinter. He had two workers load it up, and he never got out of the vehicle."

"How did he pay you? Maybe we could track his PayPal or Venmo." Abigail realized any hope of catching the assassin was slipping away.

"Um, he paid us cash."

"This is just great." Abigail slammed her fist on the table then left, slamming the door as she walked out.

Chapter 46

Dire Prediction

Once the humans and the Taurians blast jumped away from the vicinity of the rogue neutron star, Ringlow traveled back to his native system. He visited C-PU's moon, where normally, he enjoyed having the entire moon to himself and his work was peacefully routine. The chamber was lit by C-PU's bluish purple glow and by multiple view screens, on which Ringlow liked to view the cratered barren landscape beyond the bubble-shaped enclosure.

But C-PU was behaving oddly. No matter how many times Ringlow fine-tuned the data and reentered it, the super processor repeated the same dire prediction: the humans would come to their system and threaten their existence.

Ringlow rushed to another moonlike planet, a small hop from C-PU's moon around their ring of planets, and into the Overseer's chamber. The space, with its stone walls and ceiling and the glowing blue floor from which the furniture grew to accommodate the needs of the Overseer and his guests, had become all too familiar.

"I have been feeding updates into C-PU, and it has deduced an alarming prediction regarding the humans of Earth."

The Overseer was eating cube-shaped meaty morsels from a dish that was molded from the armrest of his seat. He tossed one into his mouth, chewed, then swallowed. "How could anything related to that underdeveloped race be alarming to us?"

Ringlow had never morphed to display his emotions to the Overseer, but he felt his teeth grow and sharpen as he locked his jaw into place. He remained standing with his long fingers interlocked as he tried to remove the shakiness from his voice. "One among them has or will have the ability to imminently disrupt *our* existence, and they will inevitably show up here to challenge us. Every indication is that their future path will lead them to this system. C-PU is ninety-nine-point-nine-nine percent sure of it."

The Overseer morphed as well—no horns, simply large yellow eyes peering from his massive head. He coughed on a morsel. "I have a hard time believing this. They are merely a speck we can brush away if we feel so inclined." He flicked one of his pointy over-sized fingers into the air.

Ringlow shook his head. "They are more than a speck. They are more like bacteria or a virus that can multiply and spread. Their planet is now infested with large numbers of humans and they are on the verge of spreading. They successfully sent a mission to increase the habitability of the planet to which the Taurians are heading, which will become a human colony too. None of the humans have yet departed to join that colony, so all of humanity is still located on Earth. Let's wipe them out before they show up on our doorstep."

Ringlow had admired the human species and felt he owed them for their rescue of the Taurians, but he had also witness some of their horrendous activities like the damage they were causing to their planet, harm to other species, and war amongst themselves. Any hope he had for them was now replaced by an urgency to eradicate them, his sense of self-preservation overtaking any feelings of gratitude or admiration toward the alien race.

The Overseer skewered another food morsel with a talon-like fingernail. "They were your prized species. Why do you wish to hastily end their reign on their secluded planet? Do you really think there is a high probability of them becoming a threat to us?"

"Yes. I fed a complete record of all my observations of the humans of Earth into C-PU, and it is certain that they will arrive here and cause a disruption. We are immune to a great many things, but C-PU predicts they may bring a danger from which we cannot survive. C-PU could not be specific, but I'm imagining a black hole showing up on our doorstep."

The Overseer raised his brows. "Then how do you propose we eradicate them?"

"A meteorite is an effective weapon. It's a little unoriginal—it's how they ended the reign of their dinosaurs—but it is efficient, and it leaves the potential for other life to arise and replace the dominant life forms who perish."

Ringlow had put so much hope into the success of the human race. Coming to the decision that they must be eradicated felt like he was having to euthanize a beloved pet. Although they were like a pet that was undoubtedly predisposed to violence. He had no doubt that it was necessary. One consolation was that the Taurians could continue their civilization on their new world, Nidus, without the humans. Ringlow felt an urgency to strike Earth before any humans left to inhabit the new Taurian world. There were some Taurians on Earth who would perish, but that was inconsequential.

So far in the history of the galaxy, Ringlow's people had occupied a single system somewhat peacefully and had not been threatened by the existence of any other species. Everything changed with C-PU's forecast of possible harm. He thought drastic action must be taken to prevent their future expansion.

Ringlow waited for an answer from his superior who plucked another morsel from his armrest.

The Overseer sighed. "In light of C-PU's prediction, and if you feel it is necessary, then make it so. Eradicate the humans."

Chapter 47

Coffee and Sugar

Vice President Rogan invited Abigail, Silas, and Gavin to the Oval Office for a meeting. Out of respect for the fallen president, he'd requested to keep the title of vice president instead of president, even though he had been sworn in.

His appearance was nearly the opposite of Russell's. Both were tall, but Rogan was thin and lanky to the point of being gaunt. Instead of a full head of hair, he had a thinning light-brown tuft protruding from a receding hairline, creating a widow's peak with streaks of gray on the sides.

He gave a tight-lipped smile, his crow's feet gathering in the corners of his eyes. "Thanks for coming. I haven't had a chance to talk with the three of you yet, but Russ always spoke highly of you. Especially you, Abigail."

Abigail shook his hand. "Yes, Russell was a good friend, and I miss him terribly."

Rogan nodded solemnly. "We all do. He was a dear friend of mine too. He and I didn't always see eye to eye, but he recently convinced me of the importance of what he was trying to accomplish. I want to continue his legacy."

A wave of relief permeated through Abigail and she was able to take a deep breath.

Gavin spoke up. "That's good to hear, Mr. Vice President. We were nervous about the future and if you would want to persist with the New Federation."

"I was averse to supporting his plan at first, but I am fully on board, and I think we need to continue his work to create a World Federation. It's hard when people are so divided. Sometimes, I wish there was some way to magically get everyone on the same page."

Abigail wished the same thing. She dreaded the thought of the president's legacy ending with his death. "Uniting the world is my greatest wish too. I'm worried, though, that with the president gone, our movement will lose momentum."

Rogan let out a sigh. "Now that Russell is no longer with us, the Confederation states are demanding to take over and return the United States to the way it was before he dismantled Congress."

A tingle of electricity coursed through her closed fists. She had begun to think that the assassination might have been a plot created by someone organizing in the oil states.

Gavin fidgeted in his chair. "So are the Federation states going to stand together against the Confederation and not back down?"

"I honestly have no idea." The VP shook his head. "It's hard to allocate resources for saving the world from global warming, pollution, and everything else when our people's needs are neglected. Our resources are running thin. We're really starting to feel a scarcity of all the products that come from the parts of the world we've separated ourselves from. Surviving on locally grown and produced products is admirable, but where in the Federation do we produce things like coffee and sugar? Many grocery stores are running out of produce. The oil states are maintaining trade with Mexico, who buys their oil. We had no idea how valuable Mexico's imported goods were until we stopped trading with them."

Gavin bit his lip. "This reminds me of stories my grandpappy told me about World War II. People roughed it without many necessities during that war."

Rogan leaned back in his chair and allowed a thin smile to appear, however briefly. "Back then, America also remained united against a mutual enemy. This is more like a civil war mixed with World War III. Our country is truly divided, and so is the world. China has landed a fleet in South America to retake the land we kicked them off of. They have also occupied more of the smaller countries around them. I have word that Japan sent a whaling convoy to Antarctica to make up for our interference. Russia is expanding to forcefully take over countries, like Ukraine, that were previously independent. It's a real mess. Ukrainians are putting up an admirable fight, but they're taking heavy losses and need assistance."

"It sounds like a weakened and divided America has given rise to other countries increasing their aggression," Abigail said. "They're no longer afraid we'll police the world."

Gavin straightened in his chair. "Don't we still have the armed forces, and don't we have allies?"

Silas shook his head. "I don't think a bunch of ex-whalers from Iceland will really put up much of a fight against any of those countries' naval fleets."

The VP nodded. "There's a limit to what our forces can tackle, and yes, more allies would be helpful—and allies with more resources."

Gavin glanced from Abigail to the vice president. "Well, what do we do now?"

Abigail placed her fists on the desk. "We need to pool together all the Federation's resources and continue helping each other and the rest of the world. If this is World War III, we will sacrifice our needs and try to meet the needs of others. Let's support each other and not back down. We can't let the oil states take over. Surely, we have a few allies outside of the country, like Canada."

She settled back into her seat. "There's one county I know of in the Middle East that might help. We didn't accomplish much on our naval mission, but we do have a friend in Algeria. I'm not exactly sure how he can help, but we should reach out to their president, Abdel. Also, Russell sent huge amounts of aid to Costa Rica after the hurricane. Maybe they can lend us a cup of sugar in our time of need?"

"I think you're right." Rogan nodded. "The Chinese are treading too heavily in Brazil, Ecuador, Peru, and Colombia. I think we should focus our military efforts there. Losing the rainforest will have the worst long-term impact on the world."

Silas crossed his arms. "Are you sure pissing off China is really going to help?"

The VP narrowed his eyes. "I don't care how pissed off China gets. This is a world crisis. We need to focus our efforts on what will matter for generations to come. I have finally come to realize that the rainforests belong to us all—or rather, the responsibility of protecting them should be shared by everyone. The point of our presence there will be to preserve the people's ways of life in those countries *and* the rainforest. If we gain a little support from those countries, it will be a worthwhile endeavor."

Abigail agreed. She hated considering the prospect of war over natural resources, but it would affect future generations if they failed to stand up to save a vital piece of Earth's ecosystem. She thought that perhaps she should travel there and try to use her powers to reduce the escalation of violence. She did, however, remember Rendón's warning that she wasn't bulletproof.

She studied Gavin and Silas, who sat rigidly upright and wide-eyed. Silas gripped the arms of his chair. It sounded like a war was brewing, and she wanted to keep them safe. She planned to assist the military, but she wouldn't be inviting her friends along to South America.

Chapter 48

Meltdown

Evvie had remained aboard the *Harkin*, when everyone else had departed. She was shutting down nonessential systems and setting up an autopilot to maintain orbit. It was eerie to be alone on the enormous ship. She imagined that before their trip to the neutron star, she would have been terrified of being alone in space, but she had grown to feel like she could handle the ship on her own.

She was, however, eager to step foot on firm ground after the experience of being separated from her physical body and narrowly escaping the newly forming black hole. In less than an hour, she would rendezvous with a Taurian ship that would fly her down to the planet for some much-needed shore leave. It had been too long since she'd felt a sandy beach beneath her ten human toes.

She was at a control panel when she overheard a call come through the ship's comm system: "Space Force Rangers, report. This is Vice President Rogan. Japan is asking for assistance. One of their nuclear reactors is facing a meltdown. I'm not sure what your forces can do, but you were the only help I could think of."

Brklana responded over the open channel: "Brklana reporting. Most of our team is with me. I'm at the International Space Station, where there was an air leak. We've remedied it, and we're over the Atlantic now. How can I help you?"

The vice president's voice came through with a little static. "Japan's president has issued a cease-fire and called for an end to their participation in all confrontation. Japan has declared a state of emergency, as one of their nuclear reactors is facing a meltdown. The power plant is losing containment of its reaction core after a tsunami disrupted the cooling system."

Evvie punched her comm button and spoke into her handset. "This is Evvie. I'm on my way. I'm over Australia, so I'm not too far." She shut off the comm and muttered, "So much for some shore leave."

When Evvie had been in orbit, working on her ship, she'd tried to set a course that overlooked as many beaches on the ocean as possible so she could imagine she was there. It looked like she would have to wait even longer until she would be standing on an actual beach.

She wasn't exactly sure how she could help, but she began thinking of how they had stored ice within the ship's shields when landing on Nidus. The shielding did have the ability to contain physical material.

As Evvie descended into the atmosphere toward Japan, she heard more comms come through. "Brklana here. We are sending all possible support to Japan—every ship."

The VP closed the call by saying, "Godspeed and be careful."

Evvie's was the first ship to arrive at the nuclear power station. She descended over the evacuated facility then dropped her massive ship to hover above the power plant that was on a strip of land on the west coast of the island nation. With her ship's sensors, she was able to locate the section where the temperature within the building was rising.

She lowered her ship then activated her shield, which trapped a sliver of land with the entire building that contained the breached reactor. She powered the thrusters at maximum capacity, and the ship jolted as a chunk of the building broke away from the ground. Evvie lifted the ship with the thrusters roaring. She began making slow progress, getting farther and farther off the ground, but pessimism set in because she wasn't accelerating very quickly with the extra weight. She thought perhaps she had captured too large a chunk of land, and it was weighing her ship down.

Taurian ships arrived to offer their assistance, but they could not attach any tow cables to lift the *Harkin* because of her shields. They could, however, get below and behind her ship and bump shields to add to her velocity. Her trajectory wasn't like a rocket's but more like an airplane that was gradually gaining altitude.

"This is taking too long!" Evvie reported. "The reactor in the power plant is reaching a critical point, and I have not departed from the atmosphere. If my shield fails, I'll sprinkle radioactive material back down into the atmosphere, which will affect a larger part of the planet."

Brklana called in, "Divert as much power as possible to keeping your shields up. We'll provide the thrust. Hang on. It will be a bumpy ride."

Her ship shook abruptly, but it was accelerating.

Ivanovich called in, "We are with you, Lapochka. We will work together to get you into space."

More Taurian ships showed up, their shields and engines at full power. They made contact with her shield and fired full thrusters. It did indeed become a bumpy ride as they hastily made contact. Her ship had made it higher into the atmosphere and was speeding to an even faster velocity, since there was less air to slow them down, but they hadn't reached escape velocity yet.

Evvie reported, "We're not free of Earth's gravity yet. We still need more speed. We really don't want this material falling back to Earth."

She imagined the harm it would cause if the radioactive material sprinkled back down onto land or into the sea and paused to look at the readout on her screen. "Um, I've got a problem. The temperature in the reactor is reaching a critical point. My ship has some integrity, but an explosion inside my shield would direct all of the force toward my hull. We have not achieved escape velocity. What's the ETA on the extra ships sent from the surface?"

Brklana responded, "There are ships coming from India, Australia, and America that will join our thrust effort in the next ten minutes. Five remaining Taurian vessels are almost here."

"I hope they get here soon. My computer is predicting a total meltdown with a powerful explosion in eight minutes."

"Our five ships have just made contact and are firing at one hundred percent. I think you are going to make it." Brklana's optimism helped, as well as the extra nudge from the new ships.

Evvie sighed with relief, but the moment was interrupted by a warning alarm. She reached to her controls to drop the outer shield, but she was too late. The explosion remained within her blast shield. The force knocked her against her straps as she heard the ripping sound of an explosion tear through the hull of the *Harkin*.

Chapter 49

Radiation

"Please let me see her!" Abigail pleaded.

"She's too radioactive," the nurse said. "The doctors are using all of the suits. If you went into the containment area without a suit, you would be exposed too. Ivanovich was badly irradiated when he rescued her. I don't want to treat more people with radiation poisoning today."

"Is Ivan going to be all right?"

"We think so," the nurse replied. "As I understand it, if not for him, Evvie would have died up there on her ship."

Abigail heard that he had flown his small ship into the breach of the *Harkin* and had collected her from the control room as the ship was losing air pressure. "I'm so grateful he brought her home. Is there any way I can talk to her?"

"We're placing her in an enclosure with interactive glove ports and a comm system. In a few minutes, I can take you to see her."

After the nurse led her through the hospital corridors, Abigail rushed toward the containment enclosure where Evvie lay. She had red burns on her face, hands, and arms. Abigail called though the glass, "Stay with me. The doctors are doing everything they can." She reached through the glove port to grasp Evvie's hand.

"I'm not feeling... so well," Evvie muttered. She lay with her head pressed back and her brow furrowed.

"I'm so sorry! If I hadn't given you a body, you wouldn't be experiencing this."

Evvie's face relaxed a little. "If you hadn't given me a body, I would not have experienced so many wonderful things."

"But you could have lived forever, or close to it. It's just so unfair!"

Evvie perked up a little. "A short life with you as my sister has been much better than a long and lonely life as pure energy. All of the experiences I've had are worth it."

Abigail squeezed harder. "But you could have experienced more. Why did you have to be the hero?" She realized she had vowed not to let Evvie out of her sight ever since the black hole incident, yet as soon as they'd returned to Earth, Abigail had left her in space. If she'd been on board the *Harkin*, maybe she could have done something to prevent the blast from causing so much damage. She was devastated to think that Evvie had been alone on that ship with no support.

"I did it to protect the people on this planet. The world still needs safeguarding. Keep protecting it, Abigail."

"I will. I promise." She wished she could hold her but was grateful to be able to clasp her hand through the glove.

Evvie continued, "The touch of another is something I'm glad I did not live without. And also the experiences of eating ice cream, walking on a sandy beach, and swimming in the ocean. I also haven't gotten a chance to tell you, but Fambozi and I kissed, and it was blissful. Better than ice cream."

Abigail let out a brief laugh that quickly turned into a choking sob. "If you guys are dating, you might want to start calling him by his first name."

"I'm not so sure I'm going to get a chance to do that," she whispered.

More tears streamed down Abigail's cheeks. She had a hard time getting the words out. "I hope that whatever kind of heaven Martians believe in is filled with every flavor of ice cream imaginable, sandy ocean beaches, and blissful kisses."

Evvie replied, "I have already been to heaven. It's called Earth."

Chapter 50

Funeral

A week later, the largest funeral ceremony in the history of the planet took place at Cape Canaveral. Before the ceremony, everyone mingled in a large reception hall.

Abigail had no idea she could feel so much pain as she did while saying goodbye to two friends. The president and Evvie were to be sent into the sun in a rocket capsule. Silas had customized his favorite car, the Roadster, into a space capsule, fabricated from magnesium silicate to transport their bodies though space.

Abigail kept hoping it was a nightmare from which she would wake, if only she could shake herself out of it, but she couldn't. Evvie, who had filled the role of a sister—sometimes the wise older sister and sometimes the naïve younger one who needed guidance for fitting into life on Earth—was gone. She smiled at the irony, having spent her life feeling like she couldn't fit in.

Abigail's brother walked through the crowd to face her. "I'm so sorry about the president and your friend. I know how much they both meant to you."

"Thanks, Eliot. I'm sorry I didn't believe you about your robot not being able to shoot the president. I was just so furious. Now, I'm devastated. Thanks for coming." The realization that the assassination investigation had come to a dead-end added even more ache.

Eliot nodded. "I know that I can be a self-centered brat, but I want you to know that if there's anything I can do to help, just call me."

"That means a lot. You've come a really long way, and I'm proud of you."

Silas and Gavin walked up to give Abigail hugs. They didn't speak much, but the looks on their faces said they felt terrible.

She walked over to where Max stood alone. "I'm so sorry you didn't get to see her. She mentioned you at the end."

"I hope she said something good."

"Yes, she did. She was very fond of you."

"And I was of her. In fact, I always wondered why such an advanced and beautiful being was interested in me."

"Well, you are pretty exceptional... for a human."

He allowed a tight-lipped smile to shine through his grief-stricken face. "Thank you, Abigail. I'm sorry for the loss of your sister. I can't imagine the pain you must be feeling."

"Pretty strong feelings of guilt and regret. I miss her terribly."

"I hope the pain heals with time. 'Tis better to have loved and lost than never to have loved at all.'" He blinked hard. "I will bury myself in my work and daydream about the time I was fortunate enough to have spent with her—in space and on another planet. Those are all experiences I never would have dreamed possible and will cherish forever."

"I'm glad you were there too." They hugged, and he departed toward the caskets.

Tkla, Brklana, and their baby came into the hall and approached Abigail.

Abigail wiped her eyes and put some effort into composing herself. "It's so good to see you both reunited with your baby!"

Tkla gave the infant a jiggle. "Yes, we are overjoyed to be with our little Tlana!"

Abigail attempted a smile. "JJ came very close to becoming her new guardian when we had that close call with the neutron star."

"It was a noble adventure," Tkla replied. "Thank you for what you have done. The entire Taurian race owes you and Evvie a debt of gratitude."

"She was the one with the big ship, but I'm glad I was part of the rescue mission too. Can I hold her?"

Tkla handed the infant to her human auntie. "Are you going to be okay, Abigail?"

"If I can have some cuddle time with Tlana, I might be. She is the most adorable thing I have ever seen." The infant wrapped her entire hand around Abigail's thumb and nibbled on it. Her gnawing tickled. Abigail couldn't remember the last time she had laughed. One small ray of light penetrated the heavy darkness that had been pressing down on her.

"I think she wants to eat me." Abigail poked her face closer to the baby's. "Are you sure you're not adopted and your real parents aren't *T. rexes*?" Tlana was soft and warm in Abigail's arms. Her large, inquisitive eyes locked onto Abigail's. Abigail broke the staring contest and turned to Tkla and Brklana. "I know you already have a nanny, but if you ever need a babysitter, I'm always available." She started to hand the baby back.

Brklana spoke. "If she is happy with you, then you can keep holding her for as long as she's not too fussy."

"I will. She's a comfort for me right now. Thank you."

During the ceremony, the Japanese prime minister presented a treaty to Vice President Rogan so Japan could join the Federation. He said, "No more whaling, and we will begin the transition to alternate sources of power. We will also assist in your efforts to protect the rainforests in South America."

Rogan accepted the treaty and bowed to the prime minister.

Abigail didn't know she could feel this much pain, but Evvie's sacrifice was not in vain. Evvie had saved many lives and paved the way toward peace. Japan's help with solving some of the world's problems could really turn the tide.

The Japanese prime minister approached Abigail where she sat in the front row. "It was a noble sacrifice your sister made. She showed true courage, and I will honor her selfless act until my last breath. Please accept our treaty as a symbol of a new future of world peace and unity. We pledge allegiance to the United Federation and will work in every way to end the pointless strife of humanity."

"Thank you, Prime Minister Hinata. Your words and actions mean a great deal to me. Knowing that Evvie left the world a better place because of the actions she took does help."

The ceremony ended with the rocket firing from Cape Canaveral. Inside were the bodies of Russell Randolph, the president of the United Federation, and Evvie, the Martian.

Chapter 51

Ringlow

Ringlow oversaw the mission personally, even though C-PU could have sent a pulse remotely that would have accomplished the task with little effort. He had invested so much time in studying the humans and placed so much hope in their species that he felt responsible to see the task through himself. He also wanted to redirect the asteroid in a way that was less detectable so the humans would have less time to react to its imminent collision.

In the asteroid belt beyond the orbit of Earth, Ringlow watched as his ship's shield made contact with an asteroid, which caused a chain reaction of collisions, leading to a variation in the orbit of a single large rocky body. What he hoped would appear to be a random occurrence to the humans on Earth was a precise blow to send the asteroid on a collision course with the planet. He realized with a pained smile that it didn't really matter if the humans discovered the source of asteroid's altered path. They would be more worried about their impending deaths.

Ringlow watched as the asteroid traveled for months and was nearing its destination. He knew it was a necessary preventive measure, though he couldn't help but wonder what the future would have held for the species. The Overseer had agreed that if the humans became a threat to their species, drastic action must be taken. Even though C-PU predicted forthcoming danger posed by the humans, Ringlow wondered if perhaps the supermachine could have been mistaken—not that it had ever been wrong before. Maybe the humans would have arrived peacefully in their system. Ringlow forced himself to cast the thought aside as wishful thinking.

Once the asteroid neared its destination, it became useless to speculate about humanity's future. Ringlow continued to watch the asteroid on its journey, since he had no other pressing observations to make—although he had plans to travel to the planet, Nidus, where the Taurians were completing their seeding process. Given the asteroid's remaining distance, humanity had only a couple of weeks before they and their civilization would be obliterated. So far, there was no indication that any of the humans of Earth had spotted the massive body heading their way, which was lucky. The closer it got without their detection, the better.

He would follow at a safe distance to document the impact. After that, he would visit Earth periodically to see what type of life would arise to replace the humans. Ringlow would watch and wait.

Chapter 52

The Signal

Six months after the president and Evvie had been ceremoniously sent into the sun, Silas's SETI department discovered a new signal that apparently was nothing like the message from Mars that Abigail had deciphered—the original message from Evvie.

Abigail traveled to Edmunds Air Force base, where all her adventures had begun, to see if she could decode it.

She was about to walk into the comm room but stopped. It was the room where she had listened to the first transmission that led to meeting Evvie on Mars. Abigail remembered the day of first contact fondly, among many other memorable days. She would never forget traveling to Mars, meeting Evvie, then offering the use of her genes so the energy being could acquire a physical body. Swimming in the ocean on Evvie's first day on Earth was at the top of her list too.

It pained Abigail to think that Evvie had been given a new body only to be killed long before she'd lived a full life. She closed her eyes and tried to remember every experience she and Evvie had shared during their short time together.

"How are you holding up?" Silas asked softy from the doorway.

She wiped her eyes and walked in. "I miss her so much, and I feel so much regret. I can't help but wish I could have spent more time with her before it was over."

Silas nodded. "That sounds like a tough regret to have. I do think she lived her life to the fullest."

"Yeah, I'm also angry because she was just a victim of our barbaric planet. It's truly frustrating that humanity is doomed to be such a reckless species."

"Don't lose hope. The reactor breach was an accident. It wasn't anyone's fault. Nuclear power *is* a way cleaner source of energy than coal."

"Yeah, but if we're going to harness power from potentially dangerous sources, we need to have better systems in place to prevent catastrophic meltdowns. This isn't the first nuclear disaster to have happened."

Silas reached out to grab her arm. "The world is making progress—slow progress—but have faith that we're heading in the right direction. And Evvie helped. Just look at how Japan's new commitment has turned things around."

"I wish I could share your optimism."

"I know it's hard to have hope when so much has been taken away from you. Take all the time you need to heal, but remember what both Evvie and the president died trying to protect. This planet is worth the trouble it will take to save it."

He was right. With Japan's help, the Federation had made great strides in South America, thanks to Evvie's sacrifice—a sacrifice she shouldn't have had to make. "Thanks, Silas. You're a good friend."

"I hope I'll always be here for you."

"Me too. And I'll be okay... I think. One thing that's been helping me is visiting Eliot on Dinosaur Island. I guess they never came up with a better name for it." She smiled tearfully. "Some of their animals are amazing."

"I know. I have a VIP pass to the island. It's fantastic."

"The dinosaurs are doing well in that environment. There are herds of them."

"Which are your favorites?" he asked.

"*Triceratops* and *Ankylosaurus* were my two favorites as a kid. Apparently, the specimens they have on the island are evolved domesticated versions, but they look just like I imagined dinosaurs would. The duck-billed hadrosaurs are neat because I see the resemblance to the Taurians. Spending time with the animals there has been a therapeutic experience."

"That's good to hear. The island itself is beautiful too… and the beaches."

"Yes. I spend a lot of time on the beach. It's hard, though, because I know Evvie is missing it."

"It sounds like spending time there is helping. I'm sure your brother likes having you around too."

"I didn't realize it growing up, but I guess he was neglected for attention as a kid. I'm glad to be there for him now."

Silas paused as if hoping it was okay to change the subject then gestured toward the computer. "So… this new signal is interesting. We have no idea what it is or where it's coming from."

One of the techs announced from his station, "We're trying to filter out the static, but I am afraid there is little more than static to listen to."

Abigail sat at the station and put on her headphones.

She closed her eyes and focused on nothing but the sounds. Two minutes passed while she listened intently. Then she nodded. "You're right. Barely any of the message is getting through, so it's only fragments. But I do think there are three syllables repeating over and over."

The fragments of words were so jumbled. She kept wondering if she was right about it being three syllables or if she was imagining any structure to the message at all. She looked at Silas, who had an air of hopefulness, yet his aura was lined with a dark cloud as if discouraged to know that there wasn't much hope of deciphering the message from pure static.

Abigail would sit and listen to the signal all night—for days—if need be. She focused with all her might, but it seemed the more intent her focus, the more the words were eluding her. After a while, she developed a headache, the lack of progress frustrating her. She decided that instead of focusing intently, she could relax and let her mind wander. She lost track of time. With her eyes closed, she let the static permeate through her. Just when she had nearly forgotten where she was and what her task was, the words came to life. She opened her eyes to see Silas doodling on a note pad.

"I've pieced it together!" she called, not believing what she was hearing. There was only one person who could have had any connection to the words she was hearing.

"What does it say?" Silas asked, his face showing astonishment. She smiled and cried. "It's repeating the words 'tinfoil hat.'"

About the Author

Philip Ginn has been inspired since a young age by anything related to space and science. Whether he was studying dinosaur books, watching *NOVA* or the *Cosmos* series on PBS as a kid in the eighties, or just looking into the night sky, he has been captivated by the wonder of it all. He read his first sci-fi collection of short stories (which included Isaac Asimov's *Bicentennial Man*) at the age of fourteen—some thirty-plus years ago—and since then, reading science fiction has been a lifelong interest.

To learn more about me, visit my website and sign up for my newsletter so I can keep you updated on future releases: https://philipginnwriter.home.blog

Instagram: @philipginnwriter

If you enjoyed this novel, please write a review on Amazon.

If you know someone who might enjoy this series, please recommend it to them!

Thank you!

Abigail's Complete Adventures

Homeworld

Revolution World

Godworld

Blast Jump in Time

www.ingramcontent.com/pod-product-compliance
Lightning Source LLC
Chambersburg PA
CBHW031255170626
46807CB00001B/154